USA TODAY bestselling author **Catherine Mann** lives on a sunny Florida beach with her flyboy husband and their four children. With more than forty books in print in over twenty countries, she has also celebrated wins for both a RITA® award and a booksellers' best award. Catherine enjoys chatting with readers online—thanks to the wonders of the internet, which allows her to network with her laptop by the water! Contact Catherine through her website, www.catherinemann.com, find her on Facebook and Twitter (@CatherineMann1) or reach her by snail mail at PO box 6065, Navarre, FL 32566, USA.

A Diamond in the Rough

CATHERINE MANN

MILLS & BOON

First Published in Great Britain 2018
by Mills & Boon, an imprint of HarperCollins*Publishers*
1 London Bridge Street, London, SE1 9GF

A DIAMOND IN THE ROUGH © 2018 Harlequin Books S. A.

One Good Cowboy © 2014 Catherine Mann
Pursued By The Rich Rancher © 2015 Catherine Mann
Pregnant By The Cowboy CEO © 2015 Catherine Mann

ISBN: 978-0-263-26616-0

05-0218

MIX
Paper from
responsible sources
FSC C007454

This book is produced from independently certified FSC™ paper to ensure responsible forest management.

For more information visit: www.harpercollins.co.uk/green

Printed and bound in Spain
by CPI, Barcelona

ONE GOOD COWBOY

CATHERINE MANN

To my husband, Rob, always my hero,

One

"Gentlemen, never forget the importance of protecting your family jewels."

Unfazed by his grandmother's outrageous comment, Stone McNair ducked low as his horse sailed under a branch and over a creek. Gran prided herself on being the unconventional matriarch of a major jewelry design empire, and her mocking jab carried on the wind as Stone raced with his cousin.

Alex pulled up alongside him, neck and neck with Stone's quarter horse. Hooves chewed at the earth, deftly dodging the roots of a cypress tree, spewing turf into the creek.

Even as he raced, Stone soaked in the scents and sounds of home—the squeak of the saddle, the whistle of the wind through the pines. Churned earth and bluebonnets waving in the wind released a fragrance every bit as intoxicating as the first whiff of a freshly opened bottle of Glenfiddich whiskey.

This corner of land outside of Fort Worth, Texas, had belonged to the McNairs for generations, their homestead as they built a business empire. His blood hummed when he rode the ranch. Ownership had branded itself into his DNA as tangibly as the symbol of the Hidden

Gem Ranch that had been branded onto his quarter horse's flank.

Outings on the ranch with his grandmother and his twin cousins were few and far between these days, given their hectic work schedules. He wasn't sure why Gran had called this little reunion and impromptu race, but it had to be something important for her to resort to pulling them all away from the McNair Empire.

His other cousin, Amie, galloped alongside Stone, her laughter full and uninhibited. "How're the family jewels holding up?"

Without waiting for an answer, Amie urged her Arabian ahead, her McNair-black hair trailing behind her just like when she'd been ten instead of thirty. Rides with their grandmother had been a regular occurrence when they were children, then less and less frequent as they grew older and went their separate ways. None of them had hesitated when the family matriarch insisted on an impromptu gathering. Stone owed his grandmother. She'd been his safe haven every time his druggy mother went on a binge or checked into rehab.

Again.

Damn straight, he owed his grandmother a debt he couldn't repay. She'd been there from day one, an aggressive advocate in getting the best care possible to detox her crack baby grandson. Gran had paid for her daughter to enter detox programs again and again with little success. Year after year, Gran had been as constant as the land they called home—for his cousins, too.

And she'd given each one of them a role to play. Alex managed the family lands—Hidden Gem Ranch, which operated as a bed-and-breakfast hobby ranch for the rich and famous. Stone managed the family jewelry design house and stores. Diamonds in the Rough featured high-end rustic designs, from rodeo belt buckles and stylized bolos to Aztec jewelry, all highly sought after around the country. If everything went according to plan, he intended to expand Diamonds in the Rough with international offices in London and Milan, making the big announcement at a wild mustang fund-raiser this fall. And Amie—a gemologist—was already working on designs for new pieces to meet the expected increase in demand.

Yes, the world was finally coming back together for him. After his broken engagement knocked him for a loop seven months ago...

But he didn't want to think about Johanna. Not today. Not ever, if he could avoid it. Although that was tough to accomplish, since Johanna worked for Hidden Gem Stables as a vet tech. He'd missed her this morning when they'd saddled up. Would he bump into her after his ride?

The possibility filled him with frustration—and an unwanted boot in the libido.

Gran slowed her favorite palomino, Goldie, to a trot near the pond where they'd played as kids. Apparently race time was over. Maybe now she would explain the reason for this surprise get-together.

Stone stroked along Copper's neck as the horse dipped his head to drink. "So, Gran, care to enlighten us on the reason for this family meeting?"

His cousins drew up along either side of her.

She shifted in the saddle, her head regal with a long gray braid trailing down her stiff spine. "The time has come for me to decide who will take over the reins of the McNair holdings."

Stone's grip tightened on the pommel. "You're not actually considering retiring."

"No, dear…" Gran paused, drawing in a shaky breath at odds with her usual steel. "The doctor has told me it's time to get my affairs in order."

Her words knocked the wind out of him as fully as the first time he'd been thrown from a horse. He couldn't envision a world without the indomitable Mariah McNair.

Amie reached across to touch her grandmother's arm lightly, as much contact as could be made without everyone dismounting, and Gran didn't show any signs of leaving the saddle. Which was probably the reason their grandmother had chosen this way to make her announcement.

"Gran, what exactly did the doctor say?"

Alex patted Gran's other shoulder, he and his sister protecting her like bookends. They always had.

Amie's and Alex's childhoods had been more stable than Stone's, with parents and a home of their own. As a kid, Stone had dreamed of stepping into their house and becoming a sibling rather than a cousin. Once he'd even overheard his grandmother suggest that very arrangement. But Amethyst and Alexandrite's mother made it clear that she could handle only her twins. Another child would be too much to juggle between obligations to her daughter's pageants and her son's rodeos.

In one fell swoop, Stone had realized that while his family loved him, no one wanted him—not his mother, his aunt or his grandmother. They were all looking for some way to shuffle him off. Except Gran hadn't bailed. She'd taken him on regardless. He respected and loved her all the more for that.

Mariah patted each twin on the cheek and smiled sadly at Stone since he held himself apart. "It's inoperable brain cancer."

His throat closed up tight. Amie gasped, blinking fast but a tear still escaped.

Their grandmother shook her head. "None of that emotional stuff. I've never had much patience for tears. I want optimism. Doctors are hopeful treatment can reduce the size of the tumor. That could give me years instead of months."

Months?

Damn it.

The wind got knocked out of him all over again. More than once, Stone had been called a charmer with a stone-cold heart. But that heart ached right now at the thought of anything happening to his grandmother.

Shrugging, Mariah leaned back in the saddle. "Still, even if the treatments help, I can't risk the tumor clouding my judgment. I won't put everything I've worked for at risk by waiting too long to make important decisions about Diamonds in the Rough and the Hidden Gem Ranch."

The family holdings meant everything to her. To all of them. It had never dawned on him until now that his grandmother—the major stockholder—might want to change the roles they all played to keep the empire rock-solid. He must be mistaken. Better to wait and hear her out rather than assume.

Amie wasn't so restrained, but then she never had been. "What have you decided?"

"I haven't," Mariah conceded. "Not yet, but I have a plan, which is why I asked you three to come riding with me today."

Alex, the quiet one of the bunch, frowned. "I'm not sure I understand."

"You'll each need to do something for me—" Mariah angled forward, forearm on the saddle horn "—something to help put my mind at ease about who to place in charge."

"You're testing us," Amie accused softly.

"Call it what you like." Gran was unapologetic, her jaw set. "But as it stands now, I'm not sold on any of you taking over."

That revelation stabbed pain clear through his already raw nerves.

Enough holding back. He was a man of action, and the urge to be in control of something, anything, roared through him. "What do you need me to do for you?"

"Stone, you need to find homes for all four of my dogs."

A fish plopped in the pond, the only sound breaking his stunned silence.

Finally, he asked, "You're joking, right? To lighten the mood."

"I'm serious. My pets are very important to me. You know that. They're family."

"It just seems a...strange test." Was the tumor already affecting her judgment?

His grandmother shook her head slowly. "The fact that you don't know how serious this is merely affirms my concerns. You need to prove to me you have the heart to run this company and possibly oversee the entire family portfolio."

She held him with her clear blue gaze, not even a whisper of confusion showing. Then she looked away, clicked her horse into motion and started back toward the main house, racing past the cabins vacationers rented.

Shaking off his daze, he followed her, riding along the split rail fence, his cousins behind him as they made their way home.

Home.

Some would call it a mansion—a rustic log ranch house with two wings. Their personal living quarters occupied one side, and the other side housed the lodge run by Alex. His cousin had expanded the place from a small bed-and-breakfast to a true hobby ranch, with everything from horseback riding to a spa, fishing and trail adventures...even poker games, saloon-style. They catered to a variety of people's needs, from vacations to weddings.

The gift store featured some of the McNair signature jewelry pieces, just a sampling from their flagship store in Fort Worth.

Alex was one helluva businessman in his own right. Gran could be serious about turning over majority control to him.

Or maybe she had someone else in mind. A total stranger. He couldn't even wrap his brain around that unthinkable possibility. His whole being was consumed with shock—and hell, yes, grief—not over the fact that he might lose the company but because he would lose Gran. A month or a year from now, he couldn't envision a world without her.

And he also couldn't deny her anything she needed to make her last days easier.

Stone urged his horse faster to catch her before she reached the stables.

"Okay, fine, Gran," he said as he pulled alongside

her, their horses' gaits in sync. "I can do that for you. I'll line up people to take, uh…" What the hell were their names? "Your dogs."

"There are four of them, in case you've forgotten that, as well as forgetting their names."

"The scruffy one's named Dorothy, right?"

Gran snorted almost as loudly as the horse. "Close. The dog looks like Toto, but her name is Pearl. The yellow lab is Gem, given to us by a friend. My precious Rottie that I adopted from a shelter is named Ruby. And my baby chi-weenie's name is Sterling."

Chi-what? Oh, right, a Chihuahua and dachshund. "What about your two cats?"

Surely he would get points for remembering there were two.

"Amie is keeping them."

She always was a suck-up.

"Then I'll keep the dogs. They can live with me." How much trouble could four dogs be? He had lots of help. He would find one of those doggy day cares.

"I said I wanted them to go to *good* homes."

He winced. "Of course you do."

"Homes approved of by an expert," she continued as she stopped her horse by the stables.

"An expert?" Hairs on the back of his neck rose with an impending sense of Karma about to bite him on the butt.

He didn't even have to look down the lengthy walkway between horse stalls to know Johanna Fletcher was striding toward them on long, lean legs that could have sold a million pairs of jeans. She usually wore a French braid to keep her wavy blond hair secure when she worked. His fingers twitched at the memory of sliding through that braid to unleash all those tawny strands around her bare shoulders.

What he wouldn't give to lose himself in her again, to forget about the thought of his grandmother's illness. Even if the best scenario played out, a couple of years wasn't enough.

For now, he would do whatever it took to keep Gran happy.

"Your expert?" he prodded.

"All adoptions must be approved by our ranch vet tech, Johanna Fletcher."

Of course.

His eyes slid to Johanna closing the gap between them as she went from stall to stall, horse to horse. Her face shuttered the instant she looked at him, whereas once she would have met him with a full-lipped smile, a slight gap between her front teeth. That endearing imperfection only enhanced her attractiveness. She was down-to-earth and sexy. He knew every inch of her intimately.

After all, she was his ex-fiancée.

The woman who had dumped him in no uncertain terms in front of all their friends at a major fund-raiser. A woman who now hated his guts and would like nothing more than to see his dreams go up in flames.

Stone McNair, the CEO in a business suit ruling the boardroom, commanded respect and awe. But Stone McNair, cowboy Casanova on a horse, was a charismatic charmer Johanna Fletcher had always been hard-pressed to resist.

Johanna tamped down the urge to fan herself as she stood just outside a horse stall and studied her former lover out of the corner of her eyes. Damn it, he still made her hot all over.

She busied herself with listening to a horse's heart-beat—or pretending to listen at least. The palomino was fine, but she didn't want anyone thinking she was still pining for Stone. Everyone from Fort Worth to Del Rio knew her history with him. She didn't need to feed them any fodder for gossip by drooling every time he strutted into the stables.

Lord help her, that man knew how to strut.

Jeans hugged his thighs as he swung a leg over his horse, boots hitting the ground with a thud that vibrated clear through her even from twenty yards away. The sun flashed off his belt buckle—a signature Diamonds in the Rough design—bringing out the nuances of the pat-tern. Magnificent. Just like the man. All the McNairs had charisma, but Stone was sinfully handsome, with coal-black hair and ice-blue eyes right off some movie poster. Sweat dotted his brow, giving his hair a hint of a curl along the edges of his tan Stetson. She'd idol-ized him as a child. Fantasized about him as a teenager.

And as a woman? She'd fallen right in line with the rest and let herself be swayed by his charms.

Never again.

Johanna turned her focus back to the next stall with a quarter horse named Topaz, one of the more popular rides for vacationers. She had a job to do and she was darn lucky to work here after the scene she'd caused during her breakup with Stone. But Mrs. McNair liked her and kept her on. Johanna hadn't been able to resist the opportunity to work with so many unique horses in the best stable.

Her career was everything to her now, and she refused to put it in jeopardy. Her parents had sacrificed their life's savings to send her to the best schools so she had the educational foundation she needed to pursue her dreams. Although her parents were gone now after a fire in the trailer park, she owed them. Perhaps even more so to honor their memory. Her father's work here had brought her into the McNair world—brought her to Stone, even if their romance ultimately hadn't been able to withstand the wide social chasm between them.

She had no family, not even the promise of one she'd once harbored while engaged to Stone. She had her work, her horses. This was her life and her future.

Hooves clopped as Mariah and Stone passed off their rides to two stable hands. Johanna frowned. Even though the McNairs were wealthy, they usually unsaddled and rubbed down their horses themselves. Instead, the grandmother and grandson were walking directly toward her. Tingles pranced up and down her spine. Ignoring him would be impossible.

She hooked her stethoscope around her neck. Her own racing heartbeat filled her ears now, each breath faster and faster, filling her lungs with the scent of hay and leather.

Trailing her hand along the plush velvet of the horse's coat, she angled her way out of the wooden stall and into the walkway. "Hello, Mrs. McNair—" she swallowed hard "—and Stone."

Mariah McNair smiled. Stone didn't. In fact, he was scowling. But there was also something more lurking in his eyes, something…sad? She hated the way her heart pinched instinctively, and hated even more that she could still read him so well.

Mariah held out a hand. "Dear, let's step back into the office where we can chat in private."

With Stone, too? But Mariah's words weren't a question. "Of course."

Questions welled inside her with each step toward the office, passing Hidden Gem staff barely hiding their own curiosity as they prepped rides for vacationers. Alex and Amie eyed them but kept their distance as they hauled the saddles off their horses. The twins wore the same somber and stunned expressions on their faces that she saw on Stone's.

Concern nipped like a feisty foal, and Johanna walked faster. She'd all but grown up here, following her stable hand dad around. Her family hadn't been wealthy like the McNairs, but she'd always been loved, secure—until the day her family had died when their malfunctioning furnace caught on fire in the night.

She'd lost everything. Except rather than making her afraid to love, she craved that sense of family. These walls echoed with memories of how special those bonds had been.

Custom saddles lined the corridors, all works of art like everything the McNairs made. Carvings marked the leather with a variety of designs from roses to vines to full-out pastoral scenes. Some saddles sported silver or brass studs on horn caps and skirting edges that rivaled the tooling of any of the best old vaqueros.

Her job here had spoiled her for any other place. She couldn't imagine living anywhere else. This was her home as well as her workplace.

Stone held open the office door, which left her no choice but to walk past him, closely. His radiant heat brought back memories of his bare skin slick with perspiration against hers as they made love in the woods on a hot summer day.

His gaze held hers for an electrified moment, attraction crackling, alive and well, between them, before she forced herself to walk forward and break the connection.

Red leather chairs, a sofa and a heavy oak desk filled the paneled room. The walls were covered in framed prints of the McNair holdings at various stages of expansion. A portrait of Mariah and her husband, Jasper, on their twenty-fifth wedding anniversary dominated the space over a stone fireplace, a painting done shortly before Jasper had passed away from a heart attack.

Mariah's fingers traced lightly along the carved frame before she settled into a fat wingback chair with an exhausted sigh. "Please, have a seat, Johanna. Stone? Pour us something to drink, dear."

Johanna perched on the edge of a wooden rocker. "Mrs. McNair? Is there a problem?"

"I'm afraid there is, and I need your help."

"Whatever I can do, just let me know."

Mariah took a glass of sparkling spring water from her grandson, swallowed deeply, then set the crystal tumbler aside. "I'm having some health problems and during my treatment I need to be sure I have my life settled."

"Health problems?" Concern gripped Johanna's heart in a chilly fist. How much could she ask without being too pushy? Considering this woman had almost been her family, she decided she could press as far as she needed. "Is it serious?"

"Very," Mariah said simply, fingering her diamond horseshoe necklace. "I'm hopeful my doctors can buy me more time, but treatments will be consuming and I don't want the business or my pets to be neglected."

Mariah's love for her animals was one of the bonds the two women shared. The head of a billion-dollar empire had always made time for a stable hand's daughter who wanted to learn more about the animals at Hidden Gem.

Johanna took the glass from Stone, her hand shaking so much the ice rattled. "I'm sorry, more than I can say. What can I do to help?"

Angling forward, Mariah held her with clear blue eyes identical to Stone's. "You can help me find homes for my dogs."

Without hesitation, Johanna said, "I can watch them while you're undergoing treatments."

"My dear," Mariah said gently, but with a steely strength, "it's brain cancer. I believe it's best for my dogs to find permanent homes."

The pronouncement slammed Johanna back in her chair. She bit her bottom lip to hold in a gasp and blinked back tears. There were no words.

A firm hand landed on her shoulder. Stone's hand. She didn't have to look. She would know his touch anywhere.

God, he must be devastated. She angled around to clasp his hand, but the cool look in his eyes stopped her. Apparently, he was fine with giving out sympathy, but his pride wouldn't allow him to accept any from her.

Johanna reached to take Mariah's hands instead, holding them in hers. "I'll do whatever you need."

"Thank you." Mariah smiled and squeezed Johanna's hands. "Stone will be finding homes for my dogs, but I need for you to go with him and make sure the matches are truly right for each one. It should take about a week."

"A week?" she squeaked.

Go off alone with Stone for a week? No, no and hell, no. The torture of running across him here was bad enough, but at least they had the buffer of work. Stone had stolen her heart then trounced all her dreams of having a family of her own. He'd refused to consider having children or adopting. They'd argued—more than once—until finally she'd broken things off. He'd thought she was bluffing.

He was wrong.

Did Mariah think she was bluffing, as well?

Johanna chose her words carefully. "I don't mean any disrespect, ma'am, and I understand your need for peace, especially now…" She pushed back a well of emotion. This wasn't about her. It was about Mariah, and yes, Stone, too. "You have to realize this attempt at matchmaking isn't going to work. Stone and I were finished a long time ago."

Johanna shot a pointed look at him in case he might be harboring any thoughts of using this situation to wrangle his way back into her bed. Even when she'd broken things off, he'd been persistent for a solid month before accepting that she wouldn't change her mind.

He simply arched an arrogant eyebrow before shifting his glacial gaze toward his grandmother. Only then did his eyes warm.

Mariah shook her head. "I'm not trying anything of the sort. I have trusted you with my animals for years. I've watched you grow up, known you since you were in elementary school. You also understand Stone. He won't pull off anything questionable with you watching him. Can you think of anyone else he can't charm?"

Johanna conceded, "You have a point there."

Stone frowned, speaking for the first time, "Hey, I think I'm being insulted."

Mariah reached up to pat his cheek. "If you only *think* it, Stone, then I must not be making myself clear enough. I hope you will be successful in proving yourself, but I have serious reservations."

He scratched along his jaw, which was perpetually peppered with beard stubble no matter how often he shaved. "You trust Johanna over your own flesh and blood?"

"I do," Mariah said without hesitation. "Case in point, you wanted to keep the expansion a secret, even from me."

"Just until I had the details hammered out, to surprise you. To impress you."

"Our company isn't a grade-school art project to tape to the refrigerator. You need to show me you understand the importance of teamwork and compassion. That's the reason I came up with this test." Mariah's calm but unwavering tone made it clear there would be no changing her mind. "Johanna, you'll go with him to all the interviews with prospective families that I've lined up."

"You've already found the families? You're making his test too easy," Johanna said suspiciously. "There must be a catch."

"No catch. But as for easy?" Mariah laughed softly. "That depends on you two and your ability to act like grownups around each other."

"Civility during a few interviews," Johanna echoed. "We can handle that." Maybe.

"More than during interviews. There's travel time, as well."

"Travel?" So there was a catch. She glanced at Stone who was looking too damn hot—and smug—leaning against the fireplace mantel. He simply shrugged, staying tall, dark and silent.

"These families I've lined up don't live around the corner, but the corporate jet should make the journey easier." Mariah patted her diamond horseshoe necklace. "You should be able to complete the meet and greets in a week."

Stone stepped forward. "Gran, I can handle our travel arrangements."

"You can. But you're not going to. I'm calling the shots on this. My plan. My test," his grandmother said succinctly.

Stone's jaw clamped shut, and Johanna could see the lord of the boardroom holding himself back because of his grandmother's condition.

"A week…" Johanna repeated. A week away from work, a week of more than just crossing paths for a few meet and greets. "Alone together, jetting around the country on the McNair corporate airplane?"

"I don't expect the two of you to reunite. This truly is about Stone showing me he's capable of the compassion needed to run a company." Her hand slid up behind her neck and she unclasped the chain. "But I do hope the two of you can also find some way to reconcile your way back to friendship."

Understanding settled over Johanna. "You want to be at peace—knowing your dogs are loved *and* that Stone and I won't hurt each other again."

Mariah's fingers closed around her necklace and

whispered, "My grandson's well-being is important, more so than any company."

Mariah had found Johanna's Achilles' heel. Was it an act from Mariah, to get her way? Heaven knew the woman could be every bit as wily as Stone. But given Mariah's illness, the woman did deserve peace in every realm of her life.

"Okay," Johanna agreed simply.

Mariah pressed the necklace into Johanna's palm. "Good luck, dear."

Johanna started to protest such an extravagant gift, but one look in Mariah's eyes showed her how much it meant to her...a woman at the end of her life passing along pieces of herself. The horseshoe was so much more than diamonds. It was a gift of the heart, of family, a symbol of all Johanna wanted for her life.

All that Stone had thrown away without a thought.

She pitied him almost as much as she resented him for costing them the life they could have had together.

Her fist closed around the necklace, and she stood, facing Stone with a steely resolve she'd learned from Mariah. "Pack your bags, Casanova. We have a plane to catch."

Two

Staring out the office window, Stone listened for the door to click closed as his grandmother and Johanna left, then he sank into the leather desk chair, his shoulders hunched. He couldn't believe Johanna had actually agreed to a week alone on the road with him.

Heaven or hell?

He'd started to argue with Mariah, but she'd cut out on the conversation, claiming exhaustion. How could he dispute that? If anything, he wanted to wrap her in cotton to protect her even as she made her way to her favorite chaise longue chair up in her sitting room.

The prideful air that had shone in Mariah's eyes kept him from following her. Not to mention the intuitive sense that she needed to be alone. He understood the feeling, especially right now. He and his grandmother were alike in that, needing privacy and space to lick wounds. A hard sigh racked his body as he tamped down the urge to tear apart the whole office space—books, computers, saddles and framed awards—to rage at a world that would take away his grandmother.

The last thing he wanted to do was leave Fort Worth now and waste even one of her remaining days flying around the country. Even with Johanna.

What exactly was Mariah's angle in pairing them up on this Mutt Mission of Mercy? Was she making him jump through hoops like one of her trained dogs to see how badly he wanted to run the company, to prove he had a heart? Or was she matchmaking, as Johanna had accused? If so, this wasn't about the company at all, which should reassure him.

More likely his multitasking, masterminding grandmother was looking to kill two birds with one stone— matchmaking and putting him through the wringer to make him appreciate what he'd inherit when he took the reins of the company.

He just had to get through the next seven days with his former fiancée without rehashing the train wreck of their messy breakup where she'd pointed out all his emotional shortcomings. He couldn't give Johanna what she'd wanted from him—a white picket fence family life. He wasn't wired that way. He truly was aptly named. He might have overcome the rough start in life, born with an addiction, spending most of his first ten years catching up on developmental delays—but some betrayals left scars so thick and deep he might as well be made of stone.

He understood full well his grandmother's concerns about him were true, even if he disagreed about the company needing a soft-hearted marshmallow at the helm. Although God knew he would do anything to give his grandmother peace, whatever her motivation for this doggy assignment. The business was all he would have left of her and he didn't intend to throw that away because hanging out with Johanna opened him up to a second round of falling short. His hand fisted on the chair's armrests as he stared out at the rolling fields filled with vacationers riding into the woods.

No, he didn't expect a magical fix-it with the only woman he'd ever considered marrying. But he needed closure. Because he couldn't stop thinking about her. And he was growing weary of her avoiding him.

Truth be told, he would give his right arm for the chance to sleep with Johanna again. And again. And most certainly again, because she ruled his thoughts until he hadn't been able to touch another woman since their breakup seven months ago. That was a damn long time to go without.

The life of a monk didn't suit him. Frustration pumped through him, making him ache to punch a wall. He dragged in breaths of air and forced his fists to unfurl along the arms of the chair.

A hand rested lightly on his shoulder.

Stone jolted and pivoted around fast. "Johanna? You've been there the whole time?"

He'd assumed she'd left with his grandmother.

"I started to tell you, but you seemed…lost in thought. I was searching for the right moment to clear my throat or something, and that moment just never came."

She'd stood there the whole time, watching him struggle to hold in his grief over his grandmother's announcement? The roomy office suddenly felt smaller now that he was alone with Johanna. The airplane would be damn near claustrophobic as they jetted across the country with his grandmother's pack of dogs.

"What did you need?" His voice came out chilly even to his own ears, but he had a tight rein on his emotions right now.

Johanna pulled her hand off his shoulder awkwardly. "Are you okay?"

There was a time when they hadn't hesitated to put their hands all over each other. That time had passed. A wall stood between them now, and he had no one to blame but himself. "What do you mean?"

Her sun-kissed face flooded with compassion. "Your grandmother just told you she has terminal cancer. That has to be upsetting."

"Of course it is. To you, too, I imagine." The wall between him and Johanna kept him from reaching out to comfort her.

"I'm so sorry." She twisted her fingers in front of her, the chain from the diamond horseshoe necklace dangling. "You have to know that regardless of what happened between us, I do still care about your family...and you."

She *cared* about him?

What a wishy-washy word. *Cared.* What he felt for her was fiery, intense and, yes, even at times filled with frustrated anger that they couldn't be together, and he couldn't forget about her when they were apart. "You *care* about my family, and that's why you agreed to my grandmother's crazy plan." It wasn't that she wanted to be alone with him.

"It influenced my decision, yes." She shuffled from dusty boot to dusty boot, drawing his attention to her long legs. "I also care about her dogs and I respect that she wants to look after their welfare. She's an amazing woman."

"Yes, she is." An enormity of emotion about his grandmother's health problems welled inside him, pain and anger combatting for dominance, both due to the grinding agony that he couldn't fix this. Feeling powerless went against everything in his nature.

It made him rage inside all over again, and only exacerbated the frustration over months of rejection from Johanna.

Over months of missing her.

Something grouchy within him made him do the very thing guaranteed to push Johanna away. Although arguing with her felt better than being ignored.

He stepped closer, near enough to catch a whiff of hay and bluebonnets, and closed his hands over her fingers, which were gripping the necklace his grandmother had given her. Johanna's eyes went wide, but she didn't move away, so he pressed ahead.

Dipping his head, Stone whispered against the curve of her neck, "Do you feel sorry enough for me to do anything about it?"

She flattened a hand on his chest, finally stopping him short. But her breathing was far from steady and she still hadn't pushed him away.

"Not *anything*." Her eyes narrowed, and he knew he'd pushed her far enough for now.

He backed away and hitched a hip on the heavy oak desk he'd climbed over as a kid. His initials were still carved underneath. "You've come back to offer comfort. Mission complete. Thanks."

"You're not fooling me." Her emerald-green eyes went from angry to sad in a revealing instant. "I know you better than anyone."

He reached for her fist, which was still holding the necklace from his grandmother, and drew Johanna toward him until her hand rested against his heart. "Then tell me what I'm feeling right now."

"You're trying to get me to run by making a move on me, because I'm touching a nerve with questions about your grandmother," she said with unerring accuracy. He never had been able to get anything past her. "You're in pain and you don't want me to see that."

"I'm in pain, all right—" his eyes slid down the fine length of her curvy, toned body "—and I'm more than happy to let you see everything."

She tugged away from him, shaking her head. "For a practiced, world-class charmer, you're overplaying your hand."

"But you're not unaffected." He slipped the necklace from her fist deftly.

Standing, he put the chain around her neck as if that had been his reason for coming closer. He brushed aside the tail of her thick braid. Her chest rose and fell faster. As he worked the clasp, he savored the satiny skin of her neck, then skimmed his fingers forward along the silvery links, settling the diamond horseshoe between her breasts. Her heartbeat fluttered against his knuckles.

"Stone, our attraction to each other was never in question," she said bluntly, her hands clenched at her sides and her chin tipping defiantly. "Because of that attraction, we need to have ground rules for this trip."

"Ground rules?"

She met his gaze full-on. "No more of these seduction games. If you want *me* to play nice, then *you* be nice."

"Define *nice*." He couldn't resist teasing.

"Being truthful, polite—" Her eyes glinted like emeralds. "And above all, no games."

"I thought your only agenda here was making sure the dogs end up in good homes." He toyed with the diamond horseshoe, barely touching her. A little taste of Johanna went a long way.

"I can place the dogs without you," she said confidently. "I'm agreeing to your grandmother's plan to give her peace of mind on a broader spectrum. She wants us to make this trip together, and the only way I can manage that is if you stop with the practiced seduction moves. Be real. Be honest."

"Fine then." He slid the horseshoe back and forth along the chain, just over her skin, like a phantom touch. "In all honesty, I can assure you that I ache to peel off your clothes with my teeth. I burn to kiss every inch of your bared skin. And my body burns to make love to you again and again, because, hell, yes, I want to forget about what my grandmother just told me."

He dropped the charm and waited.

She exhaled long and hard, her eyes wide. "Okay, then. I hear you, and I believe you."

Shoving away from the desk and around her, he strutted right to the door and stopped short, waiting until she turned to look at him.

"Oh, Johanna, one last thing." He met her gaze dead-on, her eyes as appealing as her curves. "I wanted you every bit as much before my grandmother's announcement. This has nothing to do with me needing consolation. See you in the morning, sunshine."

Johanna had until morning to pack her bags and get her hormones under control.

Moonlight cast a dappled path through the pine trees as she walked the gravel lane from the barn to her cabin. Her heart ached as much as her muscles after this long day. Too long.

She opened her mailbox and tugged out a handful of flyers and a pizza coupon. Laughter from vacationers rode the wind as they enjoyed a party on the back deck of the main lodge, the splash of the hot tub mingling with the trickling echo of the creek that ran behind her little hideaway house.

Since graduation from vet tech school four years ago, she'd lived in a two-bedroom cabin on the Hidden Gem Ranch, the same cabin model used by vacationers. She liked to think of it as home, but truth be told she hadn't had a home since her parents' trailer had burned down when she was eighteen. She'd lived in an apartment during her two years of vet tech training, thanks to a scholarship from Mariah McNair. Then Johanna had accepted a job at Hidden Gem after graduation, her girlhood crush on Stone flourishing into full-out love.

Day by day, she'd earned a living, marking time, doing a job she adored but never putting down roots of her own, waiting on Prince Charming to pop the question. Once he did, she discovered her prince was a frog. A hot, sexy frog. But a frog nonetheless. She couldn't blame Stone for how things shook down between them. She was the one who'd worn blinders, refusing to accept the truth until it was too late.

But with the silver chain around her neck, the diamond horseshoe cool against her skin, she could only feel the weight of impending loss, the finality of closing the book on this chapter of her life. Once Mariah died, there would be nothing left holding Johanna here. Nothing other than her tenacious attraction to Stone, but that only kept her from moving on with another man, finding a future for herself with the family she craved.

She pushed open the gate on her split rail fence. The

night air carried the refrain of square-dancing music from the sound system that fed the pool area. Maybe she needed this trip away from the ranch for more reasons than she'd thought. Perhaps this wasn't just about finding peace for Mariah, but snipping the last bonds that held her to Stone so she could move on without regrets.

She climbed the three wooden steps up to her dark log cabin, katydids buzzing a full-out Texas symphony. A creak just ahead stopped her in her tracks. She searched the railed porch, wishing she'd remembered to leave on a front light, but she hadn't expected to come home so late. She blinked her eyes fast to better adjust to the dark and found a surprise waiting for her in one of the two rocking chairs.

Amie McNair sat with a gray tabby cat in her lap, a Siamese at her feet, both hers, soon to have feline siblings when Mariah's pride joined them.

"Well, hey, there," Amie drawled. "I didn't think you would ever get home."

What was Amie's reason for waiting around? Was she here to talk about Mariah's announcement? The impending loss had to be hard on the whole family. She and Amie weren't enemies but they weren't BFFs, either. They were more like childhood acquaintances who had almost been related. And because of that connection, she felt the need to hug this woman on what had to be one of the most difficult days of her life.

Johanna unlocked the front door and reached inside to turn on the porch light. "I worked late preparing to leave tomorrow, but I'm here now." She let the screen door close again. "Is there something I can do for you?"

"Ah, so you're actually going through with my grandmother's plan." Amie swept her hand over the tabby, sending a hint of kitty dander wafting into the night air as her bracelets jingled.

Even covered in cat hair and a light sheen of perspiration, Amie was a stunner, totally gorgeous no matter what she wore. She'd been the first runner-up in the Miss Texas pageant ten years ago, reportedly the first beauty competition she'd lost since her mother had teased up her hair and sent Amie tap-dancing out on the stage at four years old. She'd tap-danced her way through puberty into bikinis and spray tans. Johanna remembered well how Amie's mama had lived for her daughter's wins.

Johanna settled into the cedar rocker beside Amie and the cats, reluctant to go into her cabin. Inside, she had nothing to do but pace around, unable to sleep because of this crazy, upside down day. "I don't have a choice but to go with Stone and the dogs."

"Sure you do." Amie kicked off her sandals and stroked her toes over the kitty at her feet. "Tell my grandmother no, that it's not fair to play with your life this way. You know as well as I do that you can find homes for those dogs all on your own."

"True enough, and of course I've thought of that. Except any…unease…I feel doesn't matter, not in light of what's important to Mariah. She's dying, Amie." The reality of those words still stole her breath for a long, humid moment. "How can I deny her anything, even if the request is bizarre?"

Amie blinked back tears and looked away, her sleek black ponytail trailing over one shoulder. "I refuse to accept she's going to die. The doctors will buy her enough time so she can pass away at a ripe old age." Her throat moved with a long swallow before she looked at Johanna again, her eyes cleared of grief. "Mariah can be reasoned with...unless you don't really want to say no."

An ugly suspicion bloomed in Johanna's mind. "Or is it you who wants me to walk away so your cousin loses?"

Amie's perfectly plucked eyebrows arched upward. "That wouldn't be very loyal of me."

"Yet you're not denying anything. What's really going on?" She hated to think Amie could be so coldly calculating, but then she'd always had the sense the woman wanted more power in the family business.

The former beauty queen spread her hands. Long fingers that had once played the piano to accompany her singing now crafted high-end jewelry. "I've never made a secret of the fact that I want my family to take me seriously." Her hair swished over her shoulder, the porch light catching on the gems in the Aztec design of her hair clamp. "I'm just weighing in with my thoughts on this whole 'test' game. This is not the way to decide the future of our family legacy."

"What's *your* test?"

"Gran hasn't told me yet. Or Alex, either, for that matter." Amie scrunched her nose. In frustration? Or at the smoky scent of a bonfire launching an acrid tint to the night breeze? "But after what she set up for Stone, I'm not hopeful mine will make sense. I'm just trying to protect us all."

Johanna thumbed a knotty circle on the armrest. "How is talking to me going to accomplish that?"

"You're the only one who has ever come close to getting through the walls Stone puts around himself. I just hope you'll make sure he's okay."

Johanna sat up straighter. "Excuse me?"

"Be sure he doesn't crack up over this."

"Crack up? Stone? He's rock-solid—no pun intended."

Amie clamped Johanna's arm in a surprisingly strong grip. "I'm worried about him, okay? He doesn't have a support system like I do. My brother and I can tell each other everything. Stone is our family, but he's never let himself get close to us. And I'm worried about him right now."

There was no denying the sincerity in her voice.

"That's really sweet of you." Johanna felt bad for assuming the worst. "I do care about Stone, even though we can't be together. He's a strong man. He will grieve for Mariah—we all will—but he will haul himself through. He always does."

Even as she said it, she couldn't ignore a niggling voice in the back of her mind reminding her that Stone's childhood had been very different from her own or that of his twin cousins. His grandmother had been his only bedrock of support.

Amie's hand slid away. "Just keep what I said in mind. That's all I ask." Cradling her cat in her arms, she stood. "Good night and good luck with your trip."

"Thank you…" She had a feeling she would need luck and more to get through the coming week. She needed a plan and stronger boundaries to protect her heart.

"Anytime," Amie called over her shoulder as strolled down the steps as though she were taking a runway scene by storm, leaving her shoes behind, her other cat following her into the night.

Scooping up her junk mail, Johanna shoved to her feet. She needed to start packing now if she wanted any chance of getting to bed at a reasonable time. Not that she expected to sleep much with her brain whirling a million miles an hour.

She'd tried to make this place her own, with everything from sunflowers in the front yard to a quilted wreath on the door. Hokey? Maybe. But she'd dreamed of hokey and normal as a kid listening to the rain rattling along the tin roof of their trailer.

She pushed her way inside. The scent of freshly waxed floors and flowers greeted her, but not even a cat or dog of her own. So many times she'd wondered why she never chose a pet for herself, just took care of other people's....

Wait.

Her nose twitched.

Waxed floors and...flowers? She didn't have any inside, not even a floral air freshener.

Patting along the wall, she found the switch and flipped on the light. A wagon wheel chandelier splashed illumination around the room full of fat stuffed furniture in paisley patterns, a girly escape for a tomboy in a dusty, mucky profession. She spun to scan the room, her eyes landing on her shabby chic sofa.

Where a man was sprawled out asleep.

Her gaze skated from the boots on the armrest, up muscular legs in jeans, past a Diamonds in the Rough belt buckle, to broad shoulders in a blue flannel shirt. For a second, she thought Stone had followed her here. A straw cowboy hat covered the man's face as he snored softly.

Although once she looked closer, she realized it wasn't Stone at all. It was his near twin. His cousin

Alex was asleep on her sofa, with a fistful of wild daisies on his chest.

As she saw him waiting there for her, she couldn't help but think, Amie and Alex didn't tell each other everything.

Three

Johanna swept the cowboy hat from Alex's face. "What are you doing in my house?"

He peeked out of one eye lazily, scrubbed a hand over his face and yawned. Stretching, he sat up, keeping his hold on the daisies, apparently in no hurry to answer her question.

Alex rarely rushed. Yet he always seemed to get crazy amounts done. He was a fascinating individual, like all the McNairs. And while he'd been in her cabin often, she hadn't expected to see him here tonight.

"Well?" She hitched her hands on her hips. "Do you have anything to say for yourself? I locked the door, so you're breaking and entering."

"As your *landlord,*" he drawled, his voice like Southern Comfort on the rocks, smooth with a bite. Stone spoke in more clipped, bass tones—like boulders rumbling. "I used my master key. I own the place."

She'd known Alex as long as she'd known Stone. She'd met all of the McNairs when her father took a stable hand job here during Johanna's third-grade year. Where Stone was the outgoing, bad-boy charmer, Alex had been the brooding, silent type, a tenacious rodeo champ even as a kid, breaking more bones by eighteen than any pro football star.

After she'd ended her engagement to Stone, she'd realized Alex's resolute nature had hidden a longtime attraction to her. Six months after the split, Alex had made his move by asking her out to dinner. She'd been stunned—and not ready to consider dating anyone. He'd taken the news well. Or so she'd thought. She was beginning to grasp how persistent, patient and downright stubborn this quiet giant could be.

With that in mind, she should have realized their grandmother's plan would not go over well with Alex. "Even though you own my rental cabin, I didn't realize landlords slept on the sofa," she joked, needing to keep things light. Her emotional well was running on empty. "Do you have a specific reason for being here?"

"I'm making sure you don't fall under my evil cousin's spell again." He swung his legs to the floor and thrust out the fistful of daisies.

Roots straggled from a couple of the stems. He definitely was a unique one with a charm all his own. At another time in her life she might have been tempted.

She took the daisies from him. "You're trying to persuade me by giving me flowers?"

"Consider it elaborate bribery," he said with a self-deprecating grin directed at the raggedy bouquet.

"You stole them out of the garden by the back deck," she shot over her shoulder as she stepped into the kitchen area to get a large mason jar.

"The garden belongs to me."

"To your family." She slid the flowers into the jar and tucked it under the faucet.

"Same thing." His smile faded. "Are you okay with this trip?"

"Your concern is sweet and I do mean that." She smiled, then jerked as water overflowed from the jar and splashed onto her hand.

"My motives are purer than Amie's were out there on the porch."

"You heard her?"

"I did, since you always leave your windows open rather than use the air conditioner." He stretched his legs out in front of him, crossing his boots at the ankles as he extended his arms along the back of the couch. "You would be wise to remember she's the most ruthless of all of us."

"That's not a very nice thing to say." She placed the flowers on the end table by the floral sofa, a perfect match for the rustic charm of her place.

"I only mean that you're my friend." He reached for her hand and tugged her down to sit beside him. "You and Amie don't have that kind of relationship. She's thinking of the family. I'm worried about you."

Johanna looked into his eyes, the same unique shade of light blue as Stone's. Though born three years apart, the men could have been twins. Alex was actually better suited for her. They had more in common. Alex ran a family ranch, whereas Stone was the king of the boardroom, such a workaholic he'd made it clear he had little room in his life for white-picket dreams.

Yet, as she sat here inches away from this incredibly sexy cowboy who'd just given her the sweetest flowers, she could only think of how much she'd wanted Stone to kiss her earlier. And Alex left her lukewarm, and it wasn't fair to keep stringing him along.

She touched his wrist. "Alex, we need to talk about—"

The front door opened with a knock in progress, no real warning at all. Johanna jolted, nearly falling off the sofa as she turned to face the intruder.

Stone stood in the open door, scowling, holding a handful of purple tulips.

What the hell?

Standing in Johanna's doorway, Stone cricked his neck from side to side, trying to process what his eyes told him. His cousin Alex sat on the sofa with Johanna. Close to Johanna. So near, their thighs pressed against each other and before she'd jolted away, she'd been leaning in, her hand on Alex's arm.

And there were fresh flowers on the end table.

Stone strode inside and tossed the tulips—ones that he'd pulled out of a vase in the lobby of the main lodge— onto the end table beside the daisies that looked remarkably like ones in the garden by the deck.

"Sorry to have interrupted…" Whatever had been about to happen. His pulse hammered behind his eyes; his head pounded in frustration over a hellish day that was spiraling down the drain faster and faster by the second.

Nibbling her bottom lip, Johanna rubbed her palms along her jeans. "At the risk of sounding cliché, this isn't what it looks like."

"What does it look like?" Stone smiled, somehow managing to keep his tone level in spite of the jealousy pumping through him.

"That Alex and I are a couple. We're not." She glanced at Alex apologetically.

That apologetic look spoke volumes. His cousin had

been trying to make a move on her. His cousin—as close as any brother—had fallen for Johanna. The thought stunned and rattled Stone into silence.

Alex stood, a gleam in his eyes just like when he'd reached the boiling point as a kid—just before he decked whoever had pissed him off. He leveled that gaze at Stone and slung an arm around Johanna's shoulders. "Who says we're not a couple?"

She shrugged off his arm. "Stop riling him up on purpose. You two are not teenagers anymore." She jabbed a finger at Stone. "That goes for you, too. No fights."

"I'm just looking for a straight answer." Stone spread his arms.

Johanna went prickly. "What this is or isn't doesn't concern you."

"Sure it does," he said, his tone half-joking, but his intent dead serious. "If you've been seeing each other and didn't bother to tell me, that's damn inconsiderate of my feelings."

Alex snorted. "Your *feelings?* You're joking, right?"

Stone resisted the urge to punch Alex in the face and forced reason through the fog. "You're yanking my chain on purpose. Why?"

"Just making a point. Johanna is important to this family and not just because she was your fiancée. If you hurt her," Alex said softly, lethally, "I'll kick your ass."

Fair enough.

They had the same goal: protecting her. Stone respected that. He nodded curtly. "Message heard and received."

Johanna whistled sharply between her teeth, like when she called a horse. "Hey, boys? Don't I get any say here?"

Stone shifted his focus from Alex to her. "Of course. What would you like to add?"

She rolled her eyes. "Nothing. Absolutely nothing. I'm completely capable of taking care of myself. Thank you both for your concern, but I need to pack for this trip tomorrow."

"Of course you can look after yourself," Stone said, gesturing for Alex to go out the door ahead of him. Then he took that moment's privacy to lean toward Johanna. "Just wanted to bring the tulips and say thank-you for caring about my grandmother's happiness."

She went still, most likely in shock, her hand drifting down to rest on top of the purple tulips. He used her moment of distraction to kiss her, just once, on the mouth, but good God, even a brief taste of Johanna was more potent than…anything. After seven months without the feel of her, his body shouted for more.

For everything.

Desire cracked like a whip inside him. He pulled back before he lost control and pushed his luck too far. "See you in the morning at the landing strip."

He closed the door behind him, the night sounds of bugs and owls, the wind in the trees, wrapping around him. He sucked in two deep breaths to steady himself before facing his cousin again.

Alex leaned against the porch post, tucking his hat on his head. "I meant what I said in there about kicking your ass."

"How serious is it? Whatever the two of you have going on?" What the hell would he do if his cousin was all-in? Or worse yet, if Johanna harbored feelings, too?

"If you care so much who she's seeing," Alex said ambiguously, "then do something about it." Without another word, he shoved away from the post, jogged down the steps and disappeared into the dark.

Stone stood on the porch, the smell of the tulips and the feel of Johanna still fresh in his senses even though he'd left her and the flowers inside. But then she'd been in his thoughts every damn second since their split.

His cousin was right. Stone was still attracted to Johanna, and it was time to do something about it.

Stone's kiss still tinged her lips and her memory.

Johanna hauled her suitcase out from under the bed and tossed it onto the mattress with a resounding thump. What the hell had he been thinking, kissing her like that? Although he hadn't lingered. Some might call it a friendly kiss. Except they had this history together....

Need coursed through her, hot and molten, with just a splash of sweetness, like the scent of the tulips she'd brought with her into the bedroom. They rested under the lamp, purple splashes of color on the white table.

She'd tried her best to tamp down her attraction to Stone these past months, which was easier to do when their paths rarely crossed. How would she survive a week of time alone with him?

She dropped to sit on the edge of her bed, the white iron headboard tapping the wall. She tugged one of the purple tulips from the bunch and skimmed it against her mouth lightly. She knew he'd certainly stolen them from a vase in the lodge, and she couldn't help but note how both cousins had snagged the closest flowers at hand. They could drape women in jewels from their family business, yet they still understood the value of a well-timed bouquet.

Stone's tulips, and his kiss, were picking away at her

defenses. Too bad she couldn't wedge a coat of armor into her suitcase to withstand the barrage on her hormones.

Laughter with a hysterical edge bubbled out of her, and she flopped back on the bed into the cushiony softness of her pink-and-gray chevron quilt. She clasped the tulip against her chest, watching the ceiling fan click lazy circles above her. She and Stone had spent entire weekends in her bed making love. She hadn't wanted to go to his quarters in the main house, not even after they'd gotten engaged, not with his grandmother in a nearby suite. So he'd taken her on elaborate trips, vowing that he did so because then he could at least feel like she was staying with him.

Now Johanna wondered if she'd known they were destined to fail even from the start. Their time together had been a fantasy that couldn't withstand the light of harsh reality.

She hadn't traveled much before Stone. During her year dating Stone, he'd flown her to exotic locales and swanky fund-raisers held by influential billionaires, a world away from her ranch and Stetson day-to-day life.

What should she expect from this trip?

She rolled to her side and stared into the empty suitcase. What did a girl take to a week of doggie dates with mystery families and her ex-fiancé? More importantly, how would she react if he gave her another one of those impromptu kisses?

A tap on the window snapped her out of her daze.

She jolted upright, her heart pounding in alarm. Before she could even reach for the cell phone her eyes focused on the face in the glass pane.

Stone stood outside like a Lone Star Romeo.

Her pulse leaped. Damn her traitorous body.

She rolled from the bed and to her feet. She shoved the window up, the muggy night breeze rolling inside and fluttering the lace curtains. "What are you doing out there?"

"I forgot my flowers. You didn't seem to want them, so I figured I would give them to someone who would appreciate them." He hefted himself up and through the window before she could blink.

She stumbled back a step, watching him eye her room, walk to the flowers then peer out the door.

Realization dawned, along with a spark of anger. "You're checking to make sure your cousin didn't come back here."

"Maybe I am." He turned on his heels to face her again. His gaze fell to her bed, right where the lone tulip lay.

Feeling vulnerable, she rushed to scoop up the flower and said, "I'm trying to decide what to pack for the trip. Since I don't know where we're going, I'm not making much progress."

"Pack comfortably." The gleam in his eyes projected loud and clear that he wasn't fooled. "If we need something more, I'll buy it for you."

"We're not engaged anymore. You're not buying me clothes or other gifts." She'd returned all the jewelry after she'd broken up with him—everything, including a yellow diamond engagement ring with a double halo setting. The night he'd given it to her, she'd thought all of her dreams of a family and a real home had come true.

She'd grown up a lot in the past seven months, alone with her disillusionment.

"Johanna," he drawled, "we may not be engaged, but you are an employee of Hidden Gem Ranch and if you're on Hidden Gem business and need clothes, the company can pick up the bill."

"Clothes for what, exactly?"

"There's a gem trade show I want to catch while we're out."

She knew how elaborate and hoity-toity those events could get. Being with him at one of those shows would feel too much like a fancy date. "I'll stay at the hotel with the dogs."

"We'll see," he said in that stubborn, noncommittal way of his just before he swung a leg out the window again. "Good night."

"Stone?"

He stopped shy of stepping all the way through the window. "Yes?"

"Thanks for the flowers." She strode closer—just to be ready to close the window when he left, not to be nearer to him. Right? "It really is sweet how much you care about your grandmother's happiness. I always admired that about you, your family loyalty."

"Glad you have good memories, not just bad."

Guilt pinched her over how their breakup had hurt him, too. She touched his shoulder lightly. "There's nothing between Alex and me."

"I'm glad to hear that."

Was it her imagination or had he swayed closer?

She pressed a hand to his chest. "That doesn't mean there will never be someone. Am I not allowed to have another relationship again?"

A smile played with his mouth. "I'm not answering that."

He looked over his shoulder at the yard.

She frowned. "Is something wrong?"

"Uh, actually—" he glanced back at her sheepishly "—I was taking the dogs for a run. Hope you don't mind they're digging up your yard right now."

She laughed, enjoying this Stone, more like the man she remembered falling for, playful and open. "We're just lucky they didn't jump my little split rail fence."

"Since they're going to be spending the next week with me flying around in a plane, it would be a good idea to remind them who I am."

She allowed herself to fall just a little more under his spell again, even if only for a minute. "That's very sweet of you."

"Sweet? First you make out with my cousin and then you call me sweet. Twice." He shook his head, tsking. "This is not my night."

Before she could help herself, she blurted out, "I wasn't kissing your cousin."

"Good." Stone cupped the back of her neck and drew her in for a kiss, the full-out kind that proved to be a lot more than mouth meeting mouth.

His body pressed to hers in a familiar wall of muscle. Her lips parted and heaven help her, she didn't regret it. She sank into the sensation of having his hands on her again, the warmth of his tongue boldly meeting hers. Kisses like this could lure her into forgetting a lot. In their time apart, somehow she'd lost sight of how intensely their physical attraction could sweep away reason.

Heat gathered between her legs until she gripped his arms, her fingers digging deep. A husky moan of pleasure and need welled up in her throat. She was so close to losing control altogether, what with a bed only a few short steps away. They may have had so many issues in their relationship, but when it came to sex, they were in perfect synchronicity.

How was she going to walk away from him after a kiss like this?

The ground tipped under her feet…or wait…Stone was stumbling into her. She braced a hand on her dresser for balance and realized Ruby the Rottweiler had both paws on the open window and she was nudging Stone in the back. Gem the yellow lab sprung up to join the Rottie, a symphony of barking echoing from beneath them. A quick glance down confirmed that Pearl the terrier and Sterling the Chihuahua-dachshund mix danced in the bushes below.

Breathlessly, she whispered, "I think it's time for you to go."

"Sleep well, beautiful." Stone winked once before sliding back out the window.

She should have slammed the window closed after him. Instead, she stood between the parted curtains and watched him gather the pack with ease. He guided the larger dogs to jump her fence while scooping up the two little ones.

No question, she was in serious trouble here with only one way to cope during the coming week. She had to make absolutely sure she and Stone did not touch each other, not even accidentally. First thing in the morning, she intended to make her hands-off edict clear. Her eyes clung to the breadth of his shoulders and lower to his perfect butt that rivaled any blue jeans ad ever.

Gritting her teeth, she slammed the window closed and spun away fast.

Damn, it was going to be a long, achy night.

* * *

The morning sun crept upward at the McNairs' private landing strip, which was located on the ranch. Johanna had given up waiting for Stone in the limousine an hour ago and had moved inside the small airport offices. The space held a waiting area, a control desk and a back room with a cot for a pilot to take naps if needed. There wasn't much else to do but sit. She could understand Stone being late to meet her, but his grandmother was here with her dogs, prolonging a farewell that already had to be horribly difficult.

Mariah held herself rigidly in control, Ruby and Gem each resting against one leg. Pearl and Sterling curled up together on a seat beside her. Johanna couldn't help but wonder how well the pack would adjust to being separated.

She checked the large digital clock above the door. The red numbers blinked nearly ten o'clock while the pilot kept busy with some paperwork outside beneath a Texas flag flapping lazily in the soft breeze. She bit back anger. She was exhausted from lack of sleep and frustrated from bracing herself to appear blasé in front of Stone.

Only to have him freakin' stand her up.

She was mad. Steaming mad. And completely confused. If he was playing mind games with her, that was one thing. But to involve his grandmother? That was plain wrong, and not like him.

Shuffling a seat to move closer to Mariah, Johanna put a reassuring hand on the woman's arm. "You don't have to do this, Mrs. McNair. The dogs can stay with you. They can stay here now and even if the time comes…" She swallowed back a lump of emotion. "Even if the time comes when you're not here. This is their home."

Mariah patted Johanna's hand. "It's okay, really. I love them enough to do what's best for them. I'll be in and out of the hospital quite often, and they deserve attention."

"Everyone here will take care of them." She held on tighter to this strong, brilliant woman who was already showing signs of fading away. She had new gaunt angles and a darkness around her eyes that showed her exhaustion in spite of keeping up appearances of normalcy with a red denim dress and boots. "You must realize that."

"I do, but I need to know they're settled permanently, for my own peace of mind." Mariah stroked the scruffy little terrier, adjusting the dog's bejeweled collar. "They deserve to be a part of a family and not just a task for the staff, or an obligation for a relative who doesn't really want them."

"They could be a comfort to you. Even if you kept one of them, like Pearl or Sterling, maybe…"

Mariah's touch skimmed from pup to pup until she'd petted all four. "I couldn't choose. It would be like playing favorites with my children or grandchildren."

There was an undeniable truth in her words and a selflessness that made Johanna ache all over again at the thought of losing her. "I wish there were more people like you in the world."

"You're dear to say that." She cradled Johanna's face in her hands. "And I wish you could be my granddaughter."

There it was. Out there. The unacknowledged big pink elephant that had sat in the middle of every one of their conversations for the past seven months. Mariah had never once interfered or questioned her decision to break it off with Stone.

If only there'd been some other way.

Johanna leaned in and hugged Mariah, whispering in her ear, "I'm so sorry I can't make that come true for you. I would have liked very much to have you as part of my family."

Mariah squeezed her once before easing away and thumbing a lone tear from the corner of her eye. "I just want you to be happy."

"My job makes me happy." True, but she'd once dreamed of much more. "If it weren't for your scholarship, I never could have afforded the training. I know I've thanked you before, but I can never thank you enough."

"Ah, dear." Mariah brushed back a loose strand from Johanna's braid. "This isn't goodbye. Even worst-case scenario, I'll be around for months, and you're only going to be gone a week. I intend to fight hard to be around as long as I can."

"I know." Johanna fidgeted with the horseshoe necklace. "I just want to be sure all the important things are said."

"Of course, but I don't want us to use our time on morbid thoughts or gloominess." Mariah smoothed her denim dress and sat straighter. "Stone in particular has had enough disappointment from the people he loves."

Johanna looked into the woman's deep blue eyes and read her in an instant. "You're sending him away this week so he won't be here as you start your treatments."

"Just until I get settled into a routine."

The closeness of the moment, the importance of this

time, emboldened her. "What if he wants to be around to support you?"

"My choices trump anyone else's right now," Mariah said with a steely strength that had made her a business-woman of national stature. "Keep Stone busy and take care of placing my dogs. Enjoy the time away from the ranch. You work too hard, and if I've learned anything lately, it's that we shouldn't waste a day."

Mariah eased the lecture with another squeeze of her hand, which Johanna quickly returned.

"Yes, ma'am."

"Good enough, and for goodness' sake, quit calling me Mrs. McNair or ma'am. If you can't call me Gran, then call me Mariah." She sighed, before shoving slowly to her feet. "Now how about we track down my tardy grandson so you can start your journey?"

"I'm sure he's on his way...Mariah." Johanna glanced at the wall clock again. This wasn't like him. Could something have happened?

Johanna's cell phone chimed from her purse, play-ing a vintage Willie Nelson love song. She glanced at Mariah, a blush stinging her cheeks faster than the fierce Texas sun. Damn it, why hadn't she changed her Stone ringtone? She should have swapped her ringtone to some broken heart, broken truck country song. There were sure plenty to pick from. She fished out her cell, fum-bling with the on button before putting it to her ear. "Where are you?"

"I'm at the office downtown." Stone's bass rumbled over her ears sending a fresh shiver of awareness down her spine. "A few unavoidable emergencies came up with work. I'll give you a call when I'm ready to leave."

Not a chance in hell was he getting off that easy, but

she didn't intend to chew him out with his grandmother listening. She would go straight to the Diamonds in the Rough headquarters and haul him out with both hands, if need be. Not that she intended to give him any warning. "Sure, thanks for calling."

She disconnected and turned to Mariah. "He's fine, just delayed downtown at the Fort Worth office. He wants me to swing by with the dogs, and we'll leave from there. Would you like to help me load the dogs in the car?"

"Of course." Mariah brightened at the task. "But please, take my limo. I'll have the airport security run me back to the house."

Johanna started to argue, but then the notion of rolling up to Diamonds in the Rough, Incorporated in the middle of downtown Fort Worth, dogs in tow, sounded like one hell of an entrance.

Her Texas temper fired up and ready, she was through letting Stone McNair walk all over her emotions.

Four

Stone hated like hell being late for anything, but crisis after crisis had cropped up at the office even though he'd come in at five in the morning to prep for his week-long departure.

Parked at his desk in front of the computer, he finished with the last details, clearing his calendar and rescheduling as much as he could for teleconferences from the road. He loved his grandmother, but she had to know the CEO of Diamonds in the Rough couldn't just check out for a week without major prep. That was the primary reason for her test, right? For him to prove he was best suited to run the company.

She couldn't have chosen a worse time.

Their CFO had gone into premature labor and had been placed on bed rest. His personal assistant was stuck in an airport in North Dakota. Their showroom was still under repairs from tornado damage and the construction crew's foreman had gone on strike.

And his grandmother was dying of cancer.

His hands clenched over the keyboard. For her, he'd put together detailed plans for taking Diamonds in the Rough to an international level, to expand the company as a tribute to his grandparents who'd been there for him over the years. Yet now she might not even live long enough to see that dream come to fruition. It cut him to the core to think he'd somehow let her down, but he must have since she felt she needed to concoct tests for him to prove himself.

His eyes slid to the wood drafting table littered with new designs, most of them done by Amie, but a few of his own were scattered through the mix. He sketched late at night, after hours, to ease the tension of the corporate rat race, more so since his breakup with Johanna. His pieces incorporated a larger emphasis on metal work and carvings than Amie's. He still included signature company jewels inlaid into the buckles, bolos and even a few larger necklaces. Each piece also carried the expected Western aura.

Amie was the true artist in the family, but his pieces usually landed well, too. Johanna had always encouraged him to design more....

He scratched his head and leaned back, desk chair squeaking in protest. What had he been thinking, climbing through her window last night like some out-of-control teenager? Except...he had been out of control, jealous over seeing her with his cousin. He hadn't thought. He'd simply acted. That kiss had left him with a need for her that clawed like metal shards scraping his insides raw. Even hearing her voice on the phone forty-five minutes ago had increased the ache of wanting her in his bed again.

A quick buzz from the temp serving as a stand-in personal assistant gave him only a second's warning before his door flung open to reveal Johanna, fire spitting from her eyes. "You missed your flight."

God, she was sexy all riled up.

"I called you." He creaked his chair back even further, taking in the sight of her in white jeans and layered yellow tank tops. "And it's a private plane. *My* private plane, for that matter. There's no way to miss a flight that's waiting for me to give the go-ahead for takeoff."

Speaking of taking off... What he wouldn't give right now to peel away those tanks of hers, one at a time, with his teeth. He'd left her place last night to give himself space to regain control. Instead, their time apart had only taken his need to another level.

"Would have been nice to know you had other plans for your day before I reached the landing strip. I could have worked, too, or slept in. Or..." She held up her hand, four leashes in her fist. "I could have let the dogs play and run around in the yard longer."

She dropped the leashes and the four-pup pack stampeded into his office. Stone barely had time to bark, "Heel, damn it!" before Gem launched into his lap, the full force of the yellow lab almost tipping his chair over. Stone regained his balance then knelt to greet the dogs. Ruby, Sterling and Pearl licked over his face with slobbery wet tongues. He liked animals—clearly, since he'd grown up on a ranch—but these guys in full force were a little much, even for him.

Barks and yips continued until Johanna dipped into sight again, regaining control of the pooches one at time until all four mutts sat in a perfect line. Which only proved she could have controlled them right away. She'd let them overrun him on purpose.

Wincing, he stood, swiping an arm across his face. He shrugged off his suit jacket. Thank goodness he hadn't bothered with a tie today.

He draped his jacket over the back of his leather

chair. "My apologies for inconveniencing you. Even if my grandmother questions my ability to run the company, I do still have obligations here that needed to be taken care of before I could leave."

"Is that what this is about?" She crossed her arms, which threatened to draw his eyes to her chest just when he needed to keep his wits about him and focus on her words. "Showing your grandmother you're indispensable?"

"That's not a nice accusation."

"Is it true?" she pressed.

Damn it, she always saw right through him. But that was only part of the picture. "My primary goal is to bring my grandmother peace. A crisis here at the office will only add to her stress level at a time when she can't afford any additional drain."

Silently, Johanna assessed him through narrowed eyes while the dogs panted, lazy tongues lolling.

"What?" he said. "You don't believe me?"

"I'm skeptical," she said slowly. "Are you still sulking because Alex brought me flowers?"

Did she have to read his every thought? "I don't sulk. I'm charming. Everyone says so."

She cocked an eyebrow. "Yep, you're sure charming the socks off me right now."

Really? He recognized a challenge when he heard one. He flattened a palm to the heavy oak desk that mirrored the one in the ranch office. "If memory serves, I charmed off more than your socks right on this desk about ten months ago."

Her jaw dropped, then clamped shut before she finally said, "Never mind. If you're finished, let's leave so we can get this trip over with sooner rather than later."

All the more reason, in his mind, to prolong this little chat.

She leaned down to gather the leashes.

Kneeling, he clasped her wrist. "Wait, you started this. Let's talk."

"Let's not." She tugged her arm free.

"Fine. Not talking is okay with me, too." Standing, he swept off his desk.

Her eyes went wide. "What are you doing?"

"You said you didn't want to talk." He fingered a button on his shirt. Sure he knew they weren't really going to have sex on his desk, but he reveled in the regret in her eyes that she couldn't hide in spite of her scowl.

She shook her head, blond hair loose and silky sliding along her shoulders. "You're being outrageous."

"Good." He untucked his shirt.

"Stop. Now," she said firmly.

Okay, he'd pushed her far enough for today, but he could see that while their love for each other might have burned out, their passion still had plenty of fire left.

He buttoned his shirt again and tucked in the tails. "Spoilsport."

"Let's clean up the floors first before we go." She brushed papers into a stack. "The pilot's waiting."

"Damn waste of an empty desk." He stacked a haphazard pile of Diamonds in the Rough promo flyers and placed them on the drafting table.

She glanced up at him through long lashes. "Are you trying to chase me off? Because if you don't stop with these stunts, I am out of here. I will place the animals because it's the right thing to do, but you, however, are on your own."

For some reason, her words caught him off guard.

He leaned back against the desk, a weary exhale bursting from him. "Honest to God, Johanna, I don't know what I'm doing. Ever since my grandmother dropped her bombshell, I've just been reacting."

Standing, she clutched a stack of files to her chest, the dog leashes still trailing from her grip. "That's understandable."

"So you're not going to threaten to leave again?" he couldn't stop himself from asking.

She chewed her lip for an instant before responding, "If you keep being honest with me, I will stay."

"Deal." He extended a hand.

She slid hers into his. "Deal."

They stood there with their hands clasped for a few seconds longer than a handshake, seconds that crackled like static in the air just before a thunderstorm.

He enjoyed the hell out of a good drenching downpour, every bit as arousing as a blazing fire.

Her tongue slid along her lips as if to soothe where she'd chewed moments before. His body throbbed in response.

She tugged her hand from his self-consciously and rubbed her fingers along her white jeans. "Where's the first stop on our journey?"

"You don't know?" He would have expected his grandmother to tell her. Yet, even without knowing the specifics, Johanna had signed on for Mariah. That giving spirit was one of the things that had always drawn him to Johanna, even as it simultaneously scared the hell out of him. Because he'd always known she was too good for him. And too wise. Eventually, she would see through him and leave.

He'd been right.

"My grandmother has put me completely at your mercy." He spread his arms wide.

She thrust the leashes at him. "Feels more like I'm at your mercy, but whatever. You can start by helping me with the dogs."

Pivoting away, she strode out of his office, those white jeans showcasing the perfect curve of her hips, her butt. His fist clenched around the leather leads.

Hell, yes, the fire between them was alive and well.

Johanna gripped the leather armrests of her chair during takeoff. The private jet climbed into the sky and she still didn't know where they were going. Yet she'd gotten back into the limousine and onto the plane with Stone and the dogs without demanding more information. She'd been grateful to use the animals as an excuse to end their sexually charged exchange in his office.

Although the confined space of the plane didn't do much to ease the tight knot of desire inside her. The plane leveled out, and she wished her own emotions were as easy to smooth. She sank deeper into the fat chair, its brown leather and brass gleaming.

Each of the pups was now secured in a designer crate bolted to the floor in the back, complete with a luxurious dog bed and a pewter bowl. Engraved nameplates marked each crate and dish. Mariah hadn't been at the landing strip when they returned. Apparently, one set of goodbyes had been as much as she could take. These past two days had been some of the most emotional Johanna had experienced. The only other days that could compare were when her parents had died and when she'd broken her engagement.

And what about Stone? She glanced across the aisle

at him, sympathy whispering through her, mingling with the frustrated passion she'd experienced in his office. Okay, to be frank, that frustrated desire flared every time she saw him, regardless of whether he said outrageous things.

He continued to work, even on the plane, just as he'd been doing when she'd burst into his office earlier. He'd opened his tablet and fired it to life, sitting on the plane's sofa. In days past, she would have curled beside him, close, touching. Now they sat on opposite sides of the jet.

As if he felt her gaze, he spoke without looking up. "We're flying to Vermont to interview a family for Gem first."

"Nice to know you're finally giving specifics for this trip. Please do carry on about Gem, Vermont and this prospective adoptive family."

He flashed a quick dimple without looking up from his tablet. "They have a newborn, so they prefer an adult dog that's already trained."

"They're wise to know that adding a puppy is like having another baby." Sounded promising. "Who's this family?"

"Troy Donavan and his wife, Hillary."

"Donavan?" she repeated in shock. She knew the McNairs had connections, but they acted so down-to-earth sometimes their power still caught her unaware. "The Robin Hood Hacker Donavan? Your grandmother chose a former criminal for her dog?"

"Where's your sense of forgiveness?" He glanced up. "His criminal past was a long time ago. He went to reform school as a teenager."

She snorted on a laugh of disbelief. "For breaking into the Department of Defense computer system. That's more than some teenage prank."

"True," Stone conceded, setting his tablet beside his Stetson. "But he's led a productive and successful life as an adult. Well, once he got past the playboy stage."

"People in glass barns shouldn't throw stones."

"I've missed your humor."

"Thank you."

She'd missed a lot of things about him, which had made her question her decision more than once. Except Stone wasn't known for his forgiving nature. While he'd made it clear he still desired her, she didn't expect he would get over being dumped or change his stance on having children. So all this flirting was counterproductive.

"We're getting off the subject," she said. "Back to the Donavans, please."

"Regardless of Troy's past, all signs indicate the Donavans are a happy couple. But the whole reason for this visit is to be sure Gem is going to a good home. They understand there's no promise the dog will be theirs."

"Good." She nodded tightly. "I have no problem leaving with her if we don't trust them to take the best care of her."

His full-out smile pushed dimples into both cheeks, his skin weathered from the sun. "I've also missed the way you get fearless when it comes to your love of animals. You never were impressed with my money. That's a rare thing."

His genuine compliment moved her as much as his touch and that was dangerous to her peace of mind. "Back to the dogs," she insisted. She pulled a manila folder from her carry-on backpack. "I have questionnaires for the families to fill out to help ensure they are a good fit."

He cocked a dark eyebrow. "A meet and greet is one thing, but you have an adoption application for them to fill out, as well?"

"I prefer the word *questionnaire,*" she said primly. "But yes, it could also be called an application."

He leaned back, arms along the sofa. "You do realize they could just buy a dog."

"They could. That doesn't mean we have to give them Gem simply because they have money. If anything, adopting Gem will show their child that love can't be bought." Tapping the folder, she sighed sadly. "It's becoming clear now that your grandmother was right to send me with you."

"What if they're awesome but Gem isn't a good fit or doesn't like them? How will you explain it to them?" he asked, appearing to be genuinely interested. "What will you tell my grandmother?"

"Your grandmother will understand. That was her reason for sending us rather than just shipping the dogs directly to the families."

"And the Donavans?" he pushed for more.

That would be awkward but not enough to make her go against her principles. "I will suggest they go to their local animal shelter to find a forever furry friend." She couldn't resist adding, "Hopefully, they'll make a huge donation while they're there."

"You've thought a lot through since just yesterday."

She rolled her shoulders in a shrug. "I'm also trusting you to roll out that charisma to smooth over any rough patches if need be."

"Somehow I don't think you're complimenting me."

Were his feelings really hurt? He seemed so confident most—all—of the time. She unbuckled and walked
across the aisle to sit beside him and oops, she hadn't
given much thought to the fact that his arms were extended along the couch, which in effect put his arm
around her.

She held herself upright to keep from leaning into
his hold. "Why don't you just keep Gem? Didn't some
client give him to you?"

"He's not really mine. He may have been given to me,
but he always preferred my grandmother." He picked up
a lock of her hair. "Truth is, Gem was a gift from a guy
who had the hots for my grandmother and was trying
to wrangle an in with the family, since she loves dogs."

"Run that by me again?" How had she not known
that?

"After my grandfather died of a heart attack, a lot of
guys made moves on Gran," he said darkly. "She was
a rich widow. Pretty. Guys were lining up. Some were
genuine," he conceded. "Some were fortune hunters."

"Yet she never remarried."

"She says no one matches up to my grandfather."

Johanna's parents had felt the same way about each
other. She wanted a love like that for herself and she
wasn't willing to settle. "That's sweet and sad at the
same time, loving that much and losing it."

He shifted in his seat. "Back to the story of how we
got Gem as a puppy…"

"Not so at ease with the emotional stuff, are you?"
How many other times had he dodged speaking about
deeper feelings when she'd just assumed he was jaded
or insensitive?

"Puppy. Gem." His firm voice made it clear he wasn't

taking her bait. He would stay in control of the conversation, going only as far as he decided to go.

"This guy thought he was being original giving me a dog to get to my grandmother. Little did he know, he wasn't the first dude to try that. The first guy brought a puppy—Gem number one—when I was around nine. The guy who'd given him to me to get to my grandmother... Boy, did that ever backfire on him. The puppy hated kids, had zero interest in playing ball or sleeping at the foot of my bed. He just wanted to go on lazy walks, which sounded boring to me at that age."

An image unfolded in her head of Stone as a little boy. And what little boy wouldn't be thrilled over a puppy? How sad he must have been to have the first Gem ignore him, reject him. He wouldn't have understood.

She leaned toward his hand ever so slightly as he toyed with her hair. "That's why all the family members should meet a pet first before deciding on the best fit for their family. Otherwise, it's not fair to the dog or the people."

"So the guy learned as my grandmother showed him the door." He wrapped the lock of hair around his finger as the jet engines hummed in the background. "The guy offered to drop the puppy off at the local shelter, which was totally the wrong thing to say to my grandmother. She dumped the guy flat and kept the puppy for herself." He smiled fondly at the memory, his gaze shifting to the yellow Labrador asleep in her crate. "So the next time a guy brought a puppy trying to win Gran over, we named him Gem II. Both Gems were her favorite walking companions."

Affection for his grandmother wrapped around his

every word. Saying goodbye to Gem would start that letting go, the beginning of a grieving process Johanna wished she could take from him or make easier. Even thinking about all the pain he would face watching his grandmother's health fail squeezed at Johanna's heart.

Before she could stop the impulse, she wrapped her arms around Stone.

Five

Kissing Johanna had rocked his world, always had. But since they'd begun this trip, he'd been the one to make the first move each time they'd touched. Having Johanna reach for him sent Stone rocketing into another orbit altogether.

He didn't need any further encouragement.

Sliding his arms around her, he breathed in her flowery scent and savored the silky tease of her braided hair gripped in his fist. The plane engines hummed an echo of the desire buzzing through his veins.

And to think, he'd almost messed this up.

His first instinct when she'd offered consolation had been to shrug off her sympathy. Then his better sense had kicked in. He had Johanna in his arms. Touching him. Sighing.

He skimmed a hand down her pulled-back hair, releasing more of that floral scent. Her slim body molded to him, the softness of her breasts against his chest so familiar. So damn perfect. He nuzzled her ear, right beside the filigreed dream catcher dangling from her lobe. Her arms tightened around him, her hand cupping his neck. Just the feel of being skin to skin sent his heart slugging against his ribs.

Her fingers stroked through his hair, and he couldn't hold back any longer. He kissed her, fully and thoroughly, with his mouth, his hands, his body. From the first time he'd touched her and tasted her, desire had pulsed through him. Stronger than any attraction he'd ever experienced. He'd known then. Johanna was special.

For years he'd seen her as only that kid wandering around the stable yard. Everything had changed the day she'd come riding in after getting caught in a rainstorm. Her clothes had been plastered to her body. He'd gathered a couple of towels to give her. Two pats in and he'd known. He'd wanted her.

Still did.

That had been two years ago, a couple of years after she'd finished vet tech school and taken a job at the Hidden Gem Ranch. A year later they'd been engaged. Five months later, she'd returned his ring.

His mind shied away from that part and back to the passion, the connection, the need. He stroked along her spine until he reached the waistband of her jeans. Her layered tank tops had ridden up to expose a patch of skin. He palmed her waist, drawing her closer. She wriggled nearer, her fingers gripping his hair, her mouth moving along his, meeting him kiss for kiss, touch for touch.

She might have only meant to console him, but she was clearly every bit as moved as he was by the moment. She wanted him every bit as much as he wanted her. There wasn't a question in his mind.

He reclined her onto the sofa, stretching out over her. Her long legs twined with his. A husky moan vibrated in her throat. Her head fell back and she arched into the press of his mouth as he kissed down her neck.

Tucking a hand between them, he slid the button free on her jeans, then flicked her belly button ring. His thumb recognized the jewelry from touch, a tiny silver boot with spurs and a diamond stud at the top. Possessiveness stirred deep in his gut. He'd given it to her early in their relationship, when she'd still wanted to keep their connection a secret. She'd been nervous about people calling her an opportunist.

That she still wore the gift stoked his passion and made him bolder. He eased her zipper down link by link then dipped his hand inside. He knew the feel of her, had memorized every inch of her, but after months without her, there was also a newness to this moment. He slipped his fingers lower, lower still until he found...

Yes.

The slick proof of her arousal set his skin on fire. Her hips rolled as she surrendered to his touch. Her husky, needy whispers caressed his ears.

Her hands roved his back restlessly, her nails scoring a needy path down his spine, tugging the hem of his shirt from his suit pants. With a frenzied yank, she popped the buttons of his shirt. He pushed up her tank tops, and bare flesh met bare flesh, damn near sending him over the edge.

This was getting out of control fast. The pilot was a simple door away. Stone had hoped to steal a kiss but he hadn't dared hope things would go this far. He needed to ensure their privacy. The sleeping area in back was small but plenty sufficient to make thorough love to her. He'd done so more than once as he'd sought to romance her around the world.

Easing his hand from her jeans with more than a little regret over losing her sweetness for even a brief break, he rolled from her, keeping his mouth sealed to hers. He tucked both arms under Johanna and lifted her against his chest. More than once he'd carried her to bed or to his desk or to a field of bluebonnets. On this realm, at least, they were in perfect synch with one another.

"Stone—" she nipped his ear with a husky sigh "—you have to know this isn't a wise idea, but for some reason I can't bring myself to say no."

"I never claimed anything about our relationship was logical." He shouldered open the door to the jet's sleeping quarters.

She cupped his face in her hands. "What do you mean by that?"

He adjusted his hold on her as he neared the bed covered in a thick comforter. Dim pot lights overhead illuminated the small jet cabin. "I've always known that you are too good for me. It was only a matter of time until you figured it out."

Her forehead furrowed. "Is that really how you felt, or are you manipulating me because I'm having a weak moment?"

Manipulating her? Is that what she really thought of him?

Her words splashed cold reality over him. This wasn't the right time to take her back into his bed again. He'd made considerable progress just now and he didn't intend to lose ground by pushing for too much too soon. If he slept with her now, she might never trust him enough for a second time…and hell, yes, he knew once would not be enough.

He lowered her feet to the ground. The glide of her

body against his made him throb all the harder, almost changing his mind and to hell with wisdom. He wanted—needed—her now so damn much his teeth ached.

Almost.

"You'll have to decide that for yourself." He backed away, his hands up between them, trying to keep his eyes firmly focused on her face rather than on the gorgeous tangled mess of her hair and the open vee of her jeans. "And when you do, if you still want us to sleep together again, just say the word and I'll be there before you can say 'let's get naked.' But I need to know you're in one hundred percent, no regrets."

He pivoted away and out the door before he made a liar out of himself and tangled up in the sheets with her for what he knew would be the best sex of their lives.

Five hours later, in Vermont, Johanna's brain was still spinning with confusion after how close she'd come to sleeping with Stone again.

Sleeping? More like unraveling in his arms at just one touch.

At least she had the distraction of a picnic lunch with the Donavan family while she gathered her thoughts. She and Stone had brought Gem along to meet them, while the other three dogs unwound in a fenced area around the guesthouse where Stone and Johanna would be staying tonight.

The late lunch with the Donavan family was an intriguing surprise. Johanna sat at a rustic picnic table while Hillary Donavan pushed her snoozing infant son in a baby swing under a sprawling sugar maple tree. Hillary was so down-to-earth she could have been Jo-

hanna's redheaded cousin, complete with freckles and
a high swinging ponytail. Johanna felt at ease, something she hadn't expected once she'd heard who they
would be visiting first.

Hillary's husband was every bit as approachable in
spite of his notorious history as the Robin Hood hacker.
Wearing a fedora with his khaki shorts and T-shirt,
Troy ran alongside Stone playing fetch with Gem in a
field of red clover.

The Donavan homestead was as understated as the
couple. A 1920s farmhouse perched on a low rolling
hill. A porch wrapped around the first floor and black
shutters bracketed the windows.

Bit by bit she saw the amenities added into the landscape so artfully she'd barely noticed. A pool nestled
near a wooded area with rock ledges and a waterfall
gave it the appearance of a stream feeding into a pond—
a clear, chlorinated pond. A child's playhouse had been
built from wood under a massive tree. A security fence
enclosed the entire two-acre property—which enabled
her to check a box on the adoption application. A lab
like Gem would need a safe place to run out her energy
with this wonderful family.

She sipped her iced tea, finally beginning to relax
now that part one of their mission appeared to be a success. The lunch together had been just what Johanna
needed to unwind after the tension of the past twenty-
four hours. The meal had been beyond delicious without
being overly elaborate. A juicy fruit salad accompanied
loaves of hearty peasant bread and deli meats, cheeses
and spreads of their choice. Fresh-squeezed lemonade.
And the ice cream… Her mouth watered as she finished
off another bite of fresh maple walnut ice cream. These

parents were clearly trying to give their child as normal a life as possible, given little T.J.—Troy Junior—was the offspring of one of the wealthiest men in the world.

Hillary wrapped her arms around her knees as she hitched her feet up onto the bench by the redwood picnic table. "We appreciate you going to so much trouble to bring Gem to us. He's such a great dog, playful but well trained."

"Thank *you* for letting us invade your home. We could have met in a park or somewhere generic for you to see Gem."

"I loved time at the park as a child, but I'm still nervous about taking T.J. out in public for security reasons." Hillary's hand fell protectively to stroke the baby's head.

The Donavan compound clearly had top-of-the-line security that could rival Fort Knox, including computerized keypads discreetly hidden and staff that could have doubled as bouncers. Johanna had never thought about the safety issue with Stone's upbringing. How difficult it must have been for his family to balance all that wealth with values. He'd clearly been born into a vast dynasty, but he had a strong work ethic. She'd always admired that about him.

Apparently, the Donavans felt the same.

"Well, Hillary, I have to say this is definitely more comfy than a park. It's generous of you to host us overnight."

The thought of being alone with Stone tonight was starting to sink in. Her skin tingled at the notion.

Hillary's gaze scanned the low rolling hills around their home. "We bought this place to give T.J. the kind of upbringing neither of us had."

Johanna angled her head to the side. "Where did you grow up?"

"Here in Vermont actually, but much more scaled back and…well…not secure." She looked back at Johanna. "I love my mom, but she was troubled. Actually, she was an alcoholic. It took us a long time to reconcile, but I'm glad we found a way to make peace before she passed."

"Oh, um, I'm sorry you had to go through that," she said, feeling totally inadequate. *Sorry* was such a lame, overused word. "Is the rest of your family still nearby?"

"My sister, yes. Troy and I have extended family, as well, the kinds of friends that are as close as relatives. We visit each other as often as we can, but we all bought vacation homes in Monte Carlo so our kids can have a sense of growing up together like cousins."

Hillary's shoulders lost much of their tension at the mention of her husband's close friends, and she launched into a story about their most recent trip to Monaco for a Formula One racing event.

The baby boy squawked awake in his swing, stopping Hillary midstory. With already expert hands, she scooped up her newborn and declared, "He needs changing and I didn't bring enough diapers out here. If you'll excuse me for a few minutes, I'll be right back."

"Of course. Take your time. I'm enjoying the sunshine." And trying so very hard not to be envious of Hillary's glowing happiness.

As if to rub salt in the wound in her aching heart, Troy noticed his wife's departure and took off after her in a slow jog, Gem loping alongside him having already transferred his doggy allegiance to the Donavans.

Stone peeled away and strode back toward her, so

damn handsome he took her breath away. Yet she knew even if he turned gray and paunchy, the essence of the man would be the same.

Strong. Driven. Accomplished. Charismatic.

And still determined to deny himself—both of them—the family happiness she craved. As much as she wanted him, she couldn't bring herself to settle for less than everything.

Taking a seat beside Johanna at the picnic table, Stone saw the wistfulness in her eyes as she watched the family tableau. He knew, without question, he'd put that pain there. Guilt threatened to drive him to his knees.

This whole afternoon of domestic bliss had been tough for him, as well, reminding him of all the times he'd seen his cousins with their parents while he sat on the periphery. He'd moved past wanting that for himself and realized he was better off not inflicting the same disappointment on offspring of his own. He knew his limitations. He didn't have the emotional capacity to be a parent, and he refused to let down a kid. A parent had to be 100 percent in. Otherwise it wasn't fair to the child. Johanna would expect—and deserved—to have a spouse every bit as committed to home and hearth as she was, rather than some stonehearted guy with a crack baby past.

He didn't want to think overlong about the man who would offer her that fairy-tale future, especially not with the feel and taste of Johanna still so fresh in his memory. The sun kissed her shoulders, which were bared in her sundress. He allowed himself at least a small indulgence and grazed his knuckles along the tanned skin, sweeping aside her golden French braid.

He cupped the back of her neck and massaged lightly. "Are you okay with the Donavans adopting Gem?"

"What do you think?" Her head lolled back into his touch. "I'm thrilled. Gem is going to a wonderful family. There's nothing not to love about this."

"I have to confess, it's going even better than I'd hoped." His thumb worked at a knotted muscle at the base of her skull. The silkiness of her skin and the light sigh passing her lips stirred him.

Her eyelids fluttered closed, her face a study in bliss. "Your grandmother will be relieved to hear the news."

"I already texted her." He waggled his cell phone before tucking it away again.

"You what?" Her emerald-green eyes snapped open, surprise and a hint of something else sparking. "That was mighty confident of you. What if I'd disagreed? I am a part of this process, you know."

"I could tell you were okay with this about thirty minutes in." His thumb brushed along her cheek before returning to the back of her neck again. "I may not be the right man for you, but I know you well."

She swatted at his chest lightly. "Then why did you bother asking when you sat down with me a few minutes ago?"

"It was an excuse to talk to you, and God knows, I wasn't going to pass up an opportunity to touch you." His voice went gravelly. His self-control was shot around her these days.

Her chest rose and fell faster in a tangible mirror of his arousal. "Why are you torturing us both this way?"

Hell if he knew the answer. "How about we both just enjoy the outdoors and sunshine? We have red clover instead of bluebonnets, but the love of the land is still here. Nothing is going to happen between us out here in the open, especially not with the Donavans nearby. There's no harm. Accept the neck massage and relax."

Some of the anger melted from her kinked muscles and she sagged back into his touch. "You always did give the best neck rubs."

"It's been a stressful couple of days." He hadn't wanted to leave Texas and now he couldn't envision what life would be like after they returned. "I sent my grandmother photos of Gem with the Donavans."

"That was thoughtful of you."

"She texted back that she's happy and relieved." And he had to confess knowing he'd eased that worry for her made him as happy as if he'd landed a big new contract. "So yes, our task is twenty-five percent complete."

"I know those photos must have brought Mariah a lot of joy." Angling toward him, Johanna stroked along his eyebrows before cupping his face. Her fingertips were callused from work, but gentle, soothing, the hands of a healer. "We may not be meant to be married, but there was—is—so much about you that's special. Otherwise I never could have fallen for you."

"Yet, here we are."

Silence settled between them, highlighting nature's sounds of branches rustling in the wind and birds chirping.

Johanna's eyes went sad, unshed tears glistening. "I wish things could be different for us, I truly do."

He agreed 100 percent. But where did that leave them? "We haven't talked about what happened between us earlier on the airplane."

"What *almost* happened," she amended.

"Right." That sure put him in his place. Still, he

couldn't stop the urge to indulge in a week of no-strings sex, to make the most of one last chance to be with Johanna. "Do you still feel like I was trying to manipulate you?"

She eased back, her hand falling from his face, and she ducked her head to avoid his touch. "Nothing's changed. We both know an affair can't lead anywhere."

"Not even a temporary fling," he said in a joke, though he was more than half-serious.

She didn't laugh. But she didn't say no, either. She simply sat in silence as the wind sent a couple of stray maple leaves skittering across the picnic table.

Hope surged through him along with a pulse of heat in his veins. He knew they couldn't have a long-term relationship, but he could feel her giving in to this week together. He pressed ahead. He just had to figure out what was holding her back. "Is there someone else?"

She choked on a laugh. "Are you serious? I live on your land, and I work at your family's ranch. There aren't any secrets."

No secrets? She was wrong there. He'd been clueless about Alex's feelings for her. "My cousin has a thing for you, and I didn't know about that."

She crossed her arms over her chest, plumping the gentle curves of her breasts along the neckline of her yellow sundress. "I told you there's nothing between Alex and me."

"But he wants there to be more." Stone's jaw clenched at the thought of her with someone else. The possibility that someone could be his cousin, and that Stone would have to watch them together every day for the rest of his life, was still more than he could wrap his brain around without blowing a gasket. "That's clear to me now. Although why I didn't see it earlier is a mystery."

"I can't control what your cousin feels, but I can assure you those feelings are not returned." She touched his wrist lightly, tentatively. "This isn't Alex's fault. People don't always make wise choices about who to… be drawn to."

"Are you talking about us now?"

Chuckling wryly, she squeezed his hand. "You truly are clueless if you even have to ask. No wonder you didn't notice how Alex feels."

Even though she insisted she didn't want Alex, Stone still had to know more. "How far did things go with Alex before you realized you weren't interested in him that way?"

For a moment, he thought she would refuse to answer his question, but then her shoulders lowered, defensiveness melting from her. Her answer was important to him, too important. His heart pounded in his ears.

"Alex asked me out once. I said no, because I'm not into rebound relationships. I also didn't want to cause trouble between the two of you."

"You care about both of us," he realized. How much did she care about Alex? Was she holding back?

"Of course I care about you both." Her hand stayed on his. Did she know her thumb stroked along his wrist? "I practically grew up on the ranch with both of you. In fact, I played more with Alex and Amie since they're younger than you. Of course I spent a lot more time studying you because of my monster crush. Sometimes it amazes me how I can know so much about you in some ways and so little in others."

He flipped his hand over to grip hers. "We saw what we wanted to see."

"I know you and Alex are as close as brothers. The last thing I want to do is cause trouble between you."

"We don't always see eye to eye on everything, but we're close. We'll get through this, too." The thought of losing any more of his family was beyond considering. "We grew up like brothers."

Except they weren't, in spite of all the times he'd wished they could be.

"You guys definitely had troublemaker moments." She grinned, lightening the mood and taking them back to safer ground. "Remember when the two of you put Kool-Aid in Amie's showerhead right before the Miss Stampede Queen pageant? I didn't think she would ever forgive either of you for turning her hair pink."

"That was Alex's idea."

"Um, I don't think so. And if it was, that's probably because you whispered the idea in his ear when he was sleeping."

Or because he'd left a gag book open to a particular page right on Alex's desk. Stone grinned. "I may have instigated some—okay, *most* of the pranks." He recognized her attempt to get off the subject and he didn't intend to lose sight of what he needed to know.

"Both of you were fantasy material for all my school friends—rich, sexy cowboys. What's not to drool over?" Mischief sparkled in her eyes. "But as you know, my crush was firmly placed on you."

"What about now?"

The pool filter kicked on, the fountain spewing higher. He looked over his shoulder and found staff clearing away the dishes discreetly. Once they left, Johanna leaned toward him again.

"You and I are not engaged anymore, and our core reason for the breakup hasn't changed. You know that," she said gently but firmly.

"Yet, we were kissing a few hours ago." Kissing and more.

She pulled her hand back. "This kind of conversation is exactly what I wanted to avoid."

"If I weren't in the picture, would you and Alex be together?" He hated the way this discussion made him feel, the jealousy, the doubts. But damn it, he couldn't let it go.

Her lips went tight with frustration for an instant. "I've already told you I'm not seeing Alex."

"I heard you." He remembered everything she'd ever said to him. "I'm asking if you have romantic feelings for him. That's different."

She shoved to her feet, walking absently toward the trunk of the maple tree before glancing back over her shoulder. "You're not going to let this go, are you?"

"You broke up with me, not the other way around." And the days following that breakup had been some of the darkest in his life.

"Your cousin and I are very much alike." She sagged against the trunk. "Too much so to be a couple."

His shoulders dropped with relief. "I'm glad to hear that...." He stood and walked to her, grabbing a branch just over her head. "Even though I know I have no rights, the thought of you being with him drives me crazy."

"Is that why you made a move on me at my place, in your office—on the plane?"

"I kissed you because I wanted to." Like now.

"And that's the first time you've wanted to in seven months?"

"Hell, no." He thought about having her every day—and every night.

"Then something changed to make you act on the impulse. Is that 'something' jealousy?" Her eyes searched him with genuine confusion. "If you can't have me, no one can?"

Put that way, he sounded like a jerk. "I don't know how to explain it other than to say that since my grandmother dropped her bombshell news on us, it feels like the world is off-kilter."

"So if your grandmother was healthy, you would still be keeping your distance, like before."

Was she hinting that she'd wanted him to fight harder to get her back? One wrong move and he could wreck the moment. The only thing he knew to do was be honest.

"Hell, I don't even really know what I mean except that we are here, together. And the thought of never being with you again is tearing me apart."

She swallowed hard, chewing her bottom lip as she stared up at him.

Stone continued, "I also know I can't just stand around and pretend to be unaffected. So either leave now or prepare to be fully, thoroughly kissed."

"I, I just… I can't." She stuttered, shaking her head slowly, sidestepping away from the tree, then rushing past him.

She couldn't be any clearer than that.

Disappointment delivered a kick to the gut even though he hadn't expected anything different.

He gave her enough time to make it inside before he released the tree branch and started back toward the main house. He only had an afternoon and dinnertime to get his head together before they spent the night alone together in the guesthouse.

One afternoon didn't sound like nearly long enough when even seven months hadn't helped him get over Johanna.

Johanna had busied herself caring for the other three dogs, taking them on a hike, feeding them, hiking again, and still restless energy whirled inside her well into suppertime.

Their evening was coming to an end with coffee on the covered back porch, a lazy ceiling fan rustling the air. Soon, she wouldn't be able to hide behind the Donavan family any longer. She would be spending the night alone with Stone.

Of course she could go to a hotel. Nothing in Mariah's agreement said she had to sleep under the same roof as Stone. She just had to help him place the dogs. Except she didn't want to cause an embarrassing scene for him in front of the Donavans....

Oh, hell, who was she kidding? She wanted to finish their afternoon conversation and learn more about why he was pursuing her now. He'd said his grandmother's terminal illness had flipped his world. If he was reevaluating, could he change his mind on things that had kept them apart before?

If so, could she trust her heart to him a second time?

Walking away the first time had nearly destroyed her with grief and loss. They were barely a day into this trip and her willpower was fading fast. She finished the last of her iced decaf coffee.

Stone set aside his empty mug and leaned toward Johanna. "We should say our good-nights. Do you have the gift from my grandmother?"

"Oh, right." She jolted and reached into her woven satchel. "We have a present for your son, to thank you both for having us here and for giving Gem a good home."

She pulled out a Diamonds in the Rough gift sack and passed it to Hillary. The bag glistened with the pattern of diamonds and spurs, the company's bold, black logo scrolled at an angle.

"How thoughtful," Troy said. "You didn't have to do this, but thanks. Hillary, how about you do the honors."

"I do love surprises." She passed over the snoozing infant to Stone.

A momentary panic flashed in his eyes, quickly masked before he cradled the baby carefully in his arms. His broad hands cupped the tiny bottom and supported the head. His sun-bronzed skin contrasted with the newborn alabaster of the baby.

Johanna's heart melted. How could it not? Her fondest dream in her heart of hearts was playing out in front of her. Stone rocked the baby in his arms as if by instinct. A lump lodged in her throat as big as the welling emotion filling her heart.

She vaguely registered the sound of rustling paper as Hillary unwrapped the gift they'd brought. Stone's gaze flew to Johanna's and held. The rawness in his eyes tore at her. She saw…pain. She saw a hurt so deep she ached to reach out and wrap her arms around him.

Clearing his throat, Stone pivoted away and passed

the baby back to Troy. Johanna shook off the daze and looked at Hillary again.

The baby's mother pulled out a box, untied the fat orange ribbon and pulled out... "A tiny rodeo buckle! How adorable."

Hillary held up the tot-sized leather belt with a rodeo buckle, the leather crafted and studded with one of Amie's originals. It was a one-of-a-kind design with a cartoon horse and baby cowboy engraved on the pewter oval.

Stone picked up the bag and tucked the box inside. "He'll have to grow a bit for it to fit."

"Thank you," Hillary said, tracing the design with her finger. "This is fabulous. We'll be sure to take a photo of him wearing it and playing with Gem."

Troy held the baby in one arm like a seasoned dad, clapping Stone on the shoulder with his other hand. "Thank you again for thinking of us for Gem. He's a great dog. And you're welcome to visit him anytime."

Stone nodded tightly. "Thank you for giving her a good home and easing my grandmother's mind."

Johanna's heart ached all over again for Stone. No wonder he was having a tougher time hiding his feelings. If they'd still been a couple, she could have comforted him, even if all he would let her do was hold his hand.

She couldn't help but be reminded of when he was about twenty-one or twenty-two and his favorite horse had gone lame. Even with the best vets money could bring, nothing could be done to save Jet. She'd found Stone grieving in the stable with his horse afterward. She'd just been a gangly teenager and hugging him would have been out of the question regardless. So she'd just sat beside him quietly, being there. He hadn't asked her to leave, and she liked to think her presence had made things somewhat easier for him.

God knew, Stone would need someone now as he dealt with his grandmother's illness, and he'd always made a point of being stoic, as if the problems rolled right off him. Mariah had been the most important person in his life, the only parental figure he'd had after his grandfather had passed away while Stone was still young.

Hillary smiled gently, tucking the belt back into the bag. "It's our pleasure to have Gem as a part of our family. He will be T.J.'s best buddy and a treasured friend." She patted Stone on the arm, seeming to understand that was as much tenderness as the man would accept right now. "The guest cabin is fully stocked with food and drinks, but please let us know if you need anything at all. Otherwise we'll see you after breakfast to say good-bye before you leave."

In the morning?

Johanna's heart leaped to her throat. Of course it was time to call an end to the evening and go to the guest-house. Resisting Stone had been difficult enough when occasionally crossing paths at the ranch. But tonight, with the memory of him cradling that tiny infant in his powerful arms?

She didn't know how she would hold strong once the doors closed behind them.

Six

Johanna's stomach tightened with each step closer to the guesthouse. A barn perched on a hill behind the Donavan's main home had been converted into a guesthouse with soaring ceilings. One side had been removed and replaced with glass windows.

Tonight, she and Stone would sleep under the same roof together for the first time in seven months. They walked side-by-side silently, not touching. But the wind twined around them as if binding them with whispering bands of air carrying his scent mingling with hers.

The desire that still simmered between them was out in the open now. Discussed. Acknowledged. She'd told him no, and he'd respected that. But to be honest with herself, she wasn't so certain she could hold out through tonight, much less through this whole week without succumbing to the temptation of one last fling. One more chance to lose herself in being with him. To immerse herself in total bliss. If only they didn't have to face the morning.

Once the guesthouse door closed behind them, there would be no more delaying. And she was feeling all the more vulnerable after watching him hold the Donavan baby. The evening seemed to have been tailor-made to play with her emotions.

Stone opened the gate to the picket fence around the guesthouse. Cuddly Sterling, impish Pearl and loyal Ruby raced up to greet them, barking and sniffing their hands. Little Pearl's head tipped to the side quizzically.

Crouching, Johanna scratched the cairn terrier's head. "It's as if she's asking about Gem. I wish there was a way to keep them all together. I have to admit I'm going to miss that goof of a dog."

"Life doesn't always work out the way we'd hoped and we're just left with doing the best we can." Stone ruffled the Rottweiler's ears, then the dachshund mix's. "Thank goodness Mariah made sure all her dogs and cats were placed in good homes."

Johanna glanced up through her eyelashes at Stone. His broad shoulders against the sentimental moonlight made for a mouth-watering silhouette. "You're right. I'm just…feeling emotional about Mariah. I know it must be so much worse for you."

He cricked his neck from side to side. "Let's get through the week as best we can."

"Of course, there's satisfaction to be found in doing something tangible for Mariah." She scooped up the dachshund. Seven-year-old Sterling cuddled closer as if sensing the ache inside her. "We should, uh, turn in. We have a lot of ground to cover this week for the other dogs."

Nerves pattered as quickly as racing dog feet as she made fast tracks along the pavers toward the guest-house.

Stone followed—she could hear the steady even tread of his long-legged stride. He reached past her, thumbed in the security code and pushed the large door wide into the sweeping great room.

Pearl and Ruby raced past, sniffing and exploring, closing in on the large dog bowl of water even though they'd had plenty to drink outside, as well. She set Sterling down to join them. Three fat, fluffy dog beds were lined up behind the sofa. The Donavans were thoughtful hosts.

As she turned toward the expansive glass wall, she couldn't help but think the winter must be magnificent with the view of a snow-covered countryside. Even now, the sight was beyond magnificent, lush and green with cows grazing. She worked with large animals as a vet tech every day and had seen farms across Texas, but even she found this place breathtaking. What would it be like to have visited these people when she and Stone had been a couple? Most of their outings had been to more pretentious social gatherings, high-end fund-raisers or business functions.

Nothing like this day or this place.

The Donavans clearly had embraced the Vermont experience, complete with dairy cows. Although not all Vermont farms came with an ice cream parlor just for their kids.

Stone whistled softly from the state-of-the-art kitchen. "When they said they'd stocked the kitchen for us, they weren't joking. Do you want something to drink? Just pick, I'm sure it's here. Snacks, breakfast pastries, fruit and ice cream. Holy cow—so to speak."

Listening to him ramble off the flavors, she realized he was doing his best to ease the tension between them. Definitely a wise idea if she wanted to get through this week with her sanity intact. "I'll take a scoop of the maple nut."

"Coming right up," he said, opening cabinets and drawers.

She walked to the kitchen island and hitched a hip up onto a bar stool. "They're a surprisingly normal family, given all their wealth."

He passed her a bowl and spoon. "Are you saying that my family is pretentious because of our money?"

"Not at all. But some of your friends…" She stabbed her spoon into the generous mound of ice cream in the blue stoneware bowl. "They looked right through my father in the stables."

Scowling, he stood across from her, his bowl in front of him. "I'm sorry to hear that."

"You were more than just sorry about it," she answered, remembering well how he'd stood up to snobs. "You did something about it. I remember this one time when I was about eleven and one of your college friends was ordering my dad around. You made sure that guy was given the slowest, least cooperative horse in the stable. The horse even sat in the middle of a stream and got the guy soaking wet. I knew it wasn't accidental on your part. Was it?"

He winked, his scowl fading. "You seem to have me all figured out."

"You always treated everyone with respect." Her trip down memory lane reminded her of the reasons she'd fallen for this man in the first place. "You took care of your own horse. But that day when I was eleven, I officially developed my crush on you."

"You never told me that story before." He shoveled a spoonful of ice cream into his mouth, his eyes tracking her every movement with an intensity that tingled through her.

"I had insecurities of my own in those days," she admitted now. It was tough to share her self-doubts around someone as confident and, yes, arrogant as Stone. "I was a tomboy, freckled and gangly, living in a trailer park. I was brought up with strong values and I loved my parents, the life they made for me."

"They loved you. The pride on your dad's face when he talked about you was unmistakable."

"Thank you…" Her eyes misted just thinking about them. She understood all too well the pain Stone was facing, losing his mother figure. "I miss them so much, especially lately."

He ate silently, letting her find her way through. She wasn't sure where her thoughts were taking her, but she felt the need to make him understand something she couldn't quite define herself.

Johanna set her spoon aside. "I know your family is full of good people, open-minded and generous. A part of me didn't want to show just how vulnerable I felt. Even growing up on the ranch, I was on the periphery as an employee's child."

She shook her head, her voice trailing off, and she ate a bite of ice cream to cover her silence. The maple flavor melted over her taste buds.

"Johanna…" He clasped her wrist. "Go ahead. I'm listening."

Licking the spoon clean, ever aware of his eyes on her mouth, she gathered her words. "It's strange how you said you felt you weren't good enough for me…. Learning which fork to use for an occasional meal at the big house is a long way from walking in billionaire circles on a day-to-day basis. Keeping up appearances during our engagement and constantly worrying I would do something to embarrass you was exhausting."

"You never let it show." His frown turned to a scowl. "Don't you think that's something I would have cared to know? We were engaged to be married, for God's sake. If we couldn't tell each other even something basic like that, then what did we even have together?"

"You're angry?"

"I'm frustrated, yes. All this time I've been thinking that I let you down." He shoved aside his bowl and leaned on his elbows, closing the space between them. "Right now, I'm realizing we let each other down. Except you weren't interested in shouldering your part of the blame."

Anger sparked along her already raw nerves. "I open up to you, and now you're pissed off? That isn't very fair."

He sidestepped around the island to stand in front of her. "Nothing about what has happened between us has been fair or we wouldn't still be hurting this much."

She swallowed hard, certain to her toes he was about to kiss her and she wouldn't be able to tell him no. They would pour all those frustrated emotions into passion. It wouldn't solve anything, but at least they would have an outlet, a release.

Except he turned and left.

Her jaw dropped.

What the hell? Stone had just walked away from her?

She almost leaped from her seat to charge after him and demand he finish the conversation. How dare he just leave? They had unfinished business....

But hadn't she done the same thing to him? Not only had she run away from him after the picnic, scared she couldn't resist the temptation to do more than kiss him. But she'd also walked out on their relationship and very publicly, at that. His words settled in her gut along with the sting of guilt. He was right. She'd let him shoulder all the blame for their breakup when she hadn't given her all to him, either.

The realization echoed hollowly inside her. She gathered both bowls and rinsed them out carefully, wishing her confusion was as easily swirled down the drain. Or that she could just shake off her worries and go to sleep like the three dogs curled up on their beds, snoring. The thought of going to her room alone was more than she could bear tonight after watching all-day family bliss with the Donavans, not just as parents but as a couple.

She yanked a blanket from the back of the sofa and curled up on the couch to count stars instead of sheep.

Stone woke the next morning with a throbbing headache and an aching erection.

His shower took care of the visible sign of his arousal, but didn't do much to cool the fire inside him. Walking away from Johanna the night before had been one of the most difficult things he'd ever done. But he'd been too angry, too on edge. He didn't trust himself and damned if he would ever put her at risk.

So he'd left her alone. He'd worked for hours before falling into a fitful sleep just before sunup.

Tossing his shaving gear into his bag, he was still steamed over his conversation with Johanna last night. He'd spent most of the night reviewing their time together and he kept coming back to how she'd broken up with him at one of his grandmother's major fundraisers. That couldn't be coincidental. If he'd known how she'd felt, he could have done things differently. Hell, he could have—

What? Given up his job and all the responsibilities that came with that? Dismissed his background and offered to give her the family she wanted? Last night he'd learned of yet another reason they weren't meant to be together.

Who would he be if he didn't run Diamonds in the Rough?

He tossed his bag on the thick four-poster bed beside a stack of discarded sketches for a new kids' line with a horse logo. The images just wouldn't come together on paper the way he saw them in his mind. Visions of a misty-eyed Johanna kept interfering, thoughts of her struggling to hold back tears when he'd held the baby.

Damn it.

He flipped open his suitcase, pulled out a pair of well-worn jeans and tugged them on. One day into this mandated week together and he was already losing his damn mind. He scratched his hands through his wet hair, needing to get his head together.

Barring that, he could at least let the dogs out.

He opened his bedroom door, wondering if Johanna was up yet. He didn't hear her so he assumed not. The wide-open barn space sprawled in front of him. The dogs sat up, one, two, three—tails wagging, tongues lolling out. They launched off their beds behind the sofa in unison but thank God, not barking. He knelt, petting each to keep them quiet. Then he snapped his fingers to lead them to the door. Walking past the couch, he almost stopped short. Johanna slept on the sofa, wrapped in a quilt, still wearing her sundress from yesterday.

His gaze stayed on her even as he waved the dogs

outside, then he turned to face her fully and enjoy a view that far exceeded anything outside. Many nights he'd watched her sleep, her face relaxed, her stubborn chin softened a bit. Her long lashes brushed her sun-kissed cheeks. His body went hard all over again, his jeans more and more uncomfortable. He needed to get himself under control before she woke.

Padding barefoot across the room, he quietly put together the coffeepot. A crystal cake plate and cover displayed a selection of pastries big enough to feed them twice over. He grabbed a bear claw, wishing his other hunger was as easy to satisfy.

As the coffee gurgled the scent of java into the air, he felt the weight of eyes studying him. He already knew. Johanna. The connection that threatened to drive him mad was alive and well.

He pulled two stoneware mugs off the hooks under the cabinets. "Sorry I woke you."

A rustle from the sofa sounded, and her reflection came to life in the window pane over the sink.

"It's okay. I was just catnapping anyway." Johanna stretched her arms over her head. "It was tough to sleep after we argued."

"That wasn't an argument. I consider that a very revealing discussion we should have had a long time ago." He poured coffee into both mugs. Black. They both drank it the same way, strong and undiluted by sugar or cream. The only thing it seemed they still had in common. He picked up both and walked toward her.

"What would talking about my insecurities have changed?" Her bare toes curled against the rustic braid rug. "Do you think our breakup would have hurt any less? I can't imagine how."

"True enough." He passed her a mug, wishing he could find a way to be with her without tearing them both apart. "Truce?"

She took the mug, wrapping both hands around the mug, brushing his fingers. The ever-ready attraction crackled. He saw it echoed in her eyes, along with wariness.

"Truce," she repeated, sipping the coffee carefully. "Where to next?"

"Travel day, actually. I've got work to catch up on this morning." Not a total lie, since he always had work. "Then we'll fly out this afternoon to take Sterling to his new family in South Carolina."

"I'm almost afraid to ask who your grandmother lined up next. The president?"

"Just a former secretary of state."

She coughed a mouthful of coffee. "I was joking."

"I'm not." His grandmother moved in influential circles. He hadn't given a second thought to the families she had chosen. They were longtime friends. But he hadn't thought of how visiting these high-profile people would go over with Johanna. How many times had he tossed her into the middle of unfamiliar, perhaps even intimidating gatherings with no warning? Hell, he hadn't even given her any direction on how to pack, just offering to buy what she needed.

He'd hoped to use this time together to find peace for his grandmother—but also to find closure with Johanna. Okay, and also to have lots of sex with Johanna until they both were too exhausted to argue about the past. Then they could move on.

Clearly, his plan wasn't working out because he was falling into an old pattern of charging ahead and expecting her to follow. She didn't trust him and if she didn't trust him, there wasn't a chance in hell they could sleep together again.

He couldn't change the past, and he'd accepted they couldn't have a future together.

Although he could damn well do something about the present. For starters, he could share the details about their travel plans. But he would have to dig a lot deeper than that to fully regain her trust.

He sat beside her on the fat sectional sofa, trying to start right now, by including her in the plan for the week. "We'll be visiting the Landis-Renshaw family in Hilton Head. They've vacationed at the ranch before. As a matter of fact, they rented the whole place once for a family reunion."

"That would be quite a who's who of family reunions."

And he hadn't even told her their third stop would be to meet with a deposed European king.

Johanna welcomed the bustle of their travel day to Hilton Head, South Carolina. Stone had arranged for accommodations in a pet-friendly beach cottage with plenty of space for the dogs to run. They would meet with the Landis-Renshaw family in the morning.

Other cottages dotted the shoreline, but with an exclusivity that brought privacy. One other couple and a small family played in the surf, but otherwise she and Stone were on their own. She'd sensed a change in him earlier as he'd shared his plans for the South Carolina portion of their trip. He was genuinely attempting to include her, rather than simply taking charge.

So far, the truce they'd declared had held, due in

large part to how he'd included her. That helped her relax, taking away a layer of tension she hadn't even realized existed. She'd been worrying about the unknown.

She sat cross-legged on the wooden deck, a dozen steps away from him. The dogs curled up around her and she checked over each of them, making sure they hadn't picked up ticks in Vermont or sand spurs from their run along the beach earlier. She finished with Pearl, the search more extensive given the cairn terrier's longer fur.

Stone walked out of the surf like Poseidon emerging from the depths of the ocean. Big. Powerful. The hazy glow of the ending day cast him in shadows, his dark hair even blacker slicked with water. She'd always known Stone the cowboy entranced her more than Stone the CEO.

But Stone nearly naked absolutely melted her.

She forced her attention back to Pearl to keep from drooling over Stone in swim trunks. Her skin prickled with awareness as he opened the porch gate and walked past her. She heard the rattle of ice as he poured a glass of sweet tea before he dropped into one of the Adirondack loungers.

"How was the water?" She released Pearl to play with the other two dogs on the fenced deck.

"Good, good." He set his glass aside. "Everything okay with the dogs?"

They sounded like any other couple catching up at the end of the day, except there was this aching tension between them. "They all checked out fine. Just a couple of sandspurs on Pearl. I trimmed their nails, and I'll want to bathe them all after they run on the beach again. Otherwise, they're all set to meet their new families."

He swung his feet around, elbows on his knees. "You're a nurturer. It's in your blood."

Her hands clenched into fists to resist the urge to sweep sand from the hair on his legs. "Are you trying to needle me with the nurturer comment?"

"I'm just stating a fact. You'll make a great mother someday."

The humid night air grew thicker, her chest constricting. "You're good with children. The natural way you held little T.J....I just don't understand you."

"I'm good with horses, too. That doesn't mean I'm supposed to be a jockey," he said wryly.

"I wasn't insinuating you should be a father. You've been honest about your feelings on that subject. It just took me a while to stop thinking I could change your mind." Hugging her knees, she studied him in the fading light.

"I've always tried to be careful that women didn't get the wrong idea about me and wedding bells...until you."

That should have meant something, but it only served to increase the ache. "You're a playboy married to your work." She exhaled hard. "I get that. Totally."

Stone went quiet again for so long she thought they might be returning to the silent truce again. Awkward and painful.

Then Stone stood, walking to the rail and staring out at the ocean. "My father."

Rising, she moved to stand beside him, wind pulling at the whispery cover-up over her bikini. "What do you mean?"

His father had been an off-limits topic for as long as she'd known him. Not even Mariah brought up the subject. Stone had always said that according to his mom, his paternity was a mystery. Was he opening up to her on a deeper level, including her in more than a few travel plans?

"I found out." His voice came out hoarse and a little harsh as he continued to look out at the foaming waves.

She rested a hand on his arm tentatively, not sure how he would react but unable to deny him some comfort during what had to be a difficult revelation. "I wish you would have told me."

"I've never told anyone."

"I was supposed to be more than just 'anyone' to you," she reminded him softly.

He glanced sideways at her. "Touché."

"Did you hire a private investigator?"

"Don't you think my grandmother already tried that hoping to find someone who actually wanted me around?"

His words snapped her upright in shock. "Your grandmother loves you."

"I know that. I do," he said with certainty. "But she'd already brought up her kids. She was supposed to be my grandmother. Not my parent."

"Did she tell you that?" She knew full well Mariah never would have said anything of the sort to Stone. Johanna just wanted to remind him of how very much his grandmother loved him.

"She didn't have to say it." He went silent for the length of two rolling waves crashing to the shore. "When I was eleven, I found the private detective's report of her search for my biological father."

"Of course she would want to know everything about you. Perhaps she was worried that he might try to take you away. Did you ever consider that?" When he didn't answer, she continued, "You said she didn't find him. So how did you locate him?"

"The report uncovered a wealth of data about my mother's activities then." His face went darker. "Suffice it to say, my mother led quite an active party life."

"That reflects on her." She squeezed his arm. "Not on you."

"I understand that." He braced his shoulders, his eyes cold with an anger Johanna knew wasn't directed at her. "I'm not a drug addict like my mother. And while I'm not a monk, I'm monogamous during a relationship. I am my own man. I control myself and my destiny."

She rubbed soothing circles along his arm. Even if this conversation wouldn't change things between them, she knew he needed to get these words out and for some reason she was the person he trusted most to tell.

She drew in a bracing breath of salty air before continuing, "How did you find out about your father?"

"My mother told me."

"That simple?"

"Apparently so. She was high at the time and to this day doesn't remember telling me." He pinched the bridge of his nose. "I was twenty-five when she let it slip about the man who fathered me—Dale Banks."

Johanna gasped in recognition. "*The* Dale Banks? The country music star?"

"My mom was a groupie back in the day." He shrugged. "She hooked up with him and here I am."

She studied his features with a new perspective. Wind whipped her hair over her face, and she scraped the locks aside. "You do look a little like him. I never noticed until now...."

"I needed more reassurance than a look-alike contest. So I confronted him."

"How did you get past his security guards?"

"I have influence of my own." He smiled darkly. "Remember the benefit concert we sponsored a few years back?"

She did the quick math and realized Stone would have been in his mid-twenties then. She couldn't imagine how difficult that meeting must have been. "You arranged that to speak with him?"

"I'm not above using philanthropy for my own good, as well."

"You don't need to be sarcastic to cover your emotions." She slid her hand to his back and tucked her body to his side as if it was the most natural thing in the world to share his burdens. And it was. She drew in the heat and salty scent of him, her senses starved after months without him. "That had to have been difficult for you, confronting him."

"I didn't. I got a DNA sample during dinner."

"What?" She looked up sharply, unable to believe she'd heard him correctly. "You tricked him?"

"Easier than forcing the matter with a conversation where he denied it and I had to prove him a liar."

He didn't fool her for a second with this blasé act.

"What did he say when you finally told him?"

"He doesn't know. Why should he? He slept with a woman he didn't know and didn't care enough to follow up."

"Stone!" She cupped his face and made him look at her. "Maybe he's changed. Perhaps he has regrets and would like to know you now."

"I don't need him in my life," he said in a cold tone that left no room for negotiation.

"Maybe *he* needs *you,*" she suggested. "People are so much more important than money or fame."

"That's right. You grew up poor but loved," he said sarcastically.

Again, he didn't fool her. She patted his cheek just a touch harder than a love tap. "Don't be a jerk."

"Maybe I'm letting my real side show." He turned his face to kiss her palm, then nipped it gently.

She wouldn't let him divert her with sex. She slipped her hand back down to his shoulder. "How did we spend so much time together and never talk about these things?"

"You were right in saying I was holding back."

She couldn't believe he'd admitted it. "Why are you telling me now? And please be truthful."

"I'm not really sure." He snagged a strand of her hair and stroked the length with gentle pressure. "Maybe because there's nothing left to lose between us. You've already ditched me. Why bother working my ass off to impress you?"

"You were working to impress me?" She couldn't resist smiling.

"Clearly, I failed." He looped the lock around his finger until he cupped the back of her head.

"Not totally." She stepped closer, unable to resist the sizzle, especially not combined with the vulnerability he'd shown in sharing what he'd found out about his father. "I did agree to marry you."

She arched up on her toes and kissed him. How could she not? Her body ached to be with him. They were two consenting adults, alone together, attached to no one else and both so very aware of the price of being together.

His arms banded around her, thick, muscled arms that held her with such gentle power she leaned closer until her breasts pressed to the hard bare wall of his chest. His mouth tasted of the salty ocean and sweet tea, a heady combination for a woman already teetering on the edge of losing control.

She sketched along the hard planes of his back, still damp from his swim and perspiration. So many nights she'd lain awake yearning to be with him again and now those restless fantasies were coming to life. Being away from home gave her the freedom to act on those impulses.

Stone caressed down her back to her hips, molding her closer to him, his arousal pressing against her stomach.

"Johanna," he groaned against her mouth. "You're killing me here. If you want to stop, we need to put the brakes on this now. It's up to you what happens next. How are we going to handle this attraction that's tearing us both apart?"

She dipped her hands into his swim trunks. "We're going to sleep together again. Tonight."

Seven

Finally, he had Johanna back in his arms again, even if just for a night. Only a fool would pass up this chance, and he was not a fool.

Taking her face in his hands, he kissed her, fully, tongues meeting and inhibitions gone. A perfect fit, just like before. Familiar and new all at once—their time apart added an edge to the need.

He backed her into the cottage, their bare legs tangling as they walked, notching his desire higher and higher with each provocative brush of skin against skin. Her fingers linked behind his neck as she writhed against him in a lithe dance of desire denied for far too long.

Impatiently, he pushed open the door with such urgency it slammed against the wall. His hands slid low, cupping her bottom and lifting her over the threshold. Once inside the cottage, he set her down, the bamboo floor cool under his feet in contrast to the heat searing through him.

Their bathing suits offered thin barriers between them, but too much right now. He bunched her whispery cover up in his hands and swept it over her head. He'd seen her in her bikini earlier—had seen her in far less—but she still took his breath away. Her simple black two-piece called to his hands, triangles begging to be peeled away.

She smiled with a siren's gleam in her eyes. "This is usually the point where you drop your Stetson on my head."

"I left it on my suitcase. Not too many cowboy hats on the beach while a guy's riding a wave."

"That's a damn shame." She traced the rope tattoo around his biceps, which ended in a lasso loop.

He and his cousins had gotten tattoos together when the twins had turned eighteen. He'd been twenty-one. Johanna had wanted to go with them. He'd forgotten that until just now. She'd wanted to get paw print tattoos on her ankle, but he'd known her parents wouldn't approve.

Tracing the length of her collarbone, he lifted the diamond horseshoe necklace she wore all the time now. "I would drape you in gems, design entire lines of jewelry dedicated to your beauty."

"Who knew you were poetic?"

"You inspire me."

She stroked up his arms. "I'm just as happy with wildflowers and bluebonnets. That day we made love in the open and you covered me in petals is one of my all-time favorite memories."

"Another reason you're special. I never have to wonder with you. I know you're here—or not here—based on me. It has nothing to do with my family or our money." He plucked the strings behind her neck. The top fell away, revealing her breasts, pert and a perfect fit in his palms.

"You're a savvy man," she gasped, her nipples beading against his hands, either from his touch or the cool swoosh of the air conditioner. "I imagine you see through the sycophants right away."

"That discernment came from practice." He thumbed along her taut peaks, teasing them tighter until she swayed ever so slightly.

She covered his hands with hers. "You shouldn't have to wonder about people that way. Thinking of you wondering, learning from practice—that makes me so sad."

"I definitely don't want you sad right now—or ever." He hooked his thumbs in the strings along her hips and snapped them before the thought formed in his mind.

Her swimsuit bottom fell away.

She kicked aside the scrap of fabric. "If I were the sort of woman who wanted to be draped only in jewels, what would you design for me?"

"Ah, now you're talking." He let his imagination take flight. "I've always liked yellow diamonds for you. I can see long earrings that trail in a sleek, thin cascade to your shoulders." He skimmed each spot with a kiss. "Each piece would echo the golden lines of your beautiful body. And a long, gold rope chain with a pendant that trails right...here...between..."

His mouth landed along the inside of one curve, then the other. Her breath hitched, her fingers twisting in the band of his swim trunks. Tugging at the elastic, she peeled the damp suit down and off into a pile around his feet.

He stepped out and then swept her up against his chest. "And since the jewelry would be for our eyes only, I dream of you in more erotic designs, as well."

"Oh, really?" She looped her arms around his neck. "I can't decide whether to be nervous or intrigued."

One step at a time, he carried her closer to the white

iron bed with a view of the water. "A thicker rope chain would circle low on your waist, resting on your hips."

"Ah, like a lasso." She thumbed his tattoo. "That works both ways, you know. I could pull you to me, especially perfect if you wore chaps and nothing more."

He arched an eyebrow. "Not very businesslike."

"We're not in the boardroom."

"True." He tossed her onto the mattress.

She landed with an enticing bounce that made all the right parts jiggle just a hint. She stretched out along the puffy quilt, her creamy shoulders propped up by a pile of seashell-patterned pillows.

Part of him wanted to take in the sight of her for hours on end, and another more urgent part of him couldn't delay any longer. He kneeled on the edge of the bed and crawled up over her, tasting his way up her bared flesh, along her stomach, teasing the diamond belly button ring with his teeth. Higher still, he took her breast in his mouth, rolling the nipple with his tongue until her needy sighs begged him for more, faster, sooner.

He glanced up to see her head thrown back, pushing into the pillows. From the flush blooming over her skin he knew she was close to coming apart. He understood the urgent sensation well and slid the rest of the way up to take her lips, his erection nudging against the slick core of her. Ready. For him. Just as he was ready for her, only her, always her.

With a hoarse growl, he thrust deep inside her.

Gasping, she grabbed his shoulders. "Stone, wait." She gripped harder, her fingernails digging into his flesh. "What about protection?"

He arched back to look into her eyes. "Aren't you on the pill?"

"Not anymore," she said. "Once we broke up and it was clear we weren't going to reconcile, I stopped taking it."

She'd thought about reconciling with him? For how long? How many opportunities had he missed to get her back only to lose her because of stubborn pride?

Have her back?

Wasn't this just about sex now?

All thoughts too weighty for him to consider with his brain muddled from being buried to the hilt inside her again.

He hadn't packed condoms.... And if they discussed this much further it was going to lead to a serious mood buster of a conversation. He rolled off her with a groan of frustration.

Johanna sat up with a gasp. "Wait." She snapped her fingers. "I saw some in the honeymooners' welcome basket on the bedside table."

Crisis averted. Thank heavens the staff had assumed they would need the romance special basket. He stayed on his side while Johanna raced into the living area, and yes, he enjoyed the hell out of the view. He'd dreamed of her, but fantasies couldn't come close to the reality of being here with her.

The sound of rustling carried from the next room before she returned. Grinning, she held a condom in one hand and a plump pear in the other. She sank her teeth into the fruit and tossed him the square packet. He snatched it out of midair then grabbed her wrist to tug her back into bed with him.

Laughing, she settled on top of him and pressed the

pear against his mouth. He took a bite, then set the fruit aside to have her. Johanna. His again.

He flipped her onto her back and thrust inside her. Gasping, she closed her eyes and welcomed him with a roll of her hips. Her legs wrapped around him, her heels digging in and urging him deeper, faster, leaving no room for misunderstanding. She wanted him, too, with the same hungry edge. He kissed her hard and insistent, the taste of pear mingling with the sweet warmth of her.

He knew her body as well as he knew his own. He'd made a point of learning each sensitive spot and how to tease her pleasure higher. And she'd done the same for him.

Touch for touch, they moved in synch with each other. Her hands roved a restless path until perspiration dotted his forehead in spite of the ocean breeze gusting through the window.

Wind chimes sang louder and louder as if kicked up by a spring storm. He whispered in her ear about husky fantasies built during nights apart, silver links binding them together, jewels hidden and found. Her panting replies—her yes, yes, yes riding each gasp—stoked the fire in him higher until his whole body felt like molten metal in a flame.

And just when he thought he couldn't hold out any longer before the heat consumed them both, Johanna flew apart in his arms. Her cries of completion rolled free, as uninhibited and natural as the woman in his arms. The sweet clamp of her body pulsing around him sent him over the edge with her.

As wave after wave crashed over him, he held her closer, absorbing her aftershocks as he slowly came back down to earth again. His arms gave way, and he rolled to his side, taking her with him.

With the wind kicking up a humid breeze and rain pattering outside, he willed his galloping heartbeat to return to normal. Except his hammering pulse wasn't cooperating. With each slug against his ribs, he knew.

He couldn't give Johanna up again, but there wasn't a chance in hell she would stay with him if she knew the worst of what he'd held back, the reason he absolutely could not fulfill her dreams and become the father of her children.

Johanna woke up to an empty bed.

She stretched under the Egyptian cotton sheets, the scent of lovemaking mingling with the ocean air blowing in through the window. Barks also echoed from outside along with the rumbling bass of Stone's voice shouting a ramble of "fetch" and "good girl."

The sun climbing high into the sky told her she'd slept in, not surprising since they'd made up for lost time throughout the night. In bed, in the shower, moving into the kitchen for food, then making love against the counter.

Her body carried the delicious ache of total satiation. Although she knew the moment she saw Stone, she would want him all over again, and she couldn't help but want to look her best. She shoved her hands through her tangled hair, which must be a complete mess since she'd gone to sleep with it still damp.

A quick glance at the clock had her rolling to her feet and racing to the bathroom. A fast washup later, she wrapped her hair and body in fluffy towels and opened the closet.

The packed full closet?

She stared at all the clothes that hadn't been there the night before. Tags showed they were all new and in her size. Stone had been busy. He'd ordered her a whole new wardrobe for the rest of their trip. He'd heard what she said about feeling uneasy and in his own way he was trying to ease that worry for her.

The barking dogs gave her only a moment's warning before Stone walked into the bedroom. So much for dressing up. She secured the towel around her and tugged the other off her head, shaking her hair free.

She skimmed her fingers along the rack of clothes. "You didn't have to do this, but thank you."

"Glad you're happy." He captured her hand and pulled her close. "And just so we're clear, it doesn't matter to me what you're wearing. In my eyes you're magnificent."

"Thank you." She arched up for a kiss. "You're one good cowboy, Stone."

"I'm trying, lady, I'm trying." He kissed her good-morning thoroughly before easing back. "I did hear what you said about going to formal functions before, and it's killing me to think you ever felt uncomfortable."

"I know a person's worth doesn't have anything to do with their bank balance."

"Damn straight." He dropped to sit on the foot of the bed, pulling her into his lap. "I imagine that's part of my grandmother's plan here, too, giving me a reality check when it comes to family values."

Her heart fluttered in her chest. He couldn't possibly be changing his stance on a family. Could he?

Afraid to wreck the moment by pushing, she changed the subject. "There's quite a range of clothes you've bought for me." She pointed to a rack with everything from jeans and slacks to sundresses and a couple of longer gowns. "Where else are we going?"

"My grandmother has a wide range of people lined up, even a couple of backups if someone doesn't work out."

She snagged an ice-blue lacy dress. "This looks fit for royalty."

"You're perceptive," he said with a grimace.

She rolled her eyes, certain she must have misunderstood. "Really? Royalty, in addition to a former secretary of state."

"Really."

She froze, realizing he was serious. "All right," she exhaled, sagging back against his chest. "If Sterling is going to the political powerhouse couple, that leaves Pearl and Ruby. Which one's getting the tiara?"

"Ruby. Enrique Medina lost both of his Rhodesian ridgebacks this year to old age. He and my grandmother are friends. He's even the one who recommended contacting General Renshaw about Sterling."

Royalty. Honest-to-God royalty. Nothing would surprise her about this family again. "What about Pearl? Is she going to the Pope?"

Stone snorted on a laugh. "I'm sure he's one of Gran's backups." He kissed her nose. "Seriously, though, I don't know as much about the last family other than that they live on a ranch in Montana."

"Are the formal gowns for the jewelers' convention that you mentioned?" Her stomach gripped at the thought. Even with the fancy clothes, she was still a farm girl who felt most at ease in her jeans, with braided hair and a horse.

"I canceled that. The variety of dresses are so we can go out to dinner somewhere nice. Just the two of us, to thank you for coming along this week to ease my grandmother's mind. Regardless of where we go from here, I will always be grateful for all you've done for Gran."

She couldn't help but be surprised again over how he was revealing more to her on this trip than she'd ever understood about him before. Had he suffered as much from their time apart? Or had confronting mortality with his grandmother's illness brought down some walls? Either way, she couldn't help but be drawn in by this man.

He tipped her chin for another kiss, one that couldn't go any further with the day slipping away, but God, she was tempted. Because she couldn't help but think these changes were too good to be true.

An hour later, Stone opened the hatch on their rental SUV to load up the dogs for their drive over to the Landis-Renshaw compound. Ruby loped into the back and he lifted scruffy little Pearl in, as well, a mesh barrier keeping them from taking over the front seat. He'd stowed their luggage in a cartop carrier. They looked like a regular family on vacation.

He rubbed the kink in his neck from lack of sleep, but he wouldn't change a moment of their night together.

The waves glistened under the power of the noonday sun and he wished they could just blow off his grandmother's plan and stay at the cottage for the rest of the week. He and Johanna had connected, just like in the past, and he was working hard to reassure her. Maybe he was deluding himself into hoping she could overlook the bigger issues if he corrected some other problems in their relationship.

To what end?

Did he really expect they would ride off into the sunset together? He had to be honest with himself and admit he wanted her back in his life on a permanent basis. But being equally honest, he wasn't sure that was possible no matter how many closets full of comfy clothes and easygoing outings he came up with.

The beach cottage door opened, and Johanna stepped out with Sterling cradled in her arms. She'd chosen a simple flowery dress, loose and classic. But she looked good in everything she wore. His assistant had ordered everything and assured him the task would be easy. Johanna had pulled her hair back in a jeweled clasp—a Diamonds in the Rough piece. And of course she wore his grandmother's horseshoe charm.

He struggled to resist the urge to scoop her up, carry her back inside and peel the dress off her. Instead, he held out his arms. "I'll take Sterling."

She shook her head, her ponytail sweeping along her spine the way his hands ached to do. "I'll hold him. I'm feeling sentimental about saying goodbye to him. I keep thinking about the day your grandmother got him as a puppy."

He closed the back hatch and walked around to open her door. "I always think of you as being there for the horses. I forget sometimes that caring for the dogs falls under your job description, as well." He leaned in the open door. "It will be tough for you to say goodbye to them, too."

"I don't have pets of my own...so yes." She stroked the Chihuahua-dachshund mix. "I have become attached. But your grandmother is wise to make sure they're placed. Too many animals end up at shelters when their owners pass away or go into nursing homes."

"We would have taken them all for her. She has to know that." Not a chance in hell would he have dumped Gran's pets at the shelter. He closed the door, perhaps a bit more forcefully than he'd intended, but the reminder of a world without Mariah cast clouds over his day.

He walked around the hood and took his place behind the wheel. He swept off his Stetson and dropped it on the console between them. Starting the car, he pulled his focus back in tight before he landed them nose first in a sand dune. Navigating the beach traffic was tough enough.

Johanna's hand fell to rest on his arm as he passed a slow-moving RV. "Clearly, Mariah has a plan in mind for them, and for your future, too. Never doubt for a second that she loves you."

He glanced at her. "She loves you, too, you know."

"Thank you—" she smiled "—but it's not the same. I'm not family."

"I'm not so sure." His hands gripped the wheel tighter, settling into their lane along the ocean side road. "She was mad as hell with me when we broke up."

"Why was she angry with you?" Johanna sat up straighter. "I was the one who ended our engagement. I made that abundantly clear to everyone."

Had she made the breakup public to spare him blowback from his family? He'd been so angry at her then, he hadn't given thought to the fact that a public breakup actually cast him in a more sympathetic light. He'd been too caught up in his anger—and hurt. "Gran said I had to have done something wrong to make you give back the engagement ring. And she was right."

The breakup had been his fault, and nothing significant had changed. He still didn't want children, and watching her cradle the dog, he couldn't miss her deep-seated urge to nurture.

He felt like a first-class ass.

Johanna adjusted the silver collar around Sterling's neck. "I'm sorry if I caused a wedge between the two of you."

"You have nothing to apologize for," he insisted, steering onto a bridge that would take them to their barrier island destination. "I'm an adult. My relationships are my own problem."

"She's trying to matchmake, sending us on this trip together." Johanna traced the top of his hat resting between them.

No kidding. "I'm sure that was a part of her plan, no matter what she said, but the rest is still true." Miles of marshy sea grass bowed as they drove deeper into the exclusive beach property of Hilton Head, the South's answer to Martha's Vineyard. "She doesn't trust me to see to the dogs, and she's right. I would have screwed it up."

"I seriously doubt that," Johanna said with a confidence he didn't feel when it came to this subject.

"I wouldn't have been as thorough as you've been." He'd been impressed and surprised during the meet and greet with the Donavans. "I wouldn't have even thought of half the things you've done to make sure Gem's in the right home and that the transition goes smoothly for her."

"Gem's going to miss your grandmother." She swept

a hand under her eyes and he realized she'd teared up. "There will be grieving on his part as well."

"Are you trying to make me just skip the rest of this trip and take the dogs home with us? Because I'm about five seconds away from doing that," he half joked. "In fact, much more of this and I'll even snatch Gem back."

She responded with a watery laugh. "Don't you dare. The Donavans are a fantastic family for Gem, as Mariah clearly already knew." She reached into her bag and pulled out dog treats. She passed two over the mesh to Pearl and Ruby, before offering another to Sterling. "They're not cutie pie little puppies anymore, and placing an adult dog can be difficult. And we definitely don't want someone taking in the dogs in hopes of gaining favor with your grandmother."

Protectiveness pumped through him. "I wouldn't let that happen."

"Of course not. You're a good man."

"Such a good man my grandmother has to test me and you dumped me flat on my ass," he said wryly.

She scooted closer, slipping her hand to the back of his neck. "I miss the happy times between us. Last night was…incredible."

What an odd time to realize she was "soothing" him the same way she soothed Sterling, using her dog whisperer ways on him. "So you do acknowledge it wasn't all bad between us."

"Of course it wasn't all bad," she said incredulously.

"Specifics." He might as well use this time to get whatever edge he could.

"Why?" Suspicion laced her voice. "What purpose will it serve?"

"Call it a healing exercise." And the hope of figuring out a way to have more with her tomorrow.

"Okay, uh…" Her hand fell back to the dog in her lap. "I appreciate the way you support my work. Like the time I'd already pulled extra hours on my shift, but the call came from a shelter in South Texas in need of extra veterinary help for neglected horses seized by animal control. You drove through the night so I could sleep before working." Her mouth tipped in a smile, her eyes taking on a faraway look. "Then you didn't sleep. You rolled up your sleeves and helped."

He had to haul his gaze away from the beauty of her smile before he rear-ended the car in front of them. "We accomplished a lot of good together that day."

"We did. And I know it was you who encouraged your grandmother to help sponsor this year's big charity event to help save the wild mustangs."

He shrugged, her praise making him itchy. "We needed a tax write-off."

"You're not fooling me." She swatted his arm.

He searched for the right words. "My family has worked hard and been very lucky. We're in a position to do good."

"Not everyone makes the same choices as your family. I don't even know that I'd fully thought about it in such concrete terms until now. Your grandmother instilled solid values in all of you."

"Very diplomatic of you not to mention what my mom or Amie and Alex's parents could have shared." Diplomatic and astute.

"I'm sorry that your mother couldn't be a true parent for you."

"Don't be." The warmth of the day chilled for him.

"She broke Gran's heart. And Uncle Garnet wasn't much better, but at least he tried to build a normal family life. He went to work every day even if he wasn't particularly ambitious." Or willing to stand up to his overly ambitious wife. "Gran always said she babied him and she wanted to be sure she didn't make the same mistake with us."

"Your aunt Bayleigh was ambitious enough for the both of them." She shuddered dramatically.

"True enough." There was no denying the obvious. "She pushed the twins for as far back as I can remember. Although I gotta confess, even their flawed family looked mighty damn enticing to me as a kid."

"You wanted to live with them."

She sounded surprised, which made him realize yet again how little of himself he'd shared with the woman who was supposed to have been the most important person in his life. If he wanted even a chance at being with her again, he had to give what he could this time.

"I did want to be their kid," he admitted. "Gran even asked them once if they would be interested in guardianship of me, but their plate was full."

She gasped. "That had to be so painful to hear."

To this day, he was glad no one had seen him listening in. He couldn't have taken the humiliation of someone stumbling on him crying. Looking back, he realized he must have only been in elementary school, but the tears had felt less than manly on a day when he already felt like a flawed kid no one wanted.

"It worked out for the best." He found himself still minimizing the pain of that experience. "Gran was a great parental figure. And my mother, well, she was a helluva lot of fun during her sober stints."

The words came out more bitterly than he'd intended. Thank God, they were pulling up to the security gate outside the Landis-Renshaw compound because he'd had about as much "sharing time" as he could take for one day. Much more of this and he would start pouring out stories about being a crack baby, who still cringed at the thought of all the developmental psychologists he'd visited before he'd even started first grade.

He was managing fine now, damn it, and the past could stay in the past.

The wrought-iron security gates loomed in front of them, cameras peeking out of the climbing ivy. He rolled down his window and passed over his identification to a guard posted in his little glass booth with monitors.

The guard nodded silently, passed the ID back, and the gates swung open. Now he just had to figure out how to say goodbye to another family pet and pretend it didn't matter that the only family he'd known would soon fall apart when his grandmother died. She'd been his strength and his sanity. She'd literally saved his life as a baby. She was a strong woman, like Johanna.

As he watched Johanna cuddle the dog in her lap, he realized he hadn't taken this dog placement trip seriously, which was wrong of him. He'd just followed Johanna's lead in shuffling his grandmother's pets to new families, not thinking overlong about the loss, just going through the motions. His grandmother, Johanna—the dogs—all deserved better than that from him.

For the first time he considered that perhaps his grandmother hadn't been matchmaking after all. Maybe she had been trying to help him understand why Johanna was better off without him.

Eight

Settled deep in the front seat of the SUV, Johanna wrapped her arms around the dachshund mix in her lap and wondered how she'd gotten drawn back into a whirlwind of emotions for Stone so quickly.

At least once they arrived, she had the next few hours with people around to give her time to regain her footing before they were in a hotel together or some other romantic setting on this trip designed to tamper with her very sanity. She had time to build boundaries to protect her heart until she could figure out where they were going as a couple. Was this just sex for the week or were they going to try for more again? If so, they still had the same disagreements looming as before.

She hugged the dog closer as she looked through the window to take everything in. Could this day be any more convoluted? She was seconds away from meeting a political powerhouse couple. The general was reputed to be on the short list for the next secretary of defense. Ginger was now an ambassador and former secretary of state. Her oldest son was a senator. Who wouldn't be nervous?

Stone, apparently.

He steered the car smoothly, but his mind was obviously somewhere else. "I never did know how Sterling ended up in my grandmother's pack."

His comment surprised her.

"One of her employees was older and developed Alzheimer's. The retirement home the woman's family chose didn't allow animals."

"That's really rough. How did I not know that story?" His forehead furrowed as he steered the SUV up the winding path through beach foliage to the main house. "I wish my grandmother would have trusted me more to see to the animals after she's gone so she could have the comfort of them now when she needs them most."

Johanna stayed silent. She agreed 100 percent but saying as much wouldn't change anything. The situation truly was a tough one. "It's sad Sterling should lose his owner twice."

"Life is rarely about what's fair," he said darkly before sliding the car into Park alongside the house.

He grabbed his hat and was out of the car before she could think of an answer. What was going on inside his head? This man never ceased to confuse her.

While she secured Sterling's leash, she studied the grounds to get her bearings before she stepped out of the car. The beach compound was grander than the rustic Hidden Gem Ranch and more expansive than the scaled-back Donavan spread. She'd seen photos from a *Good Housekeeping* feature when she'd searched the internet for more details on the Landis and Renshaw families, who had joined when the widowed Ginger Landis married the widower General Hank Renshaw. But no magazine article could have prepared her for the breathtaking view as Johanna stared through the windshield. The homes were situated on prime oceanfront property. The main house was a sprawling white three-story overlooking the Atlantic, where a couple walked along the low-crashing waves. A lengthy set of stairs stretched upward to the second-story wraparound porch that housed the double door entrance.

Latticework shielded most of the first floor, which appeared to be a large entertainment area, a perfect use of space for a home built on stilts to protect against tidal floods from hurricanes. The attached garage had more doors than an apartment complex.

A carriage house and the Atlantic shore were in front of them. And two cottages were tucked to the sides around an organically shaped pool. The chlorinated waters of the hot tub at the base churned a glistening swirl in the sunlight, adults and kids splashing.

It was a paradise designed for a big family to gather in privacy. The matriarch and patriarch of the family—Ginger and the general—appeared on the balcony porch looking like any other grandparents vacationing with their family. Relatives of all ages poured from the guest quarters. Three other dogs sprinted ahead. Not quite the careful, structured meet and greet that worked best, but clearly this home was about organized chaos.

She stepped out of the car, setting Sterling on the sandy ground while she held tight to the leash. The family tableaus played out in full volume now. She could hear a little girl squealing with laughter while her dad taught her to swim in the pool. A mom held a snoozing infant on her lap while she splash, splash, splashed a toe in the water. Voices mingled from a mother's lullaby to a couple planning a date night since grandparents could babysit.

Johanna saw her own past in the times her parents

had taken her swimming in a pond and saw the future she wanted for herself, but couldn't see how Stone would fit into it. She was killing herself, seeing all these happy families while was stuck in a dead-end relationship with a man who would never open up.

All luxury aside, this kind of togetherness was what she'd hoped to build for herself one day. Those dreams hadn't changed. Which meant she'd landed herself right back into the middle of a heartache all over again.

Stone sat at a poolside table with Ginger and Hank Renshaw, pouring over their adoption paperwork. If anyone had told him a week ago that he would be grilling them to be sure Sterling would be a happy fit for their family, Stone would have said that person was nuts.

Yet here he was, quizzing them and watching the way they handled his grandmother's dog— Correction. *Their* dog now. Sterling was curled up in Ginger's lap, looking like a little prince, completely unfazed by the mayhem of children cannonballing into the deep end while a volleyball game took place on the beach.

Stone nodded somberly, pulling his hat off and setting it aside. "It's important that Sterling get along with children."

"Amen," the general agreed, having stayed silent for the most part, a laid-back gramps in khaki shorts and a polo shirt. "We have double digits in grandkids. Christmases are particularly chaotic."

This wasn't chaos? Stone felt the weight of Johanna's eyes on him, the confusion in her gaze. He gave her a reassuring smile, and she warily smiled back, which too quickly had his mind winging back to thoughts of last night, of how damn much he enjoyed making her smile...and sigh.

He cleared his throat, and his thoughts, turning his focus back to the older couple who'd clearly found a second chance at romance.

Ginger touched her husband's arm, the former secretary of state completely poised in spite of the breeze pulling at her graying hair and loose beach dress. "Hank, we should have them test out the Rottweiler—Ruby—while they're here, as well, since he will be part of the family, sort of, by going to Jonah's father-in-law."

Ginger's youngest son had married a princess, no less. Stone looked out at the beach where Ruby splashed in the waves with another dog and a trio of preteens. "So far so good, I would say."

Ginger nodded, patting the cairn terrier in Johanna's lap. "I just wish we could take that precious Pearl, too. She's like a little Toto from *The Wizard of Oz*. The grandkids would love her and it would be wonderful to keep them together. But we know our limits."

Johanna set her glass of sweet tea back on the table. "We're going to be sure Pearl is well taken care of. Just knowing that Sterling is happy is a load off all our minds, especially for Mrs. McNair." She glanced sympathetically at Stone before looking back at Ginger. "Thank you."

The family matriarch twisted a diamond earring in a nervous fidget, genuine concern in her eyes. "I'm terribly sorry about Mariah.... There are no words at a time like this."

"Thank you, ma'am." Stone nodded tightly, emotion squeezing his chest in a tight fist. "You're offering exactly the kind of help my grandmother needs. Right, Johanna?"

He glanced at her, finding her gaze locked on a mother, father and toddler splashing through the surf together. The look of longing in her eyes slashed straight through him.

Johanna stood up quickly. "We brought a little gift, as a thank-you from Diamonds in the Rough. I'll just get it out of the car."

As he watched her race away he realized how their night together had messed with both of them. Last night had been different from their other times together, and his emotions were in revolt. He was starting to accept it wasn't totally because of his grandmother. His confusion had more to do with Johanna than he'd realized.

Strange how they'd swapped roles here, but he appreciated her interjecting. Talk of his grandmother and seeing this picture-perfect family echoed what he'd already begun to accept. Johanna was right to want this for herself. She shouldn't compromise for him.

On the plane headed for Montana for Pearl's meeting, Johanna struggled to figure out the shift in Stone this afternoon. She thought they'd reached a truce whereby they would indulge in no-strings sex for the week and deal with the fallout later. Yet, something had already changed for him.

And she had to confess, she didn't feel carefree about things, either. Watching the huge Landis-Renshaw family hurt. She couldn't lie about that.

The plane powered through the bumpy night sky and even though she knew where they were going literally, figuratively, she was now totally adrift.

She studied Stone sitting on the sofa with a sketch pad, his forearm flexing as he drew. Pearl slept on a cushion beside him, her head resting on his thigh. He was so damn enticing, he took her breath away.

"What happens now?" Johanna asked.

He glanced up. "Well, in about two more hours, we should land in—"

"That's not what I meant." Her hand fell to Ruby's head as the Rottweiler slept at her feet. Johanna would kennel them for landing or if the turbulence worsened, but for now she wanted to make the most out of the remaining time with the dogs before they went to their new homes. "Why are you avoiding talking to me? I really don't want to think that now that you've gotten lucky we're through."

His eyebrows shot upward. "You have a mighty jaded view of mankind."

"You haven't said anything to change my mind tonight," she pushed.

Eyes narrowed, he set aside his sketch pad and rolled his broad shoulders to stretch out a kink. "Who gave you such a bad impression of men, and why didn't I pick up on this when we were together before?"

"Maybe because I always gave you the answers you wanted to hear." She was realizing she had to accept some responsibility for their breakup and quit blaming him for everything.

"And I accepted them rather than pressing," he conceded, bracing his feet through another brief patch of turbulence.

"There's no great mystery to be solved." She shrugged. The muted cabin lights, with only a reading lamp over Stone, cast intriguing shadows along his rugged face. "My parents were great. My father was a good man. But for some reason, the men I chose to date always let me down. One wanted me to give up vet tech school to follow him right away, no waiting—"

"That was Dylan—"

"Yeah," she said, surprised that Stone remembered. He'd been intensely into making his mark at the company, so much so she'd decided she needed to get over her crush. She'd been living in an efficiency apartment, training to be a vet tech. It had seemed time to move forward with her life. "He couldn't even wait six more months for me to finish."

"Then he didn't deserve you."

"Damn right." She knew that now, and even then she'd felt a hint of relief since she didn't ever want to leave Fort Worth. "And the next guy I dated when I moved back to the ranch after school—"

"Langdon."

"You have a good memory." A part of her had wanted him to notice she'd grown up, had wanted him to see her as a woman rather than the pigtailed kid trailing around in the stables. Hindsight, that had been incredibly unfair to Langdon.

"When it comes to you? Yes, I have a very good memory."

"Langdon was the jealous type." And there had been reason for him to be jealous, but that still didn't excuse him going borderline stalker about it. "No need to say more."

"I disagree," he said darkly.

"Don't get caveman on me. You don't need to hunt him down. He didn't hurt me." She stared out into the murky sky for a moment before continuing, "But a look in his eyes made me uncomfortable. I could go on about the other guys in my life, but I just kept picking losers."

"Ouch," he snapped back with a laugh, scrubbing a hand along his five o'clock shadow. "That stings since I'm on that list of exes."

"One of my exes accused me of entering relationships destined to fail because I was secretly pining for you." The words fell out before she could recall them, but then, what did she have to lose at this point?

"Was that true?"

"You know I always had a crush on you." The crush had been so much easier than this.

"Crushing and loving are very different."

Her stomach lurched and it had nothing to do with the bump, bump of the plane over another air pocket. "I did love you when we got engaged."

"Past tense...." He rubbed his neck, and her fingers clenched at the memory of the warmth of his skin. "I'm still getting used to that. What about now?"

"I honestly don't know, and the way you're sitting over there all detached makes it even tougher to figure out what I'm feeling."

He stood, and her mouth went dry the way it always did when he walked her way. But instead of scooping her up, he simply moved into a large leather chair across from her. "When we were together at the beach, none of that was pretend. You can trust what we felt."

"It was real, but we're still learning things weren't as perfect as we thought they were the day we got engaged. It will take us both some time to trust anyone again."

His jaw flexed with tension. "The thought of you getting over me enough to be with someone else is not a heartening thought."

"Why do you naturally assume that the someone I should be with would have to be another person?" She wanted to grab him by the shoulders and shake him. What the hell was going on? He'd made it clear he didn't want to break up when she'd walked, and now that she was reaching out, he'd put up a wall between them. "Even after what we shared last night?"

"Is this really a discussion we should be having now?"

"If not now, when?"

Turbulence jostled the plane again, harder this time and Ruby scrambled for steady footing.

Stone rose quickly, no doubt welcoming the chance to avoid the tough conversation. "We should crate the dogs now."

Sighing, Johanna rose, too, walking to the sofa to pick up Pearl. The pup sat on top of the sketch pad, head tipped with total attitude, one ear up, one down. Johanna gathered the scruffy rascal and uncovered Stone's sketch pad.

A gasp hitched in her throat as she looked down at a page filled with all the fantasy jewelry pieces he'd described wanting to create just for her, and in the middle of it all, a drawing of her sitting in a field of bluebonnets with Pearl beside her. The attention to detail was mind-blowing, even down to the weave of her French braid.

The whole time she'd thought he was pushing her away, he'd been focused completely on her.

Stone secured the latch on Ruby's crate. The Rottweiler stared back with droopy sad eyes as she curled up on her fluffy green dog bed. He plucked a dog biscuit from the bin beside the crates and passed a treat through. This week with Johanna was getting more and more complicated and he didn't know how to return to the connection they'd enjoyed while staying at the beach.

She knelt beside him, sliding Pearl into the smaller crate with a pink doggie bed and a couple of chew toys. Just as she locked the pup in, the plane jostled again. And again. Johanna tumbled against him, knocking him back. He twisted fast to cushion her fall with his body.

Johanna stretched out on top of him. "Oh, my, that was something."

He tugged her loose ponytail. "I'm not right for you and you shouldn't settle."

"I know that, and yet here we are."

God, he knew he wasn't good enough for her and still he could already hear that voice in the back of his mind insisting he try to repair the damage that had been done in the past and clear away obstacles to their future.

She wriggled against him enticingly. "Do we have enough time to slip away into the back cabin before we land?"

He clamped a hand on her bottom, acknowledging that he was still unable to resist this woman. He couldn't envision a time he could ever keep her at arm's length. So yeah, he was a selfish bastard. "Keep moving like that and we won't need much time at all."

Laughing, she leaned down to kiss him. The turbulence dipped the plane, and they rolled, slamming against the dog crates.

The captain's voice rumbled over the intercom, announcing the need to return to their seats and buckle in until they cleared the turbulence.

Stone's low curse whispered between them before

he levered off her. He extended a hand to help her up while bracing his other palm along her back protectively to steady her as they returned to the sofa and dug out the seat belts. He took the sketch pad, flipped it closed fast and tossed it aside.

She clicked the lap belt and tugged the strap. "I felt much better for Ruby after hearing the Renshaws' feedback. Makes me hopeful that will work well, too. I wish we knew more about Pearl's family in Montana."

"Honestly, I'm surprised my grandmother isn't keeping Ruby, since that's the one dog she chose rather than adopting from someone else. I never thought to ask Gran about Ruby's history. She just said she got Ruby at a shelter, nothing more."

"Your grandmother seemed lonely after she retired from the board at Diamonds in the Rough. So I took her to the animal shelter. She chose a new friend. Ruby was a stray, no known history, but they took to each other right away."

"You're a good woman, Johanna. I've always known that, though." His hand fell on her knee.

"Don't try the übercharmer act on me." She leaned closer and tapped him on the chin.

"It's not an act," he denied even as he slid his hand under the hem of her dress, ideas flourishing for ways to please her in spite of the seat belt. "If I were just trying to charm you, I would compliment your beautiful face or your hot body...." He skimmed up the inside of her thigh, welcoming the distraction from more serious talk and concerns. If only he could lose himself in her infinitely.

"Which is all true, of course," he continued. "That's what reeled me into asking you out. But the good woman part?" He squeezed her thigh without moving any higher. "That's what kept me around. That's why I proposed. And ultimately, that's why you left me."

"What are you trying to accomplish?" There was anguish in her beautiful eyes, but a whisper of hope that spurred him on and crystalized his thoughts.

"It's a warning, I guess," he said somberly, sliding his hand from under her dress to take her fingers in his. "You are a good woman, and you deserve better than what I have to offer. But that isn't going to stop me from offering and asking again."

Her throat moved in a slow swallow. "Stone—"

"Shh." He pressed a finger to her lips. "I don't want you to answer yet. You should think. And just so you know, all I can think about is peeling your clothes away piece by piece, then making love to you in a field of bluebonnets."

"Are you really suggesting we just have sex and... drift?"

"If that means I get more time with you, then yes," he answered without hesitation. "There is no one else I'll be spending my life with. You were it, Johanna. My one shot at the whole happily-ever-after gig."

He cupped her face and drew her to him, easy to do as she leaned into him. Her fingers fluttered along his cheek, falling to rest on his shoulders. Her light touch stirred him every bit as much as her most bold caress.

Damn straight, there was no one for him other than Johanna. He deepened the kiss, her soft lips parting for him, inviting him in to taste, take and give. The warmth of her seeped into him, fanning the flames that never died. She was in his blood, now and always.

He tugged the band from her hair and combed his

fingers through the strands. The feel of her hair gliding along his hands was pure bliss, like the wind sliding over him when he rode on the open land. He played it out along her back and over her shoulders before stroking down her arms.

His hand returned to her knee and tunneled under her silky dress, along her even silkier thigh. His knuckles skimmed her satin panties, already hot from her arousal, and he ached to know what color she wore—

The plane's phone rang from beside the sofa, jarring him from the kiss and the moment. Who would call in the middle of the night? Only family and only with an emergency.

With more than a little regret, he ended the kiss and pulled away from Johanna, alarms already sounding in his mind. He angled past her to snag the phone and read the screen. He glanced at Johanna, apprehension filling his gut as his suspicion was confirmed.

"It's Amie." He frowned, thumbing the on button and activating the speakerphone. "Amie, what's up? You're on speaker. Johanna's here with me."

"Gran's in the hospital." His cousin's voice trembled, and Stone exchanged a quick glance with Johanna. "She had a seizure, Stone. It… It was…horrible. We had to call an ambulance."

Dread hit him like a boulder. "I'm on my way. I'll have the pilot turn around, and we'll be there in a few hours. Hold on, okay, kiddo?"

He vaguely registered Johanna's hand smoothing along his back.

Amie hiccupped on the other end of the line. "I'm sorry to be such a mess. It was just really frightening." The sound of her shaky breath reverberated on the crackly connection. "Alex and I can hold down the fort until you get here. The doctor says she's past the immediate danger, but…"

"I'm on my way," he repeated, pulling his focus in tight. He was the head of his family. He should be home overseeing the business and the family affairs for his grandmother, not playing games.

He owed his grandmother and Johanna better. From this point on, he was 100 percent in when it came to taking care of his family, and Johanna was going to be a member of his family.

Whatever it took.

Nine

Johanna's stomach dropped as the hospital elevator rose, taking them to Mariah.

Fear for Mariah and grief for Stone had tumbled and tangled inside her ever since the panicked call from Amie came through. And no matter how much she worried, there was nothing she could do to console Stone or make this better.

They should be bonded in the moment, leaning on each other while they were both scared and hurting, but instead she could see him drawing inward. Rather than letting anyone close, Stone took on the leader of the pack mentality that had kept him at the office late so many nights. Since he'd hung up the phone, he'd been in motion. He'd moved up front with the pilot to discuss rerouting the plane. A limo had met them at the airport driving them to the ranch to drop off the dogs and grab a quick shower.

Now, medical personnel on the fourth floor milled around the nurses' station watching over their patients through cameras and observation windows. His grandmother had plenty of watchful eyes but Stone had already started researching other hospitals and doctors without even consulting the rest of the family. God, she hoped there wouldn't be a major argument with Stone and his cousins.

The head nurse waved him through before returning to her charts. Stone had called ahead to confirm the minute morning visiting hours began. She didn't even want to consider the fact that they could have arrived too late.

Mariah looked pale and small under the stark white sheet, sleeping. Only the steady rise and fall of her chest and the monitors beeping and clicking offered any reassurance that she was still alive.

Stone swept off his hat, set it on the rolling tray and moved closer to his grandmother. His boots thudded softly against the tile floors.

Mariah's lashes fluttered upward, her eyes surprisingly clear and alert, thank heavens. "You're here." She reached out a thin hand, her skin almost translucent. "I told your cousins not to worry you. Which one called?"

"I'm not ratting anyone out," he teased softly.

Mariah laughed softly. "You three always did stick together." She looked past him and smiled at Johanna, lifting her other hand with the IV line taped down. "Dear girl, come closer. You can both do away with those gloom and doom looks on your faces."

Johanna stroked Mariah's wrist. "Of course we're worried. You would feel the same if our positions were reversed."

"True enough," Mariah conceded. "But I'm okay. It was only a case of dehydration. Nothing to do with the tumor. I let myself get run-down and just needed a little boost. It's my own fault, and I'm so sorry they scared you into coming home unnecessarily."

"Gran, you don't need to lie to me." Stone's forehead furrowed, his face bristly since he'd rushed his shower and skipped the shave. "I already know you had a seizure."

"Damn it, I told Amie and Alex not to worry you, and don't bother denying one of them told you," she groused with enough spunk that Johanna relaxed a hint. "I'm not going to die this week, so you two don't need to park by my bed and babysit me. You have work to do."

Stone dropped into the chair by her bed. "They knew how angry I would be once I found out no one bothered to call me. And believe me, I would have found out."

"You're just like me." She smiled fondly. "Tenacious."

"I'm just glad you're all right, Gran." He glanced across his grandmother at Johanna, the strain of the past few hours showing in the lines fanning from his sapphire-blue eyes. "We both are."

Mariah squeezed Johanna's hand. "Tell me about your trip so far. The pictures are wonderful but I want to hear what you think, Johanna."

Mariah was shifting topics deftly, ensuring Stone wouldn't have to battle through weightier emotions right now. Or was it Mariah who wasn't ready to face those feelings today? Johanna had never fully appreciated how alike the two of them really were. But for now, she gladly distracted both of them with talk of a safe subject.

"Well, Gem loves the wide-open space of the Dona-vans' home, and their home in Monte Carlo has a fenced area, as well. Sterling is enjoying his life as a pampered lapdog. You chose well for both of them."

Her eyelids fluttered closed for a moment before she

looked up at Stone and Johanna again with a mist of tears in her eyes. "Thank you, and I truly mean that."

"Gran." Stone leaned in. "Are you sure you want us to continue with the placements? You could keep Pearl and Ruby. Trust that we will take care of finding them new homes, if the time comes—" He swallowed hard, his Adam's apple making a slow trip down the strong column of his throat. "If the time comes you can't care for them anymore."

Johanna had to blink her eyes hard. God, maybe it was her who wasn't ready to face the big emotions in the room today. Mariah had become so dear to her. A role model. A friend.

"I'm absolutely certain that I want you to continue the plan." She smiled sadly. "I already can't give them the attention they need. Call me a micromanager if you will, but I need to know where they are and who they're with."

"Gran—" Stone's phone cut him short and he cursed softly. He pulled out the cell and checked the incoming call, before silencing the chimes and tucking the phone back in his pocket.

His grandmother touched his wrist. "Who is it? Your cousins?"

He shook his head. "It's from Montana. Probably something about Pearl. I'll take it later."

"No," Mariah said with surprising strength. "That's important business to me."

His cheeks puffed out with an exhale. "Okay, Gran. If that's what you want, but I'll be right back."

Phone to his ear, head ducked, he strode out, door swooshing closed behind him.

Mariah patted Johanna's hand. "Pull up a seat and talk to me, Johanna. How is it really going, dear?"

"What do you mean?" she asked evasively, looking away under the guise of tugging a chair over.

"No need to be coy," Mariah tsked. "Are you and Stone a couple again?"

Johanna dropped into a seat. "Wow, you really cut to the chase."

"I don't have time to dillydally around the subject." Mariah pushed the controls to raise the head of the mattress. "Even at half speed in this hospital bed, I can tell the chemistry is alive and well. I see the exchanged glances. You have to know I was hoping your trip together would fix things between you. Did my matchmaking work?"

The optimism in the woman's face was unmistakable. Johanna didn't want to give false hope, and she wasn't sure where things stood with Stone right now. "I wish I could tell you what you want to hear, but I honestly don't know."

"The fact that you didn't deny it outright gives me hope."

Johanna sagged back, rolling her eyes. "But no pressure, right?"

"You're more confident now than you were a year ago." She nodded approvingly. "That's a good thing. Your parents would be very proud of you."

She couldn't deny that Mariah's words of encouragement meant a great deal to her. "Thank you. I appreciate that, but please just focus on taking care of yourself. You're important to a lot of people."

"You've always been dear."

Johanna scrunched her nose. "You make me sound wimpy."

"I just told you I see your confidence and I meant that." Mariah studied her with perceptive eyes. "But there is a gentleness to you that my grandson needs in his life. It softens his harsher edges."

Johanna found herself growing defensive on his behalf. "Why is it that everyone assumes because his mother named him Stone he's hard-hearted?"

Mariah smiled. "And that's why you're perfect for him."

Stone ended his phone call the second he saw Amie and Alex entering the visitors' waiting room. The muted sounds from a mounted television broadcasting a talk show mingled with the soft conversations from a handful of other people in the waiting area. Fake plants and magazine racks were tucked into one corner. A coffeepot gurgled in the other.

He and his cousins had spent little time alone together since their grandmother's announcement. His gut twisted at the realization they would be meeting up in waiting rooms like this many more times in the coming months.

In light of that, any bickering between them felt like a waste of precious time. And the frustration with the Montana family that had changed their mind about Pearl? He would deal with that later.

He had Johanna's reassurance that there was nothing between her and Alex, and Stone couldn't blame his cousin. Johanna was an amazing woman.

Alex stuffed his hands in his jean pockets and rocked back on his boot heels. "You've seen Gran already?"

Stone nodded, tucking an arm around Amie, her shoulders too thin beneath her silk blouse. "She seems alert, just tired. Thank you for calling me."

Amie hugged him back quickly before stepping away. "Alex said not to bother you."

Alex shrugged. "I've got things under control here, so you can finish up your business with the dogs."

Stone held back the urge to chew out Alex for being an ass. Even his quiet cousin would have blown a gasket if left out of the loop on news about Mariah's health.

Torqued at Alex's attitude, Stone couldn't resist jabbing, "Wait until you're the one turning your life upside down to make her happy. And you know damn well you both will."

He glowered at his cousin until he was sure Alex understood he wouldn't have appreciated being left in the dark about Gran. Then, hoping to distract Amie, he asked, "Any idea from Gran about what test she has in mind for the two of you?"

Amie shuffled from high heel to high heel, gnawing her thumbnail. "She hasn't mentioned it, but you know there's no rushing Gran. She has a plan and a reason for everything she does." She looked at her hand as if only just realizing she was chewing her nails down to nothing. She tucked her fist behind her back. "Have you told your mother yet?"

"Why would I?" Stone retorted quickly. "If Gran wants to see her, she'll tell her."

Alex lifted a lazy eyebrow. "Have you ever considered we should overrule Gran? Not just on this, but on other issues, as well. You have to confess that this test thing to decide the future of a huge estate is more than a little half-baked."

Stone stared at Alex in surprise. His cousin was a man of few words, so a speech that long carried extra weight.

Amie crossed her arms tightly, a wrist full of delicate silver bangles jangling. "You can't be saying what I think. You can't intend to have Gran declared unfit to manage her affairs."

"I think we should consider it," Alex said somberly. "She even said she planned this test for you because she was afraid the tumor might affect her judgment. What if it's too late?"

Stone hated even considering it. But had he disregarded warning signs about his grandmother out of a selfish need to have Johanna back in his life? "This isn't a question we can answer on our own. We need to speak with her doctors. Agreed? Alex?"

His cousin held up both hands. "Fair enough. And about contacting your mom?"

Damn. He scrubbed a hand along his jaw. "If you want to call my mother, do it, but I have nothing to say to her. And when she does something to hurt Gran—and trust me, my mother will—it will be on your conscience."

He pivoted away to end the conversation only to find Johanna standing behind him, her worried eyes making it clear she'd overheard at least part of their exchange. He slid an arm around her shoulders. "Johanna, let's go. We need to take care of Ruby and Pearl."

The weight of Alex's jealous gaze seared his back. For his entire life, his grandmother, the ranch and time with his cousins had been his stability, his grounding force. In the span of the week, all of that was being threatened. Without his grandmother as the glue, would their family hold together?

Johanna had accused him of not understanding how she felt when she lost her whole family. For the first time, he fully grasped what she meant. The impending sense of loss left a hole in his chest. And the prospect of having his mother roll into town creating havoc did little to reassure him.

He tucked Johanna closer to his side and wondered if he could dig deep enough to keep her this time.

Johanna curled against Stone's side, resting her head on his shoulder and soaking in the feel of his fingers stroking up and down her arm. The ceiling fan in her bedroom gusted cooling air over her bared flesh. So easily, they'd fallen into old habits, tossing aside their clothes the second they crossed the threshold of her cabin.

They hadn't even discussed it or questioned it. They'd sought the blissful escape of losing themselves in each other. The ease of that unsettled her. Eventually they would have to resolve the differences that had made her walk before. The past seven months had been hell, but they couldn't just pretend the future didn't matter, even if lounging in her lavender-scented sheets with him felt deliciously decadent.

Stone kissed the top of her head, the stubble on his chin catching in her hair. "My cousins brought up something at the hospital that I can't ignore, as much as I might wish otherwise."

She glanced up at him. "What's wrong?"

"I'm going to have to tell my mother about Mariah's cancer."

"Oh, wow, I hadn't even considered that…" The last she'd heard of his mother, Jade had been living with a boyfriend in Paris. "Is she still in France?"

As best as Johanna could remember, Jade had moved in with a wealthy wine merchant about four years ago and hadn't come home since. Johanna had gotten the feeling Jade was hiding as far away from her family as she could.

Stone shook his head. "She's in Atlanta now. She went through another rehab two months ago and decided to stay near her shrink rather than go back to her fast-living wine merchant sugar daddy. Having such a large trust fund can be a blessing and a curse. Too much cash on hand to feed the habit, but plenty of money to get the best care during the next detox."

She had few memories of his mom, most of them conflicted, depending on if she was in the middle of a frenetic drug binge or somberly drained from another stint in rehab. "How do you feel about that?"

He eyed her wryly. "How do you think I feel?"

"Not happy?"

"Mariah doesn't need the drama draining what strength she has."

Johanna slid her arm around him, hugging him, her leg nestled between his. "I agree, but eventually she'll have to be told."

He nodded, his chin brushing the top of her head again. A long sigh shuddered through him. "I was a crack baby."

His stark declaration caught her by surprise, stunning her still and silent. She scrambled for the right thing to say but could only hold him tighter to let him know she was here to listen. In fact, she wished he had trusted her enough to open up before now. "Stone, I don't know what to say."

"There's nothing to say. People assume it's a poverty issue, but that's not always the case. My mother was addicted to cocaine when I was born. I didn't know that until I was an adult and saw my medical records. I just thought I needed all those developmental therapists and tutors as a kid because I wasn't as smart as my cousins." He kept skimming his hand along her back as if taking comfort from the feel of her. "My first days on this earth were spent detoxing."

She pressed a kiss to his collarbone, still too choked up to speak. Her eyes burned with tears she knew he wouldn't want to see. Thank God, Mariah had been there for him.

His hand kept up the steady rhythm. "I don't like to take medicines. I figure with a junkie mom, genetics aren't on my side as a father," he said darkly, the deeper implication clear, explaining the mystery of why he seemed so determined to deny himself a family of his own. "And what if that early addiction is still there lurking, waiting to be triggered again?"

She blinked back the tears and tipped her head to look up at him. "What does your doctor say?"

His handsome features were strained, his jaw flexing. "Not to snort coke."

She skimmed her fingers over the furrows in his forehead. "How can you make jokes about this?"

"It's better this way." He captured her hand and pressed a kiss into her palm. "I want you to understand why I'm not comfortable being a father or passing along my genes to future generations."

"Why didn't you try to make me understand before?

You have to know I would have listened without judging." Although she had to wonder. Would she have been able to accept that he didn't want children? Or would she have pushed for him to resolve his feelings in order to have things the way she wanted them?

"I thought you would run if you knew. Then you ran anyway, which only confirmed my suspicion." He threaded his fingers through her loose hair, cupping the back of her head. "Now, there's nothing to lose."

Her parents' love had been such a grounding foundation for her all her life, giving her a confidence she carried with her even now that they were gone. She'd always thought about how lucky he was to have Mariah—Johanna hadn't considered the scars he must carry because of his mother's addiction. "I am so sorry for what you went through as a baby and for all you went through afterward with your mom."

He searched her eyes. "And you aren't upset that I didn't tell you before?"

Was she? She searched her heart and decided *upset* wasn't the right word. *Disappointed* fit better. That he'd held this back only reinforced her feelings that they hadn't been ready to commit before. For whatever reason, he hadn't been able to trust her, and she hadn't looked any deeper than the surface.

She understood now that he'd never be able to give her the family she craved. His resistance was rooted in something much deeper than she'd ever guessed. But even knowing that she wouldn't be able to move them to a healthier, happier place together, she couldn't help wanting to savor this time with him. She was deeply moved that he'd trusted her enough to share this. She just wished he loved her enough to address the problem. For now though, with her emotions ripped raw, she would take whatever tenderness she could find in his arms until she found the strength to move forward with her life again.

"Not angry." She kissed him once, lightly, before continuing. "Just glad you told me now."

"You're being too nice about this." He tunneled his hands through her hair again and again in a rhythm that both soothed and aroused.

"I'm seeing things from a new perspective, questioning if I really gave you the opening to share the darker corners of your life." She took in the handsome, hard lines of his face, thinking about all the times she'd fantasized about him as a teenager. She'd idealized him and idolized him for so many years; she hadn't given him much room to be human. "I created a fantasy crush image of you and expected you to live up to that. It wasn't fair to you."

"You truly are too forgiving."

"I have my limits," she admitted. "I'm human, too."

"I should let you go, but all I can think is that someone else would take advantage—" his voice went gravelly, his arms flexing a second before he tucked her underneath him "—and there's nothing in this world I want more than to keep you safe."

"You know what I want more than anything? I want to make love to you until you can't think of any more gut-wrenching discussions for us to have." She angled up to kiss him once, twice, distracting him so she could roll him to his back. "I want us to try to be normal for a while."

"You can absolutely feel free to console me with sex."

As much as he tried to joke, she could see the raw emotion in his eyes and knew he'd pushed so far outside his comfort zone, he would need time before he could go further. So she offered him the only comfort he would allow now—an escape, a reprieve that could be found in each other's arms.

She sealed her mouth to his again. His arms wrapped around her in a flash, his hands curving around her bottom and bringing her closer. She straddled him. The pressure of his erection against the core of her was a delicious friction. Already, a euphoric haze seeped through her veins, evicting her concerns—at least for this stolen moment together.

Ten

Johanna woke to the sound of voices. Or rather one voice and a couple of different barks.

She pushed her tangled hair off her face and sat up, sheet pooling around her waist in the empty bed. Blinking to clear her mind and vision, she saw Stone's boots still on the floor, his shirt tossed over a chair. Where was his rumbly voice coming from? Maybe he was in the kitchen?

Then she heard him…from the porch. Her window was open since the night had dipped into the seventies.

"Sit…. That's right, good girl," he said, a dog bark answering.

Pearl.

"Girl, this is the last treat. You've already had four. You're gonna get sick. Yeah, Ruby, I have another for you, too. Fair's fair."

She smiled affectionately. He was sweeter than he gave himself credit for. Although with his revelations the past few days, she could understand why he was so hesitant to let down his walls and be vulnerable. His mother had betrayed him on so many different levels from the start.

The details about his birth and early years still

rocked her. It also affirmed they hadn't been ready to get married before with such secrets between them, but it heartened her that they were making progress now. He was opening up to her, and she wondered what that could mean for them as the rest of this week played out. While she wasn't ready to think beyond the next few days, she also knew they'd moved past having a one-night stand for old times' sake.

Tossing aside the sheets, she left the bed and grabbed a silky robe from a hook on the bathroom door. The sun was only just rising, but usually she would already have her coffee in a travel mug as she headed to the barn. Being idle felt…strange.

She wrapped the knee-length robe around her and padded barefoot through the living area out to the covered porch. Stone sat in a rocker wearing jeans and nothing else. His hair stood up a little in the back with an endearing bed-head look that softened her already weakening emotions. She'd missed mornings like this with him. Ruby was lounging at his feet, and Pearl slept curled up on the porch swing.

Stone glanced back at her and grinned. "Good morning, gorgeous."

"Good morning to you, too. Any news on your grandmother?" Although she assumed there must not have been any bad updates, given his happy mood.

"Amie sent a text a half hour ago. Gran's resting comfortably and will be released this morning. Alex and Amie are arguing—as expected—over which one of them will bring her home."

"I'm relieved to hear Mariah's well enough to come home. Hopefully Alex and Amie will put their competitiveness on hold for the day." She leaned a hip against the door frame, watching the low hum of activity at the lodge in the distance. She had the added privacy of a circle of sprawling oak and pine trees since she lived here. A couple hundred yards away, beyond the trees, she could hear a couple of early risers talking over breakfast. Voices and hubbub from the stables echoed from the other side of the ranch house, but everyone was out of sight.

For the most part, she had Stone to herself. "What are you drawing?"

He tipped his head for her to join him. "Come see."

She walked out onto the porch and stopped behind his chair. Looping her arms around his neck, she peered over his shoulder, surprised to find he wasn't sketching the landscape after all. He had almost finished a sketch of Pearl on the porch swing. Even only halfway done, the likeness was impressive and heart tugging. He'd captured a sadness in the dog's eyes that mirrored the sadness she'd seen in Stone's since his grandmother's announcement. He patted her hand quietly but kept the pencil in motion.

She stepped around him and settled onto the porch swing beside the terrier. She tapped the swing into motion, staying silent while Stone lost himself in the drawing. She wanted to soak up the moment and ignore the fear that this was merely the calm before the storm.

Finally, he sighed and closed the pad, looking across at her. "Sorry if I woke you."

"I wake up earlier than this for work." She reached to touch the edge of the sketch pad on the table beside him. "I forget sometimes what a good artist you are."

"The jewelry design gene in my family takes many forms," he said offhandedly.

She smoothed her hand along Pearl's back, flattening her bristly fur. "Have you ever thought about offering more input on the designs?"

"That's Amie's realm. We try not to encroach on each other's territory. The last thing we need is more competition in this family." He scratched his collar bone, drawing her eyes to his bare chest. "Besides, this is my hobby, my way of relaxing."

Her mouth watered at the flex of his tattoo along his arm and the muscled expanse of his chest. "Did you destroy the drawings of me the way you promised when we broke up?"

"You mean the nude drawings." He grinned wickedly. "What do you think?"

She wasn't sure what she thought. In the past couple of days she'd come to realize he was very good at keeping secrets and she had been very good at dodging tough subjects in the interest of keeping her fantasy alive. "Should I trust you?"

"Absolutely," he said without question. "I'm trying to make things right. And as for the drawings, I don't need any help remembering every amazing inch of you."

He angled out of the chair to kiss her with a firm, sure confidence that swirled her senses. In a fast sweep, he lifted her and settled her onto his lap. "We have about an hour before we need to head over to the house. Any ideas how we can spend that time wisely?"

She teased the swoop of bed head in his hair. "I think you may need a shower. Are you sure you don't want to hurry and help Alex drive your grandmother home?"

"I'll just leave Alex and Amie to duke that out between them."

She leaned back against his chest. She'd missed moments like this, enjoying the steady thud of his heart. "They're both so competitive. It should be interesting to watch them once their test comes. I always felt sorry for them as a kid."

"How so?" he asked. "They had everything—money, parents, a family."

Really? He was that clueless? "They had a mom who trotted them out like prize horses and a father so tied to golf and hiding from their mom they barely saw him."

"The pageant thing was a little over-the-top," he conceded.

She couldn't hold back a laugh. "You think?"

"Amie never protested—" He held up a hand. "Wait. I take that back. She complained once. She wanted to go to some high school dance and it fell on the weekend of a pageant competition."

"Did she get to the dance?"

"Nope. She won her crown." A one-sided smile kicked a dimple into his cheek. "We found the tiara in the middle of a silver tureen of grits the next morning."

"Miss Texas Grits," she quipped. "I like it. Amie is full of grit, after all." Johanna had spent so much of her life idealizing the McNairs, minimizing their struggles, feeling sorry for them on some issues, but overall envying them.

The sound of an approaching taxi pulled her attention out of their bubble of intimacy. Johanna kissed Stone quickly then eased off his lap.

She extended a hand to him. "We should go back inside before the rest of the guests saddle up for the day. I don't want to have to fight off the tourists. They'll be drooling over a half-dressed cowboy."

Her half-dressed cowboy. The possessive thought blindsided her.

The cab drove past the Hidden Gem Lodge and drew closer, as if coming to her home. Johanna hesitated half in, half out of her door. Sure enough, the taxi stopped right at her fenced front lawn. Ruby and Pearl leaped to their feet and flew off the porch, barking.

The back door of the vehicle opened and a woman stepped out, one high heel at a time. Stone's quick gasp gave her an instant's warning before recognition hit.

The reed-thin woman bore a striking resemblance to Mariah and Amie for a reason. After four years away, Stone's mother—Jade McNair—had come home.

Stone carried his mother's designer luggage into the guest suite in the family's portion of the Hidden Gem Lodge. He'd been on autopilot since the second he'd seen his mother step out of the taxi. He vaguely recalled Johanna filling the awkward silence with small talk while he grabbed his shirt and boots. His mother had said something about seeing him on Johanna's porch so Jade had instructed the taxi driver to go to the cabin rather than straight to the lodge.

His only thought had been to divert any crisis that might upset Mariah.

He put the hang-up bag in the closet and dropped the two suitcases by the leather sofa, onto the thick wool of the Aztec patterned rug. She'd certainly brought enough to stay for more than a weekend trip.

Pivoting, he found his mother standing in the middle of the floor, shifting from foot to foot under the elk horn chandelier. From nerves? Or in need of a fix? She was as thin as a bird, her skin sallow and eyes haunted but clear—her standard postdetox look. He'd seen it enough times to recognize it, and he'd seen it fall apart enough times not to bother hoping the new start would stick.

He cut straight to the chase. "Mariah needs peace, not drama. Cause her any heartache and I will throw you out myself."

Jade nodded nervously, her hand shaking as she pushed back a hank of dark hair with new threads of silver. "I'm not here to cause trouble. I heard the news about my mother's cancer from a friend."

"Are you here to make sure you're in the will?"

She sagged onto the upholstered bench at the foot of the bed. "I understand you don't have any reason to trust me, but I want to see my mother. I would also like to help if I can—and if she will let me."

She sounded genuine. But then she always did at this stage of the cycle.

"Jade, keep in mind what I said. Mariah's comfort and health come first." He turned for the door, wanting the hell out of here and back to Johanna's cabin with the dogs.

"Stone, wait," his mother called.

He stopped with his hand on the door handle. His shoulders sagged with a weary sigh. "Remember the part about no drama? The same goes in talking to me."

She stayed silent until he finally faced her again.

Jade still sat on the bench, hugging one of those fancy throw pillows women insisted on. "I'm sorry for not being a real mother to you. I regret that."

"Everyone has regrets." He understood she had to make amends as a part of the recovery process. She'd walked the steps again and again until he had the whole routine memorized. Too many times he thought she'd bottomed out enough that she'd finally begin a real recovery.

He wasn't falling into that trap again.

She looked at him uncertainly. "What? No telling me off? Handing over pamphlets for the latest, greatest rehab center? I just finished with one of the best, you know."

"So I hear. Congratulations." Time would tell, but he wasn't holding his breath.

"You've changed," she said sadly. "You're colder than ever, something else I need to make up to you."

"I'm an adult. I accept responsibility for who I am." He put his hand back on the door handle. "Now if we're done here...?"

Her eyes welled up. "My mother is dying. Can you cut me a little slack?"

"Yes, she is," he snapped, pushing past the lump in his throat. "And she doesn't need you sapping what strength she has left."

"Maybe I can bring her some comfort," Jade said with a shaky hope that hinted at the brighter spirit she'd been during some of the better times of her life. She toyed with a turquoise cascade around her neck, a piece her dad had made for her eighteenth birthday. "I have a small window here to get things right, and I'm not going to waste it."

"You can sit by her side as long as you're lifting her spirits. If you don't do that, you're gone." That's all he cared about. And hadn't he made that freaking clear the first time? Impatience gnawed at the back of his neck. "Now what else do you need from me?"

"Keep being the good man that you are." Her eyes went doe-wide as she launched into a facade he liked to call "the good mother." She deluded herself that she had something to offer. When he was a kid, this phase had been killer because it offered the false impression that she gave a damn.

"Right." He ground his teeth together, knowing Johanna would tell him to get through this. Keep the peace. At least, he thought that's what she'd say. He'd never given his mother that much airtime to know for sure.

"And Stone? Figure out how to be the kind of husband Johanna deserves because even I can see the two of you are meant to be together. I'm going to try to help here, but I know there's probably nothing I can accomplish better than you or your cousins."

Already this was seeping into drama-land. "Mom, can we stop? I need to go—"

She launched up and grabbed his arm. "You're the only hope I have left of making my mother happy. Even though I can't take credit for the man you've become—Mariah brought you up—I can take some pride in knowing I was your mother. At some point I must have done something good as your mom."

The pleading look in her eyes chipped away at him, catching him at a time when he was already raw from all the walls he'd torn down in the past couple of days. Johanna, with her healing spirit and love of family, would want him to try. She had helped so many—human and animals—without expecting anything in return.

For Johanna, he scrounged in his mind for a positive memory with his mother and came up with, "You helped me with my macaroni art project for kindergarten."

Blinking fast, she thumbed away a tear. "What did you say?"

He leaned against the closed door. "The teacher wanted us to use pasta to create scenes for the four seasons. I was mad because I wanted to draw horses so I blew off the 'homework.' The teacher sent a note home."

"You always were a good artist and smart, too," she said with pride.

He resisted the urge to say the crack baby rehab had probably shaved ten points or more off his IQ. A year ago, he would have opted for the joke. Instead, he opted for another Johanna-like answer. "You read to me. A lot. I remember that, too."

She sat on her suitcase. "What else do you remember about the macaroni art project?"

"After we finished—or so I thought—you said it needed sparkle." The memory expanded in his mind, making him smile even now in the middle of such a dismal morning. "We went into Grandpa's home studio and raided the jewel bags. You used a citrine stone for the summer sun. Silver shavings for winter snow. Tiny amethysts and rubies for spring flowers. And for autumn, we had—"

"A pile of leaves made of topazes." She clapped her hands and smiled. "When I heard you and Johanna were engaged, I called my mother and asked her to unearth those projects from a trunk I'd stored in the attic."

"You kept the project?" Stunned, he was glad he had the door at his back for support.

"All four seasons," she confirmed. "I got them framed, to be a wedding gift to you and Johanna. When you and Johanna broke up, I just kept them for myself. They're hanging in my living room. You can come see for yourself if you don't believe me." The hint of desperation in her eyes punched away a little more of his defenses.

"I believe you. That's really nice." And it was. Keeping kindergarten art didn't make up for the past but it meant something to him to know she'd held on to the memory, too.

He didn't think he could ever see her as a mother figure. That seemed disloyal to Mariah who'd done everything for him. Photos showed his grandfather had tried to fill the void of a father figure. From all he'd heard from Mariah about his grandfather, he would have kept that up....

That thought brought to mind other unfinished business between him and his mom. He'd learned time wasn't guaranteed, so he might as well go for broke. "I know who my father is."

Her McNair blue eyes went wide. "Is that a trick question where you try to get me to admit something?"

"No trick. I did the detective work and figured it out. A DNA test confirmed Dale Banks is my biological father." He still didn't know how he felt about that. Maybe it would have been better not to know than to continue to wonder what would happen if he ever confronted the guy with the truth.

Her jaw dropped. "Dale agreed to the test?"

"He didn't know about the test. I tricked him. But if I'm right, I think he already knew and didn't want to be a father, or he refused a test in the past."

She nodded.

Stone followed the rest of the thought to its logical conclusion. "And he wasn't interested in being a parent."

"I'm afraid not, son." She stood and reached to pat

his arm, but stopped just shy of actually touching him. "I'm so sorry."

He winced at the word *son* but decided to let it slide. "Apology accepted."

Yes, anger and betrayal churned inside him, but he refused to stir up drama right before Mariah came home from the hospital.

"Does that mean I'm forgiven?" Jade asked hopefully. "I know that I can't make up for what I put you through, but I would like to know you've found some peace. You deserved better."

"I have Mariah," he said without missing a beat. "I got the best."

No more blaming the past for current issues. He had to shoulder his own mistakes from now on. Which meant he had a final confession to make to Johanna, and with his blinders off, he understood she might well never forgive him. But lying to her through evasion was no longer an option.

The sun sank on the horizon like a melting orange Dreamsicle.

Johanna drew in the sweet fragrance from the field of bluebonnets. After a full day of walking on eggshells around the entire McNair family, she was more than ready to jump all over Stone's suggestion that they slip away for a ride before supper. She should have known he would choose to ride to his favorite patch of McNair land.

She slid from her horse, leather creaking. "What a great idea to come here to watch the sunset."

He swung a leg over and dismounted. He opened the saddlebag, pulled out a yellow quilt and passed it over to her. With a pat to his quarter horse's flank, he let Copper graze alongside Johanna's palomino.

She shook the quilt out onto the ground and dropped down to sit with an exhausted sigh. It seemed like aeons ago that she'd woken up to find Stone on the porch sketching doggie portraits.

"What does your grandmother want to do about Pearl since the Montana couple reneged?" She'd been surprised when he announced the family had changed their minds, but then she'd always wondered if Pearl should stay with Mariah.

He pulled two water bottles from the saddlebag before sitting beside her. He stretched his legs out, boots crossed at the ankles. "Gran expects us to proceed as planned with the backup families once we take Ruby to her princess digs."

"Sounds like Mariah really has her heels dug in deep." Johanna sipped the water, trying not to get her hopes up too high over how right this felt with his warm muscled thigh against hers while they sat shoulder to shoulder. "I have to admit, I'm surprised. I always thought Pearl was her favorite."

"Pearl was actually my mother's dog." He tipped back his water bottle, his throat moving with a long swallow.

"How did I not know that?" She thumbed the condensation on the outside of her water bottle. "I can only remember Pearl coming to Mariah about four years ago and Mariah saying offhandedly that Pearl had been abandoned by her owner."

"That's pretty much dead-on correct," he said drily. "My mother bought her from a pet store, paid a fortune for her. Thought she was getting her own *Wizard of Oz*

Toto. Once Pearl wasn't a puppy anymore, my mom didn't want her. Too much mess, too much nipping, too much trouble to take with her to France."

"That's sad to hear." Would the little terrier remember Jade? Be confused? "Shelters are full of older puppies just like that. Thank goodness your grandmother took her."

"Just like she took me."

She slid an arm around him. Jade showing up after so long must have rattled him. "Your grandmother did a great job with you. You're an amazing man."

He didn't smile or even look at her. He picked at a clump of bluebonnets and smashed them between his fingers. "It's crazy, but she blamed herself for the selfish decisions made by her adult children. I think she saw me as her second chance to get it right after my drug addict mother and my trust fund uncle who never worked a day in his life."

"You work very hard." Too hard, in her opinion.

"She still doesn't trust me to take over the company." He sprinkled the bits of bluebonnet leaves over her lap.

"She can't doubt your skills as the CEO of Diamonds in the Rough. You've expanded the company in a tough economy." She wasn't a business major, but she knew magazines had written glowing features on him.

"Mariah doubts my humanity instincts. Something you yourself have noted, as well," he pointed out. "And that stings more because I'm not sure it's something I can fix."

"Oh, Stone," she said, her heart aching over the hurt they'd caused each other. She shifted, swinging her leg over to straddle his lap. She took his face in her hands. "I never should have said that. Whatever our differences, I know you care about people. I guess that's what frustrates me most. Your refusal to see how good you are."

Unable to take the pain in his sky-blue eyes, she leaned in to kiss him, hoping he would feel all the emotion in her flowing into him. No matter how hard she'd tried to deny it, this was the only man she'd ever loved. The only man she ever would love.

His arms wrapped around her, his hands sliding up her spine and under her long braid. With deft fingers, he worked her hair loose, combing through it until her every nerve tingled to life. In a smooth sweep, he rolled her onto her back, her legs hooking around his waist. A fresh whiff of bluebonnet perfume wafted up from the press of their bodies. Already, she could feel the swell of his erection between them. What she wouldn't give to be with him, out here in the open.

"Stone," she whispered between deep, luscious kisses, "we should go back to my cabin."

"This is my land," he growled possessively, nipping along her jaw and up to her earlobe. "No one's going to find us."

"Yours?" Her head fell back, gasping. "I thought it was all jointly owned."

"We each have a section that belongs exclusively to us. This became mine on my twenty-first birthday."

"Why did you never mention that before when we came here for picnics?" She swatted his bottom lightly. God, she loved the way he filled out denim. "It would have been nice not to worry about people stumbling upon us."

He angled away, propping himself on one elbow to look directly into her eyes. "You pegged it when you said I was holding back. I planned to surprise you on our wedding day with plans for a home."

A pang shot through her chest at the fairy tale he'd tried to give her. As much as she knew she'd made the right decision then, she'd missed out on a lot of happy moments, too. Her throat burned until she cleared it.

"I would have liked that."

"Except there wasn't a nursery in my plans."

The burn in her throat shifted, moving down into a cold knot that settled in her stomach. "You know how I feel about that, and I'm beginning to understand why you feel otherwise. I've watched you for years as you helped out the staff with games for vacationers and I guess I always thought you would change your mind."

"Liking children and being a father are two different things."

She sifted through his words, wondering what he was trying to tell her by bringing her here, because clearly he had something on his mind. "But you want a space away from here, a home in your bluebonnet field."

"I never had a regular home like other kids." He picked up one flower petal after another and placed them in her hair. "Not with my mother zipping in and out of my life. A couple of times she even took me with her when she left."

"Jade 'took' you? That had to be confusing."

"Hell, yeah, it was. Especially the time the cops stopped us at the Mexican border and charged my mother with kidnapping. My grandmother had legal custody at that point."

She searched his face, shadows making it tougher with the sun surrendering fast. "Why Mexico?"

"Easier access to drugs, most likely." He said it so

nonchalantly her heart broke. "She dodged prosecution for custodial interference by agreeing to go into rehab. Again. But if we learned anything over the years, we know that unless the junkie is committed to coming clean…rehab is just a temporary, Band-Aid fix."

She kissed him again because there just weren't any words for all he'd been through with his mother. Having her here now when he was still reeling from his grandmother's cancer news had to be overwhelming. Johanna poured all her love into the kiss—and yes, she loved him so damn much, always had, ever since she was a teenager with a colossal crush that had matured into so much more.

Groaning, he trailed kisses along her jaw, her cheek, her forehead before burying his face in her hair. "Johanna, more than anything, I want to be with you out here, just us on a blanket in my field full of bluebonnets."

"Of course, I want that, too." She slid her hand between them, palming the length of his steely erection. A moist ache settled between her legs.

"Before we're together again, we need to be sure it's forever. No more pretending we could ever have a fling."

Her heart sped in her chest like a hummingbird. "I agree."

"So we need to clear up one last issue."

The little bird in her chest sped faster. The only remaining issue had to do with children. Where did she stand and how far was she willing to compromise?

"If we make love now, we don't need a condom."

She blinked in shock, certain she couldn't have

heard him right. Terrified to hope. "You've changed your mind about having children?"

"Hell, that's not what I meant, Johanna."

His eyes squeezed shut tight for an instant before he opened them again, sapphire-blue eyes so full of regret she only had a second to prepare herself before he continued.

"There's no easy way to say this. I've had a vasectomy."

Eleven

Stone knew he'd just lost Johanna. He could see it in her eyes. Just as he'd feared, once he told her everything, it was over.

That didn't stop him from trying to hold on to her. He wasn't giving her up so easily, not this time. So he sat on the quilt beside her and waited to take his cue from her. Her whole body was rigid. She shook just a little, trembling from the aftermath of a direct hit to her tender, sweet heart.

A heart he didn't deserve, no matter how much he wanted to claim it.

She blinked quickly, her eyes as green as clover even in the dimming day. "You...you did what?"

"Just what I said, and God, Johanna, I am sorry to have to say it at all." He took her hand, her fingers quivering, and he hated that he'd brought her this pain. "I had a vasectomy right after I met my biological father, which also happened to be around the time my mother checked out of rehab early again. I knew her next fall was inevitable. And I was right."

He'd been so damn sure of himself and his choices.

Her breath was as shaky as his hand. "You were so young. You still are."

Her words echoed the mandatory counseling session he'd been forced to sit through before the surgery. It made a whole hell of a lot of difference hearing it from the woman he loved instead of a well-meaning health care professional who'd made the same speech a hundred other times. He could have never predicted loving someone so much it made him question everything he'd ever believed.

"It was way before you and I started dating. Because I swear to you—" and he meant it with every fiber of his being "—if I'd had an inkling of what having you in my life this way would mean, I wouldn't have done it."

"Have you ever considered having the procedure reversed?" she asked, each word carefully enunciated, her breathing fast and shallow. Clearly, she was holding on by a thread.

"Not until I met you."

"How do you feel now?"

"If you want a child, I will do that for you." Even saying the words scared the hell out of him, but the thought of losing her scared him more. For Johanna, for their kid, he would figure it out. He refused to fail as a parent. "But you need to understand that the more time that lapses the less chance a reversal has of working. Do you have any issues with adoption?"

She shook her head, but there was still something about her stunned expression that made him uneasy. This was too much, too fast for her. She'd barely had time to process the first bombshell he'd dropped.

He waited for her to speak but she kept looking around the field of bluebonnets, the horses grazing, the circle of trees—anywhere other than at him.

Nerves strung tight, he pressed ahead. "I have two drug addict parents. I was born a crack baby. Consider me a broken model. As far as I'm concerned, I would rather fund orphanages and adoption agencies to help babies like me that didn't have a rich grandma to step in. But if you have faith I can handle being a parent, then I'm going to trust you."

"Thank you," she said woodenly. "I understand how difficult that was for you to say."

"Then why do I still see smoke coming out of your ears?"

"First of all. It's not just smoke. It's pain, Stone. Real, deep hurt." Her hands clenched into fists, and she drew her arms in closer to herself, away from him. She kept shaking her head slowly from side to side. "But yes, there's anger, too. All those months we were together using birth control, you were lying to me, letting me believe that you might be open to having a family someday even though you knew otherwise." She shoved to her feet, dusting the flower petals off her jeans in angry sweeps. "It wasn't just one lie by leaving out something in your past. It was a lie *every time we made love.* I'm having a difficult time wrapping my brain around that."

She thrust her hands into her hair, pressing against her head as she paced.

"Yes, it was a cop-out on my part not telling you." He stood, walking off the quilt and toward her, wary. "I'm an even bigger jackass than you imagined."

She stroked her fingers through her horse's mane, a nervous habit he recognized well. "Stone, I'm… I don't know what to say other than I feel betrayed." She looked up at him, her eyes so full of pain the clover-green was dewy with unshed tears. "How could you say you love me? How could you propose to me and keep something *this* important from me?"

"I intended to tell you, even though I knew it would drive you away. Maybe that's why I delayed because I knew it would make you leave me." Just as it was doing now. The hole in his chest widened until he fought back the urge to howl in denial. "Then it was too late. Apparently, it still is."

She turned to him hard and fast, fire spitting from her eyes. "Don't you get it? It's not that you had the procedure. That happened before we were a couple. It's because you lied to me, again and again. Telling me now... I don't know if that's enough. I just don't know."

"God, Johanna." His voice cracked as he reached for her.

She yanked away, her horse sidestepping sharply. "I can't..."

"Can't what?"

"I can't process this. I need air—away from you." She hitched a foot in the stirrup and swung up onto her palomino.

He didn't bother to stop her. There wasn't any use. His worst fear had happened, just not for the reason he'd expected. She hadn't left him because he couldn't father her children. She'd left him because he hadn't trusted in their love enough to tell her.

Johanna gripped the reins tightly in her hands even though she knew Goldie could find her way back in the dark. The evening had started out on such a hopeful note only to end in total heartbreak. She'd even chosen

Mariah's horse to ride as a tribute to the woman who meant so much to them all. Now she could only think of everything they'd all lost.

Goldie slowed from a canter to a trot as they neared the stables. And, oh, God, on the lanai, a wedding was taking place. The trees were strung with lights. Sunflowers and wildflowers filled the space, a live band played as the happy couple walked back down the aisle. The whole ranch would echo with music all night with the reception in a special barn built for just such catered occasions.

She'd dreamed of a wedding just like this.

Squeezing her eyes closed, she let Goldie find her way back to the stables. The regular scents of hay and leather offered none of the normal calm she found here in the barn, her realm. The noise level didn't help with the reception in full swing and some kind of party going on in the hot tub, too. She could have sworn she heard someone calling her name....

She looked back over her shoulder.

Amie was walking fast in a whispery sequined sun dress and cowboy boots only someone like her could pull off. Her brother trailed behind her, hands in his jeans pocket.

"Wait!" Amie waved, bracelets sliding to her elbow. "Johanna, I have to talk to you."

There was no missing the panic in her voice, which launched an echoing wave of panic in Johanna. "Is something wrong with Mariah?" She slid from her horse, her own boots a dusty, scarred contrast to Amie's shiny black leather.

Amie shook her head, her long hair in two loose

braids swishing. "No, she's fine. We just got a surprise visitor. The king—Enrique Medina—is in the lodge. He wants to save us the trouble of delivering Ruby so he's coming here." She clapped her hands, bracelets jingling. "Thank God we had the presidential suite available because every other room is booked. But he's here and he wants to meet Ruby, and Gran couldn't find you or Stone, and you didn't have your cell phones."

Alex put a hand on top of his sister's head. "Amie. Chill. Johanna's got it now. Right, Jo?"

Johanna looked back and forth between them and it didn't appear they were joking. "The king that wants Ruby is here now?"

Amie nodded quickly. "We can't keep him waiting any longer."

Johanna looked down at the stained jeans and sweaty white tank top. But he wanted his dog now. "Give me five minutes to throw on a dress and pull back my hair. I'll be right there."

She could do this. For Mariah, for Ruby, and yes, even for herself. She could pull this off. What a time to realize Stone had helped her unearth a confidence in herself she hadn't known existed.

By the time Stone finished riding alone for an hour, then brushing down Copper and returning him to the stable, he still had no clue what—if anything—he could say to Johanna to ease the pain he'd seen in her eyes. Pain he'd put there. He loved her and yet he'd still fallen short.

Music echoed from the barn on the other side of the stable yard, and from the sound of things, it was a wedding celebration in full swing. As if he didn't already feel lower than dirt. Had fate scheduled a wedding for tonight with the specific purpose of torturing him? Seeing the happy bride and groom stabbed at him with all he should have given Johanna. She wanted a family. She deserved to have the family she dreamed of. She had such a loving, nurturing heart. Would she leave here altogether?

She loved the ranch as much as he did.

He hadn't thought about that before. She'd been tied to the land in one way or another for most of her life. Just because he held the deed to a piece of property didn't negate all the heart she'd poured into Hidden Gem.

The only thing that kept his feet moving right now was the need to check on his grandmother.

He darted from the stable to the main lodge, boots sending dust puffing with each heavy step. And damn it, he'd left his suitcase at Johanna's. But he wasn't willing to push his luck with her tonight. He needed to get his head together first and come up with a plan to ease her heart even if that meant he couldn't have her back. He wanted her happiness above everything.

Except plans were in short supply as he climbed the steps to the massive log cabin–style lodge that had been his home his whole life. He should have taken a side entrance but his feet were on autopilot. Staff cleared away the wedding decorations on the lanai.

Pushing through the large double doors into the great room, he nodded to all the staff but didn't pause long enough to give anyone a chance to speak. He vaguely registered there was a frenetic buzz to the place that didn't seem connected to the wedding celebration since that was all taking place outside. Yet nothing appeared out of the norm. Wealthy socialites curled up on the leather sofas with cocktails. Older couples played poker in a far corner by the massive granite fireplace. He could hear laughter from the hot tub outside. Alex's business ran smooth as silk.

Only a few more steps and he would be clear of people, period, and into the private wing. He could shut himself in his suite with...nothing. He had nothing left and had no one to blame but himself.

A door opened ahead of him and his gut clenched at the thought of another confrontation with his mother. Instead, his grandmother stepped out on her own two feet, with a cane, but walking. She even wore clothes instead of a robe, a simple dress but complete with a Diamonds in the Rough signature piece around her neck. Amie hovered beside her, as if his willowy featherweight cousin could catch their grandmother.

Stone charged ahead. "Gran, what are you doing out of bed? You should be resting."

She waved him back. "I'm fine. The doctor released me as long as I use the cane."

Amie interrupted, "A walker. But she would only agree to the cane since it's one of our designs."

Stone felt like his head was about to explode. "Let me walk you back to your room. We'll talk over tea or something while you *rest*."

His grandmother patted his hand. "Stone, the king is here. In the presidential suite."

"Run that by me again?"

"Stone, we need to get moving," Amie said. "Enrique Medina decided he would come to us for his dog to save you the trouble. Johanna is doing the meet and greet now because we couldn't find you and you weren't answering your damn phone." She swatted him on the arm. "Now let's get moving to help her."

He glanced at Alex. "Do you have Gran?"

His cousin nodded.

"Thanks." Stone sprinted down the hall. Johanna had freaked out over meeting the Landis-Renshaw family. This was going to be way outside her comfort zone. While he knew she was amazing and would handle the meeting smoothly, he hated that she would feel nervous or uneasy, especially after the emotional hell they'd both been through today.

He passed by familiar framed landscapes mixed with photos, images of famous people who'd stayed at the lodge or worn Hidden Gem pieces. Finally—thank God—finally, he made it to the presidential suite. The door was cracked open enough for him to see Johanna sitting next to an older gentleman in a suit with an ascot. Johanna held Pearl, and Ruby slept at the king's feet. If Stone hadn't known the man was deposed royalty, he would have thought she was talking to any prospective pet owner.

Johanna had changed from her jeans into a simple white dress and matching white leather boots, her hair in a side ponytail, trailing a wavy blond cascade over her shoulder. She was pure Texas but with a designer elegance and poise, smiling and nodding at something the king was saying.

Stone realized he wasn't needed here. Johanna had it totally under control. Not a single nerve showed through. She wasn't even fidgeting with the diamond horseshoe that dangled on the silver chain around her neck. Something had happened to her this week. She didn't need him for confidence or help, and God, she was magnificent.

She glanced at the door as if sensing he was there. Her eyes lost their sparkle but she kept her composure. "Come on in, Stone, and hear the good news from our honored guest."

Stone forced a smile onto his face and stepped into the presidential suite. "Sir, we're honored that you would come visit us at Hidden Gem."

The deposed king had a reputation for being a bit of a hermit who lived in an island fortress off the coast of Florida. "I am so sorry to hear Mariah is having health concerns. It is a joy to have one of her dogs and my honor to make things easier for her by coming to her directly."

"Thank you," Stone answered, his head spinning from this day, blindsiding him nonstop. "It appears Ruby has found a great new companion."

Johanna stroked Pearl, still perched in her lap. "He also shared more good news. General and Mrs. Renshaw have decided they want Pearl after all. The three dogs will get to see each other at family reunions. Isn't that wonderful?"

A roaring started in Stone's head, growing louder by the second. Thoughts of his fight with Johanna, his grandmother's illness, his mother's arrival—his whole world was falling apart and there was nothing he could do about it. His eyes landed on Pearl and he knew. His grandmother needed to have this pup with her. Mariah, who'd given so much of herself to others, needed her favorite dog and needed someone to stand up, to make the decision to put her needs first. He would adopt Pearl so his grandmother could keep her near.

Even if it cost him the position as CEO of Diamonds in the Rough, he loved the little mutt and he wasn't giving her up.

"I'm sorry, sir." He strode into the room, boots thudding against the thick rug patterned with a yellow rose of Texas theme. He swiped Pearl from Johanna's lap before she could stop him. He cradled Pearl in one arm. "She's staying with me after all."

Standing, Johanna gasped. "But your grandmother's requirements…"

"I'll talk to my grandmother. She needs Pearl now more than anyone. I'll take care of Pearl during Mariah's treatments—and afterward." That last part stuck in his throat but he didn't doubt his decision. After seeing Johanna through different eyes this week, he'd learned the meaning of real love. His arms wrapped tighter around the dog. He nodded to their guest. "Thank you again for helping us rehome Ruby. Let us know if there's anything you need to make your stay more comfortable."

And manners be damned, the whole company be damned, Stone left with his dog, a dog that carried the scent of bluebonnets from Johanna.

As she listened to Mariah make small talk with the deposed King, Johanna's heart was in her throat.

At least Mariah and the twins had joined them so she didn't have to carry the conversation on her own, but it was the most torturous hour of her life. Not because she was intimidated by royalty—the man was truly approachable and, truth be told, she felt more confident now. But wondering about Stone was tearing her apart.

She couldn't believe Stone had left with Pearl, that he'd made such a beautiful and selfless sacrifice for his grandmother. He'd ignored his grandmother's test because he knew Mariah needed the comfort. Anyone who knew Mariah would understand she didn't make frivolous threats. Her test might have seemed strange, but she'd known what she was doing.

Johanna toyed with the diamond horseshoe pendant and realized Mariah never did *anything* by accident. She'd meant this test for Johanna, as well. The McNair matriarch had treated Johanna as a daughter every bit as much as she'd treated Stone as a son. This journey had brought Johanna the self-confidence to push Stone for the answers she needed, as well as bringing about an openness between them they should have had long ago.

She kept replaying the look on his face as he'd left with Pearl, remembering him telling her the story of how Pearl had come to his grandmother. As a vet tech, Johanna had observed countless people with their animals. She recognized true affection and a connection when she saw it. He didn't often show his emotions, but she'd seen the sketches he'd made. Stone was the right one to care for Pearl so Mariah could keep her during her treatment, and he was the perfect one to take Pearl afterward. No question, Stone loved the scruffy little pooch.

She'd already realized there was much more to Stone than the cowboy Casanova, stony facade he showed the world. Yet she'd let him down, as well, today. He'd told

her his secrets, owned up and offered to make amends
as best he could, and she'd panicked. She'd walked out
on a man who'd been abandoned by his mother and his
father. A man who was willing to give up his life's work
and billions of dollars to put his grandmother's happiness first. He loved his grandmother, and yes, he even
loved the scruffy little pooch enough to risk everything.

That was the man for her and she didn't intend to
wait another minute to get him back.

She stood, resting a hand on Mariah's shoulder.
"Ma'am, would you like some refreshments sent in or
do you need to rest?"

Mariah smiled at the king with a twinkle in her eyes.
"We're having a lovely visit. Refreshments would be
nice."

"Perfect. I'll let the kitchen staff know." Johanna
grasped the excuse to leave with both hands.

"And Johanna?" Mariah's voice stopped her at the
door. "Be sure to take something to that rebellious
grandson of mine."

"Yes, ma'am." Johanna smiled back at the woman
who wasn't just *like* family. She *was* family.

Racing through the lodge to the kitchen, she didn't
have to wonder where to look for Stone. She angled
through the lanai party group in full swing, vacationers
and guests from the wedding filled the place to capacity.

She stepped clear of them into the starlit night, music
from the live band at the wedding reception still filling the air. Stone loved this land and she understood
the feeling. The land all but hummed under her boots
as she saddled up the first horse she came to—a sleek
gray quarter horse named Opal. A simple click launched

the beautiful beast into motion, sure-footed even in the
night with only the moon and stars lighting the way in
a dappled path.

The wind tore through Johanna's wavy hair, rivulets
of air rippling her dress along her skin. She'd never felt
more alive and more afraid than right now. This was
her chance for everything, if she could only find the
right way to let Stone know how deeply she loved him.

Approaching Stone's favorite piece of land, the part
that belonged to him, she ducked low under a branch.
The moon shone down on Stone lying on the yellow
quilt, staring up at the sky with Pearl curled up asleep
beside him.

Her heart filled with tender feelings for the man
who'd been let down by so many, yet still had a full
heart to offer her.

Johanna dismounted. "Stone?"

"Do you know why this particular part of the land is
my favorite acre?" he asked without moving, the night
breeze ruffling Pearl's wiry fur.

She settled her horse alongside Stone's and walked
to the blanket. "Why is that?"

"The bluebonnets. They remind me of you. The
peacefulness and the sweet scent carrying along the
breeze of home." His eyes slid to her. "That's you."

She sank down beside him, sitting cross-legged.
"Stone, you take my breath away when you say things
like that."

How many times had she imagined a future with
him back when she'd been a fanciful girl? He was everything she'd hoped for and so much more. More real.
More complicated and compelling. She wouldn't trade

any part of him for the simple fantasies she'd once built around him.

"Good. You deserve the words and everything else. Whatever you want. Children. Home and hearth. Building a family. Don't settle." Even now, he fought to protect her.

He just didn't realize that she knew what was best for her now.

"I'm not settling." She wanted to reach for him but they had things to discuss first. Their reunion hadn't been a smooth, joyous coming together. It had been stilted steps toward each other because they couldn't stay away. But that was their path and she would keep on walking it. Toward her future with him. "I was hurt by what you told me today, but I shouldn't have run away. You opened up to me, and I let you down."

"You spoke the truth, though. I owe you more apologies than I can speak in a lifetime."

She hugged her knees to her chest and mulled that over for a minute, sifting through for the right words. "I guess we both aren't perfect. I tried to make you fit some high school fantasy and almost missed out on something so much better—the man you've become."

Sitting up, he captured a strand of her hair, his hand not quite steady. "Does this mean you forgive me?"

She nodded, tipping her face into his touch. "You told me you're willing to compromise with having one child—biological or adopted—however the cards land on that. I accept your beautiful offer."

He cupped her head and drew her toward him for a kiss, the closemouthed sort filled with a relief and intensity that seared straight through. "Johanna, I love you so damn much, I will do my best to be the man you deserve because, God help me, I can't live without you."

"I don't want to live without you, either," she admitted. "I've tried it. I don't like it."

"I don't want you making sacrifices for me."

"It's a bigger sacrifice to be without you." She knew that with a thousand percent certainty. No matter what the future held, she wanted Stone in her life, her heart and her home forever. He was her family.

His eyes held hers, his fingers smoothing her cheek and then tracing her lips.

"You don't know how much…" He took a deep breath and released it in a shuddering sigh. "I'll do everything I can to make this right. To give you the life you deserve."

"I know. We'll fill our home with dogs, and dote on our nieces and nephews, and yes, maybe a child of our own. But we're going to do it together."

He moved closer to her, Pearl huffing in irritation over being disturbed, then settling back to sleep. "I want to make sure you know what you're signing on for."

"What do you mean?"

"I realized tonight when I took Pearl here that somewhere along the way to being the CEO for Diamonds in the Rough, I lost sight of who I really am, lost sight of where I belong."

"And where is that?"

"I belong here, to the land, to the McNair land." He scratched his dog's ear. "I'm not a CEO who happens to be a cowboy. I'm a cowboy who happens to be an executive."

"Okay? And that means?" She wasn't certain, but

the fact that they were talking so openly gave her a new hope for their future.

"It feels crystal clear to me." He cupped Pearl's head. "My grandmother was right to give me this test. It helped me to understand. I'm not meant to be the CEO of Diamonds in the Rough."

"Whoa." She pressed a hand to his chest. "I'm completely confused."

"It's time for me to be my own man. This land, this corner, belongs to me and it's time for me to follow my destiny." He tapped her lips to silence her. "Before you think you've hitched your wagon to a broken star, I have a hefty investment portfolio of my own. And I don't see stepping away from the company altogether. I've contributed designs to the company that have landed big."

"But your plans to take the company international?"

He shook his head. "That was ego talking, the need to prove I'm better than my cousins even if I don't have parents that give a damn about me."

She reached for him. "Stone—"

"Johanna, it's okay. It's not about competing. Not anymore. It's about finding the right path. Mine is here. I want to build a home for us. Ours. A place to start our future. Not some wing at the Hidden Gem Lodge. But a place of our own to build our family."

"You have this all thought through." And it made beautiful sense.

"Even if we have a dozen children of our own, I would still like us to consider…"

"What?" she prompted.

"There are a lot of children out there who need homes, babies like I was, except they don't have a rich grandmother to pick up the pieces for a newborn going through withdrawal. It's a lot to take on. What do you think?"

What did she think? She thought this was the easiest question ever. "I'm all-in, wherever the path takes us, as long as we're together, cowboy."

*****

PURSUED BY
THE RICH RANCHER

CATHERINE MANN

To Mustang and his special boy. Thank you for
changing my life and touching my heart.

One

Nina Lowery just didn't get the cowboy craze.

Good thing she lived in Texas. All the cowboys made it easy to resist falling for any man after her marriage combusted. And never had she been more neck deep in cowboys than today as she accompanied her son to the week-long HorsePower Cowkid Camp.

Nina peeled the back off the name tag and stuck it to her yellow plaid shirt that was every bit as new as her boots. She knelt in front of her four-year-old son and held out the tiny vest with his name stitched on it.

"Cody, you need to wear this so everybody knows which group you're with. We don't want you to get lost. Okay?"

Silently staring, Cody kept his eyes on the ground, so she had a perfect view of the top of his blond buzz cut. He lifted his hands just a hint, which she took as the okay to slide his spindly arms through the vest, leather fringe fanning in the wind. The summer smell of freshly mown hay mixed with the sticky little boy sweetness of perspiration and maple syrup from his breakfast pancakes. Cody had them every morning. Without fail.

They'd been running late today, so he'd eaten his breakfast in the car, dipping his pancake in a cup of syrup. Most of which drizzled all over his car seat. But after waking up at 4:00 a.m. to get ready, then driving from San Antonio to Fort Worth, she was too frazzled to deal with the fallout of disrupting any more of his daily routine. Syrup could be cleaned later.

There were far tougher issues to tackle in bringing up Cody than combating a trail of ants.

She would do anything for her little boy. Anything. Including immersing herself in the world of boots and spurs for seven days. *Yeehaw.*

About a month ago, when her four-year-old's eyes had lit up during a field trip to a farm, she'd been taken aback. He'd been mesmerized by the horses. So Nina had devoted herself to becoming an expert on all things equine related, desperate for a means to break through the walls surrounding her autistic son.

Finding a pathway of communication was rare and cherished when parenting a child with autism.

Never in a million years would she have guessed this particular world would pique Cody's interest. Usually boisterous encounters spun him up, leaving him disoriented and agitated. Sometimes even screaming. Rocking. His little body working overtime to block the excess stimuli.

But he liked it here. She could tell from his focus and the lack of tension in his body. She'd only seen him this way while drawing. He was a little savant with crayons and paint, finding creative canvases from rocks to boxes and, yes, walls. She even had a Monet-esque flower mural down her hall.

Apparently he was a horse savant, as well.

She held out the pint-size straw hat and let him decide whether or not he wanted to take it from her to wear. Textures were an iffy proposition for him. The brush of a rough fabric could send him into sensory overload, especially on a day when there were already so many new sights and sounds, horses and humans everywhere. She sidestepped to make way for a father pushing his daughter in a wheelchair, the tyke's arms in the air as she squealed, "Giddyap, Daddy!"

Cody clutched his tiny Stetson in his hands until a long-legged ranch hand strutted past. Standing straight, his eyes tracking the man walking away, her son slid his hat in place and tilted it to the side just like the stable hand he watched. Nina breathed a sigh of relief. She'd made the right decision to come here.

The cowboy camp for special-needs kids was a clear fit for her son. The program had only started this summer, but was already receiving high acclaim. The wealthy McNair family had put their power, influence and money behind launching HorsePower Cowkid Camp on their hobby ranch—Hidden Gem. The bulk of their fortune, though, had been made in their jewelry design house that created rustic Western styles.

Cody toyed with the fringe on his vest, tracing the stamped jewel patterns imprinted in the leather. She reminded herself to stay cautiously optimistic. They'd only just arrived.

She'd learned long ago not to set unrealistic expectations. Life worked better when she celebrated individual moments of success, such as how Cody took steps toward that cowboy. A horse whinnied and her son smiled. That meant more than the hundreds of hugs she would never get.

"Cody, let's walk around and explore. We have a couple of hours to settle in before the first activity." She was used to rambling on to fill the silences. Her son did speak. Just not often. Rather than expecting Cody to answer, she was advised by the speech therapist to accept it as a pleasant surprise when he did and take heart in his advanced vocabulary choices.

Cody held up his hand for her to take and she linked her fingers around his. A rare reach-out. Her heart filled at the chance to touch her child. If Cody wanted the ranch experience, she would follow that broad-shouldered cowboy to the ends of the earth.

Weaving around the other families, she tried not to notice how many of the children were accompanied by two parents. She savored the feel of her son's hand in hers and charged ahead to a corral about ten yards away, on the periphery of the camper chaos.

Multiple barns, cabins and corrals were walking distance from the lodge. Some would call the lodge a mansion—a rustic log ranch mansion with two wings. One wing for vacationers, the other wing for the McNairs' personal living quarters. The place had expanded from a B & B to a true hobby ranch, with everything from horseback riding to a spa, fishing and trail adventures… even saloon-style poker games. They catered to a variety of people's needs, from tourists to weddings.

And now this special needs kids' camp, as well.

She refused to be wowed by the family's power.

She'd walked that path, been too easily blinded by her ex's charm. The thought of a wealthy life of ease with a handsome guy had seemed like a fairy tale and so she'd seen what she wanted to see. But her would-be prince had definitely turned into a toad, taking that fairy-tale ending with him.

Nina skirted past a half dozen children surrounding a rodeo clown passing out toy horses. Childish squeals filled the air.

"I wanna spotted pony."

"Please, please the brown one with a girl rider."

"I wike the one wiff sparkles on the saddle!"

Cody, however, kept his eyes on the cowboy. For the most part, she'd only seen chaps on men in after-shave commercials. Even in Texas they weren't common. This guy's leathers were dusty and worn, the type a man wore to work. A real man. Not an overindulged toad prince like her ex.

So okay, maybe there was something to be said for the cowboy appeal after all.

Cody's cowboy leaped over the split-rail fence in a smooth blend of instinct and strength, his tan Stetson staying firmly in place. He walked with loose-hipped confidence toward a wild horse pawing the ground, nostrils flaring. The animal clearly didn't like the sad-dle on his back and eyed the approaching man with wariness. The horse danced nervously, shifting uneasy weight from hindquarter to hindquarter, powerful mus-cles flexing. She felt her son's pulse kick in excitement. So in spite of the tremor of fear in her heart, she stepped closer to the corral.

She'd been thrown once as a child and hadn't been

a fan of horses since then. She liked to think she was a person who learned her lesson. Once burned. Twice shy.

Yet the man in front of her showed no fear as he spoke softly to the stressed beast, lulling with his hypnotic voice and gentle strokes. Her stomach gripped just as he slid onto the horse's back.

Pinning his ears back, the horse yanked hard on the reins. Now the animal was well and truly pissed.

Cody tugged his hand free. "Let go."

And she only then realized she'd been squeezing too hard. "Sorry, sweetie."

"Uh-huh." Her son walked closer to the fence, and a different fear took over. Her child had very little sense of danger.

She stifled her own anxiety and stepped closer. "Cody, we have to stay outside the fence to watch. We can't go inside and disturb the man's work."

"Kay..." Her son nodded, enraptured.

The cowboy urged the horse gently forward. The horse bucked hard but had no luck at unseating the skilled rider. His cowboy hat, however, went flying. The midmorning sun glinted off his head of thick black hair.

The kind of hair a woman could run her fingers through.

The wayward thought hit her as hard and fast as those hooves pounding the ground. She'd never bought into cowboy lore, especially after being tossed on her butt by that supposedly docile pony. Until now. At this moment, she couldn't take her eyes off the smooth flow of the ranch hand's body as he became one with the horse. He rode the frenzy without letting it take control of him, rolling naturally with the unpredictable movements. She understood the restraint and self-control it took to tap in to that Zen state in the face of such outright terror.

She carried fears of her own. Of not being able to care for her son as a single parent. Of trusting a man again after the hell and betrayal her ex-husband had put her through before their breakup and then his death in a motorcycle accident.

Those fears were nothing compared to the terrors her son faced. And the roadblocks.

Somehow she could tell this cowboy understood that fear. Knew how to ride through the moment until peace returned. He had the well-being of the horse in his care in mind at all times. And Cody was mesmerized.

So was she.

Finally—she had no idea how long they stood watching—the horse settled into a restless trot, circling the fenced area, snorting. Nina exhaled in a rush, only just now realizing she'd been holding her breath and secretly rooting for him.

Cody knelt down and picked up the man's hat, shook off the dust and held it out. "Mister. Your Stetson."

Her son's voice came out a little raspy from being used so infrequently. The cowboy tipped his face toward them, the sunshine streaming over...

Oh my.

He'd stepped right off some Wild West movie poster and into her reality. High, strong cheekbones and a square jaw, damn good-looking *power*. She blinked fast against the sting of dust in the air.

He guided the horse to their side of the fence, and her stomach flipped. Because of close proximity to the horse, right?

Ha.

She'd quit lying to herself a long time ago.

The cowboy dipped closer, extending an arm toward Cody. "Thank you, little man." His voice was like Southern Comfort on the rocks, smooth with a nip. "I'm guessing by that vest you're here for camp. Are you having fun?"

"Uh-huh." Cody nodded without making eye contact. "Spectac-u-lar."

Would the man understand? This was a special needs camp, after all.

The cowboy stroked a hand along the horse's neck. "I see you like Diamond Gem. He's a good horse, but too large for you. The camp counselors will start you out with pony rides and before you know it you'll be ready for the big leagues."

Cody shuffled his feet and tugged at the fringe on his vest.

"Thank you," Nina said. "Cody's not very talkative, but he understands all we're saying."

He looked at her, his eyes laser blue. A shiver of awareness tingled through her. Did all of him have to be so damn charismatic?

A dimple tucked into one of his cheeks. "I'm usually not much of a chatty guy myself, actually."

He'd done better with Cody today than her ex-husband ever had. Warren had been a charmer, sweeping her off her feet with extravagant gestures, making her believe in the fairy-tale ending right up until...*ribbit*. Warren was a shallow, spoiled mama's boy with too much money and too little ambition other than the next thrill. When life got real, when the day-to-day specifics of dealing with their son's autism added up, he'd checked out on the marriage. Then he'd checked out on life altogether in his reckless motorcycle accident.

Cody scuffed his little boots in the dirt, his mouth moving, repeating, "Rodeo man, rodeo man."

The cowboy dipped his head, then nodded. "Back in the day, I was. Not any longer."

Cody went silent, and Nina scrambled for something to say. For her son's sake, of course, not because she wanted another taste of that Southern Comfort drawl saturating her senses. "Then what was that show all about?"

"Just doing my job, ma'am. This was actually a low-key session," he said, his voice washing over her as he sat astride the horse, his muscular thighs at eye level... and his hips. Diamond Gem shook his head up and down, shaking the reins, a reminder that the horse, although calm now, was still unsettled. "Diamond Gem and I have been working together for a couple of weeks."

That was an *easy* session?

"Do you miss the rodeo days?" she found herself asking, unable to stop herself from thinking of all the regrets Warren had lamented over after settling down.

The dusty cowboy scratched under his hat, then settled it back in place. "Let's just say these days I prefer to spend my time communing with the animals rather than performing for people."

"And this horse? You were communing?"

"This fella was confiscated by local animal control for neglect and..." He glanced at her son. "And for other reasons. Releasing him into the wild where he would be unable to fend for himself wasn't an option. So he came here to us where we can socialize him. He's a little green and gun-shy, but we've made progress."

So he'd used the old skills to help this horse. Was he playing on her heartstrings as a part of some camp gimmick or was he as genuine as those blue eyes? She settled on saying, "That's admirable of you to risk breaking a rib—or worse—to help the horse."

The dimple twitched at his cheek again. "I may have enjoyed myself a little bit…" His eyes dipped down to the name tag stuck to her shirt. "Nina."

Her skin prickled and heat flushed through her at the sound of her name coated in those whiskey tones. What harm was there in indulging in a light flirtation with a regular guy? No risk. She was only here for a week. Although she could be imagining his interest.

It was probably just his job as an employee to be polite to the customers.

"Well, my son certainly enjoyed it, as well. Thank you." She backed up a step. "We should start unpacking or we'll miss the lunch kickoff."

"Wouldn't want that to happen." He touched the brim of his hat. "Y'all have a nice time at the HorsePower Cowkid Camp."

Her skin flushed, heating at the sound of his low and rumbly voice soothing ragged nerves. How strange to be lulled and turned on all at once. But God, how she craved peace in her life. She treasured it in a way she never would have guessed a decade ago.

And watching the lumbering cowboy ride away, she had a very real sense of how smooth and sexy could coexist very, very well in one hot package.

For the first time in months, Alex McNair was stoked about the possibility of asking out a woman. He'd been telling himself for months he needed to move on after his cousin got engaged to the only woman Alex had ever wanted to marry. But the one-night stands he'd been having lately didn't count as moving forward with his life.

He slung the saddle off Diamond Gem's back and passed it over to a stable hand. Diamond Gem looked sideways at Alex from the cross ties and let out a long nicker. He preferred to brush and settle his own horses, but his responsibilities overseeing the Hidden Gem Ranch interfered more often than not with that simple work these days. He missed free time in the saddle, but his MBA was needed here more than his equestrian skills.

And the number-one priority today? He was due to meet his grandmother for an early lunch. That took precedence over anything else. He didn't know how many more meals they would share, since she had terminal brain cancer.

With his grandmother's illness, he had to step up to fill the huge void left by their McNair matriarch. Which probably made this a bad time to think about starting a relationship, even a short-term one, but the woman—Nina—intrigued him. Her curly red hair and soft curves snagged his attention, and the memory of her berry scent lingered in his senses.

And the protective way she watched over her son drew him in at a time when his emotions were damn raw. He didn't want to overanalyze why she pulled at him. He was just glad as hell for the feeling.

It had taken him a long while to get over the fact that his cousin would be marrying Johanna. But he'd gotten past that. He had to. She would be in the family forever now. Family was too important for any kind of awkwardness to linger.

The family needed to stick together, especially with their grandmother's cancer. They needed to support her, and had to make sure the McNair empire ran smoothly through this time of transition. Giving their grandmother peace during her final days was their most important task.

Still, he couldn't stop thinking about the woman—Nina. He didn't even know her last name, for God's sake, but he sure intended to find out. He could see asking her to accompany him to his cousin's wedding. How far did she live from here? People came from all over for the camp, but the bulk were local.

Regardless, distance didn't really matter. Not to a McNair. He had the family plane at his disposal. And yet all that money couldn't give them the one thing each of them really wanted.

Their grandmother's health.

He strode toward the main house, veering off to the family's wing where he was to meet his grandmother on the porch. His boots crunched along pine straw, children's chatter and a banjo playing echoed in the distance. Branches rustled overhead. Some of those oak trees were older than him and he'd climbed those thick branches as a kid.

He neared the family porch where his grandmother—Mariah McNair—already sat in a rocking chair. A tray of sandwiches and a pitcher of tea waited on the table between the two rockers.

His gut knotted with dread over the day that rocker would be empty.

Her favored jean jumper and boots fit her more

loosely these days. And her hair was shorter now. For as long as he could remember, she'd worn it long, either in a braid down her back or wrapped in a bun on her head. But she'd undergone a procedure to drain blood buildup in her head a few months ago. Her hair had been cut short and shaved away at the surgery site.

That made it real for him. She was going to die sooner rather than later, and not of old age. That damn tumor was going to steal her from them.

"You made it," she said, clapping her hands. "Come sit beside me, load up a plate and let's talk."

"I'll clean up and be right back down." He worried about her getting sick on top of everything else.

"Now is better. A little dust and dirt isn't going to make me keel over. Besides, I've seen you messier."

"That you have." He swept off his hat and hunkered down into the rocker beside her, resting his hat on his knee, thinking of how cute that kid Cody had looked passing it back to him. "How are you feeling, Gran? Do you want more tea?"

He reached for the pitcher, noticing she'd only nibbled at the corner of a sandwich.

"I'm fine, Alex, thank you. I have the sunshine, a glass of sweet tea and one of my grandchildren here. All is right in my world."

But he knew that wasn't really true. She didn't have long to live. Months. Maybe only weeks. She'd been getting her affairs in order, deciding who would inherit what. Not that he cared a damn thing about the McNair wealth and holdings. He just wanted his grandmother.

He reached for a plate and piled on sandwiches, more to make her happy. His stomach felt as if it had rocks in it right now. "Thanks for lunch. It's a chaotic day with all the campers coming in."

"Stone surprised us all by starting that camp instead of taking over the jewelry enterprises, but in a good way."

Alex touched his hat on his knee. "That he did."

"His new life fits him. Johanna helped him see that path while she helped him with his inheritance test." Mariah set her plate of uneaten sandwiches aside. "Alex, I want to talk to you about *your* test."

"*My* test?" The rocks in his stomach turned icy. "I thought that was just a game to get Stone and Johanna back together."

At least he'd hoped so as time passed and his grandmother didn't bring up the subject of putting her three grandchildren through an arbitrary test to win their portion of the estate.

It wasn't about the money. It was about the land. A mega-resort developer simply could not get a hold of Alex's portion of the land. That, he definitely cared about.

"Well, Alex, you thought wrong. I need to feel secure about the future of what we've built. All three of you children have a stubborn streak."

"One we inherited from you."

"True enough." She laughed softly before her blue eyes turned sad. "Much more so than my two children."

Her daughter had been a junkie who dropped her child—Stone—off onto Mariah's doorstep. Alex and his twin Amie's father had been unmotivated to do more than spend his inheritance and avoid his wife.

Mariah had been more of a parent to Alex than his own.

He, Amie and Stone were like siblings, having grown

up here at Hidden Gem together. Once they'd finished college, they all turned their attention to home, working to keep the McNair holdings profitable even after their grandfather died. Each one of them had a role to play. Alex managed the family lands—Hidden Gem Ranch, which operated as a bed-and-breakfast hobby ranch for the rich and famous. Until recently, Stone had managed the family jewelry design house and store. Diamonds in the Rough featured high-end rustic designs, from rodeo belt buckles and stylized bolos to Aztec jewelry, all highly sought after around the country. And Amie—a gemologist—created most of their renowned designs, even though the McNair jewelry company was now under new management, an outsider his grandmother had hired.

Gran rocked slowly, sipping her iced tea, her hand thin and pale with spidery veins as she set the glass back on the table between them. "Now back to what I've planned for your test."

That damn test again. Stone had already passed his test to retain control of the jewelry business. Gran had made Stone work with Johanna to find loving homes for his grandmother's dogs. Yet once Stone had finished, he surprised them all by proposing to Johanna and announcing he didn't want to run Diamonds in the Rough after all. He didn't want the all-consuming ambition. The camp had been Stone's brainchild, shifting his focus to the family's charity foundation, investing his portion of the estate into a self-generating fund to run the HorsePower program while a new CEO assumed command as head of Diamonds in the Rough.

"Seriously, Gran? You're still insisting on the test? I assumed since Stone backed out and opted to live on his own portfolio you would pass the company along to Amie."

"And leave the running of the ranch to you?"

He stayed silent. The land. This place. He'd put his heart and soul into it. But that was his grandmother's decision to make. Money wasn't a concern. He had his own. He could start fresh if need be.

Except he didn't want to. He wanted his home to stay untouched by takeover from some mega-ranch theme park.

Mariah set aside her tea. "Alex, it's a simple test really. There's a competitor—Lowery Resorts—that has been quietly buying up shares of the McNair empire through shell corporations."

Alarms went off in his head. This was the worst possible time for someone to stage a takeover. Stockholders were already on edge about his grandmother's illness, concerned about the uncertain future of the McNair holdings. "A controlling percentage?"

"Not yet. But between my illness, Stone's resignation as CEO and his replacement still gaining his footing, some investors perceive a void. If our loyalties split or if they continue consolidating, we could be at risk of having our haven turned into a sideshow resort."

How the hell had this happened? His hands gripped the arms of the chair and he resisted the urge to vent his frustration. He bit back the words he wanted to spout and simply said, "How did they manage that?"

"When word first leaked of my illness, they moved fast and took advantage of investor fears. I should have seen that coming. I trusted old friendships. I was wrong. I need to move faster now. Time's too important."

He should have seen this coming. He should have

thought beyond his part of the family holdings. "We could have Stone return as CEO until the crisis with the Lowery Resorts passes."

"No, he doesn't want it, and I need to see the company settled with our new CEO, Preston Armstrong, in control before I can rest easily. The board and I chose Preston because we believe in him, but he will need time to gain investors' trust. So in the meantime, I need your help."

"You don't need to make it a test." He patted her hand, then gripped it. "Just tell me what to do for you and I'm here for you, for the family."

Smiling, she gave his hand a squeeze back, before her eyes narrowed with the laser focus that had leveled many in the business world. "The Lowery family has a vulnerability in their portfolio."

"You want me to exploit it?" His mind churned with possibilities he wanted to discuss with Stone.

"Convince the Lowerys to sell back a sizeable portion of those shares bought by their shell companies and I'll transfer all my shares of the ranch into your hands effective immediately."

He waved aside the last part of her words. "It's not about me accumulating a larger part of the homestead. It's about our family. I will not allow our land to pass into anyone else's hands."

She nodded tightly. "There's that old competitive spirit of yours. I was wondering if you'd buried it completely under that laid-back air you carry around these days."

"Hmm." He didn't like reminders of that side of himself. He picked up his tea and drank. There was still a lot of dirt inside him to wash away from those rodeo days. Things he'd allowed his parents to push him to do. Things he regretted.

"You need to be aware, the Lowery family is going to be resistant. You'll need to be careful and savvy in gaining the trust of the one chink in their armor. I've even given you a head start."

He paused mid-drink, then set his glass back down carefully. "What do you mean by head start?"

Her thumbs rubbed along the arms of the wooden rocker. "The vulnerable shares belong to the Lowery grandson. His widowed mother is the executor, and she needs to invest wisely for the boy's future—long-term."

A kid? A widow? A creeping sensation started up his spine, as if he were about to get kicked by a horse or run over by a stampede. "Gran, what have you done?"

"I investigated all the Lowerys, of course. And when I found out the grandson adores all things cowboy, I made sure a brochure for our camp landed in his mother's hands so we would have the chance to meet with them—away from the grandparents' influence."

Ah, damn. It couldn't be…

"In fact, I believe you've already met her and her son." She pointed a frail finger toward the corral, where she would have had a clear view of his morning activities.

Crap. He could almost hear that stampede gaining speed, ready to run him over.

"The lovely red-haired lady who watched you work with Diamond Gem."

Two

The sun was low and warm, piercing through the barn windows as Nina sat at a long wooden table eating supper with the other parents. A country band played twangy children's songs, a group of young campers sitting clustered in front of the small stage. Cody rocked and flapped his hands in time, having already finished his macaroni and cheese. A little girl with a pink scarf over her shaved head spun in circles with a streamer. A little boy with cerebral palsy held his new friend's hand as they danced. Three children ran up to the stage clapping.

She'd spent the morning unpacking, then eating lunch and attending camp sessions with her son, followed by pony rides, arts and crafts. They'd made belts and jewelry. And not just the children, but the adults had been included, as well. She touched the bracelet full of little charms, all Wild West themed, and a gem that was also her son's birthstone.

Between the horses and the art, her son's two favorite activities, Cody had been enthralled. The tiny sticker jewels he'd glued to the belt made an intricate repeating pattern that had even surprised the instructor.

Her son was happy, but tired from a good day. The best she could remember having in a long time. And she couldn't deny that her mind wandered back to the morning and the dusty cowboy who probably hadn't given her a second thought. But she'd kept looking for him in the crowds.

And she didn't know his name.

She stabbed at her dinner salad, covered in strips of tender steak. The big grill outside had been fired up with a variety of meats, potatoes and corn for the adults. She was wondering how the fee they charged possibly covered such a high-end production. The Mc-Nair family, or some of their wealthy friends, had to be underwriting the expense. Her in-laws were always looking for tax havens. As fast as the thought hit her, she winced. She hated how cynical she'd become, but it was hard to feel sympathy for people who wanted to write a check rather than get to know their only grandchild.

Old anger and hurt simmered. She sliced through a steak strip, took a big bite and reminded herself to enjoy this great food and the break from always staying on guard as the only person to watch over Cody.

A shadow stretched across her, giving her only a second's warning to chew faster.

"Would you like some dessert?" Warm whiskey tones caressed her neck and ears.

She set her fork down carefully and swallowed the

bite before turning around. Sure enough, her dusty cowboy stood behind her, holding a plate of blueberry cobbler—except he wasn't dusty any longer.

His chaps and vest were gone. Just fresh jeans and a plaid shirt with the sleeves rolled up. Her eyes were drawn to the sprinkling of dark hair along his tanned forearms. Masculine arms. Funny how she'd forgotten how enticing such details could be.

"Oh, hello, again." Why had she thought she wasn't attracted to cowboys?

"Dessert?"

She shook herself out of the fog before she embarrassed herself. "Not just yet, thank you. I'm stuffed from supper. I didn't expect the meal to be this good, so I snacked earlier."

He straddled the bench, sitting beside her. "What did you expect? Rubber chicken?"

The hint of man musk and aftershave reminded her of how long it had been since she'd had a man in her life. In her bed.

Shrugging, she twirled her fork in the sparse remains of her salad. "I thought since this is a kiddie camp, the cuisine would be all about catering to their finicky palates. And there certainly was plenty for my son to pick from. I just didn't think there would be such a lavish adult course, as well."

"Gotta keep the parents happy too if we want repeat customers." He cut the spoon through the cobbler and scooped a bite, his electric blue eyes on her the whole time.

She shivered with awareness. And she wasn't the only woman noticing. More than one mom cast an envious look her way.

"True enough. Well, um, thank you for checking on us…" Was this standard for all the customers? Something in his eyes told her otherwise. "I still don't know your name."

"Sorry about that. How rude of me." He held out his hand. "My name's Alex."

He said it with an intensity that made her wonder if she was missing something.

Shaking off the sensation, she folded his hand in hers and held back the urge to shiver at the feel of masculine skin, delicious. "Hello, Alex, I'm not sure if you remember but I'm Nina and my son is Cody."

"I remember," he said simply. "But it's still nice to meet you both. Officially."

She eased her hand from his before she made a fool of herself. "You must be tired after a full day of work."

"Truth be told, I'd have rather had more time outdoors rather than spend the afternoon at a desk."

A desk? She'd assumed…well, there were lots of jobs on a ranch. She should know better than to judge by appearances. It was better to get to the heart, the truth, straightaway. She glanced at Cody. "My son has autism, if you didn't already guess."

This was usually the point where people said something about being sorry and how they knew a friend who had a friend who had a kid with autism, and then they left. And that was the reason she made a point to blurt it out early on, to weed out the wheat from the chaff. Life was mostly full of chaff.

He mixed some blueberries with the vanilla ice cream and brought the spoon to his mouth. "You don't have to explain to me."

"Most people are curious and I can't help feeling the

need to tell you before Cody has one of his meltdowns."
She wet her mouth with a quick sip of tea. "It's easier
when people understand why."

"This camp is here to do what's easier for him, not
easier for us."

His words surprised her, warmed her. "Thank you.
That approach is rarer than you would think."

"Since Stone put this camp together, we've all become more enlightened." He dug into the crust covered
in blueberries.

"This place is amazing, and it's only day one. I can't
believe how much fun I had and how much I'm already
looking forward to tomorrow."

He eyed her over his raised spoon. "You sound surprised."

"I hope you won't take this the wrong way." She
picked at the knee of her jeans. "But I'm not much of
a cowgirl."

"Really? I never would have guessed," he said dryly.

"What gave me away?"

"What didn't?" He pointed to her feet. "New boots."

"New shirt too." She toyed with the collar. "I'm trying to fit in for Cody's sake, but apparently I'm not pulling it off as well as I thought."

"You're here for your kid, helping him pursue his
own interests. That's nice, no matter what you're wearing." His eyes held hers, launching a fresh shower of
sparks shimmering through her.

Then he blinked and stood. Regret stung over his
leaving, which was silly because she was only here
for a week. It wasn't as if they were going to have any
kind of relationship. Her focus should be her son. Just

because this cowboy seemed down-to-earth and un-
complicated didn't mean a thing. Not in the long run.

He glanced back over his shoulder at her, and her
thoughts scattered.

"Nina, it would be a real shame for you to miss out
on the Hidden Gem's blueberry cobbler. How about I
bring some by this evening?" He held up a hand. "And
before you accuse me of being some cowboy Casanova
with ulterior motives, we'll stay out on the porch where
you can hear your son if he wakes up. And the porch
will be very public, so there's no cause to worry about
me making a move."

"Does this kind of service always come with the
camp registration?"

"No, ma'am. This is just for you." He tipped his hat.
"I'll see you at nine tonight."

He didn't have a plan yet on how to persuade Nina
Lowery to sell her stocks to him. He was going on instinct with her, except right now his gut didn't want
to maneuver her anywhere but to bed...or on a walk.

What the hell was his grandmother thinking bringing a woman and her special-needs son here under false
pretenses? There were a dozen other ways this could
have been handled, but all those honest means were no
longer an option now that she was already here.

At dinner, he'd considered just coming clean with
her right away. Then he'd seen her eyes light up when
he'd come to sit with her. The next thing he knew, he
was chatting with her, digging himself in deeper until
it was going to be one heck of a tangle to get himself
out. If he told her now, she would shut him down, which
would be bad for his grandmother and quite frankly, bad

for him. He wanted to get to know her better. Maybe if he understood her, he would know the best way to approach her.

He couldn't deny that she was skittish. That much he knew for sure, sensed it the way he sensed when a horse was about to bolt.

Damn.

She definitely wouldn't appreciate being compared to a horse, but he'd realized long ago, his instincts with animals served him well in dealing with people too. He needed to approach carefully, take his time, get a sense of her.

Learn more about her.

Then he would know how to proceed. And that didn't stop the pump of anticipation over seeing Nina. He secured the two bags in his grip—the promised dessert.

He scanned the line of cabins that held the campers. Most of the buildings were two-bedrooms. He'd searched through the paperwork to learn she was staying in number eight. Katydids buzzed a full-out Texas symphony in the quiet night, allowing only muffled sounds coming from the lodge's guest lanai. Guests had already begun to arrive for his cousin's wedding. Between them and the campers, the place would be packed by Friday.

Spare time was in short supply. Alex stood at the bottom of the three steps in front of cabin number eight, eyeing the pair of rockers on the porch, exactly the same style as the ones on his family's longer wraparound that held a half dozen rocking chairs and four porch swings.

Guilt pinched his conscience again.

His grandmother had always been a woman of honor and manners. He couldn't figure out why she'd come up with such an underhanded test for him. It just didn't make sense, and his grandmother had always been logical, methodical. Could the cancer be clouding her judgment in spite of the doctor's reassurance otherwise?

But Alex wasn't ready to lead the charge to declare her unfit. That was a step he simply couldn't take. He would ride this out, play along and hope like hell an answer came to him soon.

He stepped up the wooden stairs, his boots thudding. He rapped his knuckles on the door, not wanting to wake Nina's son. He heard her footsteps approach, pause, then walk again until there was no question that she stood just on the other side of the door. But it didn't open.

Definitely skittish.

Finally she opened the door, angling outside and making it clear he wasn't coming in. She wore the same jeans and boots from earlier but had changed into a formfitting T-shirt with "hello" in multiple languages. Her hair was free from the ponytail, flowing around her shoulders in loose red curls.

God, he could lose himself for hours running his hands through her hair, feeling it brush along his skin. "Cobbler's warm and the ice cream's still cold. Shall we sit?"

"Yes, thank you." She gestured to the rockers, studying him with a wary smile. "You didn't have to do this."

He stopped. "Do you want me to leave?"

She glanced back over her shoulder, her hair swishing, enticing. "You're already here and I wouldn't want to deny you your dessert. Have a seat." She gestured to the table between them. "I set out some iced tea."

He thought of his talk with his grandmother earlier,

the shared tea, so few moments like that left with her. "Sweet tea?"

"The kind that was waiting for me in the fridge, compliments of your staff."

"Sweet tea is Southern ambrosia." He placed the containers on the end table between the rockers.

"One of my favorite things about moving down South." She cradled the glass in her hands, those long slim fingers drawing his eyes to her.

He cleared his throat. "What brought you to Texas?"

"How do you know I'm not from another Southern state?" She set her drink aside and took the container with her dessert, spooning ice cream on top.

"I saw your application." He could confess that much at least.

Her delicate eyebrows shot up. "Is that ethical?"

"It's not illegal, and I can't deny I wanted to know more about you. I still do."

"I guess I'll forgive you. This time." She ate a bite of cobbler, a sensual *hmm* vibrating from her as she closed her eyes.

Her pleasure sent hot lava through his veins.

"For what it's worth, I didn't read much of your application." But only because he'd been interrupted. "Just enough to make sure I got the right cabin so I can learn the rest on my own, asking you, getting to know you better while you're here. Are your rooms comfortable?"

"The place is perfect. Hardly roughing it." Smiling, she dug into her dessert with gusto.

"Hidden Gem works hard to keep authenticity to the experience while providing comfort. It may be a hobby ranch, but it's not a resort." He joined her in eating even though he'd had some earlier. Sharing the food with her here in the dark night was…intimate.

"I can see the special charm of the Hidden Gem. And hear it."

"What do you mean?" He glanced at her, surprised.

"I can't believe how peaceful this place is. That's important for my son, keeping the stimuli manageable," she said matter-of-factly.

"For his autism?" he asked carefully.

"Yes, it's moderate." She nodded. "I'm sure you've noticed his verbal impairment. He's advanced academically, especially in areas of interest like art and reading. He's only four, but he can lose himself in a book. Reading soothes him, actually…I didn't mean to ramble."

"I want to know more. I apologize if I'm being too nosy."

"Not at all. I would rather people ask than harbor misconceptions, or worse yet, pass judgment without any knowledge." She sagged back in her chair, dessert container resting on her lap. "I knew something wasn't right from the start, but my ex-husband and his family insisted he was just colicky. Then his verbal skills lagged and he couldn't initiate even the most basic social interaction with other children… We had to face facts. I had get help for him even if that caused a rift with my husband."

Her maternal instincts, that mama bear ferocity, spoke to him. He admired the hell out of that, even as he realized his grandmother might well have underestimated how hard it would be to get this woman to part with those stocks unless she was 100 percent certain her son got the best end of the deal. "I'm sorry you didn't get the support you should have from Cody's father."

"Thank you." Her green eyes shadowed with pain mixed with determination. "Early intervention is so crucial. I had to be his advocate, even if the rest of the family wasn't ready to accept the truth."

He found himself asking, "And Cody's father?"

"My ex-husband sent child support payments." She set aside the foam container as if she'd lost her appetite. "But he didn't want to have anything to do with Cody."

"Sent?"

"He died in a motorcycle crash shortly after our divorce." Silence settled like a humid dark blanket of a summer night.

"I'm sorry." Such inadequate words for the mix of losses she'd suffered, not just through the death of her ex, but in how the man had let her down.

"I like to think with time he could have accepted his son and been a part of Cody's life." Her head fell back against the rocker, her red hair shifting and shimmering in the porch light. "Now we'll never have that chance."

Time, a word that was his enemy these days, with his grandmother's cancer. "Regrets are tough to live with."

And he would always regret it if he didn't help ease his grandmother's last days.

Nina shook her head quickly as if clearing her thoughts and picked up her dessert again. "Enough about me. I don't mean to sound like my life is some maudlin pity party. I have a beautiful son who I love very much. I have a great, flexible job and no financial worries. Moving on." She scooped up some berries. "Tell me about you? How did you end up working at the Hidden Gem Ranch?"

"My family has always lived here." He couldn't imagine living anywhere else, especially after spending so much of his childhood and teenage years being dragged around the country by his parents to participate in rodeos. "I guess you could say I appreciate the quiet."

"So you're a professional cowboy? Rodeos and all?"

He'd lived a whole career by eighteen thanks to his mother's obsession with trotting her kids out into competitive circles—him with rodeos and his twin sister, Amie, with pageants. "My rodeo days are long past."

"Because?"

He shrugged. "Too many broken bones."

She gasped. "How awful. Are you okay?"

"Of course. It's all in the past. Kid stuff." As a boy, he hadn't argued with his parents' insistence that he continue to compete the moment the latest cast was removed. He'd even enjoyed parts of the competition. Most of all, he'd craved his parents' attention, and that was the only reliable way to get it. But then his favorite horse had broken a leg during a competition and had to be put down. He'd lost the fire to compete that day, realizing he'd only been doing it for his parents. More than anything, he'd wanted to go home and commune with the land and his horses.

Time to change the damn subject. "What do you do in San Antonio?"

She blinked at the quick change of subject, then said, "I'm a translator. Before I married I worked in New York at the United Nations." She toyed with the Eiffel Tower charm on her simple silver necklace. "My husband worked at the stock exchange. We dated for a year, got married, moved back to his home state of Texas..." She shrugged. "Now I help translate novels for foreign editions."

Ah, the necklace and T-shirt made sense now. "What languages?"

"Spanish, French, German."

"Wow," he nodded, eyebrows lifting, "that's impressive."

She shrugged dismissively, her hand sliding back to her neck, stroking the Eiffel Tower charm. "Words are my thing just as horses and running a business are yours."

Words were her "thing," yet she had a virtually nonverbal son. "When you said you're a city girl, you weren't kidding. Do you miss the job?"

"I don't regret a thing," she said between bites of cobbler. "I'm lucky to have a job that enables me to stay home with my son. I don't have to worry about making the appointments he needs."

"What about help? Grandparents?"

"My parents help when they can, but I was a late-in-life baby for them, unplanned. They're living on a shoestring budget in a retirement community in Arizona. My ex's parents come up with different options, ranging from some cult miracle cure one week to institutionalizing him."

"You should have their support." Since weeklong camps had started in the spring, he'd seen how stressed many of the parents were, how near to breaking.

"I have great friends and neighbors. I told you," she said firmly. "No pity party."

"Fair enough," he conceded.

She stared down into her cobbler, the silence stretching out between them. Finally she looked up. She stirred a spoon through the ice cream on the side. "Do you always deliver dessert to the campers?"

The question hung in the air between them, loaded with a deeper meaning he couldn't answer. Sure, he was here for his grandmother, but he would have been here anyway.

He settled for answering honestly. "You're the first."

"Oh." The lone syllable came out breathy, the wind lifting her hair.

He reached to catch a lock, testing the fine red threads between his fingers before stroking it behind her ear. Her eyes went wide, wary, but with a spark of interest he couldn't miss. For a long moment that stretched, loaded with temptation and want, he considered kissing her. Just leaning in and placing his mouth over hers to see if the chemistry between them was as explosive as he expected.

But that wariness in her eyes held him back. He had limited time with her. One mistaken move and he wouldn't have the chance to make it right before she left.

He angled back, pushing to his feet. "I should let you turn in. Morning comes early here."

She blinked fast, standing. "Thank you for the dessert." She stacked the containers and backed toward the door with them clutched in a white-knuckled grip. "I assume I will see you tomorrow?"

"You most definitely will."

It was only dessert. Only a touch to her hair.

And just that fast, she was tied up in knots over a man she'd met this morning. A cowboy.

God, she felt like a cliché.

Nina stood at the sink and scraped the last bite of gooey dessert down the disposal before tossing the disposable container in the trash. And God, it would be so easy to stand here at the sink and watch Alex through the window as he walked away. She'd only known him for a day. She wished she could just call it physical attraction, but she'd enjoyed talking to him. Even liked the way he could let peace settle for moments, as well.

Maybe she was simply starved for adult interaction. Her only time with other grown-ups centered on Cody's doctors' appointments or therapies. Even his play group focused on children with special needs. She wanted to give Cody every opportunity possible. But she couldn't deny her life was lonely no matter what she'd told Alex about having friends back home. The only interaction she had with others was volunteering in Cody's preschool program. Some said she should use that time for herself, and she tried. But it was easier said than done.

This week truly was a relaxing gift for her and Cody. She dropped onto the fluffy fat sofa. The cabin was cozy, comfy. A pink and green quilt—Texas two-step pattern on a brass bed. The whole place was an advertisement for Lone Star relaxation without being hokey. A colorful rag rug was soft under her feet. The lantern-style lamps and overhead light were made to resemble a flicker flame.

She should really finish unpacking and get some sleep.

Her well-traveled luggage rested on a pinewood bench. But her mind kept swirling with all the dreams she'd once stored in that case. She'd taken that suitcase with her to college, then New York City. The stickers all over the vintage piece advertised countries she'd dreamed of visiting. Warren had bought her a new set after they married, but she couldn't bring herself to throw the old ones out. After her divorce, she'd donated the honeymoon designer luggage to charity and reclaimed her old "dreams for the future" set. Those changes had felt like a reclaiming of her values and hopes.

Her cell phone chimed, interrupting her swirling thoughts. She leaned from the sofa to grab her purse off the coffee table. Her stomach leaped at the possibility that Alex might be calling. He had access to her number from her registration.

She glanced at the screen. Disappointment jabbed at her. Then guilt. She should be thankful her friend Reed was checking in on her. She and Reed had met at a play group for their children. A nice guy, a single father of a little girl with Down syndrome. His partner had left him over the stress of having a special-needs child. Nina understood the mark that betrayal left. They helped each other when they could, but they both had such very full plates.

"Hello, Reed." She propped her feet on the coffee table. "You're up late. Morning's going to come early for you getting Wendy to the bus stop."

Reed owned a bistro and took his daughter to work with him when she wasn't in school. Little Wendy loved the activity and charmed the customers.

"I'm not the only one up late," her friend teased back, his Northern accent so different from a particular cowboy drawl. "Did you lose your phone? I've been calling for a couple of hours. Just wanted to be sure you arrived safely."

"I was outside on the porch talking to…" She couldn't bring herself to tell him about Alex, not that there was much to tell. So she fibbed. "I was talking with another parent. Cody was asleep. The nights here are…idyllic."

"How did Cody enjoy his day?"

She grasped the safer topic with both hands. "He was enthralled by everything here. We're only a day into it, but I'm cautiously optimistic we're going to make a breakthrough here."

"I wish I could be there to see that."

"You have a restaurant to run."

"True enough. So tell me more about the camp."

What parts should she share with him? That she suddenly understood about the cowboy appeal? Or at least the appeal of one cowboy in particular? Reed was a friend, but not the kind of friend to whom she could say anything like that. "I was nervous coming up here that the camp would just be some overpriced excuse for parents to get a break. But it really is all about the children."

"Such as?"

"They had pony rides but let the parents lead the children around so they would feel more at ease. The menu is kid-friendly with a variety of choices so even kids with issues about texture will find something that works." And the adult fare was delicious, especially when delivered by a hot man who looked at her with hungry eyes. She hadn't felt like a desirable woman in so very long.

"That's awesome, really awesome. I'm glad you're getting this break and able to spend time with other adults. You spend too much time alone cooped up in your house."

True enough, but she didn't want to dwell on negative thoughts. She sagged to sit on the edge of the brass bed. "You must have called for a reason…"

"Can't I just check on you because you should have people looking out for you?"

"Sure you can, but I also hear something in your voice that worries me." She traced the pink and green pattern on the quilt.

"Your mother-in-law called. She'd gone by your town house and realized you'd left. She checked again this evening."

"What did you tell her?" Her mother-in-law didn't approve of her choice to keep Cody at home, and Nina knew she would just get blowback for choosing this camp. Her mother-in-law would come up with a million reasons why it was wrong.

"I said you went on a weeklong vacation with Cody. She wanted to know where. I told her to call you if she wanted details."

"Thank you." Sighing, she sagged back onto the bed, her head sinking into the pillows. "I appreciate that."

"Stop worrying. They're not going to get custody of Cody. There's no reason for a judge to pass over custody to them."

"Thank you again. I feel like I'm saying that all the time, but I mean it." She stared up at the ceiling fan slicing lazy shadows across the room, the distant echo of a band playing at the lodge penetrated the walls like a soft lullaby. "They just want to lock him away and control his inheritance. They don't love him. Not really."

"I know. And so will any judge who looks at the facts. When my partner tried to get out of helping with child support, my lawyer was on me 24/7 to keep a journal," Reed said with the unerring persistence that made him a force to be reckoned with in the courtroom. "Write a detailed accounting of your schedule and outings. Document. Document. Document. You'll have the facts on your side."

"Aye-aye, sir," she teased. "I will. Now you should stop worrying and get some sleep."

"You too. And be sure to take lots of photos of Cody."

"I will. And give little Wendy a hug from me. Tell her I'll bring her a present."

"Sure will," he said, an unmistakable affection leaking into his voice. He loved his daughter. "I'll be checking for text message photos."

"You're a good friend." And such a good man. They could have a great life together—except for the fact that they weren't attracted to each other. At all. Not a chance ever, since she wasn't a guy. "Good night, and thanks."

She disconnected the call, the taste of blueberries and the tangy scent of a certain cowboy's soap still teasing her senses.

God, on the one hand she had an amazing friend she could never sleep with. On the other hand she had a week with the hottest man she'd ever met. Too bad she'd never been the fling sort. But with the memory of Alex's touch still buzzing through her, she wondered if maybe she could be.

Three

Alex propped his boots on the office desk, the morning routine stable noises wrapping around him. Except today he couldn't get into the groove. Thoughts of Nina Lowery had him tied up into hitch knots.

He'd spent most of the night on the porch in a hammock, staring up at the stars, trying to reconcile his blaring conscience with his shouting libido. By sun-up, he'd reconciled himself to the fact that he couldn't hide his identity indefinitely. He would tell her who he was today and take it from there. It wasn't as if he'd actively tried to pry those stocks from her hands, and she had no reason to expect he would.

And he was genuinely interested in her.

What did he intend to do with this relentless attraction? It would be so much simpler if they'd just met somewhere outside the Hidden Gem Ranch. Not that he left this patch of earth often.

He cranked back in his chair, peering out in the open barn area that was more like a stadium, used for parties. The kids had worn themselves out with a morning of nature walks and a wagon ride picnic. Now they were napping in the cool barn on mats, a wide-screen television showing a video for the spare few who hadn't fallen asleep.

He scanned the familiar walls of home. Like in all their stables and barns, custom saddles lined the corridors, all works of art like everything the McNairs made. Carvings marked the leather with a variety of designs from roses to vines to full-out scenes. Some saddles sported silver or brass studs on horn caps and skirting edges rivaling the tooling of the best old vaqueros. He'd explored every inch of this place, starting when he was younger than those kids sleeping out there.

And speaking of those snoozing kids…

This would be a good time to clear up his identity issues. That much he could do—and should do— before making any other decisions about Nina.

He shoved up from his desk and walked down the hall, angling past a table of drying art projects made of leaves used for papier-mâché. Nina sat beside her son, cross-legged on the floor with a reading tablet in her hand.

Snagging a bottle of water off the snack table, Alex made his way over to her. He sidestepped sleeping children. Every step of the way he enjoyed the opportunity to look at her. Her hair was swept up on top of her head, a couple of red spirals brushed her forehead and one trailed down her neck. His hands itched to test the feel of her hair between his fingers, to tug one of those locks and let it spring back. What was she reading?

He wanted to know that as much as he wanted to touch her hair again, and this time run his fingers through the wavy curls.

Alex squatted down next to her, extending the water. "You need to stay hydrated."

She glanced up from her tablet, her eyes flickering with surprise, then happiness. She was glad to see him.

"Thank you." She set aside her book and tugged open her canvas bag to reveal three bottles of spring water. "But I'm set for *agua*."

He twisted the top of his bottle for himself. "What are you reading?"

"*Madame Bovary*."

"In French?" He thought of her speaking multiple languages.

She tapped her temple. "Keeping my skills sharp."

Cody stirred on his nap mat.

Alex froze, waited until the boy settled back into sleep with a drowsy sigh. Hesitating for a moment, Nina rose carefully. Alex gestured toward the door, tipping his head to the side in question. She tucked away her tablet and pulled out a bottle of water. Why did he feel as if he'd just won the grand prize? She followed him to the open barn doors, the wind sweeping inside as the low drone of the movie filled the air.

She lifted her drink and tapped his in a toast. "I truly do appreciate the thought even though I brought my own."

"You're a planner." As was he. He liked the regimentation needed to run this place, enjoyed the challenge.

"I wasn't always, but I have to be now." She gazed back into the barn at her son with obvious love and protectiveness in her eyes. "My son depends on me."

There was a strain in the corner of her eyes. He wanted to brush his thumbs along her cheeks until she rested. "I'm sorry you don't have more family to help out. Family is...everything."

As if he needed a reminder of the stakes for him here.

An awkward silence settled.

He'd met a woman he wanted to be with and her family posed a threat to his way of life. If she even would have him in the first place. She seemed attracted, but wary as hell—with reason.

An older cowboy brushed past, clapping Alex on the shoulder. "Hey, boss, mind if I take the afternoon off to go to my daughter's spelling bee?"

Alex waved. "Enjoy. I've got this under control."

"Great. My wife will have my hide if I don't make this, and I gotta confess, I would have been there anyway." The older cowboy's smile spread. "I'll pull overtime tomorrow."

"No thanks needed. Just tell the little genius good luck from Uncle Alex."

"Can do, boss."

Alex winced at the last word. Boss. So much for telling her on his own terms. He hung his head, wondering how she would react to his identity being revealed. Hell, he should have told her last night. Or even fifteen minutes ago.

Turning slowly, he prepared himself, surprised at the disappointment churning in his gut. He couldn't blame his grandmother either. This was his own fault... Except he didn't find anger in Nina's eyes.

Just curiosity. "You said you wanted to talk?"

Apparently she'd written off the "boss" comment to him being a foreman of some sort. He had to clear this up or it was going to explode in his face. "Let's go somewhere quieter."

Away from people who would tell her too much before he was ready for her to know. He guided her into the warm sunshine.

"Um, sure." She looked around nervously. "But I need to keep Cody in sight."

"Of course." He took her hand and tugged her toward a corral a few yards away, the only spot with a clear line of sight to the barn but also out of the hustle and bustle of ranch workers and guests.

She looked around, leaning back on a split-rail fence. "What's all the activity outside about? Seems like more than regular work and tourists."

"We host major events around here, parties, rehearsal dinners and weddings." The last word made him wince. One wedding in particular.

"Even in the middle of the camp going on?"

"Even then. We have a lot of land, more than just this one space, and we intend to keep it that way." Which reminded him of his grandmother's test as well as the Lowerys and their plans to convert the place into some Wild West theme park. "We pride ourselves on people feeling their event is private."

She angled her head to the side, her high-swept ponytail swishing. "And which event are they working on now?"

"A large-scale rehearsal dinner and wedding, actually." His cousin's wedding to Johanna. Alex was over any feelings for her, but he wanted the damn awkwardness to go away. "I bet your city-girl imagination is running wild at the notion of a country wedding."

The corners of her lips twitched. "Are you accusing me of thinking in clichés?"

"If the square dance fits." He winked.

She laughed, the melody of the sound filling the space between them and filling him up, making him want to haul her close. He needed more time with her. He just had to figure out how to balance his grandmother's request with his wish to be with the woman all week, no interference muddying the waters.

"Nina," he said, hooking a boot on the rail as he leaned back beside her, "there are all sorts of things going on at this place, including events planned for the camp parents."

She looked at him through her long eyelashes. "I read every word of the brochures and registration literature."

He allowed himself the luxury of tugging a curl, testing the softness between her fingers. "You're not interested in a spa treatment while your son naps? Or a sitter after he goes to sleep?"

Her eyes fluttered closed briefly and then steadied, staying open. "I'm here for Cody. Not for myself. I can't just turn off that mom switch."

He got that. And he sure as hell didn't expect her to neglect her son. He understood how it felt to be a kid shuffled to the side. "What about riding lessons?"

Confusion shifted across her face. "Excuse me?"

"If you want to be a part of your son's world, how about experience it firsthand? Cody's sleeping and the stable is next door." He set aside their half-drunk water bottles on the split-rail fence and called to one of their gentlest mares. A pudgy, warm chocolate–colored horse walked toward them with slow, ambling steps. And sure, Alex knew he was delaying his real purpose for speaking with her today, but he couldn't resist enjoying what could be his last chance to spend more time with her. "Consider becoming acquainted with one of our horses?"

She looked at the horse and tucked her arms behind her back, shaking her head. "No, thank you. I don't think so."

He hadn't considered that even as a city girl she might not like the ranch. "Are you afraid of horses?"

"Not afraid so much as...uncertain," she said hesitantly, holding up her hands. "My son is fascinated, so I'm here for him, but I can't say I share his fascination."

He didn't sense a dislike of horses. Just nerves and lack of knowledge. The notion of introducing her stirred him. "We all have preferences. Even if you're not an equestrian fan, I can see you want to know more about your son's world. So for his sake, give this a try." He raised his hands and linked fingers with hers, wondering why he wasn't telling her about who he was. Instead he was touching her, watching the flicker of the sun in her green eyes, and he couldn't bring himself to change course, not just yet. "We can take it slow?"

Her throat moved in a gulp. "Meaning what?"

"Just get to know Amber." He guided her hand along the mare's neck, Nina's soft skin making him ache to touch more of her. "Check out the feel of her. She's a gentle sweetheart."

Gasping, Nina stroked the horse again, reverently almost. "Wow, I didn't know. I rode a little as a child, but I only remember how scared I was and how bad it hurt to fall off. I thought she would feel bristly, but her coat is like satin."

"You've truly never been around a horse before?"

And yet she'd come here for her son, even though the horse clearly scared her every bit as much as she entranced her.

"I can feel her heartbeat." Her awe and laughter stoked him.

He kept his hand over hers, his eyes locked on her gaze, watching her entranced by the animal. "She can hear yours."

Nina turned and met his gaze. She wanted him. He could see that clearly, felt her desire crackling off her skin and into him.

Unable to resist, he dipped his head and kissed her. Just a simple kiss because they were outside and anyone could walk up to them. But damn it, this was his last chance before he would have to tell her about his grandmother's plan, and then he didn't know if he would get another opportunity. The thought of never tasting her, never knowing the feel of her was more than he could wrap his brain around.

She tasted like fresh spring water and the fruit salad from lunch. Strawberries and grapes. His hands curled around her shoulders. Soft. Warm. Such a perfect fit. Sparks shot through him, damn near knocking him senseless, as if he'd been tossed from a horse onto his head.

God, how he wanted to haul her closer, but they were out here in the open. A good thing, actually, because he still needed to talk to her. He couldn't go further. In fact, he had already taken more than he'd planned. But damn, she was tempting. And if she booted him on his ass once she found out who he was, what would he do?

The sound of a little boy's screams split the air.

Nina's supple body went rigid in his arms.

"Cody," she gasped against his mouth, pulling back. "My son. That's my son."

Frantic, repetitive screeches grew louder by the second. Nina tore out of Alex's arms and raced back to the barn.

Nina bit down the well of nausea born of pure panic. The smell of hay and dust threatened to choke her with each breath. Instead of making out with a man she'd only met yesterday, she should have been watching her son. She searched the barn, following the noise and finding her son on the far side, in a line of children waiting outside the bathroom.

Relief almost buckled her knees. He was fine. Safe.

But he was definitely having a meltdown. He needed her and she wasn't there with him. Her fault. Irresponsible. And just the sort of thing her in-laws would be watching for to claim their right to have custody of her son.

What if they had one of their private detectives here watching her now? She'd tried to keep this trip quiet, but her in-laws were cunning.

Alex raced past her, his boots pounding the earthen floor of the barn, past the now-blank movie screen, to the line of children.

He knelt in front of Cody, not touching. "What's wrong, sport?"

Her son stomped his feet, faster and faster, crying. Two camp counselors backed away, giving Cody space and looking at her with a shrug.

She resisted the urge to rush forward. Startling movements could upset Cody again, and focusing on Alex seemed to be calming him for now.

"Not his turn," Cody insisted.

Alex angled closer, not touching but using the breadth of his shoulders to block out the rest of the world and reduce distractions. "Excuse me?"

Without looking up, her son pointed at a boy wearing braces on his legs. "Not his turn," Cody gasped, tears streaking down his blotchy face. "He cut the line."

Nina stepped up and whispered, "He's comforted by rules and order."

The camp counselor, a slim blonde woman, was already sliding in to restore order, gently and ably distracting the child who'd innocently pushed to the front of the line. Or maybe not innocently. Children were children regardless of disabilities or special needs. But Nina was beginning to see that these counselors truly had the skills to manage the special issues these children faced.

"Cody," the camp counselor said softly but firmly, "breathe with me. Deep breaths at the same time I do."

And within a couple of dozen slow exhales, Nina's son was back under control again. Crisis averted for now. In fact, looking back, the meltdown hadn't been one of his worst. The teacher had read the signs and acted.

Nina knelt beside the camp counselor. "Thank you so much." Then she glanced at Alex. "And thank you for reaching him so quickly."

She forced herself to meet his gaze, tougher than she would have expected from just a half-innocent brush of their lips. But there had been so much more in the moment than she could remember feeling…ever. Though she didn't have a lot of first kisses in her life, this one ranked up there as the very best.

And the most unexpected.

One she ached to have happen again. Soon. But not with her son around. God, she was a mess.

She drew in a deep breath for herself this time. "I should take Cody back to our cabin for a while." She stepped away, slowly. "Thank you for introducing me to the horse—Amber—and for the help with my little guy."

"My pleasure." His hand cupped her shoulder, re-igniting the sparks in her belly. "After your son falls asleep, would you mind if I stopped by again?"

What? Did he actually expect they would jump in bed together because of a simple kiss? Okay, not such a simple kiss. A brief kiss that packed more of a wal-lop than most full make-out sessions.

Did he use this camp as a pickup pool full of easy marks, needy, lonely moms? But how could she ask as much with so many people around them?

"Alex, I don't think seeing each other tonight is such a good idea."

"With dessert," he said carefully. "Truth. Nothing more than dessert, and I never got to tell you what I planned when we walked outside."

"Tell me now," she pressed, even though the thought of having him come to her cabin tonight was damn tempting.

He hesitated and there was something in his blue eyes she couldn't read. "It's too noisy here. Cody's still on edge…this isn't the time."

"Okay, but just dessert. Nothing more," she said care-fully. Curious. Nervous. And yes, she wanted to see Alex again at a time when she could be sure her son was 100 percent safe and settled, because the times for her to be a woman were few and far between.

He touched the brim on his hat. "Nothing more... unless you say otherwise."

Alex tucked out of the kitchen, through the back door of the family's private quarters, carrying a container with two fat slices of chocolate-raspberry cake. He really needed to up his game if he expected her to forgive him for holding back on who he was—and if he wanted a chance in hell of a repeat of the kiss earlier. A kiss that had rocked him back on his boot heels.

Except he had no clue what tack to take with her, and he couldn't figure that out until he got to know her better. If she gave him that chance after tonight. And then there was the whole issue with his grandmother and the stocks...

Hell, this better be some damn good chocolate-raspberry cake.

He stepped out onto the back lanai, lit with brass torches to keep the Texas-sized mosquitoes at bay. He stopped short at the sight of Amie, Stone and Stone's fiancée, Johanna, all having a dessert gathering of their own. Any other time he would have been fine sitting with them. He would have welcomed the chance to smooth the waters, to prove he was genuinely okay with Stone and Johanna as a couple. They were meant to be together. He got that. Nothing he'd ever felt for Johanna came close to the intense emotion coming from his normally reserved cousin.

Amie waved her fork in the air. "Join us," the former beauty pageant queen said. "We've been waiting for you."

A family ambush? Great. "I'm on my way out for the evening. Rain check."

His stubborn twin just smiled and shook her head, her long black ponytail draped over one shoulder. "It can wait." Amie leaned to pull out a chair for him, a gray tabby cat leaping from her lap. "We need to talk."

He considered telling her no—not enough people told Amie no—but whatever she needed to say might have something to do with their grandmother.

Or God forbid, the upcoming wedding.

He set his container full of cake on the tiled table. "Make it quick. I really do have somewhere to be in fifteen minutes."

Stone had an arm draped over his fiancée's chair. "I heard Gran called you in for a special meeting yesterday."

Word traveled fast around here. How much did they know? Not much if they were ganging up on him this way.

"We just had lunch." The last thing he wanted were the details of his "test" going public. That wouldn't be fair to Nina.

"How did Gran look?" Johanna leaned forward, her fingers toying with the diamond horseshoe necklace Mariah had given her. "She went to the doctor today and it wore her out so much she wasn't taking visitors."

Alarm twisted the knot in his gut tighter. "She looked tired. But determined."

The tabby cat bounded off the lanai and Johanna shoved up from her chair to race after it, even though it was Amie's pet—a part of their ongoing battle about indoor vs. outdoor cats.

"So?" Amie licked her fork clean. "What did you and Gram talk about?"

Alex leaned back in his chair, arms crossed over her chest. "Why are you making such a production out of me having lunch with my terminally ill grandmother?"

Amie chewed her bottom lip. "We used to be able to talk about anything. We're twins."

Stone studied Alex through narrowed eyes and said softly, "Are you ditching us because of the wedding?"

Leave it to Stone to throw it out there. At least Johanna was still chasing the cat through the shrubbery. "I've made it clear I'm happy for both of you, and I mean that." Might as well go for broke. "In fact, I'm asking a new friend to come with me to the wedding."

"Who?"

"You don't know her." And Lord, he hoped Nina was still talking to him after tonight. He brushed his thumb along the top of the boxed dessert, his memory filling with that world-rocking kiss.

Stone relaxed back in his seat. "That's good to know. You're just so damn quiet it's tough to get a read off you, and we're all on edge with the new CEO stepping in and Gran's—"

Amie sat up bolt. "Gran gave you your test, didn't she?"

His twin always had been able to read his mind. Most of the time he could see right through her as well, but she had up walls today. He should have noticed before, but he'd been so wrapped up in himself. Damn it. "Amie—"

She stabbed her fork in the cake. "I knew it!" She clapped her hands. "My life is boring as hell these days, so spill. What's your test?"

Nuh-uh. His secret for now. He shoved out of his seat and grabbed the boxed dessert. "If you want to know, ask her. But I suspect if she wanted you two to know, she would have invited you to lunch." He stepped away, determined to share as much as he could with Nina to lessen the chance of this blowing up in his face. "Now if you'll excuse me, I have a date and I'm running late."

He was ten minutes late.

Gripping the arms of the porch rocker, Nina told herself it shouldn't matter. She didn't care. But she did. She'd spent the past hour since her son went to bed showering and changing into white shorts and a silky shirt that showed off her arms and legs. She'd put on makeup and dried her hair out, straightening the curls. All because of one kiss from a guy she would only see for a week.

And then?

What would life be like when she returned to San Antonio with nothing but memories? The thought chilled her.

She shot to her feet and yanked open the front door to go back inside. She refused to appear overeager—or heaven forbid—desperate.

Still, at the sound of his footsteps on her porch steps, her stomach lurched. Damn it. Pressing a hand against her butterfly-filled stomach, she realized she had to regain control. For starters, she had to be honest with herself.

Yes, she was attracted to him. Very. And clearly he was attracted to her too. She hadn't misread that. Plus, he was so different from her silver-spoon-born ex. Alex was down-to-earth, a regular kind of guy.

And he was knocking on her door.

Late.

She yanked a scrunchie off the table and pulled her hair back into a ponytail. If anything happened here, she needed to be back in control—and never let him know he'd rattled her.

She grabbed a magazine for good measure and folded it open as if she'd been casually reading before she opened the door.

Her stomach flipped again.

She stepped outside, a much safer place to be with this man who tempted her.

She took the dessert box from him and sat in the porch rocker, only to realize the pitcher of lemonade she'd prepared earlier gave away how eager she'd been to see him. She was revealing too much of herself too fast. It was time to level the playing field.

"Alex, what did you come to tell me?"

He blinked in surprise. "You sure do cut right to the chase."

"The sooner you tell me, the sooner I can have my dessert." She tried to add levity even as nerves tap danced in her stomach. Did he have to look so hot in jeans and a simple T-shirt, his Stetson resting on his knee?

"I think we've had some miscommunication." His work calloused fingers drummed along the brim of his hat. "And I don't want you to think I misled you."

An option she'd never considered broadsided her, sending a flush of mortification, anger and disappointment through her. "Oh my God. You're married." Her breath hitched as she gasped, inhaling faster and faster. She pressed her hands to her face. "I should have thought to ask. But you're not wearing a ring, and yes, I looked—"

His hand clamped around her wrist. "No, I'm not married." He pulled her hands down and held them in his. "Hell no, actually. Never have been."

"Oh." She laughed nervously, hyperaware of her hands clasped in his. "Are you trying to tell me you're involved with someone else—"

"I'm not with another woman."

Relief flooded her, so much she wanted to launch herself at him for another kiss, one much deeper than the public one earlier. A kiss where she wrapped her arms and body around him, feeling the hard planes of those muscles against her. *Oh. My.*

She needed to rein herself in and find out what he wanted to tell her first. "Not that it matters, since we just met and this isn't anything like…or…um…"

"And before you ask," he said deliberately, shoving aside the table between them and leaning in closer to her, "I'm straight."

His knee brushed hers, the warm denim against her bare skin setting her senses on fire. He'd angled so close she could see the peppering of his late-day beard and her fingers itched to explore the raspy terrain, get to know the masculine feel of him.

She clenched her fingers against temptation. "I wasn't saying… Um, I wasn't… Oh hell. It's okay by me if you're—"

He leaned in closer, his clear blue eyes holding her. "I'm one hundred percent straight and one hundred percent attracted to you."

The night air went hot and humid fast, heavy with innuendo and need. She wanted him. Her body was shouting that truth at her. She wanted to have a wild and passionate fling with this man. No complications. A simple cowboy she would only know this week. A man who was the total opposite of her privileged, spoiled ex-husband. A man she would say farewell to in a week and who could give her sweet memories to carry with her.

She squeezed his hands and said, "Okay, that's nice to know. Very nice."

"And that's why I need to clear something up before you hear from someone else. I'm not a hired hand at the ranch. I'm a McNair. My family owns the place."

Four

Alex's revelation stunned Nina silent. She snatched her hands from his.

Songs of deep-throated bullfrogs filled the quiet void as she clutched the arms of her porch rocker. Of all the things she'd expected to hear from Alex, this was last on the list. In her experience in New York City and with her ex's family, millionaire bosses didn't run around in dusty jeans.

Betrayal bit like persistent mosquitoes. The sting lingered, itching even as she told herself it shouldn't matter. She thought back, though, and all the signs were there. She'd even heard him called "boss" and let herself hear what she'd wanted. She'd heard of the McNair family but didn't keep track of all their first names.

But the heir? The McNair who oversaw the Hidden Gem Lodge? He wasn't a regular, easygoing cowboy.

And he was now the last sort of man she could consider for a fling. "You're serious? Your family owns the Hidden Gem Ranch?"

"As well as Diamonds in the Rough Jewelers. Yes, my cousins and I have run the family empire together. The Hidden Gem is my domain."

"And the rest of holdings?"

"My cousin Stone was the CEO of Diamonds in the Rough before he founded the camp. My twin sister, Amie, works for the company as a designer. We all own a portion of the portfolio, but our grandmother is the major stockholder."

Squeezing her eyes closed, she let his words sink in. Had she been dense about the "boss" part on purpose because she didn't want to know the truth or had she just been so dazzled by this man she couldn't think straight?

Hook, line and sinker, she'd bought in to the whole cowboy fantasy. Except the fantasy wasn't true at all. Alex was a rich businessman just like her ex. She scratched her arms along those imagined stings. She should go inside and close the door on him and her feelings.

Instead she opened her eyes and asked him, "Why did you mislead me?"

Remorse chased through his eyes, at least she thought it did. She wasn't sure who or what to trust right now, not even herself.

He rested his hand carefully on her wrist, squeezing lightly when she didn't pull away. "You didn't recognize me and it's rare I get to hang out with someone who thinks of me like a regular Joe Shmoe. I like to think I'm a good judge of character, but there are still people out there who only see the money."

His explanation made sense. She wanted to buy in to it and believe she could indulge in a harmless flirtation this week—maybe more. Still, the oversight rankled. "I hear what you're saying, but it still doesn't seem right."

"Does that mean you're not open to more dessert together?" he asked with a slow drawl and a half smile.

Goose bumps rose along her skin, the good kind. Could she just go with the flow here? It wasn't as if he'd claimed to be rich when he wasn't just to impress someone, and she wasn't committing to anything long-term.

"Okay," she conceded. "Since you came clean so quickly, I think I can overlook your allowing me to get the wrong idea about you. If you'd kept the truth from me for weeks or months that would be a different matter."

"Glad to know we've cleared that up."

She eased her wrist away and considered her words carefully, honestly. "To be honest, if you'd spilled the whole 'I'm a McNair' at the start, I probably would have thought you were bragging or feeling entitled."

He shuddered in mock horror. "My grandmother would absolutely not allow that."

She studied him through narrowed eyes, trying to reconcile this new piece of information about him. "You're really not a ranch hand or a foreman? You looked like such a natural."

"I'm a hands-on kind of boss." He clapped a hand to his chest. "And I'm getting the vibe that the boss issue is a problem for you."

"I'm just…unsettled." Her rocking chair squeaked against the wooden porch floor.

He leaned forward, elbows on his knees working his

hat between his hands. "It's nice to have someone to speak with who isn't caught up in the McNair portfolio."

"Sure…"

"But you're still uncomfortable."

"I'm adjusting. You live over there—" she pointed to the mansion lodge "—and I'm more comfortable in a cottage." Although her son had an inheritance that entitled him to so much more. But until she knew what the future held for Cody, she needed to be all the more cautious with his investments in case he couldn't ever work to support himself.

"Yes, I live in the family's half of the lodge. It's sectioned off into private suites." He set his hat on the table and took her hand back again, holding tighter this time. "But that's just brick and mortar, logs and rocks. It's not who we are."

"And who are you, Alex McNair?" she asked, because the image of him as a coddled rich kid didn't fit what she was seeing in him and his hands-on attitude. However, she knew how well a person could hide his real nature. "Why did you feel the need to let me misunderstand your role here for two days?"

He linked their fingers, his eyes glinting in the moonlight. "Meet me for dinner tomorrow night and let's find out about each other."

"My son is here for camp. I'm here for him, not for…" She stumbled on the word and held up their linked hands. "For whatever this is you think we might do this week."

But hadn't she just been considering a fling? Still, she needed it to be her decision, and this wasn't the kind of impulsive choice she'd ever made before.

"You're interested too. We're both adults. What's

wrong with us enjoying each other's company for the week you'll be here?"

Company? Could he mean that word as innocently as it sounded, or was there a hidden innuendo? "Do you see this program as a way to pick up vulnerable women short-term, no strings, and you get to say goodbye at the end of a weeklong camp?"

"Whoa." His eyebrows shot up in shock. "That's a lot to unpack in one sentence. I'll opt for a quick answer, 'no.'"

"No, what?" she asked suspiciously.

"No, I do not make a practice of picking up any kind of vacationer coming to the Hidden Gem. In fact, this is very atypical of me." He rubbed the inside of her wrist with his thumb. "And the last thing I would call you is vulnerable. You come off as a strong woman in charge of her life."

She rolled her eyes. "Flattery. But thanks."

"You're welcome. So, are we having dinner together tomorrow or not? After Cody's asleep of course, and under the care of one of our certified child care providers. There's a dinner boat cruise that's nice, public. No pressure."

He made the offer sound so easy. "I'll think about it."

"Fair enough." His stroke shifted from her wrist to her sensitive palm. "I'll stop by at lunch tomorrow to get your answer."

"At lunch?" She wasn't even sure what she was saying; her brain scrambled at the touch that was somehow so very intimate without being overt. What a time to realize how very little human contact she had in her life anymore.

"I happen to have gotten a sneak peek at the itinerary

from a very reliable source, and the kids are roasting hot dogs for lunch tomorrow at eleven. By noon they'll be in a saddle polishing class. Meet me while your son is settled under the attentive eye of the instructors and we can talk."

"I can't promise he'll let me leave," she said, wanting to turn the tables on him but not sure how yet. "I don't want to risk another meltdown."

"Understood. I can be flexible."

She stared at him with suspicion, chewing her bottom lip.

"What?" Alex asked.

She gave up and blurted, "You're too good to be true. It must be an act."

"Aw, Nina." His hand slid up to cup her face. "People can be genuine."

She couldn't help being enticed by the promise in his eyes. Yet pain from past betrayals welled up over how her husband and her in-laws had so deeply let her down. Worse, how they had let down precious Cody. "They can be. But they usually aren't."

He stroked back her hair, tucking it behind her ear. "Then why are you even considering having dinner with me?"

"I honestly don't know." Her scalp tingled from the light brush of his fingers, his nearness overriding boundaries she thought were firmly in place.

Their gazes met, eyes held. She breathed him in, remembering the feel of his lips on hers.

Would he kiss her again? Because if he did, she wasn't sure she could say no to anything. Her body was on fire from just having him near and a few simple caresses. He angled forward and her heart tripped over itself for a couple of beats.

He passed the dessert box over. "Chocolate-raspberry cake. Enjoy."

His lips skimmed her forehead so briefly, so softly, her breath hitched and then he was gone, jogging down the cabin steps and disappearing in the tree line.

Drawing in a steadying breath, she released it on a shuddering sigh.

No doubt about it, she had a serious willpower problem when it came to this particular cowboy.

The next day at lunchtime, Alex angled through the different stations of children enjoying camp activities from saddle polishing to panning for gold in a sandbox to using hula hoops for lassoing wooden horses. His cousin Stone had told him the activities helped with motor skills and confidence. Cody looked more relaxed today as he worked on cleaning the little saddle resting on stacked bales of hay. Nina sat on a bale beside her child, the sunshine highlighting streaks of gold in her red curls.

He was still pumped over how well the conversation had gone the night before. He'd learned a lot about her, more than she might have intended to let on. She was a wary woman and someone had obviously hurt her in the past, most likely her ex-husband. That would be important to keep in mind if Alex wanted a chance with her. He needed to tread smartly.

Nina Lowery was a tactile woman. He'd gauged her responses carefully, watching her pupils widen with arousal as he'd stroked her wrist, then massaged her palm. Her senses were hungry and he intended to feed them.

Even now her fingers were testing the texture of everything around, flitting from the bale of hay to the stirrups on the saddle.

She hadn't booted him out on his butt. She'd actually given him another chance. He was skating on thin ice with those stocks in play. It wasn't as if they were entering into some long-term relationship. She made it clear she was leaving in a week and her son filled her life.

Knowing that made him want to pamper her all the more while she was here.

Alex stopped behind Nina, resting a hand on her shoulder. "Good afternoon, beautiful."

She shivered under his hand. But in a good way.

He let his touch linger for a second before he stepped over to Cody. "You're doing a great job there, cowboy."

"Make it smooth," he said, stroking.

The instructor, a special ed teacher from a local school who'd been glad for the extra income working at the camp, stepped closer. "Cody's doing a fantastic job. I think he's having fun."

The boy nodded, his hands circling repetitive strokes over the leather, cowboy hat perched on his blond head and protecting him from the sun. "Having fun."

Nina pressed her hand to her chest, emotions obvious in her expressive eyes. "I knew this was a good idea, but I had no clue how amazing equine-assisted learning could be for my son, for all these children."

"I'm glad to hear that. My cousin worked hard searching for professionals to employ. It's important to do this right."

"Well, he succeeded." Nina smiled over her shoulder

at him. "I'm impressed with the way they've combined physical and speech therapy. And they've blended balance, posture, hand-to-eye coordination and communication skills into activities that are fun, making it seem more like play."

He hadn't thought about it that way before, but it made sense. "Horses are herd animals. They seek connections and have a way of communicating, a bond, that goes beyond words."

"I can see that." Her gaze shifted back to her child. "Most of all, I appreciate the self-confidence and self-esteem Cody's finding in these classes in such a short time. It's impressive how the different stations are geared for each child's special need. They've approached Cody with sensory activities, without overloading him." She glanced back at Alex. "But that's not what you came for. Yes."

"What?" he asked, having lost track of the conversation. He was locked in on the sound of her voice and the berry scent of her shampoo.

"Yes, I'll accompany you on the dinner cruise."

"Excellent." He folded his arms over his chest and rocked back on his boot heels.

She looked at him quickly. "You're staying?"

"This camp may be my cousin's endeavor, but it's a part of the McNair empire, happening on McNair lands. I care." He shrugged. "And it's my lunch break. I'd like to spend it with you. If that's okay?"

"Sure," she said, her eyes wide with surprise. "We could take a walk? The counselors encourage parents to step away today. You know that, since you've read the itinerary."

"Guilty as charged."

She laughed softly before kneeling to talk to her son, detailing where she was going and how long she would be gone, as well as what to do if he needed her. Cody nodded without looking away from his task.

"Cody," she said, "I need to know you understand."

He turned toward her and patted her shoulder with a clumsy thump, thump. "Bye, Mom."

Her smile at the simple connection stole the air from Alex's lungs. Then she stood, spreading her hands wide. "Lead the way."

Victory charged through his veins. He cupped her elbow and steered her around the different play stations, the controlled chaos of childish squeals all around them. "After yesterday's incident I thought you might be hesitant to go too far away."

"I feel more confident today than yesterday. So, would you like to show me around the place?"

"Actually, yes, I have something I believe you'll enjoy over by the pool area." He steered her along the path back to the main lodge, tree branches creating a shady canopy. "You'll still be able to see your son, but indulge yourself, as well."

"I don't have my swimsuit with me right now and a swim is on the schedule for later. I'll burn if I go twice."

"That's not what I mean." He gestured to the rustic canvas cabana off to the side of the pool area. "We're here for a couples' massage."

"What?" Her voice squeaked. No kidding, *squeaked*. Nina cleared her throat and tried again. "You must be joking."

"Not at all." He grinned wickedly. "My first choice was to fly you to my favorite restaurant for lunch, but

I knew that would be pushing my luck. So I opted for something here at the resort you would enjoy for an hour."

Horrified that she could have so misread him, she held up a palm and backed away. "We are *not* going to have massages together. God, I can't believe I trusted—"

"Wait." He grabbed her wrist, chuckling softly. "I'm not that clueless. Sorry for teasing you a bit there. If you pull back the curtain, you'll see it's just shoulder massages and a light lunch. Simple. No need to take off our clothes…unless you want, that is."

Her hand lowered. She'd been played, but in a funny way. She crinkled her nose. "You *are* a bad cowboy after all."

He held up his thumb and forefinger. "Just a bit."

Alex escorted her past the luxury pool area. One side of the tall stone fountain fed a waterfall into the shallow end of the pool. A hot tub bubbled invitingly on the other side of the fountain. Her in-laws were wealthy, but in a more steel-and-high-rise resort kind of way. Nina respected the way the McNairs had preserved the look of their place, even if it meant limiting customers. He stopped outside the cabana just as the curtain swept wide.

An older woman stepped out, frail, with short gray hair. Nina backed out of her way, but Alex urged her closer.

"Gran," he said, leaning in to give the older woman a kiss on the cheek.

So this was the indomitable Mariah McNair. The flyers about the camp had included the story of the senior McNairs' romance and how they'd built their dynasty.

Mariah had run the business side while her husband, Jasper, had been more of the artisan. The photo in the welcome packet bore only a passing resemblance to the woman in front of her, a woman whose health was clearly fading. Although her blue eyes were every bit as sharp and vibrant as her grandson's.

"Alex." Mariah smiled, looking frail but relaxed, a sheen of massage oils glinting on her neck. "Introduce me to this lovely lady."

Something flickered in Alex's eyes, but Nina couldn't quite figure out what. "Gran, this is Nina Lowery. Her son, Cody, is here for camp this week. Nina, this is my grandmother Mariah McNair."

The McNair matriarch extended a thin hand, veins spidery and blotched from what appeared to be multiple IVs. "It's a pleasure to meet you, dear. How is your child enjoying HorsePower?"

"Nice to meet you as well, Mrs. McNair." Nina shook the woman's cool hand and found the quick return clasp to be stronger than she would have expected. "My son is having a wonderful time, thank you. I'm amazed at how quickly the camp counselors have put him at ease."

"I'm glad to hear that." Mariah tucked her hands into the pockets of her loose jean jumper. "Leaving a positive legacy is important." She nodded to Nina. "Nice to meet you, dear. You'll have to pardon me, but I'm going to take a nap now." She waved to a younger woman behind her. Her nurse? An assistant?

Mariah walked slowly away, the other woman hovering close to catch her if she stumbled.

The pain in Alex's eyes was tangible.

Nina's parents had been older when she was born, so her memories of her grandparents were dim, but she recalled the grief of losing them, first to dementia, then to death. Nina touched his arm. "It's tough watching those we love grow older."

Alex rubbed the back of his neck. "She has cancer. Terminal."

"Oh no. Alex, I'm so very sorry."

He glanced over at her. "Me too. Nobody is ever okay with losing a loved one, but to be robbed of the years she should have had left is…just…" He rubbed the back of his neck hard. "Ah hell, I think I'm more than ready for that shoulder massage now."

And suddenly it was the most natural thing in the world to tuck her hand in the crook of his arm. "That sounds like an excellent idea. You'll have to pardon me if I'm antsy. I've never had a massage before. Lead the way."

He swept the canvas curtain aside, to reveal a massage table, two massage chairs and a team of massage therapists, just as he'd promised. The grandmotherly pair waited off to the side in simple black scrubs with the Hidden Gem logo on the pocket.

The canvas walls were lined with Aztec drapes. The music of Native American pipes drifted through the speakers and muffled sounds outside. Cooling fans swished overhead.

Nina eyed the massage chairs warily, designed for her to straddle, her back exposed and her face tucked into a doughnut-style cradle. Warily, she smiled at the therapists before sitting. The leather seat was cool, but the cover on the face cradle was cottony smooth with a hint of peppermint oils that opened her sinuses with each inhale.

Alex sat in the chair beside her, face in the cradle,

strong arms on the rests. Her view of him was limited, but then every bit of him intrigued her. It had been so long since she'd had a man in her life, the masculine details made her shivery all over. The dark hair sprinkled on his arms made her want to tease her fingers along his skin.

Clearing her throat, she shifted her eyes away from temptation. A tray of finger foods as well as glasses of green tea and lemon water with straws waited on a long table in front of them.

Never in a million years would she have expected him to come up with this idea. She heard the light rustle of footsteps as each masseuse took her place and whispered softly, "I'm going to start on your shoulders now. Let me know if you require more or less pressure."

At the first firm touch, Nina all but melted into the chair. Wow. Just wow. "Alex, this is…unexpected and incredible."

"Unexpected in what way?" His voice rumbled from beside her.

"That you thought of this and that you're here too, I guess," she answered, the last word turning to a low groan of pleasure. She reached for the lemon water and guided the straw through the face cradle for a sip. The scent of massage oils filled the air. Sage, perhaps?

"A good massage was crucial back in my rodeo days if I wanted to walk the next day. Even once my years on the circuit ended, I found I was still addicted."

She'd seen him on the wild horse that first day, but hadn't thought about his rodeo days. She turned her head enough to sneak a peek, her eyes roving over his body, envisioning those strong thighs gripping resistant bulls. She also thought of the kinds of falls he must have taken. He'd mentioned broken bones and she couldn't hide a wince at the pain he'd felt. She noticed a tiny scar peeking out of his hairline along his temple. Had he gotten that from a bad spill?

The masseuse gently guided her face back into the padded cradle of the chair and kneaded the tight tendons along her neck. The stress of so many weeks flowed down her spine and away from her body. "This really is heavenly and just what I needed." Her mind went a little fuzzy with relaxation, and her eyes slid closed, voice getting softer with each word. "Funny how I never thought about how little actual physical contact I have in my life these days. Not even hugs…"

Every deep breath she drew filled her with the scent of peppermint, sage and Alex's aftershave. The relaxing massage, the tempting smells and images of this oh-so-physical man made her warm with pleasure.

There was something intimate about sharing this experience together, yet safe because nothing more could happen while they were being massaged. But during the dinner cruise tonight? And afterward?

She'd already broken so many personal rules when it came to this man. How much further could he entice her to go?

Five

Alex knocked on the cabin door, a bouquet of wild-flowers in his hand, wrapped in paper and tied with some kind of string the lodge gift shop had called raffia. He'd even written a card for her, including a poem he'd found in French about a beautiful woman. He wanted to make the flowers special, more personal.

If ever a woman needed some pampering, it was Nina.

That instant during the massage when she'd commented on how rarely she was touched had been a serious gut check moment of all the things she was missing in her life, down to the simplest   touches. He'd witnessed firsthand how hard she worked for her son, how she'd restructured her whole life to be his first and fiercest advocate all on her own. Alex burned with the need to make her life easier.

At the same time, all this made him nervous after Johanna's rejection. And now with Nina, it meant even more that things go well. He wanted to get this right, all the way down to a French poem.

The door opened and he felt the wind knocked clear out of him as surely as if he'd been thrown off a bull. "You look...amazing."

His eyes swept over her, her red curls gathered up into a loose bunch on top of her head, one curl trailing down her cheek. She wore a simple black wraparound dress that brushed the top of her knees. He recognized the long gold chain from the ranch's jewelry store. His pulse ramped up at the thought of her going to extra trouble to prepare for their date.

"It's nothing fancy. I didn't pack with a dinner cruise in mind." She toyed with the link chain, stepping back.

"If this is simple, I'm not sure my heart can take anything more." Truth.

"Save the bull for the rodeo ring." She laughed, taking the flowers from him and burying her face in the bouquet. "Thank you, they're lovely. I'll put them in water while I get my shoes. Sorry I'm not ready yet, but you are early," she called over her shoulder as she walked to the kitchen.

His eyes held on the gentle sway of her hips. He ached to walk up behind her and brush a kiss along the vulnerable curve of her neck.

"I came early to introduce you to the sitter, who ought to be here in just a minute. I thought it would be best if I brought her by to spend time with Cody before he goes to sleep, in case he wakes up while you're gone." He peered out the window to check for the care-

giver, then sat beside Cody at the kitchen table where
the boy drew using an iPad program.

His little fingers flew across the screen tracing lines,
picking and shading with different colors. His concentration was so intense his wiry body didn't move other
than for his tiny fingertips. He wore cowboy PJs, and
his blond hair was spiky wet from a bath.

Nina turned on the faucet and filled a hammered
metal pitcher with water, the flowers already tucked
inside. "That's very thoughtful—and insightful. Thank
you. I had planned to speak with her, of course, but
having Cody meet her is even better. Is she one of the
camp counselors?"

Alex glanced out the window again and stood to get
the door for their guest. "Actually I brought the best
babysitter I know. The one I trust above all others." He
tugged the door open and waved her inside. "This is
my sister, Amie."

The impulse to ask Amie had surprised him. His sister had merely hummed knowingly, seeing right through
him. But she hadn't pumped him for information about
the date. She'd merely asked what time.

His twin rushed into the cabin in a swirl of perfume
and some long shirt-dress thing. Funny how she always said she hated the beauty pageant days yet she still
glammed up like the runway queen she'd once been.

She hugged her brother quickly before walking to
Nina standing stunned at the sink. "I'm Amethyst—
Amie. Nice to meet you, Nina." She approached Cody
more slowly, carefully, aware and sensitive. "And this
must be Cody."

Nina set the pitcher in the middle of the table and

tucked the card into her purse. "My goodness, thank you for coming. I'm sorry if your brother pressured you."

"Not at all. I love kids. Although I feel robbed not to get more time with Cody, since he'll be going to sleep soon." Amie angled her head to look at his drawing.

Nina pulled a list from the counter. "I expected to have him in bed before you arrived, but I wrote down my contact info and all his favorite soothers. He has a special weighted blanket—puffy blue—for bedtime or watching TV. It's a sensory issue."

Amie took the list and placed it on the table in plain sight. "Weighted blanket. Got it." She tucked into the chair beside Cody slowly, adjusting her whirlwind demeanor. She slipped a boho bag off her shoulder and set it gently on the table. "Cody, do you like cats? I'm the cat lady around here."

"Cats?" he asked without looking up from his art project that was taking shape into a herd of horses racing in a circle around a little boy. "How many?"

"I have four at home." She held up four fingers, then pushed down two fingers, talking as if he were looking at her. "But I brought two itty-bitty kittens with me."

Cody looked to the side, toward her but not at her. Nina smiled and Alex slid an arm around her waist, whispering in her ear, "I told you she's great with kids."

Amie carefully lifted two young kittens from her boho bag. The orange tabbies wore little sweaters made of socks and were cradled in a lined box. "They stay warm by keeping close to me. These are strays we found in the barn. Actually there were four. Johanna is bottle-feeding two and I'm bottle-feeding the other two."

She pulled out a couple of tiny bottles and raised her

perfectly plucked eyebrows expectantly as she waited for his response.

"Oh," Cody gasped, rocking forward on the bench for a closer look. "Kittens? I like kittens. Cat lady has kittens and I like kittens."

Alex chuckled. "Does Stone know he's taking bottle-fed kittens on his honeymoon this weekend?"

Amie glanced up, her long black braid swinging. "They'll be weaned by then, silly. I'll have the four until they get back."

Nina leaned in to sweep a finger down each fuzzy orange back. "Will you keep them?"

"I'm not that much of a crazy cat lady. I already have four of my own." Amie cradled one in her hand and positioned the mini bottle to its mouth. "We'll get them spayed and neutered and find them good homes."

Cody sat cross-legged on his chair, the rocking barely discernible as he ran one finger along a kitten's back just as his mother had done. "So soft."

Nina cautioned, "Be careful, Cody. Gentle."

Amie scooted closer. "Would you like to feed her? I'll hold the kitten and you hold the bottle."

"Yes, yes, yes." He held out his hand, wriggling his fingers.

"Cody," Nina said. "I'll stay to tuck you in."

"Feeding the kittens. I want to feed the kittens. Don't wanna go to bed yet." His words dwindled as he took the bottle, his eyes focused on holding the bottle to the kitten's mouth. "Then gonna draw pictures of kitties."

Nina touched the top of her son's head lightly, smiling her thanks to Amie. "That sounds wonderful, Cody. You're going to have a great time with Alex's sister."

Alex's sigh of relief mixed right in with Nina's. Her

body relaxed as tangibly as earlier when they'd gotten massages. The tension drained from him, as well. Bringing his sister here had been the right call. Nina and her son fit with his family a way that boggled his mind. Things were happening fast with Nina, and he had no desire to slow down, just keep going with the ride. He would deal with his grandmother's test later.

For tonight, he would have Nina all to himself.

Nina's toes curled in her simple gold sandals as she sipped a glass of merlot on the paddle boat dinner cruise. She had a closet full of lovely dresses from her New York City days, but they were all back at her house. Yet Alex's heated looks made her feel attractive.

Alive. Even in the simple way they sat in silence now, enjoying their meal under the stars. She swirled the wine in the glass, then set it back on the table as the paddle boat made its lazy way down the Trinity River, lights twinkling from houses along the shore. The dinner cruise had tables inside and outside. But she'd opted for the moonlight and a filet mignon, the evening so different from her daily life. She loved her son, but this was such a treat after so many peanut butter sandwiches.

Things had felt so easy these past two days. Exciting and restful all at once. Alex had a slow swagger approach to life that seemed to accomplish so much more than anyone else racing around.

His twin sister had that same gift, but with a Bohemian flair instead of the down-to-earth cowboy ways of her brother. Nina had been stunned to see Amie show up in a sparkly long shirt worn as a dress along with thousands of dollars' worth of bracelets and draped necklaces. She didn't look much like a babysitter. But she'd brought orphaned kittens, teaching Cody to connect with other living beings.

There was something unique, something special about this family. And they were drawing Nina in despite the wealth and privilege, despite all the things she'd swore wouldn't be a part of her life again.

The engine roared, shifting gears as the paddle boat angled around a bend in the river. The tables were bolted to the floor, even though the glide across the water was smooth. Electric sconces flickered like candlelight in the centerpieces. Seating was limited, exclusive, only a couple of dozen tables total. Each corner offered privacy and intimacy, with the strain of live music muffling other conversation. How many proposals had been made on this riverboat?

And where had that thought come from?

She searched for something benign to say so her thoughts would stop wandering crazy paths. "Your sister is nice. You two appear to be close."

"Very close. We're twins."

The slap of the water against the hull mixed with the ragtime tunes from the musicians.

"Right, of course there's a special bond between the two of you." She tore at a roll, pinching off a bite. "Where are your parents? I haven't seen them around."

His face neutral, he answered, "They travel a lot. My father is a trust fund baby through and through. He has an office and little responsibility. My mom enjoys the finer things in life."

"I thought perhaps your father had retired, since you and your cousin run things."

Alex choked on his water. "The notion of putting my father in charge of a lemonade stand is scary." He shuddered, setting his glass back on the table. "You'll see them when they come for the wedding."

She set her roll down carefully. "Excuse me?"

"At Stone and Johanna's wedding this weekend. My parents are flying in." He smiled darkly. "They're big on showing up for the parties and flying away to the next vacation when things are tough."

She reached for his hand to offer comfort, but he leaned back and took his drink again in a not too subtle avoidance of sympathy. That simple gesture tugged at her heart even more than his words.

He drained the rest of his wine and set his glass down again. "Do you have any siblings?"

She considered pushing the point, then shook her head. "I'm an only child with no cousins." She'd hoped to have a big family of her own, with lots of siblings for Cody. "My parents had me late in life. They'd given up on ever having a child and wow, I surprised them. I know they love me, but they had such a deep routine by the time I came along, I definitely upset the apple cart—"

She stopped short as a waiter silently tucked in to refill their wineglasses before slipping away.

Alex turned the crystal goblet on the table. "You mentioned they'd retired to Arizona. I'm sorry they aren't here for you now as you parent alone. The support of family would make life easier for you."

"We're doing fine on our own." How strange that she and Alex had more in common than she'd thought. Both raised by distant parents who didn't quite know what to do with their kids. But there was so much more about him she didn't understand and so little time for this fling of hers.

"What?" he asked, the clink of silverware echoing from the next table. "Do I have food in my teeth?"

"Sorry to stare." She laughed softly, the wine and night air loosening her inhibitions enough to admit, "I'm just pensive tonight. I'm curious. Why are you going to all this trouble to romance me when I'm leaving so soon? I believe you when you say you don't use the camp for easy pickups. So what's going on here?"

"Is there something wrong with wanting to spend time with you?" Her charmer cowboy had returned; the storm clouds in his eyes from mentions of his parents long gone. "I enjoy talking to you and honest to God, it's been a while since I've found someone who piqued my interest."

"And that's all there is to it?" She leaned both elbows on the table, resting her chin in her hands while she searched for answers in his blue eyes…

And within herself, as well.

He met her gaze dead-on. "I'm attracted to you. I don't think I'm wrong in believing you feel the same. So we're dating. We have limited time together, so I'm cramming a lot of dates into one week."

"That's true." The wind stirred, carrying the strains of music and hints of lovebird conversations from a couple of tables over.

He toyed with her hand doing that tempting little move massaging her palm. "And for two of those evenings I'm already committed to attending my cousin's rehearsal dinner and wedding. I'm hoping you'll be my date for both events."

In spite of the warm summer evening, her skin chilled. "Is that what this romance is all about? Winning me over so you'll have a date for the wedding?"

"No, God. Of course not," he answered with undeniable sincerity. "I would have asked you out this week regardless."

She wanted to believe him, but then she'd believed her husband right up to the moment he rejected their child and walked out the door. "You can be honest with me. I prefer to know the truth."

"I am being honest about wanting to ask you out." He hesitated, jazz filling the silence until he continued. "And yes, it'll be nice to have you there to ease any awkwardness in my family. I briefly dated the bride."

"Ouch." Nina winced. "That could be uncomfortable to say the least."

He waved a hand. "Stone, Johanna and I have all made peace about this. I just don't want others assuming things that aren't true. Any feelings I had for her were passing and are over."

She saw only honesty in his eyes, his words ringing true. And even if he did still carry a bit of a torch for the bride, shouldn't that be a relief? It would make this week less complicated. Nina could have her romantic fling with no worries of entanglement.

So, why did she still feel a slight twinge of jealousy? Pride urged her to make light of it. "If you need me as a shield of sorts, you don't have to go to all of this trouble. Just say so and I'll be your amorous date. I'll pick up an incredibly sexy dress and look adoringly into your eyes."

"Nina, stop." He held her hand firmly and stared straight into her eyes. "I want to be here with you. And I want you to be my date for the rehearsal party and wedding because I enjoy your company."

She scrunched her nose. "Forget I said anything. Let's talk about something else."

"No, I need to be honest about this and I need for you to believe me."

"Good, because honesty is the most important thing to me."

He glanced down for an instant before meeting her eyes again. "If there wasn't wedding, I would still be asking you out, pursuing the hell out of you, because you are a fascinating woman. And please, please find that incredibly sexy dress. Except it will be me and the other men there staring at you." He lifted her hand and kissed her knuckles. "Now, would you like to dance before they serve dessert?"

"Yes, I would like that very much." She squeezed his hand and stood, letting the music tug her along with his words. Because all those jealous thoughts and wondering what he might be up to didn't matter. Tonight was a rare treat. To be out and romanced.

The band segued into a slow song as if anticipating her preference...her need. The small dance floor already held four other couples, but everyone was in their own private world. She'd thought she had that with Warren. God, she'd been so wrong.

Shaking off thoughts of her ex, she stepped into Alex's arms, determined to enjoy the night and stop thinking about the future. The heat of his palm on her back urged her closer, until her breasts skimmed his chest. He tucked her near him, resting his chin against her temple, the rasp of his late-day beard perfectly intimate against her skin.

No words were needed and in fact, she didn't want to speak. She soaked up the manly sensation that had been so lacking in her life for so long, the scent of Alex's aftershave mixing with a hint of musk. The strong play of his muscles under her hands as they danced. Her body flamed to life. Embers so long buried she'd assumed them cold and dead were stoked to life, igniting a passion. And not just for any man. She wanted Alex. This week was her only time with Alex McNair, and she should make the most of it.

The absolute most.

Something had shifted in Nina between the main course and dessert. She'd become…intense. All he'd done was ask her to his cousin's wedding. She hadn't even read the French poem yet. She'd tucked it in her purse, and as far as he could tell, she hadn't taken it back out.

He walked silently beside her up the flagstone walkway to her cabin. She hummed the music from the boat but didn't speak and wasn't sure where they were headed next. Especially after that out-of-the-blue outburst of hers offering to be his arm candy at his cousin's wedding.

Her speech would be burned in his memories as one of his favorite moments in life. Ever. She was amazing. Sexy and funny. Loyal. They hadn't known each other long, but in two days she'd turned his world upside down until he couldn't stop thinking about her.

Although there was still the issue of her son's stocks. She didn't even appear to know Cody had them or she would have said something. Her not knowing would only make it harder for him to offer to buy them.

Alex was a businessman, a damn good one. He always had a plan—everything from a five-year plan down to a plan for the day. But with Nina, he'd been flying by the seat of his pants without even reins to hold on to. He wasn't normally impulsive, but Nina made him want to forge ahead, throwing away rationales and agendas. He would figure out the issue of his grandmother's quest later. It would all come together. It had to.

The creak of the rocking chair sliced through the night sounds. His sister sat on the front porch under the outdoor light.

The former beauty pageant queen spread her hands. "Welcome home. You should have stayed out later." She carefully tucked her padded box with kittens back into her boho bag. Long fingers that had once played the piano to accompany her singing now crafted high-end jewelry. "Cody was an angel. We fed the kittens. Then he drew pictures of them. There's one for you on the counter, and I hope you don't mind that I kept one for myself. He's a regular little Picasso."

Nina grabbed the banister and walked up the steps. "Surely it wasn't that easy."

"He woke up once, asked for a glass of water. He really wanted to feed the kittens again." She adjusted her back, bracelets jingling. "I didn't think you would mind, so I let him, and then he went right back to sleep. We had fun. Truly."

Nina took Amie's hands. "I can't thank you enough for making the evening special for him too. Change is difficult for him, but you made the night magical with your kittens. I wish I'd thought to take a picture."

"Don't worry. We took tons of selfies. I'll forward them to you. I mean it when I say I enjoyed myself. I'll bring the kittens by again." She tipped her head to the side. "I would like to do a sketch of him, if that's okay with you."

"Of course."

"Good. It's a plan. I have this week off work for the wedding, so I'll see you around." Amie swept in a swirl of elegance. "Good night, you two. I'm going to head back before I turn into a pumpkin."

His sister patted him on the face as she walked down the steps, brushing aside his thanks before she wound her way back to the main house.

He turned to Nina to ask if she and Cody would go on a ride with him tomorrow, but before he could speak, she kissed him. Not just a quick kiss or peck on the cheek. She wrapped her arms around his neck and pressed flush against him. Her mouth parting, welcoming and seeking. And he damn well wasn't saying no.

Moving her closer, taking in the give of her soft curves, he deepened the kiss, sweeping his tongue against hers. Tasting and exploring. Wanting. The chemistry between them had been explosive from the first moment he'd laid eyes on her. With Nina, he was alive in the moment—the future be damned.

A throaty moan of pleasure vibrated through her into him. This kiss was the kind a couple shared when there was going to be more. But while he'd known things were moving fast between them, he hadn't expected to move this quickly. Her hands slid over his shoulders, digging into his shirt, sliding lower.

Sweeping back her hair, he kissed along her jaw. "This is not the reaction I expected."

"Good." Her head fell back to give him freer access, the gold links of her delicate necklace glinting in the porch light against her pale skin. "The last thing I ever want to be is predictable."

He trailed one finger along the path of those gold links, lower down her throat and collarbone, all the way to the curve of her breast. A slow shiver went through her, and it was all he could do not to put his mouth on the leaping pulse at the base of her throat.

"You're so incredible. You damn near bring me to my knees." Even if he hadn't come close to understanding her yet… God, how he wanted to.

She toyed with the top button of his shirt, as breathless from the touches as he was. "What if I said I don't care about your money and I don't have room in my life for another person? But I'm okay with having a fling this week?"

His body shouted hell yes, but his brain insisted this was too good to be true. And what if he wanted more than a week? How had she turned the tables on him so quickly? "You're really propositioning me? For the week only?"

"You may not believe me, but I don't do this kind of thing often." She nibbled her bottom lip. "But there's chemistry between us. With this window of time away from the rest of the world, it seems meant to be. For now."

He looked for doubt or hesitation in her green eyes and found fire instead. Pure fire. "When do you propose we start this fling?"

She wriggled closer, backing him toward the cabin door. "What about now?"

Six

She was actually doing this. Having her first official fling.

Sure, she'd been married, but she'd dated her husband for nearly a year before sleeping with him and he'd been her first. Her only. Even the thought of Warren threatened to freeze her with nerves, so she pushed away those memories. Nothing would steal this opportunity from her. This was a fantasy getaway with a fantasy-worthy man, a slice of time away from the real world. She deserved this. Needed it, even, with a physical ache she hadn't known was there until Alex made her feel all that she was missing.

Nina reached behind her to fumble for the cabin door without ending the kiss. She was an adult with few chances to feel like a woman anymore. Right now, with Alex's hands cupping her bottom, she wasn't sure she'd ever felt like this before.

He nibbled her bottom lip. "I'll get that."

Before he finished the sentence, he'd swung the door wide, his hands returning fast to her bottom. He lifted her until her feet dangled and he walked her across the threshold. One step at a time, he moved deeper into the room until the backs of her thighs hit the sofa and he lowered her, leaning with her and stretching out over her. All of it so fluid they never broke contact. Her nerves hummed with arousal from the weight of him. His hands tangled in her hair as he kissed her deeply, thoroughly.

Her body ached for release. Not just release, because she could take care of that alone, but the completion that came from sex. From a man's hands on her body. From this man's hands.

He angled up onto his elbows, murmuring against her neck. "I don't want to crush you."

Her fingers skittered down his back, tugging his shirt from his pants. "I like the feel of you on top of me."

In particular the warm press of his muscular thigh between her legs. She arched her hips ever so slightly. Pleasure rippled through her.

Alex picked up on the nuance and nudged closer. "And I like being here."

She purred her approval against his mouth. "Thank you for the flowers."

The wildflowers' sweet perfume mingled with the rustic air of the log cabin. And there was that note she'd never gotten to read. What had he written to her?

Alex stroked her hair back from her face. "You deserve more pampering."

"You've pampered me to bits today."

"I have plans for tomorrow, if you're game."

"Let's focus on the right now."

"And what is it you need, Nina?"

"More of this." She skimmed her mouth over his.
"And this…" She tucked her hands into the waistband
of his slacks. "And this…"

She writhed against his leg, the pressure giving the
perfect stimulation to the aching bundle of nerves.
His growl of appreciation sent molten desire pumping
through her veins. She met him kiss for kiss, stroke for
stroke, exploring the feel of his hard-muscled body.
She kept waiting for him to steer them toward the bedroom, but he seemed content to make out—with some
seriously heavy petting. His hand smoothed aside the
top to her wraparound dress, his fingers tucking inside her bra. The rasp of his work-roughened fingertips sent sparks shimmering along her skin, her nipples
pulling tight.

She couldn't remember how long it had been since
she indulged in just old-fashioned necking. He was
stroking her to a fever pitch, her body moving restlessly under him.

"Alex," she whispered, "let's move to the bedroom."

Or to the spa tub in her bathroom. Her imagination
took flight, the naked visions in her mind bringing her
closer to the edge. Still, Alex didn't move to leave the
sofa. In fact, his head dipped and he captured her nipple in his mouth, rolling it with his tongue and teasing
gently with his teeth. Her back arched into the sensation, pressing her more firmly against his leg.

Bunching the hem of her dress in his hand, Alex
skimmed against her panties. She thought about her
mismatched bra and undies, wishing she'd indulged in
some new lingerie at the gift shop instead of a necklace.

Then she felt the full attention of his eyes focused on her as he dipped inside her panties. The intensity in his eyes relayed how much he wanted to make this happen for her. That care aroused her every bit as much as his skilled fingers stroking her until she couldn't hold back the orgasm exploding inside her. She bit her lip to hold back her cries of completion as he caressed every last aftershock from her. With a final shiver, she sagged back against the leather sofa, her body melting into the cushions with the bliss of completion.

Her breath came in ragged gasps and she dimly registered him smoothing her clothes back into place. Then he stood and cool air washed over her. She elbowed upward and he touched her shoulder lightly.

"Shhh, just relax." He kissed her on the forehead, pulled the unopened card out of her purse and set it beside the pitcher of flowers on the coffee table. "Good night, Nina. Lock up after me."

Before she could collect her stunned thoughts, he'd left. Shock chilled the pleasure as she lay on the sofa, her arms sprawled and one leg dangling off the side. What the hell had just happened?

She gathered her dress together and sat upright. Alex was definitely the most confusing man she'd ever encountered. Not that she was doing any good at understanding herself these days either.

She swept aside her tousled curls and reached for the card on the coffee table. She popped the seal and withdrew a folded piece of paper, not a card at all. But a poem written in French. Her eyes scanned and translated...the romantic words about an ode to a beautiful woman.

Her fingers crimpled the edges of the paper as the words soaked into her brain.

She'd just convinced herself to have her very first fling. But she'd indulged with a gentleman bent on romancing her.

Walking away from Nina took every ounce of self-discipline Alex possessed. But the night had spun out of control and he needed time and distance to plan his next move with her.

He jogged down her porch steps, putting space between him and the mind-blowing image of her sated on the sofa. Yes, he wanted her—so damn much his teeth hurt—but he hadn't expected her to offer a fling. And he certainly hadn't expected to start caring about her and her son. Ducking under a low branch, he made faster tracks through the trees on his way back to the lodge, glowing just ahead.

Pursuing a relationship with Nina was a train wreck in the making. Eventually she would find out about his pursuit of the shares in Cody's trust fund—the details of which his grandmother had emailed to him this afternoon. So much so he felt like a damn financial voyeur. His grandmother could lose the company if he told Nina now and she walked away.

It wasn't just about keeping the ranch for himself. He would do anything to make Gran's final days peaceful. Now he'd put all that at risk by starting a relationship with Nina. And he couldn't deny the truth. He didn't regret pursuing her, not for a second, and he had no intention of stopping.

He halted midstride, his eyes narrowing. Turning on his boot heels, away from the house, he walked toward the stables instead. With luck a midnight ride would burn off the steam building inside him.

Because the next time he faced Nina, he needed to be absolutely calm and in control of himself.

"Horse rides, Mama. Horse rides," Cody chanted the whole way from lunch to the afternoon activity, clutching Nina's hand so tightly her fingers went numb.

The sun baked the ground dry as she led Cody from the picnic area to the stables. Nina's nerves were shot. She hadn't slept the night before, tossing and turning, wondering why Alex had walked away from her. She hadn't heard from him or seen him all morning. She wondered if they were still on for their plans he'd mentioned the night before. He'd said he wanted to see her and she'd agreed.

She absently chewed her already short nails. Her son had been wound like a top since he woke up. For the past few days they'd ridden ponies and worked on their equine skills. Today, he would ride a larger horse.

Nina's stomach was full of butterflies. She knew he was ready, but still. She tried not to let her own fear of horses taint the experience for him.

As she neared the corral, children clustered around their counselors, each camper wearing a different color shirt according to the group. Cody broke free and raced to his teacher. His confidence was already growing. And his joy. Even an inkling of joy from her pensive son was pure shimmering gold.

Parents had been encouraged to step back today, so Nina stopped by the split-rail fence.

"Hello, Nina?" Amie's voice called to her through the masses.

Nina searched the faces down the line along the rail. She angled and walked past other parents until she reached Alex's sister, standing with another woman. Part of Nina winced at the possibility Amie might ask about the date, but another part of her insisted this was an opportunity to learn more about Alex. And hopefully figure out her own feelings in the process.

"Hello," Nina said. "Thank you again for babysitting last night."

"My pleasure, truly." Amie set her sketch pad on the corral railing and hooked arms with the other woman. "Let me introduce you to Johanna Fletcher, soon to be Johanna McNair. You wouldn't know she's supposed to be the pampered bride. She insists on working in the stables right up to the day before the wedding. Johanna, this is Nina Lowery. Her son is that adorable little blond-haired camper over there—the one I told you I want to draw a sketch of today."

Nina stifled a gasp as she realized this was the woman Alex had mentioned briefly dating. Curiosity and something greener prompted Nina to study the leggy, down-to-earth woman. Johanna and Amie were total opposites, yet there was a scrubbed-clean glamor to Johanna in her frayed jeans, worn boots and baggy T-shirt.

Johanna laughed, swishing her blond braid over her shoulder. "The substitute vet tech doesn't arrive until then. I'm here for my animals. Stone knows that."

Nina shook off the jealous thoughts and searched for something to say. "This camp you and your fiancé have started is simply amazing."

Johanna's smile beamed. "We both consider ourselves lucky to have the means and opportunity to make a difference for children."

"Well, you certainly have made a difference for Cody. I'm grateful your staff was able to fit us in at the last minute when I called on Wednesday."

Johanna's forehead creased for a moment before she smiled again, stepping back. "Well, I should get to work. Amie, we can talk about the extra guests later." She waved quickly. "Nice to meet you, Nina."

Nina waited until the vet tech was out of sight before turning to Amie. "Did I say something wrong?"

"Not at all. I think she was just confused over how you got into the camp last week. There's usually a long waiting list."

"Oh, good, I was afraid I'd made things awkward, since she dated Alex."

Amie arched a perfectly plucked eyebrow. "You know about that? Not many do."

"He mentioned it to me."

"How interesting that he told you." Amie leaned back against the rail, her turquoise and pewter necklace glinting in the afternoon sun. "She and Alex went out once, purely platonic, though, because she was still on the rebound from a breakup with Stone. She also didn't want to cause trouble between the cousins. And truth be told, she never really got over the crush she had on Stone. Clearly."

"Crush?"

"She practically grew up here. Her father was the stable vet tech before her. Johanna has loved Stone for as long as I can remember. Sometimes romance happens slowly over years." Amie toyed with her turquoise necklace, her eyes pensive. "And sometimes that connection happens in an instant."

"My parents were the love-since-childhood sort." She remembered her plan to find out more about Alex and asked, "What about yours?"

Amie's smile went tight. "They met in college. My mother always said the second she met him, she knew he would be hers. My father was considered a catch and my mom is quite competitive."

How did a person respond diplomatically to that? "From the tone of your voice, I take it to mean competitive isn't a good thing."

"Not in her case." She snorted inelegantly. "She may truly love Dad, but she sure loves his money. It's weird to think how she likes the wealth but carries this huge chip on her shoulder, insecure from feeling that she never accomplished anything on her own. So she pushed us to find the success she felt she'd been cheated out of by living the life as a cossetted queen with a sugar daddy."

Whoa. Nina rocked back on her boot heels. "That's... unfortunate."

"Don't feel sorry for her. You haven't met my mom." Amie crossed her feet at the ankles, her brown riding boots immaculate. "Have you ever watched that reality show series about babies in beauty pageants? That was my life. From the beaded gowns to the questionably adult dance routines to pixie stix poured into cola to keep me awake at nap time."

"For real?"

"I have shelves of tiaras and trophies to prove it." She straightened and struck a quick beauty queen pose. "I even have a special row for my fake teeth she had made when my baby teeth fell out."

There was something sad about not enjoying the precious gap-toothed smile of an innocent child. "It doesn't sound like you were on board with those plans."

"I'm only marginally messed up by her stage mom ways." Amie waved aside Nina's concern. "I went to college and double-majored in art and business. I wasn't summa cum laude, but I finished on time. I have a job. Alex is the one who had it far tougher than I did."

Nina's stomach clenched. "What do you mean?"

Amie glanced into the corral where children were being lifted onto placid mares and ponies. "Have you ever watched the rodeo circuit? It was sure nothing like that. Before the age of eighteen, my brother had broken more bones than an adult football player. Or at least it seemed that way. And to keep our parents happy, he kept climbing right back on again."

Nina pressed a hand to her tight throat, thinking about her son's joy today and envisioning Alex as a child being pushed by adults. "I'm so sorry. For both of you."

"Don't be." Amie shrugged an elegant shoulder dismissively. "We didn't starve. We weren't abused. We lived a life of privilege and accolades. I just wanted you to understand why sometimes we're a little bit off when it comes to relationships and expressing our feelings."

Nina wasn't sure what to say in response, looking around nervously, seeing a pigtailed girl with muscular dystrophy benefitting from the rhythm of the dun-colored pony she rode. The girl smiled from the saddle, her eyes dancing with each step of the pudgy pony. An older boy missing an arm worked on his balance riding a surefooted mare. Kicking up a steady stream of clay, the blue roan mare walked around the pen, seemingly sensitive to the needs of the boy.

Alex and his sister downplayed themselves and their lives, but this family clearly worked to use their money and power for good. And this clearly good woman was sharing so much about herself and their family. Nina felt like a fraud.

"Alex and I have only known each other for a few days," Nina blurted out.

"Right." Amie picked up her sketch pad off the rail and backed away one poised step at a time. "Like I said, some fall faster than others." With a wave, she spun away, sketch pad under her arm.

Nerves clustered in Nina's stomach over the mention of relationships and commitments. No surprise, since her ex had trounced her ability to trust. This was supposed to be a fling.

And yet she couldn't help searching the grounds for a glimpse of him.

A rush of warm air over her neck gave her only an instant's warning before...

"Good afternoon, beautiful."

Alex braced his hands on Nina's waist as she turned fast to face him. Waiting to touch her again had made for a torturous twelve hours. He'd always considered himself a methodical man, but in a few short days this woman had flipped his world upside down.

His late-night ride hadn't helped him find any answers for balancing his grandmother's request and his driving desire to pursue Nina for more than just one night. Until he came up with the right approach for addressing the stock purchase, he wanted to do everything in his power to win her over, not just physically.

Her eyes were wary as she met his. "Thank you. I wondered where you were this morning."

"Taking care of business for the wedding." He stroked her waist lightly. "Now I have a couple of hours this afternoon free to spend with you."

Her chin went up. "If you think we're just going to pick up where we left off after you walked out without—"

He tapped her lips. "I have other plans for the day and hope you're amenable."

"To what?" she asked warily.

"A tour of the McNair property while your son's busy with his lessons." Maybe then she would understand how important the ranch was to him, and then she would understand how this legacy compelled him. "Amie is staying nearby in case Cody needs anything. She said it's the perfect opportunity to sketch him."

"You've thought of everything." She looked around. "Are we going on a drive?"

He shook his head slowly. "Your son is riding today. I think he would be proud to see his mom give it a go, as well."

Her nose crinkled. "You're playing dirty pool, using guilt on me.

"Is it working? Because your chariot awaits, beautiful lady." He stepped aside, gesturing behind him.

Her eyes went to the large bay-and-white horse behind him. The gelding was tied to a rail post swishing his tail from side to side. Nina studied the horse incredulously.

"Do you actually expect me to ride him?" Her voice

squeaked, her wide eyes still fixed on the bay. Not surprisingly, the gelding's tack was gorgeous. The light tan saddle contained an elegant inlaid depiction of a horse herd at a full-out gallop. The cantle, skirt and fender were plated with etched silver, complementing the plates of silver ornamentation on the bridle. Alex and the bay looked like a scene from an old Western movie. Yippee-ki-yay indeed.

"I thought we could both ride together and that would make you feel more secure in the saddle." Had he pushed too hard? It had seemed like a good idea this morning.

She glanced over at her son, then back at the horse. The gelding was calm enough that Nina didn't run screaming in the other direction.

Chewing her lip, she nodded tightly. "Okay, sure. If Cody can conquer his fears to step out in public, I can do this."

Alex slid his hand behind her neck. "Nina, you are so damn incredible."

"Yeah, yeah, whatever." She grabbed his arms and tugged him toward the horse. "Now hurry up before I change my mind."

With a cowboy whoop, he grasped her waist and lifted her over the split-rail fence. He took his time setting her on her feet again, letting her slide down the length of his body. The press of her soft curves and the swing of her red wavy curls had his body on fire in an instant. He didn't regret walking away last night, but he sure as hell looked forward to the day he wouldn't have to.

"Nina, this is Zircon. He's an American paint." He stroked the white horse with brown markings. Zircon's

nearly solid brown face was interrupted by a long cres-
cent stripe below his right eye. Zircon shook his head,
a rumble that radiated all the way to his tail. He looked
lazily at Alex, tongue hanging out of the right side of
his mouth. "He's solid and sweet as you can tell. I trust
him with a second rider, but we'll keep it short for him
and for you. Are you ready?" Alex touched Zircon's
tongue and the horse came to full attention, tongue
back in the cheek.

Alex waited for her verdict. She glanced at her son,
clearly in his element, atop a horse. And sure enough,
Amie sat with her back against a tree, sketch pad in
hand.

Alex gripped Nina's elbow. "He's fine. Happy. He'll
be busy for the next hour on a scripted walk to the creek
and back. What about you?"

"Yes, let's do this before I lose my nerve." She
pressed her hand to the horse's body and slid her foot
into Alex's linked fingers.

She was tense and not particularly pliable, but he'd
helped worse. He hefted her up and secured her, quickly
mounting up behind her.

Zircon stood steady. Not a move. "Good boy," he
praised softly before sliding his arms around Nina, his
cheek against her hair. "How are you doing?"

"You have experience if this horse freaks out.
Right?"

"Of course." He breathed in the berry smell of her
shampoo as he clicked for the horse to start forward

"Okay, good." She grabbed the pommel and horn
fast. "You know there are a half dozen women around
here who are green with envy—and not afraid of
horses."

"Where? I don't see anyone but you." He slid a palm to her stomach and urged her to lean into the circle of his arms. "You still aren't relaxing. Why don't you grab a chunk of mane with one of your hands? It'll help you connect to Zircon and you'll gain some more balance."

"Truthfully?" she said through her teeth. "I'm trying to figure out why you're doing this, since you left last night when I made it clear you could stay."

Her right hand moved toward Zircon's mane. She twined her fingers around the locks of bay-and-white mane, her breathing easing ever so slightly.

"You did." He rested his chin on her head, looking out at the grassy stretch of earth, the creek, the trees that had lived here longer than he had. Zircon walked on calmly, responding to the slight pressure in Alex's legs. He started to angle the horse toward the open field. Toward where he and Nina could talk. He was torn between this woman and his obligation to this land. "And there will come a day when I take you up on that."

"But not last night." Her back went starchy stiff against his chest.

"There's a difference between thinking you're ready to take a step and actually being ready." Arm wrapped around her, he urged her closer.

The press of her bottom against him was sweet torture. The roll of the horse's steps moved Nina's body against him until he throbbed with arousal. A low growl slipped between his clenched teeth.

She laughed softly. "Serves you right."

"Well, damn. I think I irked your feelings. Sorry about that." He chuckled softly. His arm slid up just under her breasts. "I guess we'll have to…talk and get to know each other better."

She tipped her head, her expression quizzical. "Talking would be good. Tell me more about what it was like growing up here."

"Well, my grandmother believed we needed to learn every inch of the farm firsthand." He guided the horse around a fallen tree and into an open field of bluebonnets. Zircon's ears flicked back and forth. "We shadowed the staff. Sometimes it was fun, sometimes not so much. She said she didn't want any spoiled trust fund babies taking over the family business."

"Good for her."

He nudged Zircon to the left past a fat oak, birds flapping from the trees up into the clear Texas sky. "One summer she got us all chickens and we learned to start a chicken coop."

"Seriously?" She relaxed against him, laughing.

"To this day we call that 'the Summer of Eggs.' We had to collect them and learned how to cook the eggs as well—scrambled, fried, then graduating to omelets and quiche."

"I like that your grandmother had you boys learn, as well."

Did she know that she'd loosened her grip on the horn, and one hand had slid to rest on her thigh? He didn't intend to point that out. Her shoulders and body started to move with Zircon's gait and not against it. Nina was a natural when fear wasn't her main focus.

"She and my grandfather built this business from the ground up." As the words rolled from his tongue, he realized his reason for bringing her here. It wasn't about riding a horse. It was about hoping she would understand his motives. Hoping that she would be able to forgive him for holding back part of his reason for seeking her out. "The ranch is actually Gran's. My grandfather was the jeweler/craftsman. Together they blended that dream into an empire." Alex's neck kinked with nerves as he considered how far to take this conversation.

"That's lovely, seeing their differences as strengths to be blended."

"You said your husband grew up pampered."

"Did I?"

"I believe so. You mentioned his wealthy parents and their need to control." He swallowed hard before venturing into that damn dangerous territory. "Would that be the Lowerys of Lowery Resorts?"

She glanced back in surprise. "Yes, actually they are. Cody too, since he inherited his father's portion of the holdings."

Alex forced his hands to stay loose on the reins. "And you're the executor or are his grandparents?"

"I am, and God," she sighed, sagging back into a slump, "the weight of that worries on me. The doctors still don't know exactly what the autism means for his future. Will he be able to support himself? Live on his own? I don't know the answers, so I have to be very careful with that money. He could have to live off the investments for the rest of his life."

Her words hammered at Alex with a reality he hadn't considered until now. He'd been so busy thinking about what was best for his grandmother and the ranch, he hadn't given a thought to worrying about that four-year-old boy. This wasn't about the McNairs versus the Lowerys. This involved a sick old woman and a special-needs child who might never be able to support himself. That truth sliced clean through him.

They were well beyond the bluebonnet field and

walking through a rocky, unstable area. Zircon's ears were pinned back. Guilt weighted Alex's shoulders down and dimmed the beauty of the day. So much so that he lost track of the path in the land he knew as well as his own hand.

So much so that he didn't see the arc of the rattle-snake between the horse's hooves until it was too late.

Seven

Nina's heart leaped to her throat.

She felt the horse coil beneath her, almost mimicking the motion of the rattlesnake. Zircon's muscles exploded forward and he reared back. Ears pinned flat against his head, the paint pawed the air. Alex banded one arm around her to hold her secure and the other held the reins. He said something, some kind of command to Zircon, but she could only hear the roaring in her ears and the hammering of her heart as the world tilted backward.

She was going to die. Fall off the horse. Break her neck. Make her son an orphan. She'd stepped outside her comfort zone and would pay the price. A scream welled in her throat. She squeezed her eyes closed to fight vertigo, every muscle in her body tensing. She grabbed a fistful of mane, holding so tightly that her knuckles were bone white.

Zircon's hooves slammed down again, jarring her teeth, pushing her forward and off balance. She tried to stabilize her body weight on Zircon's neck but barely caught her breath before the horse bolted forward. She slammed back against the hard wall of Alex's chest, knocking the air from her lungs.

"Alex!" she choked out.

"Stay calm," his voice rumbled against her ear. "Hold tight and remember to breathe."

Faster and faster, the horse galloped along the path, then off. Zircon's gait was hurried, erratic. The horse was hardly running in a straight line and his ears were still pinned in fright. Earth and dirt flew past her vision. They raced through an open field, toward a creek. The wind whipped through her hair, but she hadn't been tossed off. She wasn't dead from a broken neck.

Yet.

Alex had her locked firmly against his chest, and her heartbeat raced as fast as the horse. "It's okay, Nina. I've got this. You're all right. Zircon will run himself out. We just need to stay seated."

She heard him and slowly began to believe him. Her nerves battled with a long-buried urge to enjoy the ride and ignore the risks. Just live on the edge. Which was exactly what they were about to do as Zircon readied to cross the creek. The horse pushed off the thin creek's bank. Instinctively Nina shifted her hands up the horse's neck, grabbing its mane and leaning forward into the jump.

Zircon went flying over the creek and landed smoothly on the other side. Had she squealed or screamed again? She didn't know, but the world was sparkling. This felt like flying.

The drumming of the hooves reverberated through her as Zircon nimbly galloped around fat oak trees. They approached another clearing. Alex gathered the reins and pulled the horse's head to the right. Zircon's head turned sharply and his legs followed. Nina watched the horse's nervous eyes soften. Alex kept the horse turning to the right. The circle became smaller and smaller. Bit by bit, the horse slowed. Then stopped, snorting and pawing at the ground.

Alex slid from the saddle and lifted her off, setting her quickly on the grass before kneeling beside his horse. His hands skimmed along the front legs, left and right.

Nina covered her mouth. How could she have forgotten about the snake so quickly? "Is he okay? Was Zircon bitten?"

Alex shook his head. "It doesn't appear so, thank God. The rattler just spooked him." He glanced over his shoulder. "Are you all right?"

"I'm fine, only a little surprised. And very grateful no one was injured, especially Zircon." She reached out tentatively and patted the horse's neck, the satiny coat soothing to the touch. Frothy sweat pooled beyond the horse's ears and around the bit.

Rising, Alex stood beside her again, stroking her cheek. "I'm so damn sorry that he went out of control so fast."

"You kept us all safe. And truth be told, once I got past the initial startle, I actually enjoyed the ride. I didn't expect to feel like that."

"Like what?" He stepped closer, his hand drawing her nearer.

"My skin tingled all over," she said with only a sliver of space between them.

He smiled, the corners of his eyes crinkling. "You're a horsewoman after all."

Laughing softly, she angled closer, her nerves igniting at the simple brush of her breasts again his chest. "A horsewoman? That's taking things a little far based on one ride."

He tapped his temple. "Trust me. I have a sense for things like this."

"Perhaps next time we ride we can take things a little slower and see how it goes."

"You're willing to ride again?" he asked with clear undertones.

"Absolutely I am." Her body damn near ignited with thoughts of last night, of taking things further. "In fact, I'm looking forward to it."

"You're going to be sore after today's experience." His hands slid down her back, lower, pressing her hips to his.

"Probably. Where's your masseuse?"

"I was thinking of something else to relieve tension later tonight, if you're game."

While she wanted to be with him, she was confused after his departure the evening before. Things were moving so fast, and she was the one who'd wanted that, wanted a fling, but she needed to understand *his* intent better. She needed to make sure they were on the same page. "About last night—"

"Things moved fast, I get that."

"They did, and I have to confess I'm not used to that. So maybe I sent some mixed signals. I was married, but my life has been focused solely on my son since then.

This week has been…different. I guess what I'm trying to say is that I didn't want you to leave," she admitted. Since she was living on the edge today, she might as well go for broke.

"I didn't want to go."

Finally she asked the question that had plagued her through a very sleepless night. "Then why did you?"

He tugged his hat off—how had that stayed on through the crazy ride?—and thrust a hand through his hair. "It's difficult to explain, other than to say this week doesn't seem like long enough."

"But it's all we have." She hadn't considered more. Even the thought of being vulnerable in yet another relationship made her feel as if the world had tilted again. She backed away from him. "I have a life and a home in San Antonio."

Although that life felt mighty far away at the moment.

He slammed his hat back on his head. "You're right. Forget I said anything. Let's live in the moment."

The tension in her chest eased and she leaned against him. "One day at a time. I like that."

She arched up on her toes to kiss him, enjoying the way their mouths met with familiarity, fitting just so. His arms slid around her, his hands warm and strong palming low on her waist. Her breasts pressed to the hard wall of his chest, and her mind filled with memories of the night before, of his touch, his intuition about just how to set her on fire.

Her senses, still so alive from their mad dash, burned all the hotter. "Alex…"

"Nina…" he whispered in her ear, his beard stubble rasping against her cheek. "I want you here, now, but we're too close to the camp and there are other riders out."

She gasped, jerking away. "Oh my God, the kids are out riding." She pressed a hand to her forehead. "How could I have forgotten?"

"But we have a date for later." He pulled her back into his arms and traced her bottom lip. "I told you, I have a plan for reducing tension. Trust me?"

God, how she wanted to. "I'll see you tonight after Cody goes to sleep."

Eight hours later, Alex held his hands over Nina's eyes, hoping she would enjoy his idea for their evening together. He'd brought dinner to her and Cody first, enjoying the chance to get to know her son better. They'd eaten barbecue and played with toy horses Alex had brought as a gift until Amie arrived to babysit again.

Nina had smiled more broadly over his present to her son than she had over the chocolate strawberries he'd brought for their dessert. He couldn't help being drawn to her devotion to the boy after the way his own parents had ignored their children except for when he and Amie were trotted out to perform.

He wasn't going to have many more opportunities to be alone with Nina with his cousin's wedding right around the corner. Even the small family service would still take up all their time over the weekend, relatives pouring in left and right. Not to mention the bachelor party and rehearsal dinner.

Thoughts of family were the last kind Alex wanted right now.

Nina had made it clear she only wanted a week together, and that was likely all they would have once she knew how badly his grandmother wanted her son's shares in the McNair Corporation. He'd considered just offering an exorbitant amount of money for them, but their own finances were tangled up in investments. Selling them off to liquidate cash would be unwise fiscally, and unfair to their own investors. He was caught in a loop of damned if he did and damned if he didn't.

So he did the only thing he knew to do. Focus on letting Cody have the best camp experience possible. Get to know the child better.

And pamper Nina for whatever time they had together.

She clasped his wrists. "Where are we going?"

"Almost there," he said, stopping in front of the sauna attached to the family's private pool house. "Are you ready for more relaxation?"

"I think so."

He lowered his hands and opened the door to the small cedar room. A tray waited with water bottles beside a stack of fat towels.

Everything had been prepared as he'd ordered. "This is our family's private sauna. No one will bother us here. I thought you might be sore after being jostled around on Zircon. Your choice, though, if you'd rather not."

She turned in his arms to face him, smiling. So easy to please and so at home in the places he loved best. She fit in here seamlessly. "I think it's a fabulous idea." The emerald green of her gauzy blouse made her eyes sparkle. "You have a knack for knowing just what I need. But I'm curious, what do *you* need?"

Her provocative question hung in the air between them.

His eyes fell to the deep V of her shirt, which had

been drawing his gaze all night long. A long lock of hair had slipped loose, the curl pooling just above her breast as if it were providing a path for his touch. "I need you, Nina. Just you."

He walked her into the sauna, the temperature still moderate. For now. His temperature? Definitely notching higher the longer he looked at her.

She stroked along his shoulders, her touch making his skin tighten everywhere. "I've got to know, though, are you going to walk out on me again?"

"Not unless you ask me to." He kicked the door closed, sealing them inside the low-lit cubicle.

For good measure, he went back and locked it.

"Doubtful." She arched up on her toes to nip his bottom lip. "I'm warming it up fast." She winked at him. "I think we're both way too overdressed for this sauna idea of yours."

"I'd like to help you with that." An understatement.

She lifted her arms in an unspoken invitation for him to peel off her loose blouse. He swept up the gauzy fabric and tossed it aside on the bench, his eyes never leaving all the creamy pale skin he was unveiling.

His breath caught in his throat at the sight of her breasts in white lace. High, luscious curves. "You look every bit as beautiful as you felt last night."

He'd been reliving those moments in his head all day long. Even more, he'd been looking forward to making even more memories with her tonight.

Her fingers walked down his shirt. "You don't have to shower me with compliments."

"I want to…if I spoke as many languages as you do—" he tugged the zipper on her jeans, down, down, revealing white bikini panties "—then I could tell you again and again how beautiful you are, how much I want you, how often thoughts of you distract me at work."

"You have quite a way with words no matter what language you're speaking."

She worked free the buttons on his plaid shirt, one at a time, her knuckles grazing his skin and tempting him to toss aside restraint. Then her cool hand slid inside his jeans and restraint was absolutely the last thing on his mind. She curved her hand around his throbbing erection and he bit back a groan as she stroked.

Growling low in his throat, he eased her down to sit on the bench and knelt in front of her, tugging her boots off one, then the other. Her new leather boots were starting to have a worn-in look, as though she belonged here. In his house. In his arms.

She flowed forward, sweeping aside his loose shirt, then leaned back again, eyes roving his chest with obvious appreciation. Kicking aside his own boots, he tugged his wallet from his pocket and pulled out two condoms, then placed them on the bench.

Her pupils widened with desire.

He peeled off his socks and shucked his well-worn jeans before standing naked in front of her. Her smoky smile steamed over him hotter than the sauna. She trailed her fingers down his chest, down his stomach, gently brushing his erection. He throbbed in response, her touch sweet torture. She trailed her hand lower down his thigh, muscles contracting at her caress. Urgency pumped through his veins.

Lifting her hand, he pressed a kiss to the inside of her wrist, feeling the pulse beat hard against his lips. Then he stepped back to turn up the heat on the sauna, coils heating the stones, a water fountain trickling down to send bursts of steam. Bottles of oils lined a rack before the fountain—eucalyptus, citrus, birch and peppermint.

Choosing eucalyptus, he drizzled oil over the stones before turning back to her. Anticipation curled through him. Finally he had her all to himself, naked, alone, his for the taking. They'd been building to this moment since the first time he saw her. And in spite of all the reasons they didn't stand a chance in hell at having more, he couldn't stop wanting her.

He reached to the stack of fluffy white towels in the corner and spread two out on the bench. He reclined her back, using an extra towel to make a pillow. He stretched out over her. Flesh to flesh. His eyes slid closed for a moment.

Then thoughts gave way to sensations. The scent of her berry shampoo. The creamy softness of her neck when he pressed his lips to her pulse. She hooked her leg around his, her foot sliding up and down the back of his calf. He finally gave in to the temptation to taste her, along her shoulder, nudging aside a bra strap, then the other, baring her breasts to his mouth, his touch. She arched up with a husky moan and he reached underneath her to unhook her bra and toss it aside.

Sweat beaded along her skin, glistening. Perspiration streaked down her neck, then between her breasts. One droplet held on the tip of her nipple. He dipped his head and flicked his tongue, catching the droplet and circling, laving. Her head fell back and a moan floated from her lips.

Nina nibbled his earlobe. "No more waiting." She passed him a condom. "We can go slow after. And from the count of what you pulled from your pocket, you're intending there to be an after."

"At least that much," he vowed. "And whatever else you want."

"Perfect," she purred, trailing her fingers down his arms and guiding his hands to hurry up.

He tore open the wrapper, and her hands covered his as she helped him sheathe himself. She hitched her leg higher, hooked on his hip, bringing her moist heat closer. His forehead fell to rest against hers as he pushed inside her. Her breath came faster and faster, flowing over him. He thrust deeper, deeper still and her hips rolled against his, inviting him to continue. He thrust and she moved with him, synching into a perfect, driving rhythm that had him clenching his teeth to hold back. She'd said they could go slow next time—and there would be a next time—but he wasn't finishing now until he'd satisfied her.

The steam billowed off the rocks, filling the small room, air heavy with the scent of eucalyptus and sex. Perspiration gathered on his forehead, a droplet sliding off to hit the towel under her. Their slick bodies moved against each other, his pulse hammering in his ears. He swept her hair from her face, capturing her mouth and soaking in the feel of Nina.

Just Nina.

He braced himself on one elbow to keep his weight off her and slide his other hand between them, caressing her breasts and lower. He stroked the slick bud, circling and teasing, her purrs of pleasure urging him to continue. Just when he thought he couldn't hold out any longer, her gasps came faster and faster. Her fingernails dug into his back, scratching a light but insistent path as her head flung back. She cried out in pleasure, her orgasm pulsing around him, clasping him tighter and hurtling him over the edge into his own release.

His arm gave way and he lay fully on top of her, thrusting through the final wave of ecstasy. His breaths shuddering through him, he buried his face in her neck and rolled to his side, holding her close. Already hungry for the next time and wondering how long he could keep her here and the world at bay.

Because more than ever, he was certain that a week with Nina would never be enough.

Tucked to Alex's side, Nina trailed her fingers along his muscular arm, the scent of eucalyptus steaming through the sauna. She was already nearly halfway done with the weeklong camp. Then she would have to walk away from the Hidden Gem—from Alex.

This place was like a fairy-tale getaway, a Brigadoon, too good to be true and destined to disappear when she left. Alex made her want things she'd decided were not meant to be. Scariest of all, he made her want to risk her heart again and she didn't know if she could take another betrayal.

A sobering thought at a time she was determined to live in the moment.

She slid her hand down to link fingers with Alex. "We should get dressed soon and head back. Your sister must be getting sick of babysitting Cody."

"No hurry." He kissed their clasped hands. "Amie adores Cody and she owes me."

"For what?" she asked, hungry to know more about him.

A smile tugged at his mouth. "When we were seventeen, she didn't want to win the Miss Honey Bee

Pageant—and given how many pageants she'd won in the past, it wasn't arrogant of her to assume she would run away with that crown. But back to that time. She didn't want to go because the Honey Bee Queen had to attend the county fair and she wouldn't be able to attend homecoming."

Nina drew circles on his chest, perspiration clinging to their skin. "What did you do?"

"Nothing awful. We went boating the day before the competition, and we stayed out so long we got sunburned. I told Mom the engine stalled. Amie looked like a lobster. Mom made her compete anyway. Just slathered her in more makeup. Amie got second runner-up."

"Seriously?" The story was funny and sad all at once.

"Scout's honor." He held up his fingers. "I offered to cut her hair, but she nixed that, so we opted for the sunburn instead. I was never sure if she opted out of the haircut idea out of vanity or because Mom would have just bought a wig."

"People call you quiet and reserved, but you're really quite funny."

"I guess I have my moments." He kissed the tip of her nose, then picked up a hand towel and gently—methodically—wiped the sweat from her body. "So I take it you approve of the sauna?"

"Very much. Is there anything Hidden Gem doesn't have? Seriously, sauna, massage therapist, airplane, catered dinners, even that well-stocked gift shop, so there's no need to leave for anything. This is like nirvana."

His smile faded. "There are others who would say this place should be modernized."

"In what way? There's every convenience possible."

She couldn't imagine anywhere more restful or entertaining.

"There are no theme parks or casinos. A high-rise could fit a lot more people into the space, make more money, attract big acts to perform."

The mention of high-rise tourism made her think of her in-laws, the last people she wanted intruding on this moment. "You can't possibly agree with that. It would take away the authenticity and the charm."

"It's good to hear you say that."

The fierce intensity of his kiss took her breath away and made her wonder about the reason for his sudden shift in mood.

She gripped his shoulders, questions filling her mind. But before she could ask, a cell phone rang, jarring her. Not her ring tone. His. Sounding from his jeans on the floor.

He murmured against her mouth, "Ignore it."

Oh, how she wanted to. "It could be your sister. Cody might need me."

"You're right. Of course, we can't ignore it. I should have thought of that too."

Rolling from her, he sat on the edge of the bench and scooped his jeans from the floor. Nina stroked his broad back and traced the light scratches she'd left along his shoulder blades.

He answered the cell phone. "Amie, is something wrong with Cody?"

Alex clicked on the speakerphone and Nina sat up beside him, concern and maternal guilt chilling her warmed flesh.

"No." His sister's voice was tight with nerves. "Not at all. He's fast asleep."

Nina relaxed against him, resting her cheek on his shoulder, her hand on his chest.

"Glad to hear it," Alex said, sliding an arm around Nina. "Then what's up?"

"Prepare yourself," she said with a heavy sigh. "Mom and Dad are returning home from their trip a day early. They've already landed in Fort Worth but didn't want to make the drive out to the ranch tonight. They'll be here first thing in the morning."

His jaw tight, he turned off the speakerphone and brought the receiver to his ear. "We'll need to band together to keep things calm for Gran…"

Curiosity nipped. He'd mentioned issues with his parents, but his reaction seemed…strong. It was only a day early. Surely that wasn't a big deal. But the muscles bunching along Alex's back told her otherwise.

Nina pulled a towel from the stack and wrapped it around herself. But there was no escaping the sensation that her Brigadoon was fading.

Eight

Alex hadn't eaten breakfast yet and he already had indigestion.

He paced restlessly around the family lanai, brunch prepared, he and his sister waiting with Gran for their parents' arrival. The morning sun steamed droplets of water off the lawn from the sprinkler system. Making love with Nina had been everything he expected and more. He'd always been such a methodical man. But the instantaneous combustion between him and Nina rocked him back on his boot heels. And before he could get his bearings, his parents opted to put in an early appearance.

His mother had a way of being less than pleasant to the women he dated, which was strange, since Bayleigh McNair wasn't what anyone would call an overly adoring parent. Regardless, he didn't want Nina subjected to that, especially not now while they were still finding their way around whatever it was they had going.

A persistent crick pinched at his neck. He should have been better prepared for his parents' arrival and how he would handle them meeting Nina. They'd been due in tomorrow anyway, but he'd been taking things one day at a time this week. That sort of impulsive living wasn't his style.

Gran reclined in a patio lounger sipping tea, her breakfast untouched on the small table beside her. His indomitable grandmother was so frail she looked as if a puff of wind would whisk her away. He needed to make sure this breakfast—the whole wedding weekend—went smoothly. No drama. This was his family and they were at their best for his grandmother.

Stone's mother would be a wild card. Her behavior was always hit or miss depending on if she was using drugs or fresh out of rehab. Thus far she'd been clean for six months. If she followed past patterns, the fall was due any day now.

Maybe it wasn't fair of him to expect Nina to put up with his family's volatile dynamics, especially since weddings always multiplied drama. Except after last night with Nina, he couldn't bring himself to waste even a minute of the remaining week. He needed to persuade her they had something special—because he was going to have to come clean with her about the stocks soon.

Why couldn't Nina have come to one of the other camp sessions? Although she wouldn't be here at all if his grandmother hadn't orchestrated Nina's arrival. He couldn't imagine never having met her. So whatever it took, he would get through these next few days and maintain the peace for his grandmother.

And figure out a way to keep seeing Nina after the camp ended.

First, he had to get through welcoming his parents. They kept a suite here as well but were rarely in attendance. They preferred penthouse hotels around the world.

A limousine cruised up the oak-shaded entry road, turning toward the private drive and stopping near the lanai. While the others drank mimosas, Amie drained her simple orange juice and refilled the crystal flute. Stone and Johanna—lucky ducks—had bowed out of breakfast claiming a meeting with the caterer.

Clouds drifted over the sun as the chauffeur opened the door and Alex's mother stepped out in a flourish. Bayleigh McNair believed in making an entrance.

His mother breezed up the stairs. Collagen-puffy lips and cheek implants had changed her appearance until she looked like a distant relative of herself. Not his mother yet eerily familiar.

Alex stepped beside Gran's chair, wishing his presence alone could keep her safe and make her well. Her hand trembling, Gran set aside her teacup with a slight rattle of china, watching her grandchildren protectively. Alex patted her shoulder.

His father stepped alongside his wife, wearing a crisp suit as if he'd dressed for work. Ironic as hell, since Garnet McNair carried an in-name-only title with the company, some kind of director of overseas relations. Which just meant he could pretend he worked as he traveled the world. Mariah only requested he wine and dine possible contacts and charm them. On the company credit card of course. His parents were masters at wringing money out of Gran.

She was a savvy businesswoman, so Alex was certain she knew her son's game. And equally certain it had to break her heart, given how hard she and her husband had worked to build the family business. It was no wonder she felt the need to put her grandchildren through tests before handing over her empire.

Bayleigh swept up the lanai stairs—perfect. There was no other word to describe his mother. Not a hair out of place. Makeup fresh, a bit thicker each year. And always, always, she stayed almost skeletally thin—thanks to hours on the treadmill and a diet of cottage cheese and coffee. What the treadmill couldn't fix, she took care of with liposuction and tummy tucks. The rest of her was beige—blond hair, tanned skin, and off-white or brown clothes depending on the time of year.

He often wondered how his mom managed to keep those white outfits clean with kids around. Gran was always dusty and never minded if they'd just eaten chocolate ice cream when they gave her a hug.

Gran and Nina had a lot in common.

Bayleigh's heels clicked across the tile as she briefly hugged each of her children, leaving a fog of perfume in her wake. She dabbed her eyes with a tissue as she swooped down on her mother-in-law. "Mother McNair, how are you feeling?" She kissed Gran's cheek and then sat in a chair next to her. "I'm just so glad you're still with us for the wedding."

"No need to start digging my grave yet." Gran didn't show any irritation, only a sardonic smile of resolution. "I've got some life left in me yet."

Garnet knelt beside his mom. "Mother, please, let's not talk about unpleasantries." He took her hand in his. "I'm glad to see you looking so well, enjoying the sunshine." She glanced up at the sky. "Well, what little bit is peeking around the clouds."

Her smile turned nostalgic. "You look so much like your father, Garnet. I miss him every day even after all these years."

Although her son hadn't inherited much in the way of work ethic from his mother or father, Alex had heard his grandmother blame herself for pampering her children. He didn't agree. Not completely. She might have been indulgent in those days, but his father and aunt should have taken responsibility for their own lives. Alex passed his mother a cup of black coffee.

Bayleigh cradled the cup and inhaled the scent as if filling up on the smell alone. "We came early to help, since the bride doesn't have a mother of her own. And Mother Mariah is so very ill. Of course we all know Stone's mother can't be trusted to show up sober. So I thought I should come a day early to make sure all is in order."

Bayleigh sipped her coffee.

Garnet stayed silent, not surprising, and filled a plate with quiche and fruit. The sound of crunching footsteps sounded just before Stone jogged into sight from around the corner of the house.

Stone took the steps two at a time up to the lanai. "Sorry I'm late. Johanna is still working out details with the caterer. She'll be here when she's through. Thank you for coming, Aunt Bayleigh, Uncle Garnet." He swept his hat off and kissed his grandmother's cheek before loading up a plate of quiche, two danishes and melon slices. "I'm starving. Glad y'all saved me some food."

Amie sipped her crystal flute of orange juice. "Good

thing you got here before Aunt Bayleigh drank all the coffee."

Bayleigh scowled. "Amie, must you be unpleasant?"

"Always," his sister answered without hesitation. "Mother, Johanna and Stone are adults. I believe they can manage to plan a small wedding on their own."

Bayleigh set her china cup aside. "Well, I imagine if they're not set on impressing anyone, that's just fine."

Amie's eyes narrowed. "Then Johanna and Stone will exceed your expectations."

Garnet cleared his throat and slid a hand along his wife's back.

"Forgive me, Amie." Bayleigh patted her daughter's knee before picking up her cup again. "I'm just getting antsy to plan a wedding for one of my children, but neither one of them shows signs of settling down. I hope you don't wait too long, daughter dear. Your biological clock is ticking."

"Mother, you surprise me. I thought you were concerned about me wrecking my figure." Amie's barb was unmistakable and there was no stopping the mother/daughter battle once it started rolling.

Bayleigh eyed her daughter over her coffee. "Amethyst, your pageant days are long past."

Alex's twin shot blue fire from her eyes at her mother. "Maybe I should look into a sperm donor."

Their father's mouth twitched, but he didn't look up from eating his food while reading his morning news on his tablet. "Don't rile your mother. The weekend's going to be long enough as it is."

Stone set down his fork long enough to say, "Alex has been seeing a single mother here with her son at HorsePower Cowkid Camp."

Alex grasped the change of subject with both hands, grateful to steer the conversation onto relatively safer ground—ground that wouldn't upset Gran. "Hey, cousin, that's no way to treat the man planning your bachelor party."

Not that he was really all that stoked about the party, which surprised the hell out of him. All he really wanted was to find Nina and Cody.

Amie laughed softly. "She would have figured it out soon enough anyway when you showed up at the rehearsal dinner with your redheaded bombshell in tow."

Alex shot his twin a glare. "You are not helping, Amie."

"A redhead." Bayleigh winced. "Well, if you have ginger children we can always fix that with a quick trip to the hair salon. Tell me more about her."

Alex didn't like the gleam in his mother's eyes one bit. Protective urges filled him. "Are those storm clouds overhead? Maybe we should move brunch inside."

His mother patted her hair. "Not even the threat of drenching will distract me from finding out more about this woman. You didn't answer my question, son."

"Mother." Alex leaned forward. "Her name is Nina and you *will* retract your claws and leave her alone. Don't pretend you don't know what I'm talking about. No interfering in my personal life. Period."

"Of course." Bayleigh pressed a hand to her chest with overplayed innocence. "I just want grandchildren. I dream of the days I can buy little smocked dresses or tiny cowboy boots."

"That subject is also off-limits," Alex said firmly. "As is your intent to choose their mother. I mean it."

His father looked up from his iPad for the first time. "This week's going to be interesting."

His grandmother's keen blue eyes took in all, and he hated that she'd witnessed the sparring, even if it was par for the course with their family gatherings. Alex wondered if maybe there was more to Gran's test than he'd originally thought. Could this be some sort of reverse psychology? Maybe she didn't want the stocks? Or had plans for another way to get them?

Could she be testing his honor to make sure none of his father's screwed-up values were running through him?

Damn, that stung.

He'd always been the different one, not a part of Diamonds in the Rough. But he'd thought his grandmother respected how he'd channeled his own work ethic and values into turning Hidden Gem into an asset to the empire and a tribute to their land.

Hell, he didn't know what to think right now. He just wanted to get this breakfast over with so he could spend time with Nina.

Rain pattered on the barn roof, and Nina cradled a cup of coffee with rich cream and two spoons of sugar. Sitting at a rustic picnic table in the café corner area, she'd been eating a pastry while watching her son. The children were scattered throughout the stalls that had been set up petting-zoo style. Each kid had been partnered with his or her choice of a pony, donkey, dog, chickens or even a rabbit to brush, hold or pet. Four stalls down, Cody ran a bristly brush along a miniature donkey, a teacher close at his side, instructing.

Nina wasn't needed now. Her son was enjoying independent play. She should be happy and go back to her cabin to read or nap with the rain soothing her to sleep. She'd certainly gotten very little sleep last night. She set down her coffee with a heavy sigh.

Her stomach had been in knots all day over the influx of McNairs and what that did—or didn't—mean in regards to her relationship with Alex. Whether making love or just talking, she'd enjoyed being alone with him. Solitude would be all but impossible now and she felt that she'd been robbed of her last few days left for a fling.

Except if it was just a fling, she shouldn't be this upset.

Thunder rolled outside, and Nina looked at her son quickly to make sure he wasn't upset. Some of the other children covered their ears, one squealed, but Cody was lost in the rhythmic stroking of the donkey's coat.

The barn door opened with a swirl of damp wind, and Alex ducked inside, closing the door quickly. He shook the rain off his hat, scanning the cavernous space. His eyes found hers in an instant and he smiled, his gaze steaming over her in a way that said he was thinking of last night too. She started to stand, but he waved for her to stay seated as he walked past her to her son.

Alex nodded to the teacher and let her angle away before taking the teacher's place beside Cody. Nina threw away her coffee and padded over silently, curious about what he intended to say.

And yes, eager to be near him.

Alex picked up a second brush, smoothing it over the donkey too. "I wasn't much of a talker either when I was younger," he said softly. "I know it's not quite the same as what's going on in your mind. But I wanted to let you know I understand that even when a person is quiet, he still hears. That's part of what I enjoy most about the animals here, in the quiet with them, it's easier to hear."

"Yes." Cody's little hand smoothed steadily. "My mommy broughted me here."

"You have a smart mommy. But I don't know you as well as your mom does. So, while I know you're listening, I can only guess what you would be interested in hearing. For all I know, I could be boring you talking about fishing when maybe you prefer soccer. It's okay for you to be quiet, but I would appreciate a hint on what you would like to talk about."

Cody set aside the brush and stroked the donkey's neck. "Donkey's nice."

"You like activities with horses, ponies, donkeys? You're okay with me talking about them?"

"Uh-huh." He kept rubbing the donkey without looking away.

"Okay, then. My cousin Stone has a quarter horse named Copper. My sister, Amie, has an Arabian named Crystal." He listed them in a way that Nina realized gave Cody a connection to each McNair. Since Cody loved the animals, he would have positive associations with the person. "My favorite is the Paint, named Zircon. My grandmother has this thing about naming every person and animal after a gemstone. She likes themes and patterns."

"I like patter-ins," Cody whispered, drawing the last word out so it had a third syllable.

"Okay, let's talk about the gem pattern names. People call me Alex, but my name is Alexandrite and my sister Amie is Amethyst. My grandmother even had dogs that had similar names."

"Dogs?" A spark lit in Cody's eyes and he tipped his head toward Alex. "Where are the dogs?"

"My grandmother is sick, so new families are taking care of three of the dogs. My cousin Stone has the fourth dog named Pearl, and my sister takes care of Gran's cats."

"Can I pet the doggy?"

Alex grinned. "How about puppies? Someone dropped a box of border collie mix puppies on our land a couple of weeks ago. They must have thought we would be a good home for them since one of our ranch hands has a border collie that works with him. Would you like to see the pups?"

Cody nodded quickly, eyes wide. "Uh-huh."

Nina's heart all but squeezed in two as Alex went out of his way to lead Cody to the pen of fuzzy border collie mix puppies tucked in the office. She stayed out of sight so as not to disrupt the moment. Two puppies played tug-of-war over a toy. Another flopped back over belly catching a ball, ears flopping. Alex showed her son different ways to play gently with the small fluff balls. Cody had such little time with male role models.

Alex made her ache and yearn for things she'd thought she could never have again. The ranch was well equipped for taking care of puppies and kittens who needed homes, and even helping struggling young moms and special-needs children, but she had to remember for her and for the puppies—Hidden Gem was a temporary stop. Only the McNairs stayed here. Like the puppies, Nina and Cody would be moving on to a different home and this place would be just a nostalgic memory.

An hour later, Nina took photos of her son riding a mechanical bull—with the bull set on a very slow speed to buck and turn. She could already envision one of these images reproduced onto a large canvas in her living room, surrounded by smaller photos from throughout this incredible week.

Would Alex be in any of those pictures? Could her heart take that kind of bittersweet reminder?

The rainstorm had ended a few minutes ago and since Cody was the last of the children to take a turn on the mechanical bull, the head camp counselor called out, "Line up, by your groups. Blue ponies here. Yellow ponies there. Green. And then red."

The children raced toward the door in a loose cluster, pent-up energy radiating off their little bodies. A girl in a wheelchair whizzed by, pumping the wheels faster and faster, pigtails flying.

Nina felt Alex's presence a second before he put his hand on her shoulder.

"Who are you sending the photos to?"

"A friend at home." She held up the cell phone. "Reed and I met at a support group for single parents with special-needs children."

"Reed?" His jaw flexed. "Should I be jealous of this guy?"

"No, we're just friends. Good friends who try to help each other, but we're only friends." She tucked away her phone before taking his hand, wishing she could do more. But anyone could walk in, and children were within eyesight. "I wouldn't have been with you this week if there was someone else."

"Good, I'm glad to hear that." His thumb slid around to stroke the inside of her wrist. "Did you get your turn on the mechanical bull?"

She blinked in surprise. "Um, no. That activity was just for the kids."

"I own it." He patted the saddle. "Do you want to try?"

"I'm not going to put on some *Urban Cowboy* sexy ride show for you."

He grinned, a roguish twinkle in his blue eyes. "I wasn't proposing anything of the sort—especially not with kids nearby. But even the mention is filling my mind with interesting ideas." He squeezed her hand. "For now, how about a regular slow ride?"

Somehow he made even that sound sensual. Irresistible. She approached the mechanical bull tentatively, touching the saddle.

Alex's hand fell to rest on her shoulder. "There are different speeds. We take this as slow as you want to go."

She glanced back at him. "Are we still talking about the bull?"

"Do you want us to talk about something else?"

Her stomach flipped and she looked away. "I guess I'm riding the bull."

"All right, then. Climb on. Grab hold and we'll start her slow."

"Okay, but no pictures." She stepped into the stirrup and swung her leg over, sitting, half sliding off the other side before righting herself with a laugh. "I never was much of one for carnival rides."

"Let me know if you want to stop." He turned the knob, setting the bull into a gentle rocking motion that started to turn.

"I tossed my cookies once on the Ferris wheel," she confessed as the bull circled.

"I know where the mop is."

"An almighty McNair mops floors?" she teased, trying not to think about the day they'd ridden the horse together.

He increased the speed. "Gran brought us up with down-home, work-ethic values. We had jobs on the farm as kids and teenagers, just like everyone else, and we had to start at the bottom, learning every stage of the operation."

She gripped tighter. "What did your parents have to say about that?"

"Not much as long as the big money kept flowing their way."

"Your father didn't work?" That seemed so atypical compared to what she'd seen from Alex working up a sweat on the ranch in addition to his desk work running the place.

"My father has an office. He makes business trips, but does he work? Not really. I guess Gran wanted to make doubly sure the grandkids turned out differently. And we did. Although we always thought Stone would run the company, he decided to run a nonprofit camp instead."

She read rumors of a new CEO outside the family being hired to run Diamonds in the Rough, but she hadn't paid more than passing attention. "That must have been a huge disappointment to your grandmother not to be able to pass along her legacy to her children."

"It was—and is. But she's happy about the camp. Who wouldn't be proud of this? It's amazing, innovative and rewarding. I just want her to be at peace in her final days." Shadows chased through his blue eyes.

"All that parents want is for their children to be happy and try their best."

His eyes met hers. "Not all parents."

"Are you saying your grandmother—"

"Not my grandmother. My parents." Looking down, he scuffed his boots through the dirt. "Let's talk about something else. Like how's that bull feeling? Ready to take him up a notch? If you can still talk, it's obviously not going fast enough."

She shook her head quickly. "I think it's time to stop."

He switched off the controls and the bull slowed, slowed and finally went still. Alex reached up to help her down. "I'm going to miss you tonight while I'm at the bachelor party."

She slid down the front of him, enjoying the feel of their bodies against each other, her mind firing with memories from the night before. "I thought men lived for those sorts of things."

"I would rather be with you tonight." His warm breath caressed her neck.

She pressed her cheek to his heart for just a moment, listening to the steady thud. "That's really sweet of you to say."

"My thoughts are far from sweet." He growled softly in her ear, "I'd love to see you after the party if it's not too late."

His words rang with an unmistakable promise and she didn't have the least inclination to say no.

Nine

Alex knew he was in trouble when he couldn't stop checking his watch for the end of the bachelor party. He wanted to spend the evening with Nina and Cody. But he owed Stone this traditional testosterone bash. Stone was more like a brother to him than a cousin, so for now, thoughts of Nina and her son needed to take a backseat.

The party was being held in a private lodge behind the Hidden Gem ranch house. Cigar smoke filled the room along with round poker tables. A buffet full of food and a bar stocked with the best alcohol and brews stayed stocked throughout the night. Country music piped through the sound system, a steel guitar still audible over raucous laughter, the clink of glasses and the whirr of a few electric card shufflers at work.

Garnet, Stone and Preston Armstrong, the new company CEO, sat with Alex at one table. Four more tables held longtime employees from the Diamonds in the Rough Jewelry and the Hidden Gem Ranch. Stone had insisted on the bachelor party being held the day before the rehearsal dinner, not wanting any of his friends to be nursing hangovers at his wedding.

Preston threw his cards down, gray eyes tired from concentration. "Fold. This is the lamest bachelor party ever."

Alex laughed, tossing turquoise and white chips into the middle of the table. The chips clinked and fell haphazardly in a pile. "You're just pissed because you're not winning."

"You could have a point there," Preston conceded, shoulders sagging.

Stone passed new cards to the remaining players. "My orders for the evening. Nothing but booze and cards."

"Not even a movie?"

Stone grinned devilishly. "Haven't you heard? I'm saving myself for marriage."

"Yeah, well, what about the rest of us?" Preston barked.

Stone shrugged, finishing his drink. He rattled the leftover ice in his glance. "Have your own bachelor party, and you get to make your own rules."

"Not going to happen," Preston insisted, palms up as he pushed back from the table. "While y'all finish this hand, I'll use the time to become reacquainted with the bar."

Garnet tossed in his hand. "I'm out too. Another drink sounds good."

Alex looked at the two pairs in his hand and slid a few more chips to the middle of the table. "I'm happy for you and Johanna." He paused to look at his cousin across the table. "I hope you know I mean that."

"That's good to hear," Stone answered, his voice hoarse with emotion. Stone's features flattened as he stared at the pile of chips, avoiding Alex's gaze. "You mean as much to me as any brother ever could."

"I'm sorry it even had to be said. She and I were too much alike to ever be a couple. Any feelings I thought I felt were more habit than anything else."

Because Alex knew now that anything he'd thought he felt for Johanna paled in comparison to what he felt for Nina.

"Well, loving a woman is rarely easy." Stone peeled his eyes up toward Alex.

Alex rubbed the cards in his hand. The plastic of the cards hummed, seeming to drown out all the other sounds of the bachelor party. "I'm learning that."

Stone set his cards facedown. "The mom with her son here at the camp?"

"Forget I said anything. And for God's sake, don't let anybody say anything more to my mother." Alex tipped back his drink. While it looked as though he had been slamming back vodka all night, his drinks had all been water. He wanted a clear head for later. He wanted to enjoy Nina. Their time together was short and he didn't need a single sense dulled. "This is about you tonight, cousin."

Stone pushed his cards into the middle. "Well, damn, then let's bail and go riding. You and me, like old times."

Now, that sounded a helluva lot more appealing than sitting here. Alex scraped his chair back, but had to ask, "Is it fair to leave Preston stuck with my father?"

"Preston's the boss now." Stone stood, his smile widening. "That's the beauty of having found my own path, cousin. Johanna and I answer only to ourselves and each other."

"Good point."

They clinked glasses, drained the contents and left the party. And Alex couldn't help thinking how damn important family was to him.

Even more important than the ranch? Or were they inextricable? Hell, if he knew the answer.

Stone and Alex hadn't been on a night ride in years. When they were kids, they used to steal away, ride deep into the night to get away from their respective parents. There was something calming in taking to the trails together, even if they didn't speak a helluva lot to each other.

Alex glanced over at his cousin. "Are you ready?"

Stone was preparing to mount Copper, his sorrel quarter horse.

"I bet you I can still whup your ass from here to the creek," Stone said, steadying himself on Copper. He tightened the reins, creating a curved arch in Copper's neck. The horse was sheer power.

The quarter horse danced with anticipation, sock-covered legs shifting from side to side, issuing a challenge.

"I doubt that. You're rusty these days." Alex absently stroked Zircon's neck. Zircon turned his head to nuzzle Alex's knee.

"It is my bachelor party, you know," Stone said dryly.

Alex smiled lazily. "All right. On my mark, though."

Stone nodded, urging Copper next to Zircon.

"One. Two. Three. Go."

Zircon leaped forward, seeming to read Alex's thoughts. That was what had always made horses easy for him. The nonverbal communication. The unexplainable connection.

From the corner of his vision, he could see the glint of Copper's tack. Stone was a stride ahead of him. Collecting his reins, Alex opened up Zircon's pace.

Zircon's ears pinned back as the horse surged forward. Finally Alex gained on his cousin as they drew closer to the creek. Memories of riding with Nina, of kissing her out here in the open on McNair land filled him. He had to see her tonight. No matter how late. Even if just to slide into bed with her and listen to her sleep.

The sensation of the gallop reverberated through Alex's bones. Shaking his thigh. Wait. The buzz wasn't from the connection of hooves and ground. It was his cell phone vibrating. *Damn.*

"Stone," he called out. "Hold on. Someone's calling."

As Alex slowed Zircon to a walk, the familiar ringtone replaced the hammering of hooves. Amie's ringtone. Amie who never called this late at night unless it was important. Or if there was trouble.

Hands shaking, Alex retrieved the phone from his pants. Stone slowed Copper, his face knotting with concern.

Alex took a deep breath. "Hello?"

Amie's voice pierced through the receiver. "It's Gran. She's got a horrible headache and the nurse is concerned. You know Gran never complains. We have to take her to the emergency room. It's faster than calling an ambulance. Please, you have to get here. Now."

"Stone and I will be right there." Alex looked at his cousin. "We've got to get to Gran. Something's wrong."

Stone nodded, his jaw tight with worry. Both men turned their horses back toward the barn. This time, they raced for another reason. For family. And Alex could swear Zircon burst quicker than he ever had before.

While she waited for Alex, Nina stretched out in her bed reading a Spanish translation of an American romance novel, work and pleasure all at once. She'd quickly become accustomed to having adult conversation at night and missed him.

And yes, her body burned to be with him again.

She glanced at her cell phone resting on top of the quilt. He'd said he would text when he was on his way so he wouldn't startle her. He was always so thoughtful, and the way he understood Cody made it tougher than ever to think about the end of the week. A lot could happen in the next few days.

Look how much already had.

Her cell phone vibrated on the bed—she'd been afraid to keep the ringer on for fear of waking up Cody. She scooped up her cell and found an incoming text. From Alex.

Delayed. Gran has severe headache. Going to ER.

Nina's fingers clenched around the phone, her heart aching for him. She texted back quickly.

So sorry. Prayers for your grandmother.

She wished she could do more, say more, have the right to go with him and comfort him. It was obvious his grandmother was like a mom to him. He spoke so highly of her and clearly admired her. Alex had to be going through a lot. How amazing that he still had so much to give both her and Cody this week between the wedding, his work and his grandmother's declining health.

Nina clutched the phone to her chest, flopping over to her back to watch the ceiling fan blades swirl. Had she been wrong to cut herself off from dating for so long? Did she even know how to answer that question when she couldn't even imagine being with any man other than Alex?

This was becoming such a tangle so fast when she'd been determined to never again to make an impulsive decision, to allow herself to be swept off her feet.

The phone hummed again and she pulled it up fast, elbowing to sit up. Hoping that it was Alex with good news.

Except it was an incoming call from her friend. "Hello, Reed."

"Hope I'm not calling too late."

"Not at all. I'm just reading, feeling lazy." She turned off the e-reader and set it on the bedside table. "Is everything okay at home?"

"I had to call. Those photos of Cody are incredible." Reed's favored eighties radio station played in the background. "I'm signing Wendy up. They had to put her on the waiting list, though. You sure were lucky to get a slot."

Nina thought back to her flurry of packing and preparation when the surprise slot and discount fee came open so quickly. "They told me there was a last-minute cancellation."

"And a waiting list a mile long."

She sat up straighter. "I don't know how to explain it, but I can put in a good word for you with the McNairs. I've, uh, gotten to know them this week."

"That would be fabulous, sweetie. Thanks. I wouldn't ask for myself, but it's for Wendy." He paused. "You're doing okay, then?"

"Cody's thriving. I'm doing great, enjoying the change of scenery." She used to travel often with her UN job. She missed that sometimes, and that made her feel guilty. It wasn't Cody's fault. The support group where she'd met Reed and learned to cope had changed her life and saved her sanity. "Wendy will love it here and so will you."

"Glad to hear it. Well, keep those photos coming. Night."

"Night," she responded, disconnecting and flopping back again. Her thoughts swirled and she felt she was missing something in her exhaustion.

She couldn't account for how she'd gotten the slot this week, but she knew everything about meeting Alex McNair felt as though it was meant to be, each day more perfect than the last. She was tired of being wary and cautious. Her time with Alex had been a personal fairy tale and she wasn't willing to question that. He was different than her frog-prince ex-husband. Alex had to be.

Sleep tugged at her and maybe a bit of denial too, because she just wanted to enjoy her remaining days here and let the future wait.

With only the moonlight in his bedroom to guide him, Alex tugged off his shirt, which still held the scent of smoke from the bachelor party and a hint of the antiseptic air from the hospital. The ER doc had diagnosed Gran with dehydration. An IV bag of fluid later, they'd released her to come home under the care of her nurse.

Or rather she'd insisted nothing would keep her from making the most of the wedding weekend with her family. She would check with her doctor every day and she already had round-the-clock nurses staying at the house. But she was dying and no amount of meds would change that.

Anger and denial roared through him. He didn't want to stay here and he didn't feel like sleeping. He yanked a well-worn green T-shirt from the drawer and tugged it over his head. The grandfather clock in his suite chimed three times in the dark. Regardless of the time, he had to see Nina.

He opened the doors out to his patio, leaped over the railing and jogged across the lawn toward her cabin. He had a key. She'd given him one for tonight right before he left. The full moon shot rays through the oak trees, along the path. Most of the cabins were dark. The only sounds were bugs and frogs. He took the steps up to Nina's two at a time and let himself inside quietly.

He checked on Cody first. A buckaroo bronco lamp glowed on the dresser. The boy slept deeply, his blond hair shiny in the soft light, his room cool and his weighted blanket on top of him. Nina had told Alex once that the cocooned feeling helped her son with serotonin production or something like that he'd meant to read up on.

He closed the door carefully and stepped into Nina's room. She was beautiful, princesslike even. Her bold red curls piled around her neck. Causal. Desirable. She was asleep on top of the covers, her cell phone in her left hand and her e-reader on the bedside table. She had on a light pink *C'est La Vie* T-shirt with a picture of the Eiffel Tower. The shirt barely covered her thighs. He thought about taking her there. To Paris. To Rome. And so many other places. To bed.

If she could forgive him for his half-truths this week.

Sitting on the edge, he eased the covers back. "Nina, it's me."

"Alex," she sighed, her voice groggy as she rolled toward him to portion of the bed with the quilt pushed aside. "How's your grandmother?"

Her concern was apparent, even if she wasn't fully awake. Damn.

"Gran is at home resting peacefully in her own bed. She was just dehydrated from the summer heat." He tugged the covers over Nina, kicked off his shoes and slid into bed beside her. "I hope you don't mind that I'm here. I know it's late, but I missed you."

"So glad you came." She cuddled closer, her arm sliding around his waist. "Missed you too."

Her warm soft body fit against his, the sweet smell of her shampoo filling every breath. He stroked her back in lazy circles, taking comfort in touching her. Hell, just being with her. His body throbbed in response, but she was asleep. So he gritted his teeth and tried to will away the erection.

Easier said than done.

She wriggled closer with a sleepy sigh. He bit back a groan. Maybe coming here and expecting he could just sleep hadn't been such a wise idea after all.

Her leg nestled between his. The soft skin of her calf added fuel to his already flaming fire. He ached to be inside her, to hear those kittenish sighs of pleasure mixed with demands for more. She was a passionate, giving lover. He wondered what it would have been like if her last name wasn't Lowery and she'd just been a regular mom bringing her son to camp.

She slid her hand down his side over his hip, wriggling against him. Was she dreaming? The thought of her having sensual dreams turned him inside out. But he couldn't take advantage of her that way.

Then her hand slipped around to cradle his erection.

He grasped her wrist and willed himself to move away. "Nina, you're dreaming."

Her eyelashes swept up and she smiled at him. "Dreaming? Not hardly."

Her voice was groggy, although she was very obviously awake. She unzipped his pants and wrapped her fingers around the length of him. His eyes slid closed and he allowed himself a moment to enjoy the sensation of her touch. The outside world would be intruding soon enough. This could well be his last chance alone with her before she dumped him—or his family scared her away.

"Nina…" he groaned, his arms going around her as he rolled to tuck her beneath him. "I need you."

"How perfectly convenient," she murmured in a husky voice, "because I've been dreaming of you and I need you too. Now. Inside me. I've been thinking about you all night long."

He fished out his wallet and tossed a condom on the bed before sweeping her underwear down. She kicked them aside with an efficient flick. And his whole body shouted to thrust inside her. But he needed to imprint himself in her memory—her in his own—in case this was their last time together.

No. It couldn't be their last night together. He refused to entertain the possibility.

He kissed along her jaw, her neck, then lower, between her breasts and lower still. Her breath hitched as she picked up his intent seconds before he nuzzled between her legs. He blew a light puff of air over her and she shivered, her fingers sliding into his hair, tugging lightly. She arched up as he stroked and laved. Each purr and moan and sigh from her had him throbbing with the need to take her. Her head thrashed back and forth on her pillow, her pleasure so beautiful to watch.

Then she tugged at his shoulders, scratching, urging him breathlessly, "So close. I want to come with you inside me, but I can't hold out much longer."

He didn't need to be told again. Pressing a final intimate kiss to her, he slid back up her body, nipping along her stomach and her breasts. Her hands impatient, she took the weight of him in her palms stroking, coaxing until he growled in frustration.

Smiling with feminine power, she sheathed him with another arousing stroke. He covered her, settling between her thighs, waiting even though holding back was pure torture. Finally she opened her eyes and looked straight at him. Holding her gaze, he pushed inside her velvety warmth with a powerful thrust. And damn, he was glad she was near her own release, because his was only a few strokes away. He moved inside her, again and again, her legs wrapping around his waist, drawing him deeper.

The bed creaked and the ceiling fan blew cool gusts over his back. But even blasts from the air conditioner couldn't stop the heat pumping through his veins. He saw the flush of impending release climbing up her neck, and he captured her mouth, taking her cries of completion, his own mixing with hers.

Perfection. Nina. Coming undone in his arms.

Rolling to his side, he held her to him, the aftershocks rippling through them. The night sounds of bugs and frogs sounded along with a gentle patter of a rain shower starting up again. He smoothed his hand over her hair, her face tucked against his chest until eventually her breathing returned to normal, then slower as sleep grabbed hold of her again.

So much weighed on his heart—between his grandmother's illness and the impossible position she'd put him in. He couldn't wait another day to unburden himself, even if he knew Nina was sleeping. And yeah, maybe he also needed to test out the words to find a way to tell her when the time was right. "Nina, I need to tell you something."

"Mmm," she answered, her eyes closed. Her arm draped limply over him.

He knew she likely couldn't hear, but still he confessed everything his grandmother had asked him to do, how torn he felt, how much he wanted her... And the unheard words didn't make him feel any better. So he just held her until the sun started to peek from the horizon. He needed to leave before her son woke. Alex had to prepare for his cousin's rehearsal dinner.

And for the proverbial storm that his mother brought to every occasion.

Nerves made Nina restless about her date with Alex. Her hand shook as she swept on mascara, leaning toward the mirror and praying she wouldn't end up looking like a clown this evening. She had tried out a makeup tutorial from the internet to update her look since she didn't get out much these days. Winged eyeliner. Classy and timeless but she would have to watch the sweat this weekend.

It was only a date. She was just Alex's plus-one for his cousin's rehearsal dinner. Except it wasn't just any party. It was a McNair affair, an exclusive event.

And Nina was sleeping with him. They'd gone beyond a one-night fling. And he'd left her the sweetest note on her pillow, in Spanish this time. Not perfect, but perfectly adorable. He'd complemented her beauty while sleeping and said she would be in his thoughts all day. She'd already tucked the note into her suitcase along with the card he'd given her with the wildflowers.

So yes, she wanted to be at her best and only had the limited wardrobe she'd packed for a children's cowboy camp.

She'd taken two hours this morning to race around and find new dresses to wear to the rehearsal party and the wedding, and an outfit for Cody tomorrow. She'd thought she misheard Alex when he said he wanted her son to attend the wedding, and she was more than a little nervous for her child. But Alex assured her it would be a casual affair with a Texas flair Cody would enjoy. There would even be three other children there.

It was almost as if she belonged here. With Alex.

A dangerous thought. They'd only known each other a few days. But she damn sure intended to leave an indelible impression on his memory.

She clipped on a brass bracelet with Spanish inscriptions, another acquisition from Diamonds in the Rough, and smoothed her loose chevron-patterned sundress. She admired her freshly painted toenails peeking out of her strappy sandals and stepped out of her bedroom into the living room, then stopped short, her heart squeezing at the sight in front of her. Alex and her son, both catnapping.

Cody curled up on the sofa, hugging his blanket and wearing new puppy dog pj's she'd picked up for him during her shopping spree this morning. The actual wedding rehearsal had already taken place and she'd skipped that to prepare her son before Alex came by to pick her up.

Alex snored softly in the fat leather chair, his booted feet propped on the ottoman. Her gaze skated from his boots, up muscular legs in khakis, past a Diamonds in the Rough belt buckle, to broad shoulders in a sports coat. A Stetson covered his face. He looked so much like his cousin Stone it would have been easy for someone to mistake the two men for each other. But she would know her man anywhere.

Her man?

When had she started thinking in possessive terms like that? And after such a short time knowing him?

They'd stolen late-night dates, but his days had been taken up with work and she'd focused on Cody's camp—other than keeping her cell phone in reach at all times, treasuring each quick call or text from Alex.

Oh God, she was in serious trouble here.

He tapped his hat upward and he whistled softly. "Nice!"

"Thanks," she said, spinning, the skirt rustling along her knees, "I guess it's time?"

"The sitter is already warming Cody's supper in the kitchen." Standing, Alex walked toward her, eyes stroking her the whole way. "And I queued up his favorite videos, since he'll probably be up late because he napped."

She stepped into the circle of his arms. "Is there anything you haven't thought of?"

"I sure hope not. I'm doing everything in my power to ensure that this evening is as pleasant as possible to make up for having to spend time with my mother."

"She can't be that bad." Certainly not as bad as Nina's in-laws. They'd been distant while she was married, but grew outright hostile after her divorce. And now? They barely acknowledged Cody existed. They rarely spoke to her. "I'll be fine."

He squeezed her arm. "Okay, then. But if you need me to rescue you from her, give me a sign. Like tug on your earlobe."

Laughing, she hooked arms with him, then ducked her head in to say hello to the sitter before they left. One of the camp counselors had agreed to watch Cody.

After a short walk to the open air barn full of family and friends, Nina found herself searching for his parents. Curious after all she'd heard. Alex went straight for them as if to get past the introductions and move on. An older couple stood together under an oak tree strung with white lights. The pair was easily identifiable as his parents by the resemblance. Although their idea of casual sure came with a lot of starch and spray tan.

"Mother, Dad," Alex said, placing a possessive hand on Nina's back, "this is Nina Lowery."

Bayleigh McNair was a beautiful woman, no question—except for her beady eyes, which moved around quickly, assessing without ever meeting Nina's gaze. "Lovely to meet you, dear. How long have you and my son been seeing each other?"

"Mom, I already told you she's here with her son for Stone's new camp." His hand twitched ever so slightly, even though his voice stayed amiable.

"So you just met this week." Eyebrows raised, Bayleigh looked at Nina as if she were a gold digger.

Indignation fired hot and fierce. How unfair and judgmental. And Nina had no choice but to keep her mouth closed and be polite. "We met my first day here. I thought he was one of the ranch hands. Can you imagine that?"

"How quaint." Bayleigh half smiled.

Amie joined them, the feathers on her skirt brushing Nina's legs. "Mother, you're being rude. Stop it or I'll wear white shoes after Labor Day."

Her mother sniffed, looking offended. "No need to be obnoxious, dear."

Alex's father folded her hand in his. "Nina, it's lovely to meet you. And your last name, Lowery... If I remember correctly, you married into the Lowery Resort family."

"Yes, sir." She shook his hand briskly, then twined her fingers in front of her. She wasn't comfortable talking about money the way these people were. That was her son's money, her ex-husband's wealth. She'd grown up in a regular middle-class neighborhood.

Garnet clapped his son on the shoulder. "That's mighty big of you, son, letting the competition in here this way."

Nina frowned. "Competition?"

Bayleigh swatted her husband's arm. "Leave the poor girl alone before Amie threatens us again. You heard Alex say she's here with her child, you know, for that *special* camp. For *special* kids."

Nina bristled. That last comment went too far. Digs at her were one thing. But her son was off-limits. Was this woman that clueless or deliberately baiting her?

Alex's father hooked arms with his wife to steer her away—thank heavens. "We should check on Mother. Inside."

Bayleigh patted his hand. "I know it's so hard for you to see her that way."

Garnet's chin trembled and he leaned on his wife. Amie cursed softly and walked into the barn full of tables and a dais.

Alex's jaw flexed and he hung his head, sweeping his hat off to scratch a hand through his hair. "I am so damn sorry for my mother's behavior. It's inexcusable." He dropped his hat back on his head. "I wouldn't blame you if you wanted to leave now."

Nina rocked on her heels. "I have to confess, she's a lot to take in all at once, but I'm fine. There's plenty to celebrate here and other people to meet. Let's have fun."

"That's diplomatic and kind of you." He caressed her shoulders, comforting and arousing at the same time. "Is there something I can do other than gag my parents?"

As angry as his mother had made her, Nina could let it go. The woman was superficial and catty. However, Nina's mind was quietly turning over the "competition" thing Alex's father had mentioned. What had she missed? She thought about how Reed had insisted spots at this camp were impossible to come by. Had someone in the McNair organization wanted to keep the competition close?

Certainly there was no way Alex would know about her relation to the Lowerys, was there? She shook off the suspicion.

Alex was clearly hurting now over his mom's behavior, and it wasn't fair to blame him for his mother or take out her frustration on him. "I know your parents are grieving too. People are rarely at their best when they're hurting."

His hands slid up to cup her face. "That's more generous than she deserves. More generous than I deserve too, because I should have given you a stronger warning."

"You're not responsible for your parents." Now that her anger had faded to a low simmer, she saw the pain they'd caused him. "Are *you* okay?"

He folded her hand in his. "I'm a big boy. I know my parents. I just want better for Gran, especially now."

"Your grandmother *has* better. She has *you*." Nina took in the angles of his face, touched by the wind and sun, nothing affected or fake. "And she has Amie—I like your sister."

His mouth twitched. "She's a character."

"From everything I've seen of Stone and his fiancée, they've made your grandmother very happy with their wedding. And I assume seeing you there with a date on your arm will reassure her, as well." Another suspicion blindsided her, one she hadn't considered. "Is that why you've been pursuing me? To make your grandmother happy by having a date at the wedding?"

He hesitated, then shook his head. "I'm not sleeping with you to make my grandmother happy." His throat moved in a long swallow. "But there is something important I need to tell you once we're alone."

Ten

The three hours since Alex had said they needed to talk had passed at a torturous snail's pace. Nina wondered how much longer she could hold out waiting to hear what Alex needed to tell her. Good or bad? But if it had been good, wouldn't he have told her right then?

Her mind raced with darker possibilities. Had she allowed herself to get too excited over him? Overanalyzed his gestures? Made too much out of a few days?

She swiped sweat from her brow, searching for the restroom to make sure her mascara and eyeliner hadn't dripped into raccoon eyes after all the dancing she'd done. The live country band had started their first set with a Garth Brooks classic and Nina had thrown herself into the fun with both feet, telling herself to enjoy every moment she could before her time with Alex ended. She'd had fun, but after almost an hour on the dance floor, Nina was certain she looked like a train wreck.

She slid around tables full of guests enjoying after-dinner drinks and coffee. The desserts were all shaped and decorated like jewels. The event was lavish but personal, and touching, reminding her of all she'd once dreamed of having when she started her life with Warren.

Her imagination had been running wild all evening through dinner. Coveted camp slots? Lowerys competing with McNairs? A grandmother who wanted to see her grandchildren settled before she died.

Nina's instincts shouted that something was off, but she couldn't figure out exactly how she fit into the picture. And this wasn't the first time Alex had said he wanted to talk to her. Her heart beat faster, her chest going tight.

She tugged open a door and instead of a bathroom she found an office, with a desk, chairs—and Amie sprawled on the rust-colored velvet sofa. Her eyes were closed, but she was clearly awake. Tear tracks streaked through her makeup.

Nina stepped into the room and closed the door quickly behind her. "Amie?" she asked, walking to the sofa. "What's wrong? Are you all right?"

"Hell no." She peeked out of one eye, dragging in deep breaths. "But I will be."

Kneeling, Nina touched her arm. "Is there something I can do? Get you a tissue? A drink?"

"How about a pair of lead shoes, preferably men's size twelve?" Amie said bitterly, sitting upright and swinging her feet to the floor, tucking her feet back into her high heels.

"Ouch. Sounds bad." Sounded man-bad.

"Nothing I can't handle. I'm usually better at controlling my emotions, but there's so much going on..." She eyed the dartboard, strode over with determination and grabbed a handful of darts from the tray and plucked three from the target. "Next best thing to lead shoes? A dart, right in the face."

Nina winced. "Um, I'm not sure that's legal."

Amie backed away from the board. "I'm not going to stab him literally. Just imagine his face right there..." She lined up the toss. "...Bull's-eye. Every time. Rage does funny things like that."

"Remind me never to make you mad." Nina raised her hands in surrender, offering Amie a playful smile.

"Ah, honey." Amie turned fast and gave Nina a hard hug, one of the darts in Amie's fist scratching a little against Nina's back. "I would never hurt you. You're too nice."

"Do you mind if I ask which man made you mad? Family?" She saw a no and finished, "Or someone else?"

"Someone—" Amie pitched a dart "—else." She launched another.

"I'm sorry. I know how much it hurts to be betrayed by a man." Nina's ex-husband had left a river of pain in his wake, one she was still fording.

Amie avoided Nina's eyes, charged up to the board and pulled out the darts one at a time. "You're a strong, beautiful woman. Don't let anyone in my family walk over you."

Nina's nerves gathered into a big knot of uncertainty about Alex's secret. She churned over a million possibilities, but regardless of which one was true, they all led to the same ending.

Alex was going to break things off with her. Of course he was. He'd clearly just needed a date for the night. He had something to prove to his mother. To Johanna. Nina was just arm candy.

She'd wanted a fling, and Lord, she'd gotten it. This one week and one week only. And it was over. Her stomach plummeted worse than when Zircon had spooked.

What a time to realize she wanted more. What a time to realize how easy it would have been to have a life here with Alex.

Alex guided Nina out onto the dance floor, having ached to have her in his arms all night long. He had feelings for her that were about more than sex. He cared about her. Admired her even.

And he had to be honest with her, even if that cost him the ranch. He wanted his grandmother to be happy, but he couldn't do that at the expense of his honor. Seeing the strength and commitment—and love—Nina showered on her son made Alex realize he needed to man up.

"Let's dance outside, where it's less crowded," he said, clasping her hand and steering her into a dance under the lit oak trees.

The night was beautiful, the air cooler and the music a little quieter outdoors. Two people sat on a bench talking, and another couple danced, but none of them were close enough to overhear.

She was stiff in his arms, reserved and dodging his gaze. His mother had clearly done damage as usual. God, where did he even start?

"Nina—"

"Go ahead," she blurted out, her legs brushing against his.

He paused, angling back to look into her eyes. "Go ahead and what?"

"Go ahead and break things off with me. That's what you wanted to tell me, isn't it?" she asked, her face void of expression. She'd already built a tall wall between them. "You don't have to make this any more awkward than it already is. We had a fling and it's over. You don't need me to be your plus one at the wedding tomorrow. Dance with your sister, enjoy your family."

He pressed his fingers to her mouth. "That's not what I wanted to say at all."

A flicker of uncertainty sparked in her green eyes. Something that looked like cautious hope. "Then what is it?"

"I owe you an apology for not being up front at the start."

"I thought we discussed that already. You hid the fact that you weren't just a ranch hand. But we moved past that." Her fingers clenched, bunching his shirt in her hands. "It was a minor misunderstanding."

This was tougher than he'd expected but long overdue. "When my grandmother's cancer was first diagnosed, stock prices dropped because of concerns about the future of the holdings. My cousin and my grandmother thought they'd tracked the purchasers of those stocks to make sure no one group amassed a portion large enough to risk gaining control of the company."

Her eyes went from wary to resigned. "Something went wrong."

"Lowery Resorts has been buying up McNair stocks."

Her feet stopped moving altogether. His words hung between them, his gut heavy with guilt.

"My in-laws." Her hands fell to her sides; her fists clenched.

"In a sense. Your son's trust fund uses the same investment broker. He used shell corporations to buy up stocks for your son as well as your in-laws. The stocks that went to your son slipped under our radar."

"Until now." She sagged to sit on a rustic wooden bench. "It's no accident that I'm here, is it?"

He sat beside her, his hands clasped between his knees. "No, my grandmother made sure you received the brochure and the scholarship."

She met his gaze full on, her chin set but her eyes glistening with unshed tears. "And your role in this?"

"My grandmother wants me to encourage you to sell those stocks back to us."

Her eyebrows pinched together. Her face was impassive. The wall from earlier sprang back in full force. Damn. "Why didn't you just say that from the start? We could have negotiated."

"We didn't think you would agree." How had this ever made sense to him? He should have known this was a train wreck in the making from the start. He should have passed it over to the lawyers and accountants and let them handle it. Emotions screwed up business. "It's a great time to buy but not a good time to sell. In all honesty, it wouldn't be in your son's best interest to sell."

"Why is there an issue with having other stockholders?"

"Think about the resorts your in-laws build and look at Hidden Gem." The thought of his home being turned into a tourist trap made him ill. "We have a problem."

"More than one apparently." Sighing, she blinked fast and slumped back against the bench. Her mouth opened slightly, allowing a breath of words to escape. "How much of what we shared was even real, Alex?"

"God, Nina, how can you even ask that? My grandmother not only wanted me to persuade you to give up those stocks, but she led me to believe my inheritance depended on it, like a test to prove how badly I wanted my piece of the family business. But I couldn't do what she asked. I pursued you in spite of her test. I'm being honest with you now. I never wanted those stocks to come between us." He reached for her only to have her flinch away. His worst nightmare come true. He'd told her the truth and she hated him for it. Not that he could blame her. It sounded awful when he laid it out. If he could only make her see he cared about her. About her kid. It wasn't about the stocks anymore. It never had been. He was falling for her and her son.

Footsteps sounded behind him, and Nina looked over his shoulder, distracted. He glanced back to find his sister racing toward them, a ringing purse in her hand.

"Nina, you left your bag back on the sofa. The sitter has been trying to reach you. She called me too."

Nina shot to her feet, her eyes wide with alarm. "Did Cody wake up? I need to go to him."

Alex knew his sister well, and even though she appeared poised, he could see the signs of blind panic. Something was wrong, very wrong. He stood beside Nina.

Amie clasped Nina's hands. "No, it's not that. I'm sorry to have to tell you this, but Cody is missing."

Alex's nightmare just got a whole lot worse.

"Cody!" Nina shouted into the night, her voice hoarse, her heart raw. Holding a flashlight, she walked alongside Alex into woods.

The staff was checking every inch of the lodge and the cabins. The family and guests were searching the grounds. She was running on fumes and fear. Other voices echoed in the distance shouting her son's name, but she knew too well even if he heard, he very well might not be able to open up enough to answer.

Her world was collapsing. Her son had wandered off. The sitter had put him to bed, and she was positive he hadn't gone out past her. His window was open. And he was gone.

Nina had been frantic and tried to bolt out to begin searching, but Alex had remained calm, held her back and reminded her that an organized approach would cover more ground faster. Ranch security had been notified and a grid search was under way.

Knowing that everything possible was being done hadn't made the last hour any less horrific. She'd allowed herself to be charmed and distracted by a man who was only using her, and now her child was in danger. She would never forgive herself. Served her right for believing she was in another fairy tale.

Alex swept his larger spotlight across the path leading to the creek they'd once soared over on a horseback. Nausea roiled. The thought of her son drowning...

She bit back a whimper.

Sweeping the spotlight along the creek, Alex stepped over a log. "We'll find him. We have plans in place for things like this, grid searches and manpower. We'll find him before you know it."

"This is my fault." And there was nothing anyone could say to convince her otherwise. She walked alongside the water, shallow, probably not deep enough to be a worry, but everywhere was dangerous to a boy with little understanding of fears or boundaries. "I should have been with him tonight."

"It's impossible for you to be with him every minute of every day," Alex pointed out logically. "The sitter has excellent credentials too."

And yes, he was right. But that meant nothing to a mother in the grip of her worst nightmare. "That's not making me feel any better."

"This kind of thing happens even when there's a houseful of adults watching." His spotlight swept over a trickling waterfall, no sign of her son. "You can't be attached at the hip."

"Intellectually I know that. But in my heart? I'll never forgive myself."

A rustling in the woods drew her up short. She struggled to listen, to discern…A rabbit leaped out of the brush and scampered away. Disappointment threatened to send her to her knees. Alex's arm slid around her to bolster her.

She drew in a shaky breath and regained her footing. "You can relax. I'm not planning to sue the camp. I just want to find my son."

"Nina, God." He took her arm. "Lawsuits are the last thing on my mind. I'm worried about Cody." His voice cracked on the last word.

"I shouldn't have said that." She pressed her fingers to her throbbing head. "I'm terrified and on edge."

"Understandably so." Having reached the end of the creek, he turned back, sweeping the light ahead of them, up along trees with branches fat and low enough for a child to climb. Owl eyes gleamed back at them. "Later we'll figure out if there's fault and if so, that employee will be dismissed. Right now we can only think about one thing."

"I appreciate that you're able to keep such a cool head." She swallowed down her fear and forced herself to think about the search for her son.

"You know, Stone and I wandered off once."

She realized he was likely trying to calm her by making aimless conversation, but she appreciated the effort, grounding herself in his deep steady voice. "Really? Where did you go?"

"Into these woods." His footsteps crunched as he backtracked toward the ranch again. "We planned to live off the land like cowboys, catch fish, build a fire and sleep in a tent."

"Obviously you made it home all right."

"A thunderstorm rolled through and drenched us. We got sick on the candy we packed, since we didn't catch a single fish." Flashlights from other searchers sent splashes of light through the trees, voices echoing. "And we had so many mosquito bites Gran made us wear gloves to keep from scratching."

"What gave you the idea to try such a dangerous thing?" she asked, on the off chance that would give her some insight to where her son might have wandered off to.

"We were boys. Boys don't need a reason to do stupid things," he said dryly.

"While I can agree on that," she answered with a much-needed smile, brief, then fading, "I think something made the two of you run off."

Alex sighed. "Stone's junkie mom had just threatened to take him again, and when I asked my parents to file for custody, they said no," he recounted with an emotionless voice at odds with his white-knuckled grip on the massive flashlight as they drew closer to the corrals. "Gran even asked them once too. But no go. Anyhow, that day, we decided for twenty-four hours we would be brothers."

His story touched her heart with a sense of family she'd never had, and while it didn't excuse his keeping secrets from her, she could sense the conflict he must have felt over the stocks and the ownership of a place that meant so much to him.

She leaned against the corral rail, her flashlight pointing downward. "Thank you. For trying to distract me while we search—"

Alex held up a hand. "Shhh…Nina. Listen."

She straightened, tipping her ears to catch sounds carried on the breeze, to parse through the people shouting for her son, the four-wheeler driving.

And puppies mewling.

She gasped. "Puppies. He's—"

"With the puppies," Alex finished, already sprinting toward the barn where the children had played with livestock.

Where he'd shown Cody the litter of puppies.

They'd checked here earlier and hadn't seen him. Could they have missed him? Or maybe he hadn't made his way here yet when they came through the first time?

Nina raced past him and yanked open the barn door. "Cody? Cody?"

Alex waved to her. "Over here. Asleep behind bales of hay holding a puppy."

She tore across the earthen floor, dropping to her knees and soaking in the sight of her son curled up around the fuzzy black puppy. He wasn't with all of the puppies. He just had one and they'd missed him. Somehow they'd overlooked him, but she wasn't going to second-guess. Not now. She was so damn grateful to have her child safe. Tears of relief streaked down her face, mixed with pent-up emotion from the entire week. She slid down to the ground, unable to escape reality.

She'd found her son—and now she needed to leave.

Eleven

Perched on the edge of Cody's bed, Nina tucked her son in for the night. He stared back at her as he rhythmically touched the top of his blanket, completely unconcerned. She should never have left him this evening. Shudders pulsated as her thoughts wandered on what could have happened. But Cody was here.

Safe.

She didn't take that gift of safety for granted for even an instant. This evening could have ended so horribly. She should be happy. Relieved. But she was still so shell-shocked by Alex's revelation and the hour of terror looking for her son that she could barely function. Nina let out a breath she didn't realize had been locked in her chest.

She smoothed Cody's hair and he let her touch him without flinching. "Please don't wander off without telling me, okay? I know it's difficult for you to talk, but this is important. I need to know where you are."

"Want that collie puppy," he whispered, and pulled a piece of paper from under his covers. He'd drawn a puppy playing in the barn. The detail was stunning, capturing the border collie perfectly. So much talent.

If only they'd found that picture earlier, it would have steered them right to him. "We'll get a puppy when we're home, okay, sweetie?"

Cody sat up, hugging his puffy blue blanket. He shook his head. "Want a puppy here."

Her heart tugged at all the things she couldn't give him. "Oh, my sweet boy, it's beautiful here and I love your pictures so very much. But we have to go home."

His eyes darted from side to side, stopping to stare at the outfit on his dresser. Fresh blue jeans sat beneath a brand-new yellow cowboy shirt. A brand-new kid-sized Stetson hat rested on the top of the pile. Pale tan rope circled the base of the hat, the ends joined by a silver horse charm. New brown cowboy boots with a matching fringe vest sat next to the clothes. "The wedding. I have new clothes. We gotta go to the wedding. With the kitty lady."

His jaw jutted.

She could see him ramping up and needed a way to calm him. "We'll go to the wedding. You will get to wear your new outfit."

"Okay, okay."

"But I need you to promise me you won't wander off like that again. You could have been hurt. I was very scared for you. I need you to say the words, Cody. Promise me."

He avoided her eyes, but he nodded, lying back down again. "Promise."

"Good boy." She patted the blue blanket. "It's time to go to sleep. Night-night. I love you so much."

She could speak multiple languages, but words were so hard to find to get through to her precious child. What would she have done tonight without Alex's support?

Ah, Alex. The heartbreaking cowboy. Now, there was a touchy subject. Her stomach tightened as her brain tried to make sense of her conflicting emotions.

Backing away from Cody's bed, she adjusted the Buckaroo Bronco lamp on her way out. She closed the door softly. Sagging back against the panel, she let the tears flow, wishing the pain could be uncorked so easily.

A movement deep in the living room snagged her attention and she saw Alex rise from the sofa. Had it only been a few hours ago he'd come here to take her to the party? She'd dressed with such hope and silly expectations from a tube of mascara.

He walked across the floor and wrapped his arms around her. She pushed against his chest in a half-hearted attempt to make some kind of point. To get back at him for seeming so perfect and being so very flawed. Even worse, dishonest. Was he really just another frog-prince?

Crying harder, she pressed her face against his chest to muffle the sounds so her son wouldn't hear. She twisted her hands in his shirt.

Her legs buckled and his arms banded tighter around her. He smoothed her hair and mumbled words against her head. He backed closer to the living area until he sat in the fat armchair and pulled her into his lap. She continued to cry, not the hard racking sobs anymore, but the silent slip of tears down her cheeks. His hands roved up and down her back rhythmically.

As she shifted, her face brushed his. Or maybe his brushed hers and their mouths met, held. She should pull away. This was a bad idea for a thousand reasons that would only lead to more heartache. But this was her last chance to feel his hands on her, his mouth. She didn't want lies, excuses or half-truths. She didn't even want to talk. She wanted this. This man might not have what she needed from life, but she would take this moment of pleasure for herself before she left. She'd come a long way from the woman who'd married Warren and hoped for the best.

She looped her arms around Alex's neck as she wriggled closer. Neither of them asked if it was right or wrong. Their bodies spoke, communed, and his hands clasped her hips, shifting her until she straddled his lap. He bunched her dress up, his fingers warm on her skin, twisting the thin barrier of her underwear until the strings along her hips *snapped*.

Without breaking their kiss she fished in his pocket for his wallet and found a condom. With sure hands she unbuckled that rodeo belt and unzipped his pants. He growled his approval against her mouth.

Then frenzy took over and she lowered herself onto him. Inch by inch. His hands on her hips, her hands on his shoulders and yes… Her head fell back as their hips rolled in sync. Faster and faster. The heat and need built inside her, all the pent-up emotion from the night, crushed dreams and disappointment leaving her raw.

Soon—too soon and yet not soon enough—she felt

the rise of her orgasm building, slamming through her, riding the wave of all those emotions. She sank her teeth in Alex's shoulder to keep from shouting out. His hands clenched in her hair, his fists tight as she felt his release rock through him.

In the aftermath, she kept her face tucked into his neck while he stroked her back. Even though she would be attending the wedding tomorrow, she knew...

This was goodbye.

Wedding photos and receiving line complete, Alex was finally free to mingle before dinner and dancing kicked into high gear. He knew more about weddings than most men. After all, the Hidden Gem hosted them on a regular basis. And he focused on every damn detail tonight to keep from thinking about the hole in his heart over losing Nina. Last night had put him through the emotional wringer—from their fight, to Cody wandering off, and then to making love with Nina in a frenzied moment that had goodbye written all over it.

Damn straight he needed to think of something else to keep from walking away to lose himself in a bottle of booze in the solitude of his suite. So he focused on every detail, making sure the wedding and reception went off without a hitch.

And damned if he wasn't too aware of Nina and Cody's presence anyway.

Even knowing she'd only attended because her son had been emphatic about it didn't stop the rush of pleasure having them here. The kid was something else. Who'd have thought he would dig his heels in on wearing his new clothes and attending a cowboy wedding? Cody looked as though he belonged here, at Hidden

Gem Ranch, with his cowboy outfit. Guilt struck at Alex, rattling through his chest. He had to focus.

The vows Johanna and Stone had spoken were from the heart, the ceremony in the chapel brief. One groomsman and one bridesmaid—Alex and Amie. The bride wore a simple fitted lace dress with a short train. The loose, romantic waves of her hair complemented the airiness of her dress. Elegant. Understated. Her lone bridesmaid wore a peach-colored dress in a similar but simpler style, to the floor without a train.

Stone and Alex wore tan suits with buff-colored Stetsons for when they were outside. This event was about the bride and groom, their style, making memories on their day.

At the end of the service, as Alex escorted his sister out of the church, he felt the weight of Nina's gaze, felt the hurt he'd caused her. More guilt. More shame. And he didn't know how the hell to make it right and he didn't know who to turn to for guidance.

Silently he and Amie walked to the barn where the rehearsal dinner had been held. All of the decorations from the night before were still in place, plus more. Gold chandeliers and puffs of white hydrangeas dangled from the barn rafters. Strings of lights crisscrossed the ceiling, creating an intimate, dreamy atmosphere. Bouquets of baby's breath and roses tied with burlap bows graced all the tables. The inside had been transformed into rustic elegance, with gold chairs and white tulle draped throughout.

There were rustic touches as well. At the entry table next to the leather guest book, seating cards were tied to horse shoes that had the bride and groom's names engraved along with the wedding date. A cowbell hung on a brass hook with a sign that stated Ring for a Kiss.

A country band played easy-listening versions of old classics.

But Alex was in no mood for dancing. Not if he couldn't have Nina in his arms. She'd made it clear last night after she'd booted him out of her bed that she was leaving right after the wedding. She'd only stayed this long for Cody. Alex poured himself a drink and found a table in the far back corner. Isolated. He would have to move up front with the family soon enough. For now, he could be alone with his drink and his thoughts.

"Mind if I join you?" His father stood beside him.

"Um, no, not at all." He gestured to an empty chair. "Have a seat, but Gran will insist we move up front to the main table soon."

"Then we might as well enjoy this as long as we can." Garnet tipped back his drink. "You look like you could use some support—or advice. Woman troubles?"

"There's nothing anyone can do." Alex sipped the bourbon, watching Nina and Cody talk to the bride. The little boy touched the bridal bouquet with reverence.

Memories of walking the ranch looking for Cody gut-kicked Alex all over again. He'd never known a fear that deep. Or a relief so intense once they'd found him.

Rattling the ice in his glass, Garnet followed Alex's gaze before studying his son hard. "People think your mother married me for my money and that I live off my inheritance. And they wouldn't be totally wrong on either of those points. But you know what, son?"

Alex met his father's piercing gaze—the McNair blue eyes—and finally saw a little of Gran in there. "What, Dad?"

"It's none of their damn business. Bayleigh and I may not live our lives the way others would, but it works for us." He thumbed his wedding ring around his finger. "We have a happy marriage. I did learn that from my parents. Pick the right person for you and to hell with everyone else's expectations. This is your life."

Alex wasn't sure how to apply the advice to his own personal hell, but he appreciated his father's effort. "Any reason you never thought to have this kind of father-son talk with me before now?"

"You didn't need it then." Garnet shrugged, adjusting his bolo tie. "Now I believe you do."

"It's not that simple with Nina." There. Alex had said it. Acknowledged that he and Nina were—or had been—a couple. He wanted her in his life.

"Sure it's every bit as simple as that. Buy the stocks from her. Pay more than they're worth and give that boy some extra security." Garnet's practicality sounded more and more like a McNair by the second. Maybe everyone had underestimated him. "So what if the ranch has to scrimp on mechanical bulls for a while? Big deal."

"You make it sound so easy." Very easy. Doable.

"Because it is." Garnet set aside his drink. "Your grandmother only said get the stocks back in the family. She didn't say who had to buy them. If you need me to chip in, consider it done."

And Alex could see his father meant it. He was offering to help. Alex clapped him on the shoulder, the advice solidifying in his mind with utter clarity. "Thanks, Dad. Really. But I think you already gave me what I needed most with your advice."

"Then what's holding you back?"

"I need for Gran to be at peace with this. Ever since I met Nina, it's stopped being about the ranch. It's about giving Gran peace."

His father nodded, gesturing to the front of the room where Gran held court with the bride, Amie—and Nina. Family. That was what meant the most to Gran.

This plan might not be what she'd had in mind, but his grandmother had always respected leadership and honor.

And love. There it was, no hiding from the truth anymore. Yes, it was impulsive and fast, but he'd never been so sure of anything in his life. Alex loved Nina. He loved her son as well, and he intended to do whatever it took to become their family.

Nina twisted her hands together, nervous at the attention from the McNair matriarch. Sweat began to build in her palms. Did the woman know her plans had been uncovered? Mariah was so fragile; it was easy to see how a person would do anything to make her final days as drama-free as possible.

Then again, damn it, if that had been the woman's goal, why come up with elaborate tests for her grandchildren to prove their loyalty to the family? Mariah's process of inheritance seemed to invite problems. Frustration simmered, balancing out the empathy. Nina's emotions were a huge mess today.

Mariah took Nina's hand in her cool grasp, her skin paper thin and covered with bruises from IVs. Despite her frailty, Mariah's grip was firm, confident. A true businesswoman. "I'm so glad your son was found safely."

"I appreciate all the help searching. This week has been a dream come true for him. I understand I have you to thank for getting him into the program."

Mariah's eyes went wide at Nina's frank approach—

and then she smiled sympathetically. "I'm sorry that life has to be so difficult for you."

"Life is hard for everyone in some way, ma'am. I love Cody. I have a good job in my field that allows me to stay home with my son. My life is good."

Life is good. This was what Nina had repeated over and over to herself as she dressed for the weekend. She desperately tried to convince herself that she didn't need anything else besides Cody and work. Tried to tell herself that was all she wanted. That it was enough.

"Then why are your eyes so sad?"

How could she tell the woman about the doomed affair with Alex? She couldn't. "My in-laws will use the incident with Cody getting lost to try and take him away from me. They think he would be better off in a hospital, coming home on holidays and weekends. And they want control of his inheritance from his father."

What was it about this woman that made Nina spill her secret fears?

"That has to be so incredibly frightening for you. They sound like they're using the issue of institutionalizing him as a power play."

Nina nodded. "They are." She looked at the deathly ill woman in front of her and saw complete clarity in her eyes. Nina didn't want to burden her, but honesty might allay Mariah's concerns about those stocks more than all this behind-the-scenes game playing. "Ma'am, with all due respect, if you wanted Cody's stocks, why didn't you just approach me and give me a chance to be a reasonable businesswoman?"

Mariah's pale blue eyes went wide and she gripped her cane. "So Alex has told you." She smiled, bringing color back to her pale face. "Good for him."

What? "I'm confused. You wanted to keep this a secret but you didn't?" Nina didn't appreciate having her life manipulated, regardless of how ill the older woman was.

"I want to apologize for bringing you here under false pretenses. My grandson is so introverted. He communes with the animals more than people, and that's a part of what makes him so successful at running the Hidden Gem. But he also needed a nudge outside his comfort zone. I hoped forcing a meeting between the two of you would help him move forward with having a life that doesn't center on work 24/7. Life's too short, too precious." Mariah leaned closer. "You must realize by now that the crush he had on Johanna was born more out of convenience than any real passion. When I see the two of you together—" her eyes twinkled with life "—now, that's passion."

How could Nina tell Mariah the test backfired? They'd broken up. He'd lied to her...for a few days. Then come clean. Could she forgive that? After her marriage, she had issues on that front, no question. But Alex had shown more compassion and honor in a week than her ex had displayed in their entire marriage.

Mariah squeezed Nina's hand and continued. "I took advantage of your desire to help your son. That was wrong of me."

"You were desperate to do anything for your family. I understand that feeling." As Nina said those words, she felt the truth of them settle deep in her soul. Life wasn't about black and white, right and wrong. It was about flawed humans doing their best, one day at time.

Now if she could just find a way to make Alex understand that her love for him was every bit as strong as her love for her son.

If he could understand that, they would be able to find a way to work through this tangle.

Together.

A box in his arms, Alex knocked on Nina's cabin door with his boot. Moonlight sparkled through the branches overhead. Now that he had his compass firmly planted, he'd accomplished a lot in a few short hours, busy as hell setting things into motion all while seeing his cousin off at the end of the wedding. But then a rancher was a multitasker by nature. He didn't want to waste another second. He had to win Nina over and keep her in his life.

Hopefully forever.

She opened the door, her hair wet from a shower, wearing pj shorts and a loose shirt. And she'd never looked more beautiful.

"Mind if I come in?"

She stepped back, opening the door wider to reveal packed suitcases by the sofa. Her vintage bag sported large stickers displaying sites from around the world. "We need to talk."

God, he hoped that was a good sign.

"Let's sit on the sofa. I have a few things to show you."

Her face gave nothing away as she padded silently beside him. Either she was egoing to boot him out on his butt. Or, if she somehow still had a shred of hope for their relationship, she was going to make him work for it.

Fine. Ranchers were well versed in hard work. He

was putting everything on the line tonight now that he knew exactly what he wanted.

"Nina, I realize I royally messed things up between us. I should have been honest from the start. I let my fear for my grandmother cloud my judgment, and that's the last thing she would want."

She rested a hand on his arm. "I understand—"

No way was he giving her a chance to let him down easy or tell him she'd already called a cab. He plowed ahead, situating the box he'd brought beside him. He needed to bring out everything he had. Now.

"I'm not sure that you do understand just how much you mean to me and how much I value the woman you are, but I'm hoping this will show you." He reached into the box and pulled out a book. "This is from the family library. It contains the French poem I gave you on our first date."

He set the leather-bound edition on her coffee table.

She traced the gold lettering on the front. "I thought you looked up the poem on the internet."

He would have laughed at that if he wasn't still scared out of his mind she had one foot out the door already. "That certainly would have been faster. But the journey is well worth the effort."

Next, he pulled out a box of Swiss chocolates and a Violet Crumble candy bar from Australia. "These came from our gift shop, but they're just a sampling of places I want to take you and Cody. I know you've given up a lot of dreams for your son, Nina, and I'd like to give them back to you. I want to ride in the Swiss Alps with you and make love under the stars. I want to take Cody to Australia and show him a whole other kind of cowboy to enjoy."

He meant it too. He'd stuck close to home ever since leaving the rodeo circuit, finding peace at the Hidden Gem. But he wanted to see more of the world through Nina's eyes.

Her hands went to her heart, but she stayed silent.

"I also want Cody to learn to love the ranch here."

"He already does," she said softly.

"Good, but I want him to feel a part of the history of this place." He pulled out a heavy woven blanket. "This is a Native American blanket made by one of our local artisans, quite heavy, and I thought it might be of comfort to Cody. And even if the blanket doesn't suit him, I want this to be a symbol of how much I care for your son."

Tears welled in her eyes as she took the blanket from him and clasped it her chest. "Alex, you don't need to say any more. You've already—"

He touched her lips to quiet her, hoping maybe he was getting through to her. But he had a lot to make up for and he wasn't taking any chances on screwing this up too.

"I worked to pull this together tonight and intend to see it through because it's important to me that you know how much you mean to me, Nina." Deep inside the box, he withdrew a manila envelope. "This contains the proposal my investment broker just sent to yours."

She took the envelope and pulled out the papers, her hands trembling. She scanned the documents, then gasped. "Oh my God, Alex. Why did you offer to pay such a ridiculous amount for Cody's stocks? I thought you said your cash flow was tied up right now?"

"I did this because it's the right thing to do," he answered simply. "Cody is an amazing kid. I hope with every fiber of my being that with you as his advocate, he will have a future full of independence. But I know that's not a given. So I did what I could to help him."

She cocked her head to the side. "You really did risk your inheritance by pursuing me instead of taking your grandmother's 'test.' You're not trying to buy me off?"

As if that could even be done? He knew her better than that. This was a woman with deep values and a huge heart. "Nina, I would do just about anything for you. But this was for Cody, because that boy has come to mean a lot to me. Because I want the best for his future too."

A future Alex hoped he would be a part of.

She tucked the papers back into the envelope and set them on top of the blanket. "You didn't put your own finances at risk for this, did you?"

"I'll be fine. Hidden Gem will be fine. It's a done deal." His grandmother was ecstatic. Now he just prayed it was enough to keep Nina and Cody in his life.

She smoothed her hand along the envelope. "I don't know what to say to that other than thank you."

He rested his hand over hers. "You could say you forgive me."

She drew in a shaky breath. "I wish you could have been open with me from the beginning, and especially as we got to know each other, but I can understand how deeply torn you must have felt the effects of your grandmother's illness."

"You're too forgiving." His hands slid up her arms as he started to hope this could work out after all. "I have one more thing for you in the box. Are you still interested?"

She smiled. "Most definitely."

God, how crazy that he was nervous over this part when he knew with every fiber of his being it was exactly what he wanted. But then nothing had ever been this important. He reached in to pull out a dozen yellow roses.

"I know that red roses are supposed to signify love, but we're in Texas, and the yellow rose is our flower. I very much want you to be my Texas rose. Now. Always. Because in spite of my quiet tendency to keep to myself, I have fallen impulsively, totally in love with you, Nina Lowery."

The tears in her eyes spilled over and she launched into his arms, the flowers crushing between them and releasing sweet perfume.

Her mouth met his and she kissed him once, twice and again, before pulling back. "Oh God, Alex, I love you too. Your strength, your tenderness, the way you always put others first, which makes me want to be your champion, giving back to you the way you give to so many others."

His heart pounded with relief and happiness. How did he get this damn lucky? "I have a plan. We can see each other every week while we work out details. If you don't want to move I can look into opening a Hidden Gem in San Antonio."

She gasped. "You would do that for me?"

"For you, absolutely." He cupped her face in his hands. "I want what's best for you and Cody. We can figure that out together."

She set aside the crushed flowers and pulled out one long-stemmed bud that had survived. "Actually my job enables me to live anywhere. So I was thinking more along the lines of a long-term rental of one of the cabins. You and I could...date." She trailed the flower under her nose and then provocatively between her breasts. "Get to know each other better. Turn this fling into an all-out affair."

"Ah," he sighed, anticipation pumping through him. "I can romance you. Win you over."

"You've already won me over. Lock, stock and barrel, I'm yours." She traced a rosebud along the side of his face. "And *you* are mine."

* * * * *

PREGNANT BY
THE COWBOY CEO

CATHERINE MANN

To my family—my world

Prologue

Two months ago

Amie McNair had never considered a one-night stand. Until now.

A champagne fountain gurgled beside her as she stared across the ballroom full of partiers gathered to celebrate her cousin's engagement. The night had been fun so far, but too similar to so many other glittering events that she attended in her work. She'd been thinking up an excuse to leave soon so she could trade her silky dress for the comfort of cotton pajamas. The jeweled choker at her throat was a gorgeous piece, but the yellow diamond at the base of her throat felt heavy. Tight. Like a collar keeping her neck in check. She liked her longer, bohemian-style pendants.

Those mundane thoughts scattered when he entered the room.

The broad-shouldered man striding confidently through the arched entryway pulled the air from her lungs. The connection was instantaneous. She wasn't quite certain why, but she forgot all about a desire for cotton pj's or the need to tug off her necklace. Her nerve endings sat up and paid attention.

Sure, he was tall, dark and hunky. But her world was filled with commanding, powerful men—from the cowboys that worked on her family's Hidden Gem Hobby Ranch, to the executives who worked in the family's Diamonds in the Rough jewelry-design empire. This man certainly measured up, from his muscled chest in the custom-tailored tuxedo, to the black Stetson he swept from his head and passed to an attendant near the entrance.

Yes, a Stetson and a tux.

And a boldly handsome face, tanned, with a strong square jaw. A face that had been lived in. His coal-black hair had a sprinkling of silver at the temples. That hint of age shouted wisdom, resolve. *Experience.*

A shiver tingled through her, gathering in all the right places.

Yet, in spite of all that, she found herself drawn most to his eyes. Even from halfway across the ballroom she could see they were a mesmerizing mix of gold and green that shifted ever so slightly with the chandelier sparkling overhead. She'd worked with amber that color in her jewelry designs and the changeable nature of the hue fascinated her. His gaze swept over her, past, then back again.

Holding.

That shiver inside her turned into a full-fledged fire. Her hand trembled and she set aside her champagne glass, her body already drawn forward in an undeniable magnetic pull. The urge to find out more about him propelled her feet across the room in time with the live band playing a classic Patsy Cline love song. Amie walked beneath the oversize, multicolored paper lanterns that decorated the room, toward the mystery man as he angled past guests in tuxes and formal gowns.

Other women noticed him, too, some of them watching every bit as intently as she did. But his eyes stayed on her as he closed the gap one bold step at a time.

Who was he? She knew most of the guests but didn't recognize him. Still, enough people nodded in greeting to him for her to know he wasn't a party crasher.

His gaze stroked over her, his hazel eyes gliding along her body like whispery smoke, confirming the awareness was reciprocated. She let herself relish the feeling, because honest to God, the last year had drained her. The grief over her grandmother's cancer, over the impending loss of the most important person in her life was heavy. Too heavy. From tip to toe, she hurt over losing her grandmother and, knowing Gran's legacy, her company was in the process of being handed over to a new CEO. So much change. Not the way her family's business was meant to be handled.

But right now, for the first time since her grandmother had announced her terminal brain tumor, there was a distraction from that ache in her heart.

A compelling, fascinating distraction.

She stopped in front of him, only a few inches apart. The crowd was so thick around them, the hum of their conversation and the band's tune created a false bubble of privacy. He held his silence, just looking back at her with a furrowed brow. Nice to know she wasn't the only one baffled by this moment.

She certainly didn't believe in love at first sight, but she couldn't deny the chemistry, the intense attraction, the connection that felt like more than simple lust. She understood physical attraction but considered herself beyond those superficial types of relationships. After all, her mother had trotted her across pageant stage from toddler days. Hair teased. Makeup. Ruffled custom dresses and shiny tap shoes.

Amie had been judged on her appearance, her walk, her smile for longer than she could remember. She'd seen enough backstabbing beauties with a Mona Lisa smile to know that the true value of a person went much deeper than the surface. Even knowing that, she couldn't deny how much she wanted this man.

She meant to say hello or introduce herself or ask his name. Instead, she glanced at his hand. No wedding ring. No tan line. "Are you married?"

A dark eyebrow lifted in a brief flash of surprise.

"Are you?" His voice rumbled between them with a hint of twang.

Local? Not quite. But definitely from a nearby region. His voice tripped along her senses, a deep tone that shivered against her skin.

She shook her head. "I'm not married."

"Me neither," he answered simply, without touching her. "Are you seeing anyone?"

She liked that it mattered to him. That said something good about him. "No. Are you seeing anyone?"

"Only the woman in front of me."

Oh. Damn. He was good. A small smile teased the corners of his mouth.

She wasn't sure exactly who moved first, but somehow her hand was tucked in the crook of his arm and he led her to the dance floor where they moved silently, their bodies in tune, step for step, through a slower country-music classic. The thick clusters of bright paper lanterns made the room glow with a rainbow of colors.

She breathed in his scent, clean but spicy, too. Masculine. Heady. His touch warmed her where he touched her waist. Her hand.

How long had it been since she'd felt a man's hands on her?

The energy between them crackled like static along her skin. Each chord from the string band strummed her oversensitive senses. She breathed in and he breathed out. Their steps synced effortlessly, her body responding to the slightest movement of his, shadowing his steps as she fell deeper into the spell of his gaze.

The dance gave her rare moments of pleasure in a year of hellish hurt and worry. No wonder she'd been drawn to him. She needed this. And in the same way that she could follow his steps, her body anticipating his next move, she could tell that he needed this, too. It was in his eyes. In the way his hand spanned her waist.

A step and swirl later and they were in the hall, then tucked in the deserted coatroom.

Then in each other's arms.

The dim lighting cast the room in shadows as she arched up into his kiss, his arms strong around her, but loose enough she could leave if she wanted. But the last thing she wanted was to stop. Pleasure pulsed through her at the angling of his mouth over hers, the touch of his tongue to hers. The kiss went deeper, faster, spiraling out of control in the quiet of the coat closet—a seriously underutilized space since it was spring in Texas.

Still, someone could walk in, and while she wasn't an exhibitionist, the possibility of discovery added an edge to an already razor-sharp need. The muffled sounds of music and partiers wafted under the door. She pressed herself to the hard planes of his body.

His arms moved up and he cupped her face, looking at her with those intense hazel eyes. "I don't do this sort of thing, tuck into coat closets with a stranger."

She covered his mouth with her hand. "We don't need to make excuses we have no way of knowing are true. This moment just…is. I don't understand why. But we're here." She took a deep breath of courage and said, "Lock the door."

Without a word, his hand slid behind him and the lock clicked in the long closet. The simple sound unleashed her barely contained passion. She looped her arms around his neck and lost herself in the kiss again. In the feel and fantasy of this man.

Her breasts tingled and tightened into hard beads of achy need. She couldn't remember when she'd been this turned inside out. She was thirty-one years old, not nearly a virgin. But she was unable to resist the draw of this stranger. The hard length of his erection pressed against her stomach, a heavy pressure that burned right through the silky dress she wore.

She couldn't deny where this was headed or that she wanted this. Him. Now.

His mouth traveled down her neck, then along her collarbone. "Condom. In my wallet," he said, his hands grazing under her breasts. "I'll get it."

He started to ease back and she stopped him, gripping his lapels.

"Let me."

Slipping her hand into his tuxedo jacket, she let her fingers stroke across the muscled heat of his chest. This was a man, the very best kind, powerful in body and mind. She tugged his wallet from inside his jacket and considered for an instant looking for a name, …but her thoughts were scattered by his hands over her hips, gathering her dress. She plucked out a condom packet and tossed his wallet to the floor.

His hands were back on her just as fast, roving, keeping the flame burning.

She unzipped his pants as he lifted her hem. Her gown bunched around her hips, he hitched her up onto the small corner table where the coat check would normally pass out tickets during colder months. The wood was cool against her legs and then she slid them up and around his waist as he pressed against her, into her, with a thick pressure that sent a moan rolling up her throat.

It wasn't an elegant coupling. Her need was frenzied and his matched hers. This was crazy and out of control. And perfect. She lost herself in the pleasure, her senses heightened until everything felt…more. The tangy scent of his aftershave swirled inside her with every breath. Music muffled from the other room serenaded them, syncing their bodies into the most fundamental of dances.

And then thoughts disintegrated, the pace speeding, rising, bliss swelling inside her until she bit her lip to hold back a cry of pleasure that would betray their hideaway at any moment. He skimmed down the shoulder of her dress, dipping his head to take her breast in his mouth. That warm, moist tug took away the last of her restraint. Her head falling back, she surrendered to the orgasm sparkling through her like the facets off a diamond. The hoarse low sound of his release as he thrust deeply one last time sent another shimmer through her, leaving her languid, replete.

Using a last whisper of energy, she lolled forward. Her head rested on his shoulder as she waited for her racing heart to slow. His hands glided up and down her spine, easing her back to her feet, holding her up.

He smoothed her dress into place again and pressed a kiss to her temple. "We should tal—"

She shook her head. "Please. Don't say anything." She tugged her capped sleeve back over her shoulder and skimmed along her hair, the French braid having stayed miraculously in place, right down to the jeweled flower pin she'd clipped to the end of the braid. "Let's go back out. Go to separate sides of the room. And when, or if, we meet…it will be for the first time. Let this be what it is."

A fantasy. A once-in-a-lifetime crazy encounter— and she didn't want to hear it was commonplace for him. Didn't want to think about what she'd just done. Not while her body still trembled with pleasure and her heartbeat pulsed an erratic rhythm.

She didn't wait for his answer.

Reaching behind her, she simply unlocked the door, tucking out and around. Her legs were less than steady as she made her way back to the ballroom, and the sound of his footsteps close behind her didn't help. Was he following her? Was he going to insist or make a scene?

A mix of anticipation and dread made her chest tight with nerves.

The cool blast of the air conditioner in the hall rushed over her heated skin, goose bumps rising along her arms. The band still played, having picked up the speed with vintage Johnny Cash.

And before she could clear her head, she realized her grandmother had blocked her path. Mariah McNair looked regal but frail as she clutched her cane.

The tangy scent of masculine aftershave teased Amie's nose. Was it wafting from him behind her? Or just clinging to her body to remind her of what she'd done?

Her grandmother gripped the cane in a hand bearing sparkling jeweled rings. One of them was an amethyst heart Amie had designed as a teenager. With her other hand, Mariah took hers in a cool grasp, her skin paper thin and covered with bruises from IVs. Despite her frailty, Mariah's grip was firm, confident. "Amie, dear, I was just looking for you to introduce you. But I see you and Preston have met."

Foreboding iced out residual passion. "Preston?"

Her brain worked overtime to make the pieces fit any other way but the one she feared.

Yet the magnetic, compelling man she'd just given herself to in a coat closet stepped around her, his eyebrows now pinched together as he whispered, "Amie?"

Her stomach dropped as if she'd just fallen down an elevator shaft. Dawning realization robbed her of speech, her mouth bone dry.

Her grandmother squeezed Amie's hand as she smiled at Preston.

"I'm so glad you've had a chance to get to know our new CEO." Mariah extended her hand to the man. "Welcome to the Hidden Gem Ranch."

One

Two Months Later

Preston Armstrong was not a fan of weddings. Not even when he'd been the groom. Since his divorce ten years ago, he was even less entertained by overpriced ceremonial gatherings. He considered himself a practical businessman. That mind-set had taken him from a poor childhood to the top of the corporate ladder.

So, attending a marriage ceremony and seeing Amie McNair front and center of attention as a bridesmaid took his irritation to a whole deeper level—even now at the reception. Especially given that she'd ignored him for the past two months.

And most especially since she looked sexy as hell in a peach-colored bridesmaid's dress. Weren't those gowns supposed to be ugly, hated by bridal attendants around the world? But then, beautiful Amie with her luscious curves and confidence could probably make a burlap sack look sexy as hell. She'd won all those beauty-pageant titles for a reason.

Although he thought she was more alluring now with her at-ease boho look than the old runway-glitz photos that still periodically showed up in the social pages. Even her signature-designed coral teardrop earrings and necklace held his attention. Particularly the way that pendant nestled between the swell of her breasts.

He tipped his aged bourbon back, the sounds of the reception wrapping around him as he put in his required appearance at the McNair wedding event. He glanced at his watch, figuring he had to put in another half hour before he could check out and head back to the office. It was quiet there at night. He got more work done.

If Amie would talk to him alone for five damn minutes, he could reassure her that the closet encounter would never have happened if he'd known who she was. From the horrified expression on her face when her grandmother introduced them, clearly Amie didn't want anything to do with him either.

Business and pleasure should be kept separate. Always.

He didn't have the time or patience for awkwardness. He was confident. In charge. But that had all changed the minute he'd looked across the social function and saw a woman who'd flipped his world upside down.

This whole wedding week had gone to a new level of uncomfortable, to say the least. Being around Amie at work, they could keep things professional, if tense. It wasn't easy with all those thoughts of their explosive encounter hammering through his memory, but he managed to keep his boardroom calm intact.

However, the parties this week reminded him too much of that night he'd met her at the newlyweds' engagement shindig.

He'd meant it when he'd told her that impulsive encounter wasn't the norm for him. While he wasn't a monk, impetuous sex with strangers had never been his style. He'd spent a large part of his adult life married and monogamous. Then after his divorce, affairs had been careful, sensual but civil, with no long-term expectations.

He had affairs. Not hookups. And he sure as hell didn't have anonymous sex with a woman more than a decade younger than him.

Until Amie. Nothing about her followed a familiar pattern for him.

Keeping his hands to himself today was an exercise in torture, just as at work. Hints of her sucker punched his libido. The soft scent of her perfume lingering in his office after a meeting. The heat of her as she stood near him in a crowded elevator. And the list went on since she worked in the same building, her role as a renowned gemologist crucial to some of the most popular Diamonds in the Rough jewelry lines.

Up on the small stage in the oversize barn, the country band returned from their break, taking their place again and picking up instruments. Although to call it a barn didn't do the space justice. The reception was being held at the McNairs' hobby ranch, Hidden Gem, so the place was high end rustic, just like the company jewels.

Gold chandeliers and puffs of white flowers dangled

from the rough-hewn rafters. Strings of lights criss-crossed the ceiling, creating a starlit-night atmosphere. Bouquets of baby's breath and roses tied with burlap bows on the tables made him recall his earlier thought about Amie classing up a burlap sack. The inside had been transformed into rustic elegance, with gold chairs and white tulle draped throughout.

At the entry table next to the leather guestbook, seating cards were tied to horseshoes that had the bride's and groom's names engraved along with the wedding date. A cowbell hung on a brass hook with a sign that stated, Ring for a Kiss.

Good God. He wanted out of here. He knocked back the rest of the bourbon.

Amie's cousin Stone McNair, the former CEO of Diamonds in the Rough, was the groom, and there was no doubt he believed in all this forever, happily-ever-after nonsense as he twirled his blonde bride around on the dance floor.

At least the ceremony in the chapel had been brief. One bridesmaid and one groomsman—Amie and her twin brother, Alex. Amie's dark brown hair was loose, in thick spiral curls that made him want to tug just to see what she would do.

To hell with standing around. He might as well confront the awkwardness. It wasn't as if she could run away from him here.

He set aside the cut-crystal glass and strode through the crowd, a who's who list of Texas rich and famous. Just like that night two months ago, he made his way to her, this time determined for closure rather than a start of something.

Getting her semi-alone here shouldn't be too tough.

The exclusive venue had plenty of dark corners arranged for privacy so guests could visit and catch up.

He stopped behind her, smiling over her shoulder at the mayor. "I'm sorry to interrupt, but Miss McNair promised me this dance."

Amie gasped, her mouth opening to protest. But Preston took her hand and pulled her onto the dance floor before she could speak. He hauled her out in front of the small chamber orchestra, moving quickly before the stunned expression could melt from her elegant face. Before a closed, frosty one took its place. He'd watched that transformation too often over the last eight weeks and it was time to put an end to it.

He slid an arm around her and drew her close, those dark brown curls brushing him. "You look lovely tonight. Especially for being stuck in a bridesmaid's dress."

"It would have been nice to be asked if I wanted to dance. What are you doing?"

"Dancing with the groom's cousin. A perfectly acceptable move, nothing to draw attention to us. Unless you cause a scene out here in front of your whole family, our business acquaintances and some mighty prominent politicians."

Which he definitely did not want her to do. Then, he would have to let her go. And he liked the feel of her in his arms again too much to have her walk away yet.

"Fine," she conceded, blue eyes predictably turning to ice as she spoke. "Let's dance for appearances. Gran's always saying it's good for the company if we show a unified front."

Oh, he had her here for more than appearances and business. He was going to find a way to get past her cold shoulder. He couldn't stop the attraction, and chances were slim to none that he would be able to act on it. But he could damn well do something to disperse the tension between them.

He hoped.

Preston sidestepped another couple and swept her to a less crowded corner of the dance floor, mindful of the security guards posted around the perimeter of the event. "It's quite a party tonight. Congratulations to your cousin and his bride on their nuptials."

If Stone hadn't given up his role as CEO of Diamonds in the Rough, Preston wouldn't have been here. And the job was damn important to him. His job was all he had after the crash and burn of his personal life.

She smiled tightly, her body stiff and unyielding in his arms. "We do have all the tools for a first-rate wedding at our disposal."

The bride's thirty-thousand-dollar tiara had been custom designed for the event; in fact, a delicately understated piece that Amie had worked on personally for weeks. The tiara alone had created industry buzz and media coverage alike, a key piece in the company's new bridal collection.

"Do you realize this is the first time we've spoken about anything other than business?" He respected her work ethic, and discovering that admirable trait about her made this all the more difficult. Unlike her father, she was more than a figurehead. Amie contributed immeasurably to the company, so Preston crossed her path. Often.

She angled closer and for an instant he thought maybe... his pulse sped. His gaze dropped to her mouth. To her lips, parted.

And then, too soon, her breath teased against his

neck as she whispered, "I just want to make it clear, we won't be heading for the coat closet tonight."

There was no mistaking her determination. Too bad her method for delivering the news had him ready to sweep her off her feet and back to the cabin he'd reserved on the property for the night.

"I'm quite clear on that after your big chill these past two months." His hand twitched against her waist, the memory of her satiny skin still burned in his memory. "I'm just glad to know you're finally willing to acknowledge it happened."

"Of course it happened," she hissed between pearly-white teeth. "I was very much there."

The brush of her body against his was sweet torture. "I remember well."

Shadows shifted through her sky blue eyes. "Did you know who I was that night?"

Her words slowed his feet, stunning him. He picked up the dance pace again and asked, "Is that what you've thought all this time? That I played you on purpose?"

"Forget I said anything." She pulled back. "It doesn't matter now."

He strengthened his hold. "Not that you would believe me regardless of what I say. Although it was more than clear you didn't know who I was, and if you had, that night wouldn't have happened." He touched her face lightly. "And that would have been a damn shame."

They stood so close, their mouths only a couple of inches apart. He remembered how good she tasted—and how complicated that had made things for them the past couple of months. Having an affair with her would be a bad idea, given he was her boss and she was the granddaughter of the major stockholder.

But God, he was tempted.

So was she. He could see it in her jewel-blue eyes and the way she swayed toward him an instant before she stepped back.

Grasping his wrists, she pulled his arms from her. "I'm not sure what spurred you to reminisce right now since you don't seem to be the type to get sentimental at weddings. But now is not the time or the place for this discussion."

His eyebrows rose in surprise. "You're willing to talk then? Later?"

She held up a hand. "Talk. Only. I mean that."

"Let's step outside—"

"No. Not here. Not tonight."

He reached for her, sensing already she was just putting him off again. "Amie, if this is another stall tactic—"

"We'll have our secretaries check our calendars and schedule a lunch next week. Okay? Is that specific enough for you? Now, I need to check on my grandmother." She spun away in a swirl of peach silk.

Standing in the middle of the dance floor, he watched her walk away, the sway of her hips and those million-dollar legs peeking through a slit in the dress. Stepping off the dance floor, he wondered what the hell he hoped to gain in a conversation with her. An affair, given their work connection, was a bad idea, but he wasn't in the market for anything long term. Not again.

He charged back to the bar for another bourbon on the rocks, ignoring a waiter's offering of the evening's signature beverage, a Mouton Rothschild favored by the couple. Tonight, bourbon would do just fine. Marriage hadn't worked out well for him. At all. Just ask his ex.

He was too absorbed with work, too much of a loner. After all, a boss couldn't party with his subordinates, which put a serious dent in any kind of social life. He wanted to say that's what had made him so susceptible to Amie that first night, but he knew it was more than that. He was a man of control. Calm. Yet, the second he'd seen Amie, he'd claimed her with that first look in an explosive chemistry that went beyond any he'd experienced before, even with his ex-wife.

No wonder his marriage had failed early on. He'd made a fortune and in the end it hadn't made a bit of difference when things mattered most.

Rather than subject their daughter to a divorce, he and his wife had tried to hold it together for their child. But theirs had become a marriage in name only. Eventually, his ex had found someone else. She'd told Preston her new love would at least be around, which was better for Leslie than an absentee father. He'd bought into that, feeling guilty as hell and incapable of giving his child what she needed.

He'd replayed that decision a million times over, wondering if he'd fought harder for his marriage, for his child, if life could have turned out differently. Guilt piled on top of more guilt.

His baby girl had flown out of control during her teen years. Drugs, alcohol, sex. He'd tried grounding her, taking away her car, her allowance. He'd planned to take a vacation week to spend time with her, let her pick the vacation spot. She'd turned him down.

He should have persisted. He'd thought about it. Then it was too late.

Leslie ran off with her boyfriend the day after graduation, seventeen years old, pregnant. She'd ignored all offers of help and advice, determined to put her parents and the lifestyle she hated behind her. She hadn't cared about wealth or private jets. Hadn't wanted her own driver or a massive home. She'd even snubbed a doctor's care.

She and her baby boy had died seven months into the pregnancy. Premature delivery. Something with the placenta presenting first. His daughter, Leslie, bled to death. The baby lived for two days before dying.

The Armstrong portfolio was worth billions and his daughter and grandson had died from lack of prenatal care because she hated him that much. So much, she wouldn't take a penny or the most basic advice from him.

Some days the senselessness of it made it nearly impossible to hold back the rage.

The pain.

His child. Gone.

His ex blamed him. Damn it all, but he blamed himself, too.

So he put one foot in front of the other and existed.

Until that moment he'd seen Amie McNair. What was it about her? He wasn't the type to fall for a pretty face. But she was more than that. Not that he'd known as much that night. He'd just looked into her eyes and he'd seen...

Something that scared the hell out of him. Something worth going back for.

A risk he couldn't take again.

Pushing her grandmother's wheelchair down the hall to the family quarters, Amie took comfort from the ever-present scent of oak and pine that permeated the main lodge at Hidden Gem Ranch. The family wing could be accessed privately from the outside, but tonight, she'd taken the easier path through the lobby, waving to the night desk clerk on duty.

Now, as they passed through double doors that required a pass code, Amie could still barely breathe after how close she'd come to kissing Preston right there on the dance floor in front of everyone. She did not need people gossiping about the two of them. Especially not now. Damn him for rattling her. She needed to keep a cool head for her grandmother's sake.

Amie had never been known for her restraint.

She'd been sorely tempted to steal one more passionate moment with him before the inevitable conversation he'd insisted on having. But then her stomach had started churning and she'd made the excuse about secretaries and calendars before bolting.

Throwing up on his shoes would have been the worst way to tell him their night in the coat closet had created a baby.

Somehow, in spite of the condom, she was undeniably pregnant. She hadn't been with anyone else in six months, so there was no question about the paternity. She needed to tell him soon and agree on a plan before she shared the news with her grandmother.

Amie glanced down at her grandmother's gray head, her body frail from cancer, her once-long hair now short, just beginning to grow back from the latest round of treatments and surgeries that had only delayed the inevitable. "You overextended yourself this week, Gran."

Amie backed into her grandmother's suite of rooms, a decorative set of cattle horns on the door, an old joke of Gran's from her days in the corporate boardroom when a competitor had called her bullheaded. Gran had proudly taken to displaying this set on the front of her chauffeur-driven vehicle. These days, they resided on her door, still a reminder of her strength.

"Of course I did." Gran reached back to pat Amie's fingers on the handle, hand trembling. "I would rather die a day or two earlier than miss making the most of my grandson's wedding festivities."

"Well, that's blunt." Amie maneuvered the chair along a Persian rug, past a long leather sofa, the fireplace roaring with a warm blaze despite the summer temperature outside. Her grandmother appreciated the ambience and didn't mind the extra warmth in her more frail condition.

"You're one to talk considering you are just like me, stubborn as hell."

"I'll take that as a compliment, thank you very much."

Gran would be happy about the baby, no question. But Amie worried about the future because there was no way the critically ill woman would live long enough to see her great-grandchild's face. Amie couldn't bear to add more concerns. Beyond making her final days peaceful, stress was also a danger to her already fragile health. Amie needed to get her life together and develop a plan regarding Preston's role in their child's life. In this much, at least, she could be like her grandmother. Strong. Driven.

Calculating.

As the wheelchair rolled to a stop, Mariah folded her hands in her lap again. The bedroom was at once familiar and alien with its soaring high ceilings in rustic woodwork, supported by exposed beams in a darker wood. A two-tiered cast-iron chandelier hung over the living area, casting a warm glow, with lights that looked like gently flickering candles. Two wingback chairs bracketed the stone fireplace where she'd shared secrets and hot chocolate with her grandmother. But now there were additions to the place—a wheeled hospital cart of medical supplies and a leather recliner where the night nurse usually kept watch.

No doubt, Gran's caregiver would report in as soon as Amie sent her a text.

"Can I help you get settled? Bring you anything before I call for the nurse?" She took out her phone but wanted to stay. Wanted to visit the way they used to, never caring how late the hour.

Her eyes burned as she blinked away unexpected tears.

Her grandmother gestured for her to sit. "Amie, I've lived a full life. Of course I would have liked to have more, or at the very least live these last days in full health. But I'm making the most of the time I have left. I've seen one grandson married and have hopes the other grandson will be settled soon."

Ouch. No mention of her granddaughter. Just that Stone was married, and Alex had found the perfect woman. She swallowed hard.

"Alex and Nina are happy, and her son, Cody, is precious." She was happy for Alex. Her twin's joy was her joy.

"It's good to see a child here in the house again. I've missed the laughter of a little one."

Did her grandmother know? Was she hinting for an admission or just referencing Cody? Shooting to her feet, she turned away to hide any telltale expressions on her face. Amie picked up the pewter pitcher on the bedside table and refilled her grandmother's water glass, unable to pull her eyes away from the photo of her grandparents on their wedding day. "You should turn in early and conserve your strength for the family breakfast tomorrow."

"I'm resting now and my strength isn't going to return," she said with a dry laugh. She sipped her water, cleared her throat and continued, "I don't have to sleep to relax. Let's talk."

"About what?" Her skin prickled. She sat on the chaise at the end of the four-poster bed that had been converted into a queen-size hospital bed. Unwilling to think about that—and how hard life had become for her beloved grandmother, Amie bent to breathe in the delicate scent of lilies of the valley in a big bunch on the nightstand.

Gran set aside her glass of water. "Stone and Alex have both passed their test to assure me they can handle their share of the inheritance, that they can carry on the McNair tradition in the spirit I would wish."

Her cousin Stone had surprised them all by stepping down as CEO of Diamonds in the Rough and developing his nearby land. He'd started an equine therapy camp for children with special needs. Her twin brother, Alex, had gained their grandmother's trust to keep running the Hidden Gem Ranch and opened up parts of the facility for Stone's camp.

"Ah, so now you get to the reason for this conversation." She sagged back, clutching a decorative pillow protectively. "What do you have cooked up for me?"

"You don't need to look so worried." A smile lighting her sapphire-blue eyes, Gran smoothed her grandmother-of-the-groom turquoise satin dress, the hem heavy with silver embroidery that mimicked a Diamonds in the Rough necklace she favored.

"Of course I'm worried. And more than a little curious. You saved my test for last for a reason, I'm sure.

I assume that's because my challenge is the most difficult. Or I'm the most difficult to deal with." A bitter memory from her past seeped in. "Mom always coveted that slot to perform last in a pageant to keep me foremost in the judges' minds. After the bar had been raised as high as possible, she figured I would know how well I had to perform to win."

Like the year her mother had changed Amie's baton-twirling act into a fire-throwing stunt—just half an hour before Amie took the stage—since another girl had done a great baton act. Amie would have never guessed her mother could find a way to light the ends of her batons on fire in thirty minutes. But with Mc-Nair wealth and a helpful hotel concierge, anything was possible for a demanding pageant mother. Amie hadn't burned down the building or set herself on fire, but she hadn't won and she'd been scared as hell.

Gran's smile faded and sympathy filled her eyes. "The test I have in mind isn't like your mother making you compete in all those beauty pageants."

"Isn't it?" Amie said bitterly, then felt guilty right away. It wasn't her grandmother's fault. "Never mind. Forget I said that. I know you're not like Bayleigh... You love me, so whatever you're doing must be for a reason."

"Your mother loves you, dear, she's just…"

"Self-absorbed." There was no denying the truth. "I've acknowledged that and moved on. I'm an adult and I accept responsibility for my own feelings."

Gran tipped her head to the side. "You say that, but until this moment, I never realized this test would make you feel as if my love is conditional…like your mother's."

"Does that mean I'm off the hook with my challenge?

You'll fire Preston and put me in charge?" she asked, only half joking.

"Oh dear, you always did have a great sense of humor," Gran said affectionately. "This isn't about my love for you. Love isn't about money. You have millions with your trust fund and personal earnings. This is about figuring out where you best fit professionally in the business."

"What if I do like Stone and decide to build my own future?" She just wished there was something else she wanted to do, but she lived and breathed to work at Diamonds in the Rough.

Or at least she had until Preston showed up and took away the job she'd hoped for as her own.

"That's your choice. But keep in mind Stone still took his test because he knew that would put my mind at ease. These requests of mine are because I love you and I want the best for you."

Amie sighed, exhaustion stealing through her. "I do know that, Gran."

Her grandmother's shoulders braced. "This week Preston Armstrong is traveling in support of the unveiling of our new line. I want you to go with him."

She waited for the rest and…nothing. "That's it?" Amie asked, incredulous. "That's my test?"

"Yes, be civil. Don't cause a scene. Truly show the world that we're a unified force, even away from the office, and stockholders will be reassured."

"A week on the road with no scenes." She'd kept her distance from him for two months, she could do so for longer.

"That's all."

"You're letting me off rather easy," she conceded,

hoping she could finish up some design work on the trip since she'd been working night and day on a secret collection—a labor of love that she worried wasn't right for Diamonds in the Rough.

"I don't think so." Her grandmother shook her head. "Not considering the cold shoulder you've given him these past couple of months."

She could have sworn she'd kept that from her grandmother. Mariah wasn't at the office often at all. Amie had imagined—hoped—her chilly reception would be perceived as businesslike.

She'd guessed wrong. "I apologize if you think I haven't been receptive to your new CEO. I thought I was simply being professional."

"Don't try that innocent act with me," Gran snorted. "You won't even stay in the same room with him unless forced by a meeting. I'm not sure what your differences are and I don't need to know. We are very lucky to have lured him away from his job in Oklahoma. It was a big sell convincing him this job would increase his corporate appeal as a man of serious net worth and business importance. I do not want to lose him at Diamonds in the Rough, as our stocks continue to rise since we announced he was taking the helm."

"Rising at the expense of firing some of our most loyal, long-serving middle management," she reminded her grandmother.

"And I can see you're still bitter about that decision to consolidate here and expand other offices."

Amie pressed her lips together to keep from arguing with her grandmother, something that would only stress her out since clearly this battle was already lost.

Gran nodded wearily. "Reconcile with him. Because,

like it or not, he is the CEO, and if having you there upsets the flow of business, well, I can't have that."

The full weight of her grandmother's words sunk in. "Are you threatening to fire me?"

And just as troubling, what did Preston have to do with this? Had he been pressuring Gran to nudge her out of the company? Or to find another angle to wrangle his way into her bed?

His approach tonight might not have been coincidental. He could have set this whole thing up, damn him. Anger fired hotter inside her, almost a welcome relief after the frustrated passion, fear for her child—and grief for Gran.

"Let's not borrow trouble. Focus on the week and learn to forge a friendship with Preston."

Friendship? With the father of her child from a one-night stand? And how was he going to react to the news of the baby? Gran's request might not even be possible. "What if Preston doesn't agree? Or if he's antagonistic?"

Her grandmother smiled with a narrow-eyed determination Amie recognized well. "Then you'll just have to win him over. Because, like it or not, your days of avoiding him are done."

Two

Hands jammed in his tuxedo pockets, Preston strode away from the barn to the resort cabin where he planned to spend the night. Most of the guests were either staying in the main lodge or in one of the bungalows scattered around the property.

He'd done his duty at the reception, put in an appearance. With luck, he could pull out his laptop and log some extra hours preparing for his upcoming business trip. He would try to numb his mind and body against the attraction. Just being near Amie at the wedding had desire pumping through him. He needed to come up with some kind of plan to work with her without this eating them both alive, but damned if he knew which way to turn. For now, burying himself in reports and numbers would have to do.

The reception was still going strong in the towering barn, music and conversation swelling out into the night. The lodge itself held two wings, one for family suites and the other for guests. Then the cabins offered larger, more private space, farther away from the din of the ongoing party.

A movement from the family quarters snagged his attention, a shadowy figure charging across a first-floor veranda. The moonlight cast a glow, illuminating the unmistakable silhouette of... Amie. She paused at the railing, scanning the grounds. She was looking for him—that was clear the second her gaze landed on him.

Her shoulders went back, her breasts straining at the strapless dress, teardrop earrings brushing her bare shoulders. She flicked her long hair over her shoulder, her eyes narrowing. She stomped down the porch steps, hem of her bridesmaid's gown in her fists and hitched to her knees so she could storm closer all the faster. Something had lit her fuse. He wanted her attention back on him anyway.

He stopped in his tracks and waited. Anticipation pumped through him. Even mad, she was incredible, a sight not to be missed. Besides, there was something about knowing he got under her skin this much. That he'd put all that spark and fire inside her.

She stopped in front of him under the shade of a sprawling oak strung with white lights. Her breasts rose and fell rapidly, enticingly. "Are you responsible for this?"

Responsible for what? He could hardly think with her so close, her heaving breasts nearly brushing his chest. He would only need to move one step closer. "You'll need to narrow that down for me."

"You said on the dance floor that we need to talk soon." She jabbed him in the chest with one finger.

He grabbed her finger. "And you said our secretaries need to set up a lunch next week."

"Did you know that couldn't possibly happen? Did you pressure my grandmother into making me travel with you around the country this week?"

He dropped her hand. He didn't know what the hell she was talking about. He was heading out for a week to launch a new line for Diamonds in the Rough, but he'd made no plans to take her along. Apparently she thought otherwise for some reason.

Still, that didn't explain her angry reaction. They'd worked together for two months. Why was she so upset about this trip? He was missing something and he wasn't sure what.

But he intended to find out. "Why would I go out of my way to insist on that?"

"For a week of repeats of our encounter in the coat closet two months ago."

Righteous indignation steamed through him. "Have I pressured you in any way that would make you assume that I would disregard your wishes? Because I take the issue of sexual harassment in the workplace damn seriously."

"No, you haven't done anything inappropriate," she acquiesced, chewing her full bottom lip. "But you sounded determined tonight. I just had to know if you're manipulating me behind the scenes as well."

Unable to resist taunting her, he stepped closer, letting his gaze linger on her mouth as their bodies brushed. "Should I have?"

A light flashed in the night sky and an appreciative

murmur went up from a crowd gathered on the western lawn. The fireworks show had started to celebrate the nuptials.

"Quit twisting my words around." She tipped her face toward him without backing down, her creamy skin lit by the purple-and-white lights sparking overhead. "I don't like being played, that's all."

He swept a stray lock of silky dark hair over her shoulder, his knuckles skimming her soft skin, the teardrop earring cool across the top of his hand. "I take this to mean we're going on a business trip together this week."

The crowd watching fireworks cheered as a series of pops and bangs ended in a giant red heart burning into the cloudless Texas sky.

Her eyebrows pinched together, her gaze never wavering to watch the display. "You really don't know about my grandmother's plan for us?"

Gently, he gripped her shoulders and turned her so she could see the bright red heart before it faded. While she watched, he leaned closer to speak into her ear.

"I have no reason to lie to you." In fact, he just wanted to open a dialogue with her so they could figure out how to work together—or resume the affair. He couldn't help but wonder if part of the reason they kept sparking off each other was that they hadn't let all that attraction run its course. "It's been tough breaking through your walls these past two months, but I wouldn't go to someone else to take care of that problem for me. And I certainly wouldn't worry a terminally ill person with my concerns."

She turned to face him again, giving him a clipped nod, some of the tension easing from her while the orchestra played a Mozart piece timed to coordinate with the explosions in the air.

He leaned back against the tree trunk and jammed his hands into his pockets and away from temptation. "Now catch me up to speed about what's going on with this business trip, since it appears to involve us both and Diamonds in the Rough."

"My grandmother has insisted that I accompany you for the unveiling of the new line to reassure the stockholders that the McNairs fully endorse your leadership." Sighing, she perched a hand on her hip.

Preston's gaze fell to her waist, the dips and curves of her so damn alluring his mouth watered. "That's a sound business decision on her part. What's the problem?"

He didn't understand why she was so upset. She'd worked hard on the new line, had invested a lot of time and creative energy toward putting it together. She deserved to see the first public reactions to her work.

But she shook her head. Visibly upset.

"The problem is… She's an amazing woman and I just want to do what she needs." She blinked back tears, making her blue eyes shine in the reflected light from the soaring roman candles in a multicolored display. That sheen in her gaze made him want to hold her.

"Amie?" He resisted the urge to reach for her, half certain she would bolt. "Losing someone you love is not easy. I'm sorry about your grandmother's illness."

"Me, too." She swiped her wrist over her eyes, smudging mascara. "So we're traveling together this week for the unveiling tour. Just the two of us."

"Apparently so." He wondered what her grandmother was up to with this last-minute idea and why she hadn't discussed it with him first. "To Los Angeles, New York City and Atlanta. It may be for the best. We have to figure out how to work together without all this tension."

He had sensed that Amie was working on a private project these last few weeks and he wondered why she hadn't shared any details. That kind of closed-off creativity didn't benefit the larger company. He needed her communicating more.

Had that been Mariah McNair's intent, to smooth the business waters before she passed away? It wasn't such an odd wish. The woman did live, eat and breathe the business, even from her sickbed.

Amie crossed her arms over her chest, her breasts pushing even harder against the fabric. "We've been doing fine so far at the office."

"Are you serious?" These had been some of the most tense workweeks in his life. He'd never had personnel problems—until now. Until her.

"Has my work performance been in any way substandard?"

"Of course not," he admitted, not mentioning the way she'd retreated to her office for long periods at a time with her door closed. "But it would help workplace morale if you didn't act like you want me dead."

Her shoulders sagged, her eyes softening. "I do not want you dead."

"Then how exactly do you want me?" He stepped closer, his eyes falling to her mouth, to her full lips. Amie McNair had a way of knocking the props out from under him by just walking into a room, and he was damn tired of tap dancing around the subject. He was too old for games.

The fireworks on the lawn churned faster, shot after

shot popping and exploding, sending showers of sparks into the night sky. The fireworks reflected in Amie's eyes as she stepped back, expression iced over again. "If we're going to be away for a week, I should start packing."

Turning, she marched across the grass, her beautiful body illuminated by white lights in the sky that turned on and off, on and off.

Just like Amie herself.

Amie was exhausted to her toes. Not just from the wedding but from the shocking talk with her grandmother to the confrontation with Preston.

She was truly going to spend a week alone with him.

Closing her bedroom door, she finally let her guard down. Kneeling, she held out her hands for her cats, a gray tabby in her lap, a Siamese at her feet, both hers, and Mariah's two Persians as well. Yes, she was just shy of a crazy-cat-lady starter kit, but her furbabies brought her comfort. With a final stroke along each feline's arched back, she stood. She'd loved growing up on a farm with animals all around, even if her room was far from rustic, a jewel box of a space, from the strands of multicolored glass beads around her bed, to the stained-glass insets in the high windows above her reading area.

Walking out of her shoes, she reached behind her to unzip the bridesmaid's dress. She shimmied it down and kicked it aside. She sagged to sit on the edge of her bed. She flopped back on the bed, the silk of her camisole and tap pants soft against her skin still tingling from Preston's touch. Damn it, she hated losing her composure. And to lose it twice in one night?

Her hand slid over her stomach. No baby bump yet, but soon more than just her breasts would be swelling. And her hormones were out of control, leaving her tearful most of the time and nauseated the rest of the time. Her figure would soon be evident to everyone. No more pageant jokes about her size.

She'd been the first runner-up in the Miss Texas pageant over a decade ago, reportedly the first beauty competition she'd lost since her mother had teased up her hair and sent Amie tap-dancing out on the stage at four years old. She'd "Good Ship Lollipopped" her way through puberty into bikinis and spray tans. Her mama had lived for her daughter's wins.

She didn't even want to think about her parents' reaction to her pregnancy.

There wasn't anything she could do about it tonight and she truly was exhausted. No matter how much she slept, her body demanded more. She reached on the bedside table for her mouth guard by the phone. Tension had made her grind her teeth at night since she was seventeen and entered higher-stakes pageants.

She'd already seen a doctor to confirm and start prenatal vitamins. The appointment had been scary and exciting at the same time. Preston deserved the opportunity to be a part of his child's life from the start—if he wanted. She would have to tell him about the baby this week. It wasn't fair to wait any longer. This was his child too. She would just have to find the right time. His reaction would also have a lot to do with how she presented the news to the rest of her family.

If only she knew him better, knew how he would react, how he would want to proceed. She was capable and prepared to take care of the baby herself. But she didn't want her child to live with a father's rejection.

She squeezed her eyes shut and buried her face in her pillow, wishing she could will herself to sleep faster.

The phone rang on her bedside table, jarring her. Was something wrong with her grandmother?

Flinging back the covers, she grabbed the receiver and pulled out her mouth guard. "Hello?"

"Amie?" her twin brother's voice filled her ear. "Are you okay?"

"Of course." She tugged the covers back up again. "Why do you ask?"

"You left the reception before it was over. That isn't like you."

They always had been in tune with each other's moods. Her brother wasn't normally a chatty person, so for him to call, he must sense something was up. But she wasn't ready to tell him. It wouldn't be fair to tell anyone before Preston.

"Gran was tired, so I took her back to her room, then I decided to slip out. I did see the fireworks display though. It was a beautiful touch." No way was she telling him about Gran's test. He would worry, wonder—question. "I hope you don't mind that I left the hosting duties to you."

"Of course I don't mind. We're family. You've been carrying more than your fair share of the McNair face time for Hidden Gem business this past year. The reception was winding down by the time you left. Mother and Father were in their element entertaining anyway."

"They do like to play the head-of-the-family role."

Their parents lived off a trust fund, tightly managed by Gran's lawyers. Their cousin Stone's mother also lived off her trust fund, working to stay clean after multiple stints in drug rehab. Leaving the bulk of her estate to her grandchildren was a huge vote of confidence from Gran that Amie didn't take lightly. Her grandmother's respect meant everything to her.

Amie was determined to do better by her own child than her stage mom, Bayleigh. Without question, Mariah was the better role model.

Amie tucked the phone more securely under her neck. "Was there anything else?"

"What was up with you and Armstrong on the dance floor? Any progress getting along better with the new boss? He's really not such a bad guy. We had a good time playing cards at the bachelor party."

"Have you been talking to Gran?" she asked suspiciously.

"No, I just got to know him better with all the wedding parties this week. We talked some."

"Talked about what?"

He laughed softly. "You sound nervous."

The twin bond was sure a pain in the butt sometimes. "I'm not nervous. I'm just exhausted." Really exhausted. She'd never been as tired in her life as she'd been the past few weeks. "Good night, Alex. Love you." She hung up the phone and resisted the urge to pull the covers over her head.

Someone was going to guess soon and her secret would be out. She needed to control the telling.

Sunday morning, Preston waited beside the limo, outside the Hidden Gem Ranch. It wasn't like Amie to be late. Ever. She was always one of the first at work and last to leave. But she'd kept him out here hanging around for over twenty minutes.

He definitely wasn't accustomed to anyone making him wait. Maybe she was playing a mind game?

The door to her quarters opened and she backed out onto the veranda, her curvy bottom wriggling as she juggled her purse and some kind of bag. Turning, she faced him and started forward, wearing turquoise high heels, pencil jeans and a flowy white shirt with multiple strands of signature McNair necklaces. The long loops of her necklaces drew his eyes down her body, hinting at the curves that lay beneath the shirt.

As always, he braced for the fact she damn near took his breath away.

His eyes fell to the little pink leopard-print carrier that wobbled back and forth to the side as something fuzzy and shadowy moved around inside. He frowned. "I thought you said you were packing clothes? Not livestock."

Stopping in front of him, she lifted up the frilly carrier. "Clearly this isn't large enough for a horse. I sent my bags ahead to the airport. This is one of my carry-ons. It may come as a surprise to you, but I do not travel light."

He opened the limo door for her. "You're one of those types that takes a cute little dog everywhere."

"Don't let my cat hear you call him a dog. He hates that." She slid into the long leather seat.

"You travel with a *cat*?" He dropped into the seat across from her and stared at the carrier beside her. This woman never failed to surprise him in every way possible.

"Are you saying cats miss their humans less than dogs?"

"No—" he chose his words carefully "—cats are more independent. More easily left on their own."

"Well, I won't be leaving this one." Her chin tipped. "If you have a problem with that, you can be the one to call off the trip." She flashed a thin smile at him. "Could you possibly be allergic?"

Was that her plan? To get him to bail? It would take a lot more than a feline to make that happen. Still, he couldn't help digging. "I am not allergic to cats—or dogs, for that matter. But surely someone on the staff can handle that. You have other pets."

"This one is special." She unzipped the top and the fluffy Siamese's head popped out. The cat yawned and stared at Preston with blue eyes just as intense as Amie's. "He's old and has diabetes. He needs his injections."

Guilt kinked his neck. "I'm sorry for leaping to conclusions." He shook his head. "But I have to confess, I still don't get it. You have the money for fancy pet sitting, including injections. So you need his company? Don't you have two or three other or a dozen other cats? There are varying accounts around the office of how many. How did you pick which one to bring?"

"Four. Just four," she said tightly. "My other three cats are staying with Gran. But I only trust Johanna with this one since she's a vet tech, and as you know, she is on her honeymoon. Other than her, there's no one I trust to administer the medication who's also familiar to Roscoe—"

"Roscoe? I thought your family named all people and animals after gems." Her brother was actually Alexandrite and she was Amethyst. Even their horses had gemstone names.

"My grandmother and my parents did that with the names. I don't. Trust me, learning to write Amethyst in preschool wasn't easy. So, this is Roscoe. It fits." She smoothed a hand over his head. "I know I could hire some high-end pet sitter for him, but his diabetes gets worse when he's stressed, and when he misses me, he stresses."

"We can't have that happening." He scratched a furry ear and the cat erupted into a low, humming purr.

"This is not a joke," she snapped, hugging the carrier closer. "I couldn't bear it if he passed away while I was gone. I'm important to him and he's important to me."

He rested his hand on her knee. "I'm not laughing at you. I'm just wondering if the cat is going to need jewelry for the galas too."

"Ha-ha. I'm not taking him to work with me." Her gaze flicked to his hand and she chewed her bottom lip. "Just traveling and keeping him in my suite."

"You genuinely seem to care." And that made her all the more attractive somehow.

"I do." She lifted his hand from her knee, but the flush on her neck showed she wasn't unaffected. "Now, can we get going? The plane is waiting."

He let the air crackle between them for an instant before signaling the driver. It was going to be an inter-esting—and tempting—week.

Three

Amie buckled her cat's carrier into the seat beside her on the luxury jet, larger than the McNair family's plane, with more space for the lengthy travel planned for the week. Plush leather seats. A semicircular sofa around a dining table, with a galley kitchen off to the side. Even a small shower and sleeping area curtained off.

Other than a pilot behind the bulkhead wall, she was alone with Preston for all of the flights. Day and night. She sagged back in the leather recliner, the sounds of Preston across the row tempting her to look. Just sitting in the limo with him had been tempting. That's why she had strengthened her defenses. She had to. What would this week—even the past two months—have been like if she wasn't pregnant? Would she have eventually fallen under the spell of the sexy, brooding CEO in spite of the fact he ran the company she'd once hoped to head?

Unlikely once the pink slips had started being handed out to employees. Sure, he was getting results, but she still wasn't convinced his way was the best way. Maybe she could use this week to find out his future plans for the company. And if they involved more of his hatchet style of leadership? She hoped to persuade him to find a compromise that didn't gut the heart of the family business.

She jammed earbuds in to prevent further conversation and closed her eyes against the morning nausea. She *felt* Preston settle in his seat. Instinctively, she reached for the volume control, pressed the button and tried to lose herself in the music. Anything to dull her interest in the man sitting across from her. She kept her eyes shut, and tried her best to relax her jaw. To be natural and unconcerned even though her nerves were raw.

This was really happening. She'd wondered how she would tell him about the baby and now it was clear that conversation would have to happen this week. At the end of their travels, because if she told him sooner, the rest of the trip would be impossible to withstand. She had to use this time to find common ground, a peace of sorts before telling the rest of the family.

Easier said than done.

He was an arrogant man. A fair boss, but distant. Cool. She wanted and needed more in her life. She'd been left with no choice in her distant parents. But she'd seen her grandparents' marriage and the way they loved their family unconditionally. She would settle for nothing less for herself or her child.

The plane taxied and took off smoothly. Amie thought she might just get away with listening to her favorite folk music all the way until lunch. And if he lost himself in work, maybe she could pull out some of her own sketches for the collection she hadn't shared with anyone else. Ideas were buzzing in her head for the snake-themed coils she'd designed, the patterns of their markings inspiring interlocking pieces for multicolored chains in precious metal. They were more urban and sophisticated than the rustic luxury items that were the company cornerstone, potential crossover items into a younger, more international market while staying true to her roots.

She hadn't shared them because what if they ventured too far off the mark? Weren't as good as she hoped? She didn't think she'd get sacked for stepping outside the design aesthetic, although with Preston at the helm...who knew? Her bigger concern was that she'd spent time designing pieces that would never be made. The artist in her mourned that.

Then she felt a gentle tug on an earbud. A sideways glance revealed Preston with the earpiece dangling between his fingers.

His face was open, receptive. "Now that we're settled for the trip, do you want to tell me why you've gone out of your way to ignore me since that night in the coat closet?"

Leave it to a man—and a billionaire CEO at that—to be direct.

"We work together. It isn't wise to pursue a personal relationship." The sight of him in a black suit and leather cowboy boots threatened to take her breath away even now. She had continued to want him over the past two months. That was part of the problem.

All that male arrogance and remorseless reorganization hadn't done nearly enough to make her body stop wanting him.

"Amie, clearly we have to find a less antagonistic way to be in the same room." He draped the earbud over her armrest, just a hairsbreadth away from her arm. "I assume that's why your grandmother sent us on this outing, to keep drama out of the workplace."

"Drama?" She plucked the other earbud out and resisted the urge to toss something at his head. "Are you calling me a drama queen? I am a professional in every way at the office. You're the one who thinks I'm plotting your death."

"Okay, we've agreed you don't want to tie concrete blocks to my ankles and throw me in the Trinity River, but you're still a professional dripping ice every time I walk into the room." He leaned on his armrest, coming closer and pinning her with a laser gaze. "I wouldn't put up with this from any employee, male or female, no matter who they're related to. I find nepotism to be abhorrent, in fact."

Nepotism? The word seared her. She worked twice as hard as anyone else to prove otherwise and still she couldn't catch a break. If she didn't love the family company so much, she would have left long ago. "I apologize if I've been less than cordial or in any way taken advantage of my family connections."

"There's that ice I was talking about. Combined with a beauty pageant answer—carefully worded."

She smiled tightly, irritated and turned on—and scared. "Well, you're the one asking for world peace."

"Just a cease-fire."

"I want that, too." She needed it. For their child's sake. "I'm just not sure how. This probably sounds strange after what we did two months ago, but I really don't know you."

The steel in his gaze lightened. He leaned back in his chair, hands crossed over his chest. "Ask me anything you want to know."

"Anything?" *How would you feel about becoming a daddy in seven months?* Probably not wise to lead with that one.

"Sure," he said. "On one condition."

Damn. She'd known this supposed cease-fire was too good to be true. "I am not sleeping with you again just to find out your favorite color."

"I didn't ask you to," he pointed out. "My condition is simple. For every question you ask, I get to ask one as well. You can even choose who goes first."

Sounded fair, and as he'd mentioned, all those pageants sure had given her a wealth of practice in dodging sticky questions. "All right, why did you take this job when you were making more money at the sportswear corporation in Oklahoma?"

"Your grandmother is quite persuasive. I don't need the money. But I do need a challenge."

"Is that what I am to you? A challenge?"

He smiled, hazel eyes glinting. "That's another question when I haven't asked you anything."

"All right, your turn." She sighed warily, her tummy flipping with nerves and a hint more morning sickness. "Ask away."

"What's your favorite color?"

She blinked fast, waiting for the other shoe to drop. "Seriously? That's it?"

"Do you want a tougher question? Something more personal? Because I can think of more than one of that sort."

"Fuchsia," she blurted. "My favorite color is fuchsia. What's yours?"

"Don't care."

"Then why ask me my favorite?" She couldn't help but wonder.

"I've found I can tell a lot about a person by their choice. I catalogue those picks, like crayons in a box, and track the trends. It's like analyzing data in the workplace."

"Wait. Seriously?" She held up a hand as something else occurred to her. "You're working for a jewelry empire and you don't care about the nuances of beauty in jewel tones? Just an overall trend of some Crayola personality test?"

"I care about tracking sales data. I'm not a designer. I have people for that. A good boss knows who to promote based on job performance—not bloodlines." He hinted at that distrust of nepotism again. "What made you choose to stay in the family business rather than strike out on your own?"

She searched for the right words to explain something innate. "It's in my blood, all I can ever remember wanting to do. In fact, my earliest memories are of accompanying my grandfather to work."

"What did you do at the company as a toddler?"

"You'll have to wait. It's my turn to ask. Based on all that cataloguing of favorite color trends, what do you think would be your favorite color—if you ever decided to choose one?"

"What?" He looked at her as if he was dizzy from following her through a maze.

"What type of person are you? If I'm fuchsia, what are you?"

"Um, navy blue, maybe dark gray."

Why did she want to know? "You didn't think about that, did you? I believe you just made up an answer."

"Prove it," he said smugly, crossing his arms over his chest. Even through the black shirt, she could see the outline of muscles in his arm. His smile was genuine, if not a little playful, and his eyebrow cocked with such arrogance that she couldn't look away.

She scrunched her nose. "You're not playing fair with this question game."

He leaned forward again, closer this time. "I don't know the answer to your color question and I really want to get to my question. What did you do with your grandfather at work?"

She found herself drawn in by the timbre of his voice as much as the steel in his eyes. "He asked me to help him make a necklace for Gran's birthday. Picking out the stones. Choosing which of his designs I liked the best. It was...magical."

"Your grandparents are important to you." He was a perceptive man.

She needed to remember that.

"My grandmother is the primary reason I'm here. She and Gramps were more parents to me than my own—which is no great secret to anyone who's been around for any length of time. I hate that I'm missing even a day with her on this trip, but this is what she wants."

"If making your grandmother happy is that important, that brings me back to my first question. Why have you been avoiding me?"

There was no more hiding the truth from him or herself.

"I'm not sure how to be in the same room with you without thinking about the day we met."

Amie's admission still rattled around in Preston's brain even hours later after they'd checked into their Los Angeles hotel on California's renowned Gold Coast. He paced around the sitting area between their rooms, picture windows overlooking the water. Crystal, brass and high-end upholstery filled the place. He wasn't much on décor, but he knew "good" when he was around it. He hadn't grown up with this kind of luxury, but he'd grown accustomed to it over the years climbing the corporate ladder.

A knock sounded at the door. "Room service."

Preston went to admit the catering staff, allowing them to set up the wet bar with a tray of fruit and vegetables, plus a selection of finger sandwiches and teas. He'd asked what a light lunch would be for a woman and he had to admit the spread looked good. There would be food at the gala tonight, but he thought Amie might like something ahead of time.

Tipping the servers, he went to Amie's door and knocked.

"Amie?" The door nudged open. It must not have been latched in the first place.

A silver ball of fur streaked past his feet.

"Roscoe!" Amie streaked just as fast, wearing a T-shirt and cotton shorts that were…short. He probably shouldn't have noticed that when she was chasing her escapee cat.

But her hair was in a topknot on her head. No jewelry anywhere. And she had a down-to-earth appeal that kicked him square in the chest. It took him a minute to move past that and notice that she sidestepped a baby grand piano and one-of-a-kind furnishings like a shifty running back, finally pouncing on Roscoe before he slipped into Preston's room.

"Those were some moves," he drawled, trying hard to lift his eyes from the sight of her bare thighs.

"I might not have had to move so fast if I'd had a little help." She arched an eyebrow at him, no trace of makeup on features that didn't need it.

"I was...distracted." He couldn't help a slow grin at her glare. "I'll help now though. Do you need his carrier?"

He peered inside her bedroom and noticed a spread of papers on her bed. Sketches of jewelry designs that she'd inked in with bright, bold colors in snakeskin patterns.

"Wait." She hurried over, brushing past him even as he moved into her room. "I don't need the carrier."

He couldn't take his eyes off the sketches. "You did all these?"

It was a significant amount of work. They weren't rough sketches. They'd been drawn in meticulous detail, large enough to really see the interlocking-chain design.

"It's nothing." She started gathering the papers, stacking them hurriedly, but carefully, too. Even as she juggled a cat in her arms.

"Nothing?" How could she write off such obvious hard work as nothing? "I hope you're not taking them to a competitor."

He was only half joking. Why else would she be trying to whisk them out of sight?

"Don't be silly." Skimming aside all the papers, she secured the cat in her bathroom, closing the door. "I saw the lunch spread out there." She yanked a black silk robe off the top of her suitcase, colorful clothes exploding out of it in every direction. "It looks delicious."

A curious response. Preston tucked it away, not wanting to risk upsetting the accord they were trying to find.

"I hoped there would be something you would like." He followed her back out into the living area.

She slipped her robe on, covering up her luscious bare legs. But when she turned and smiled at him, he had to admit that was just as much of a treat.

"As it happens, I am famished."

Later that evening, he twisted open a bottled water, waiting for Amie to finish dressing for their evening out—although thinking about her a door away showering? Not wise. Not when they had to spend so much time together.

He'd already changed into a tuxedo for the gala at the Natural History Museum. It was almost like taking Amie on a date—well, for him, anyway, since work permeated every aspect of his adult life.

A date?

Was that what this week was about? Starting up a relationship with her in spite of the fact he was fifteen years her senior—and her boss? Damn it, he didn't want to be that cliché. But he couldn't get her out of his mind.

The door to Amie's room clicked and…damn.

He set his bottle down slowly. The sight of her knocked the wind out of him. He'd spent so much time keeping professional distance, sometimes the impact of her just caught him unaware. She carried off a boho style all her own. One of a kind in so many ways.

She stood in the doorway, wearing a rhinestone halter top attached to a filmy peach skirt to the floor. Buff-colored cowboy boots peeked out with diamond anklets around them. Her hair, normally loose, was gathered in a tight braid and fell over her right shoulder. Only Amie could carry off such an eclectic pairing.

God, she was magnificent, and his body fired to life in answer. Who was he kidding? He noticed her every minute of every day—whether she was in no makeup and a T-shirt, or dressed to impress.

He pulled a rose from the arrangement on the wet bar. "You look damn hot and I bet you know it."

"Your flattery overwhelms me." She rolled her eyes but took the flower anyway, bringing it to her nose and inhaling. "Mmm."

"Plenty of people flatter you. You want to be respected for more than your looks or being a McNair, and I see that. Now, let's go wow the business world." He extended his elbow.

She stared at him in confusion for three blinks of her long eyelashes before she tucked her hand around his arm. "Lead the way."

He guided her to the penthouse elevator and tapped the button, the touch of her hand searing through his jacket. "I meant it when I said your work speaks for itself, no last name needed."

"Thank you, Preston. I appreciate that, truly," she said as the door slid open and they stepped inside. Together. "You know all about my family—thanks to our infamous nepotism— "

"I didn't say your family doesn't deserve their jobs—well, other than your father." He shrugged, wondering why he felt the need to shoot himself in the foot. "Sorry if that offends you."

"I can't condemn you for speaking the obvious." She snapped the bud off the long stem and tucked the flower into her long braid that draped over her shoulder, anchoring it with ribbon at the end. "I'm curious, though… Back to our questions game, what about your family?"

He went still for an instant, weighing his words. "No chance of nepotism in my family. There was no family business to join into. My father worked for a waste disposal company, injured his back and went on disability. My mother worked for a cleaning service. Mostly cleaning condos for a real estate company."

"It sounds like they had a difficult time financially." She leaned back against a mirrored wall, the lights glinting off her sequined top.

They had, and he'd been so determined to do differently by his family, sometimes he'd forgotten the positive parts of his childhood. "My dad may have been laid up, but he studied with me every day. He wanted to make sure I had more choices than he did. Than my mother did."

"Where are they now?"

The floors counted down as they descended toward ground level where their car waited, elevator music tuned to the Mozart station.

"I bought them a condominium in Florida, complete with maid service." He may have failed his ex and his daughter, but he'd done right by his parents.

"You support them? That's really lovely."

"I have more than enough money. Why wouldn't I?" His gaze dipped to the small of her back, visible in the mirrored wall behind her.

"Not everyone would. Do you get to see them often?"

"Not as often as I would like." He pulled his eyes

back up to her face, lingering for a second on the rose tucked in her hair. "I think you owe me about a dozen questions."

"All right, then ask," she answered with an ease that said he was making progress breaking through the awkwardness between them.

There was a chance for...hell, who was he kidding? He wanted a chance to have her again. In a bed. The attraction wasn't going away. It increased every day and was wrecking their work environment. Tonight was just a reminder of how damn hard it was to be professional with her. He wanted to free her from the layers of fabric, feel her body against his again.

"I'm going to save my questions for later, after work." He swept his arm toward the lobby, already looking forward to the ride back up the elevator.

Amie had been a part of Diamonds in the Rough since graduating from college with a double major in art and business. But until recently, she hadn't given a lot of thought to the expanded business that went into marketing the product. She'd assumed the pieces would come together for her at the right time, especially after her cousin had stepped down to pursue his own dreams.

God, that was brave of him to do.

She felt like a coward right now, afraid to tell Preston about the baby. This week was supposed to be about finding that courage, and the more time she spent with him, the more questions she had.

She stepped out of the limo in front of the Natural History Museum, the red carpet filled with LA elite and top players in Hollywood. Diamonds in the Rough collections would be displayed throughout. The evening passed in a blur of schmoozing, seeing her rustic gem designs and others artfully showcased throughout the Southwest exhibit—beside everything, from a stuffed longhorn steer, to a locomotive light, to portraits of the diverse people who'd shaped Western history.

She was a part of this, the McNair legacy, and she couldn't deny Preston was in command. He owned the room, quietly and confidently, alongside some of the most famous men and women in the country. Hooking them. No doubt there would be Diamonds in the Rough pieces adorning actors and actresses at music and movie awards shows.

By the end of the night, she felt light, excited about the business in a way she couldn't recall since she'd been a child making a necklace with her grandfather. She just wished she knew what Preston thought of her designs when he'd seen those sketches earlier in the day. Why hadn't he said anything?

But he had been thoughtful so far on this trip. The questions game had helped her learn things about him. The lunch he'd ordered—so obviously full of chick food that he'd selected items with her in mind—had been a sweet gesture, and so welcome, considering that her appetite really kicked in later in the day.

The business part of the event was winding down and the attendees were free to explore the museum for the remaining hour the company had rented the venue. Amie hooked arms with Preston, wondering if maybe, just maybe, they were going to find level ground after all.

She stared upward in wonder at the butterfly exhibit. Monarchs and a zillion other kinds she'd never thought to learn the names of glided, landed, soared again. Her imagination took flight along with them. "This museum was a genius idea for the display."

"It's about art. You design art every bit as beautiful, Amie."

She stopped, turning to face him. "I think that's the nicest thing you've ever said to me."

A half smile ticked a dimple in his craggy, handsome face. "Considering how little we've talked, that's not saying much."

"You know, you haven't been exactly accessible, yourself." She wanted to touch him, to stroke those strands of gray at his temples and see if they had a different texture.

"What do you mean?" All hard edges, he made such a contrast to those delicate yellow butterflies drifting behind him.

"You're a broody and moody workaholic." Even with butterflies as a backdrop.

"I'm the boss. I have to maintain a certain professional distance, and I'm certainly not going to set a bad example by taking long lunches and checking out early," he said with more of that broody moody authority. His mouth formed a tight line that she wanted to tease open.

"It's more than that." She tilted her head to the side, wondering if it was her imagination that his eyes lingered on her outfit now. And had all night, even amidst the A-list guests with plunging necklines. The thought sent satisfaction and desire through her. "You're not the warm fuzzy, approachable type."

"No. I've staked my reputation on being a leader not a team player. Besides, I'm also fifteen years your senior. You realize that, right?"

Did that bother him? She hadn't thought about it beyond thinking how well he carried it. The gray streaks at his temples, the hard, defined angles in his face. And those keen, calculating eyes. The man exuded pure sex appeal and would no matter what age. But she couldn't just dismiss what he'd said.

"The years between our birth dates would be an issue if I was a teenager. Ew. And illegal. But I'm far beyond that stage of life. So I don't see it as an excuse for distant behavior—" she took the plunge for her baby "—outside the office."

His eyes narrowed. "So you're saying outside the office is okay?" He took a step closer, still not touching but near enough that one deep breath would brush her chest against his. "Because I was under the distinct impression you didn't want to pursue the relationship because I'm the boss. And quite frankly, I agree that's problematic on a lot of levels if not handled carefully."

"Of course," she murmured, having thought through all of them. "You're right."

He studied her for a long moment, eyes so perceptive she wondered if he could pluck her secret thoughts right out of her head. Instead, his voice lowered to a level that hummed along her skin.

"But you're open to discussion," he pressed. "What are we going to do about working at the same company when there's still this connection?"

A butterfly landed on his shoulder and in that moment he was so very approachable. So much so, she couldn't think about anything but how scared she'd been since that stick turned pink.

"I guess that's what this week is supposed to be about."

She sure hoped he had answers, because she couldn't seem to figure out any.

Only one answer ever sprang to her mind when she got this close to Preston. And it had a lot to do with what he called a "connection." On her end, it felt more like a riot of emotions combined with raw lust and—quite honestly—a little bit of magic.

What else could explain her attraction to the off-limits cowboy CEO with a butterfly on one shoulder?

She chewed her bottom lip and before she could second-guess herself, she arched up onto her toes for what could be the last kiss she would ever have with Preston.

Four

Preston had Amie back in his arms again and the feel of her was better than any memory he'd held on to of that night in the coatroom. And his memories had been pretty damn awesome.

Her lips parted under the press of his, yielding in a way that could only happen when they were kissing and she wasn't snapping at him, just purring. Right now, with her mouth under his, there were no arguments. No doubts. Even in her yielding, she was sure of herself. Of the kiss. The silken stroke of her tongue along his told him as much while he skimmed a touch down her bare arms and up again, her halter top giving him delicious access to her shoulders. The slender warmth of her neck.

He breathed her in, deepening the kiss.

The press of her curves against his body sent his pulse into overdrive. The exotic scent of her musk- and-clove perfume tempted him, begged him to touch her. Everywhere. He enjoyed the silkiness of her hair as he stroked his hands over her braid. But he needed to touch more of her. Needed to feel her skin against his. She leaned into his fingertips as he ran them down her spine. Her nimble fingers played along his neck and over his shoulders. Every touch sent snaps of electricity through him until he backed her into a wall, his body shielding them from view if anyone walked in.

He hadn't tasted her enough that first time. Hell, he could kiss her for days and not get enough of her taste. She was such a flash of bright color in his world that he could see her like a damn kaleidoscope even behind his eyelids as they kissed.

More than that, she intrigued him. This woman who was won over by butterflies more than flowers or extravagant gifts. So different than his other relationships. She was unique. Special. And he should be old enough to know better, but still, she drew him in. Age and their work connection and his own shortcomings in relationships be damned. He wanted her, ached to have her.

And from the way she moved, Preston could tell Amie wanted it too. Her touch spurred him to take the chance. He kissed along her neck, nipping her shoulder. "Let's go back to the hotel. That is completely not the workplace and a helluva lot roomier than a coat closet."

Her head fell back and she blinked fast, long black cyelashes fluttering to focus. "What?"

"I want to take my time with you." His hands glided down her bare arms slowly, resting finally on her hips. A smile snaked across his lips. "I want to live out every fantasy I wish we'd had time for two months ago."

"Ohmigosh." The fog from her eyes cleared and horror replaced passion. "What did we just do?"

"We kissed. Like two consenting adults who've been going damn crazy with frustration for the past two months trying to ignore the connection." He was losing ground fast and needed her to understand. "This is not about a repeat of the coatroom. This is about two adults attracted to each other. That's all."

She raised an eyebrow, face turning cold. Like marble. "Do you sleep with every person you're attracted to?"

He hadn't considered she might wonder about his motivations. It seemed odd that such a confident, sexy woman could have insecurities, too, but as he thought back to those sketches she'd tried to hide from him, he had to wonder. "I meant it when I said I'm not a one-night-stand person and I believed you were being honest, too."

"You're saying we should...what?" She angled her head to the side, butterflies swirling behind her in a display. Her blue eyes steeled against him. "That we go on dates? That we sleep together?"

"Honestly? I was thinking we would do both." There would be issues to deal with, datingwise, but he wasn't a man who tolerated sneaking around.

"What about all the things you said earlier?" She backed out of his embrace and crossed her arms over her chest defensively. "You're my boss and older than I am. That you're not a team player."

Good question. And that meant she was considering it. He was closer to winning. "We keep our relationship separate when we're at work with a little less ice and obvious static. We're both professionals."

She shook her head, the rose slipping loose from

her braid. It tumbled to the floor behind her, landing silently. "It isn't that simple."

It felt simple enough to him, especially seeing the way her fingers trembled lightly as she skimmed them across her lips where he'd just kissed her. His gaze followed the path of that sensual touch, hungry to show her how very, very simple—elemental—this could be.

"Why not?" he asked instead, thirsty for more of her. "What's the harm in trying a date? Or more. See what happens? Can't be more awkward than the past two months."

Indecision flickered through her eyes, just a flash before she held up a hand. "Don't try to win me over with your corporate pitch. I am not okay with the way you've cleared house and tampered with the family culture at McNair. You can save your closing-deal number. I know how you operate, and who knows, maybe my head's next on the chopping block."

"That's not in the cards," he said without hesitation.

Her throat moved in a slow swallow of relief. "Well, I'm not some account to win over."

"You most definitely are not." She was more. So much more.

Amie shook her head. "Save it."

A tight line smoothed her plump lips into an expression that he couldn't readily identify. Pain? Hesitation? He wasn't sure. And while he realized he would have to put his plans on hold for now, he was not giving up. Not on this woman.

Amie broke his gaze, turned around and made for the door. She stepped on the flower, smearing the red petals on the ground.

Preston stared at the ground, breathing in the scent of roses for a moment while he contemplated his next move.

The ride back to the hotel in the limousine was awkward, to say the least. Amie couldn't stop thinking about the kiss in the butterfly gallery. How much she wanted to take Preston up on his proposition. In fact, she very well might have if she hadn't been pregnant. But she was and she had to keep that in mind at all times for her baby's sake.

Preston sat across from her, giving her space. Although she could sense he was only biding his time. She'd watched him at work often enough to know his tactics. Telling him to back down wouldn't work. She needed to come up with a plan of her own.

Soon.

Her cell phone rang inside her pewter handbag. The bag, while stylish, was full of essentials. She batted around a mess of receipts and makeup, digging for the ringing phone. In the seat next to her, she dumped her lip gloss, mints and amethyst-and-pearl compact. Finally, the purse was empty enough to find her phone. She fumbled with the turquoise clasp. Her grandmother's name flashed across the screen. Her gut clenched in fear.

She grabbed the phone and answered fast. "Gran, it's late in Texas. What's the matter?"

Preston's forehead creased and he looked at her, a question in his eyes. She averted her gaze. Now wasn't the time to worry about Preston. Not when her grandmother was this sick.

"Nothing's wrong, dear." Her grandmother's voice

came across weaker but steady. "I'm just calling to see how the party at the museum went."

"The party? You're calling for an after-action report now?" she asked incredulously. "It's after midnight there, Gran. We can talk tomorrow. You should be asleep."

Her grandmother snorted on the other end of the line. "All I do is lie around in bed and rest. It wrecks my sense of day and night."

"Are you feeling all right?" Amie lowered her voice, wishing for a moment of privacy. Her grandmother's illness was hard for her to deal with. She hated to think of her grandmother awake in pain.

"You just saw me this weekend. I'm the same."

Dying. Moments ticking away while Amie was stuck going to parties. It wasn't fair. She wanted to be at her side. To soak up the precious, borrowed time with her grandmother.

"And I'm going to worry about you every single hour of every day because I love you and you're so very important to me."

"You're a sweet girl. My only granddaughter. I was so excited when you were born."

"Sweet? Me?" She laughed softly. "Not really, but then neither are you. I like to think I inherited my feistiness from you."

Her grandmother chuckled along with her, then laughed harder until she coughed. Clearing her throat, she continued, "I am proud of you and I believe you can make this work. Now, tell me. How is it going?"

"The LA party was a success. The museum setting was brilliant." The kiss with Preston was incredible, but that part would not appear in any reports. "The photographer took lots of photos. You should have them on your computer to look through in the morning. If you're still having trouble resting, some pictures may have already arrived."

"Photos of you with Preston? I want to see how the two of you work together."

Alarms sounded in her head. Had her grandmother picked up on some vibe between her and Preston? She couldn't possibly know about the baby. Amie settled on a simple answer. "We were a unified front for the company."

"So you're working through the differences that fast? I'm not buying it, dear."

"We're trying." She looked across the limo, her eyes meeting his. Had he been watching her so intently the whole time? Concern etched in his face. Genuine concern. It'd be so easy to let her guard fall, even now. "For you, Gran. Now, please, get some rest. We won't let you down."

The line disconnected and Amie realized more than her baby's well-being was at stake here. Her grandmother's peace of mind needed to stay in the forefront. They needed to smooth things over. And fast. She could make it through the week, smile for pictures with him. Amie couldn't afford to weaken again around Preston. She had to stay strong and make sure every step was taken on her terms. She needed to reclaim some control.

Preston angled back, his arms along the leather limo seat. "Everything okay?"

"Sure. No crisis." The last thing she wanted to tell him was that she suspected her grandmother could have ulterior motives beyond solidifying business relations. "She just wanted to check in."

"And that's all?" His hazel eyes narrowed in disbelief. The shadows in the limousine softened his features, making him seem more approachable. "I don't think so."

"What are you? Psychic?" She gripped the edges of the seat as the limo turned a corner. The driver took the corner hard, and she lurched toward Preston.

"I just know." He lifted his index finger to the side of his temple and tapped twice. "It's part of what makes me the boss," he said, his confidence filling the seat as tangibly as his broad shoulders.

"That—" she paused for effect, then grinned "—and your arrogance."

He laughed, apparently not daunted in the least. "Confidence is important. You're one to talk, by the way."

She opted to ignore that part. "Aren't you going to ask why she called so late?"

The smile faded from his handsome face. "Tell me."

"She's having trouble sleeping because she's in bed so much." And Amie wanted to be there with her to keep her company, but her grandmother wanted her here for whatever reason. For a test. "It tears me up inside to think of her confined like that. She's always been such a vibrant, dynamic woman. She's the one who taught me to ride. Alex, Stone and I would spend hours out on the trails with her and Gramps."

"I'm sorry. This is such an unfair way for her life to end."

"I'm grateful she can still talk, that she's still herself. The thought of…"

The limousine stopped short, and Amie fell forward, landing her onto Preston's lap. He reached out to catch her instinctively. Heat flooded her cheeks as his warm hands helped her back to an upright position. This was exactly the kind of situation she needed to guard herself against. Thank heaven they had arrived at the hotel. Amie was exhausted with worry for her grandmother, her child and her feelings.

She peered out the window only to realize they'd stopped a couple of blocks short of the hotel. Preston frowned, but she was closer to the window separating them from the chauffeur. She tapped on the pane, signaling the driver.

The window slid opened. "Yes, Mr. Armstrong? Miss McNair?"

"Is there a problem?"

The uniformed driver scratched under his hat. "There's a pileup that has traffic blocked ahead of us and there's no backing up. I'm afraid we're stuck until it clears. The minifridge is stocked."

Alone? In the limo with Preston for who knew how long?

Amie snatched up her pewter clutch bag. "We'll just walk. The hotel is only two blocks and this highway congestion is never going to let up."

The chauffeur looked to Preston, who shrugged. "Whatever the lady wants."

Amie stepped out into the warm night. Whatever she wanted? If only life could be that simple.

Preston shot out of the limo, stunned at how fast she'd bolted. No way in hell was he letting her walk around the streets of LA alone, regardless of how safe the area was supposed to be. It was still a city, far different from the open spaces of Texas. Besides that, she looked exactly like what she was—an extraordinarily beautiful and wealthy woman, both of which could attract the wrong sort of attention. Five sprints later, he'd caught her, her sequined top glinting in the night.

He shortened his strides to measure his pace to Amie's as he scanned the traffic-jammed street. The famous LA traffic was no joke. People honked their horns, and music with heavy bass from a parked car filled the night air. The hotel was located in a good section of LA, but his instincts still stayed on alert. There were plenty of places, even in the good areas of the city that could be a threat to two pedestrians. He placed a palm on the small of her back possessively as they walked. He glanced at her, narrowing his eyes and daring her to argue. "If you don't want my hand on you then we get back in the limo."

She sighed, tucking her handbag against her side. "We need to set some ground rules for the rest of this trip."

At least she was still talking to him. That was progress over the past two months of the great chill. "Such as?"

He continued to scan the area as they walked down the empty sidewalk. They had made it one block away from the limo. The street signs were caked brown from the smog. To a native Oklahoma kid, cities like LA felt dirty and overcrowded, even in the upscale areas. The sooner they were back at the hotel, the better. Maybe he could convince her to stay for a glass or two of wine in the hotel's restaurant.

"We have to work together for years to come," she said with her chin jutting, exposing her elegant neck.

He wanted to kiss her, starting at her neck. The taste of her two months ago and in the exhibit this evening wasn't nearly enough. Preston's attention wandered from her neck to the seductive swish of her filmy skirt.

Her boot heels clicked against the pavement, a steady drumming sound that matched the evenness of her voice. "We need to figure out how to make that happen without the attraction interfering."

"I still don't see what that has to do with denying the pull between us altogether."

"You mean have an affair."

"We *are* adults. Sex happens sometimes." The more he thought about it, the more it made sense. Even though they worked together, there was an equality to their stance since her family was the major stockholder. And she clearly didn't want a long-term relationship, thank God, since he'd already been there, wrecked that with his ex-wife. "Fighting the attraction isn't working. An affair makes sense."

"That brings me back to my original point. Affairs more often than not end…messy." She clutched her purse to her stomach. "We can't afford that."

"Then we agree that when the time comes to move on, we'll be cordial." He guided her past other pedestrians making their way down the sidewalk. Blue-and-red lights flashed in the distance as first responders pushed through the backed-up traffic to get to the three-car pileup.

"Preston, I hear what you're saying, but it's not that simple anymore." Her throat moved with a long swallow. "We can't afford to take that risk. The stakes are too high. Far too high."

There was such worry in her eyes, an unmistakable fear. Panic tore at her face.

He squeezed her elbow lightly. "I think that until

we face this head-on and give it a try, the tension will only get worse and interfere with the job all the more."

"Spoken like a man who doesn't take no for an answer."

"I didn't imagine what just happened or what happened two months ago."

She glanced up at him, her eyes full of more of that worry he didn't understand—but a yearning he understood all too well.

Chewing her bottom lip, she glanced at him. "Preston, can we go back to the original plan of getting to know each other better and take it from there?"

"Are you asking me to win you over?" The prospect filled him with a rush of excitement and hope.

"No," she said quickly, "I didn't mean that, exactly. Just...just... I'm asking you to be honest."

He measured his words, searching for the best way to win his way around her. "Okay, but on one condition."

"What would that be?" she asked warily.

"That we use this time together as dates. Real, honest-to-God, get-to-know-each-other dates. You'll see firsthand that we can balance work and romance."

Her jaw dropped. "Dating? You're serious."

"Absolutely, take our time."

She fidgeted with her purse gripped in her hands. "And when you say take our time, how long are you talking?"

"However long it takes. Trust me, I don't take this lightly. I'm not the type to let relationships into the workplace, never have been. You're just that damn amazing."

"Flattery already? I haven't agreed yet, so you can hold back on the wooing." For the first time since the kiss in the exhibit, Amie looked relaxed. Receptive.

The smile on her face reached her eyes, setting them aglow in the muted streetlight. She shoved him with her shoulder playfully. This was the Amie he wanted to get to know.

"I only speak the truth." God, she was mesmerizing. So much so, it was hard as hell to see anything but the stars shining in her deep blue eyes.

So hard he almost missed the shadowy figure lunging from behind a billboard. The man was broad, built and hardened by the streets. His frenetic eyes focused on Amie with a repugnant leer. On instinct, Preston stepped in front of her. Crooks like this never risked leaving people alive to identify them, especially when drugs were making their decisions for them.

The man loomed in front of them, a knife in hand, waving it menacingly. Erratically. "Give me your cash and jewelry now and nobody gets hurt."

Five

"Amie, get back." Preston pushed her behind him, the street lamp casting a halogen halo over the man with a knife, his face shadowed by the brim of a ball cap. "We don't want anyone to get hurt."

Fear chilled Amie so thoroughly her boots felt frozen to the pavement. She stared at the jagged-edge blade glistening in the night.

"Then pass over your money, dude, and quit screwing around here." The broad shouldered young guy stood close, looking from side to side, jittery. The rest of the world oblivious or uncaring. Or perhaps too busy rubbernecking over the three-car pileup to notice a simple purse snatcher by a trash can.

In a flash, Preston swept a foot behind the guy, knocking him to the ground, stunning Amie with the speed and power. Preston stomped a foot on the crook's

wrist, pressing until the criminal screamed. His fist un-
furled and he released the jagged knife.

The clatter of metal on concrete released Amie from
her daze. She sprinted toward the flashing lights at the
car accident. Surely there had to be a cop there who
could assist.

"Help, please," she called out, waving one hand and
hitching the hem of her layered skirt with the other.
"Someone tried to rob us. My...boss has him restrained.
The man had a knife. My...date...has him restrained."

A few heads turned, two rescue workers returning
to their efforts to dislodge a woman from a smashed-up
car. But one cop disengaged from the accident scene.

"Yes, ma'am?" The policeman with a shaved head
and steely jaw jogged closer.

Thank God. She waved for him to follow her.

"Over here, by the closed toy store." Her heart in her
throat, she raced back to Preston.

A small crowd had gathered around the fallen thief,
suddenly interested, after all. The onlookers hungrily
digested the scene, pointing and murmuring at Preston,
who had the young man pinned to the ground with his
knee planted on the guy's back, gripping the assail-
ant's hands.

The officer and Amie pushed past the crowd, walking with determined footsteps to Preston. Relief de-
flated her fear, but even relief didn't keep her knees
from trembling as she thought of how wrong this could
have gone. And she had a baby to think about now.
Preston's baby. If something had happened to either of
them... She started toward him, needing to touch him
and feel him vibrantly alive. But he shook his head,
keeping her at bay until he passed over the crook.

"Officer," Preston said, "that's his knife there. You'll find his prints since he didn't bother to wear gloves. I didn't touch it."

The policeman knelt beside them and secured the man's hands with cuffs. "I've got this now, sir. I'll be right back to take your statements." He read the guy his rights and walked him to a police cruiser.

Standing, Preston straightened his jacket and cupped her shoulder to steer her away from the subdued criminal. "Are you hurt, Amie?"

"I should be asking you that." She pressed her hands to her chest, vaguely aware of camera flashes in the background. Photos of the wreck? Cell phones were everywhere these days. "You're the one who took on the man with the knife. Thanks to you, there's not a scratch on me. You acted so quickly. I thought we would have just handed over our money."

"He was high on something." Preston's jaw flexed with tension. "I couldn't trust him to walk away, not even in this crowd."

"I'm just glad you were here with me. I'm sorry I forced us to walk and put you in danger."

"It could have happened anywhere, anytime. All that matters is you're okay." He clasped her elbow and nodded to the policeman. "We should go inside to wait for the cops to take our statement. The last thing I want is for someone else to try a repeat."

"Of course. I know I've already apologized, but I am so sorry for leaving the limo." Guilt pinched tighter than her boots as she strode through the lobby doors of their hotel, passed a small group of guests peering out the windows onto the street outside. The posh interior felt like a different world. "Where did you learn to defend yourself like that?"

"I grew up in a neighborhood where you had to look out for yourself." He gestured to a green velvet sofa by the window overlooking the street.

"Still, that was such a risky move to make." She sank onto the couch and smoothed her skirt. "You could have been injured—or worse."

"Less risky than trusting a twitchy user to let us go unharmed. My only concern was keeping you safe." He sketched a finger down the braid trailing over her shoulder. "I could see in his eyes he was never going to let us walk away and risk having us ID him. He wanted you. I couldn't let that happen."

Unable to resist, she leaned her cheek against his hand. "Thank you for keeping us safe."

"Us?"

She bit her lip, realizing she'd almost let it slip about the baby at a totally awkward and public time. "Us— as in you and me." She stood quickly when the door to the hotel opened, relieved at the intrusion. "I think I see the officer coming this way to speak with us now."

Amie sat on her bed, cloaked in her favorite black silk robe, absently stroking her cat. The cat purred loudly, but refused to lie down on her lap. He was fidgety.

She felt just like Roscoe. He refused to sit down, to commit to a direction. Just like her. She couldn't stop thinking about this evening, either. About the whole varied experience. Her kiss with Preston. Her grandmother's desires. Her child. The man with the knife. All of it swirled around her head.

"Oh, Roscoe, what am I supposed to do?"

The cat nudged her hand in response. "Thanks, kitty. That's clearly very helpful. Great advice."

She stopped petting the cat, pushed herself off the bed and made her way to the minifridge. Water. She needed some water.

Things with Preston were more complicated than ever. She wanted to be with him. Wanted to let herself give in to him.

It wasn't that easy. Her own happiness wasn't the only consideration. She unscrewed the water bottle cap and took a swig of water.

Roscoe slinked off the bed and rubbed up against Amie's legs, threading around her feet with determination. He let out a low mew. He sounded more like a kitten than an old cat.

"All right, Roscoe, let's get you settled for the night. I've got your favorite treats."

Whenever they traveled, Amie made sure to pack the best assortment of toys for the cat. He was so loyal, her constant companion. She dug around Roscoe's traveling bag and pulled out a can of tuna, a bowl, a can opener and a blue mouse toy.

Absently, Amie drained the tuna water into the bowl and set it on the ground. The cat rushed the bowl, eager to lap up the treat. Roscoe didn't actually like the fish, just the water. Small indulgences.

Which, if she were being honest, is what she wanted with Preston. A small bit of fun.

It was more than that though. The way he looked at her tonight when her grandmother had called. He had such genuine concern in that handsome face of his. In those kind hazel eyes. And he had saved her. Stood up to that mugger without a moment's hesitation. So protective of her already.

And that was part of the problem. If she had let it slip that she was pregnant, Preston would stay close to her for the baby's sake. She would never be able to tell what he really felt for her. And selfish as it was, she wanted to know. Needed to know.

Glancing at the clock, Amie realized she was late in giving Roscoe his insulin injections. She readied the needle, scooped Roscoe up and pinched the extra skin around his neck. The cat was perfectly still.

"Good boy. You're such a good boy. I always know what to expect from you, Roscoe," she said softly as she slid the needle into his scruff.

"Brave kitty. That wasn't so bad, was it?" She capped the needle and rubbed under his chin. Roscoe circled once on her lap, sat down and purred.

She still had to figure out Preston. Tomorrow, in New York City, she would get to know him better. Which was what she had started to consider just before she'd realized she was pregnant. Baby announcements could wait a while longer. There was something about him that made her want to hold out. Just a little longer.

Preston hadn't found much sleep after the holdup. Instead, he had paced restlessly around the suite replaying events and how damn wrong the evening could have gone. How something could have happened to Amie. And how deeply that would have affected him.

She'd come to mean more to him than he'd realized. So much more.

He was still processing that after their flight across the country to New York City the next morning. Their event wasn't until tomorrow evening, which normally meant he would fill the free day with work. However, he found himself wanting to spend every moment with Amie. When he couldn't sleep the night before, he'd heard her moving about in her room for a long while, but just as he weakened and started to knock, all noise ceased. She settled for the night, leaving him to his thoughts and an aching need to be with her. The trauma of the attack must have worn her out, because she slept during most of the flight, too.

Now that he had New York City at his disposal, he didn't intend to waste an instant of his time alone here with her.

Figuring out what to do for one of the wealthiest women in the country hadn't been easy, but then he'd always enjoyed a challenge.

He'd arranged for a rickshaw to take them to Central Park to attend a Wild West film festival. The muggy day had eased with the setting sun, a pleasant breeze added to the wind from the ride. The *click, click, click* of the cyclist pedaling along the street was rhythmic, lulling. Amie sat beside him in killer shorts and heels with a flowy shirt that the wind molded to all her beautiful curves.

She leaned back, her high ponytail sleek and swinging with the pace of the horses. Her eyes took in the scenery. "I love New York, I always have."

"Always?" He propped a foot up on the other seat across from them, not remembering the last time he'd relaxed in the city. Hell, most people he knew probably wouldn't even recognize him in khaki shorts and a polo shirt. He'd spent all his time in planes, boardrooms and carefully chosen social functions for years.

"My grandparents used to bring Alex and me here as kids. We would see a show, do some shopping." Her blue eyes turned sentimental as they passed Rockefeller Center, a lighter blue as she offered him a small smile.

"I can see why that would give the town good memories."

She glanced at crowded streets as tourists jostled for pictures. "My grandmother always let me choose my own clothes, no worries about impressing a pageant judge."

"You didn't enjoy any part of the pageants?"

"To be honest, I did at first. I liked that my mom spent time with me. I enjoyed the attention. And I really enjoyed getting to have a Mountain Dew and Pixy Stix if the pageant ran past bedtime and I needed a pick-me-up." She shrugged sheepishly, her shoulder brushing his in the confines of the small rickshaw. "Later, though, I wanted to enter the competitions that included talent and grades and community service. But my mother told me that would be a waste of time. I stood a better chance at the ones based only on looks." She stopped short and held up an elegant hand, a silver bracelet wrapped from wrist to elbow. "I don't mean that to sound vain. Scratch everything I said. I shouldn't have—"

"I heard what you meant." And he couldn't imagine ever having said something like that to his daughter. That kind of behavior was inexcusable. "You're clearly a talented artist and intelligent individual."

She snorted inelegantly. "You have to say that because my grandmother owns the company."

"No, actually, I don't," he said with a raised eyebrow as they turned in to Central Park, the sound of street musicians drifting on the wind as the sunset hour turned the sky to golds and pinks. "If I didn't believe in your work I would have moved you to another department."

"Even if that made my grandmother angry?" she pressed.

Did she really think he was only pursuing her for her grandmother's approval? He could clear that much up at least. "My condition to signing on was I have complete authority over hiring."

"But my father still works for the company and we know he doesn't do anything." Her cheeks flushed with color.

And he understood that. She had one helluva work ethic he respected.

"Your father doesn't get a salary from the company coffers so it's not an issue for me. He has an office where he holds social meetings with possible connections. I can live with that."

"It's awkward," she said through clenched teeth, absently toying with her bracelet. "I don't want to be an embarrassment."

He slid his arm along the back of the leather seat and cupped her shoulders. "There's not a chance anyone can miss your work ethic and talent. The other designers are solid, and the occasional design from your cousin adds variety. But the sales numbers for your designs speak for themselves, putting you at the top of the heap."

She glanced at him, her mouth quivering, tempting him. "Thank you. I appreciate that."

"Just stating business." Which meant that wouldn't be a good time to kiss her. He searched for a distracting subject to keep him from kissing her in front of all of New York. Not that anyone would care. "What about vacations with your parents?"

"We went to my pageants and my brother's rodeos together."

"But what about vacations?"

"They took those on their own to have together time as a couple, which is great, of course. And if Alex or I won, then all the better."

So her parents only had time for her and her brother if they were competing like show horses? He didn't like the sound of that at all. No wonder she was so concerned with rising to the top of the company. It wasn't about success but the only way she would know to feel valued.

She rested a hand lightly on his knee. "What about you? What kind of vacations did you go on as a kid?"

His body leaped in response to her touch and it took him a second to focus on her question. "My folks didn't have much money, but we went camping and trail riding. You may remember me telling you my mom worked for a cleaning service. She worked overtime cleaning offices for a stable, so we got discount rates and we could ride. It was actually therapeutic for my dad's injury."

"Your mom sounds awesome." She smiled with that million-watt grin that had stolen his breath from across a room. "So you're the real-deal cowboy. Is that what brought you to Diamonds in the Rough?"

"It was part of the allure of the job offer." He liked riding to unwind after a long day at the office. It gave him peace of mind.

"So, where are we going?"

"Wild West film festival in Central Park. Our first date."

"Date?" Her delicately arched eyebrows shot upward.

"What we talked about last night. Dating. Spending

time together. How did you put it?" He scratched his temple, then pointed. "I'm 'wooing' you."

The bicyclist braked to a stop close to the Sheep Meadow portion of the park, an open field teeming with people, with plenty of visible security. After last night's scare with the purse snatcher, he'd wondered if he should just lock them both up in their suite. But he also knew too well he couldn't control everything. So he would keep her close. Which was how he wanted her.

Snagging a folded blanket and tucking it under his arm, he jumped to the ground and extended a hand for her. She stepped down gracefully, her slim fingers resting in his, her unique silver-and-turquoise ring a walking advertisement for her talents. They walked side by side through the crowd to find a seat. Some were in chairs but others sprawled on blankets. His preference for tonight. He saw her eyes landing on a food vendor and he waved for an order of pizza and bottled waters before they sat down for tonight's first feature under the stars.

He spread the red plaid blanket while she arranged the food. Families and couples dotted the field. A few strollers and kids running in the last light of day. Some people had brought extravagant picnics, complete with linen, silver and candelabra. But most of the attendees had just showed up in jeans with a blanket. Amie seemed content with their spot. She extended her legs and bit off the end of a slice of pepperoni pizza, chasing the oozing cheese with her mouth. Groaning. Pleasure obvious.

"Oh my God, this is the best piece of pizza I have ever eaten in my life."

"So you're a sucker for a pizza pie," he said, lifting up a piece for himself. "I did not expect that."

"And I didn't expect this for a date, but it's perfect. Just what I needed after all the stuffiness of the airplane travel and galas."

"I thought you would enjoy the fresh-air venue after so much time indoors."

She nodded, swiping her lips with a napkin. "The downside to office work is missing being outside. My brother managed to blend both, running the ranch."

"I agree one hundred percent. That's part of what drew me to Texas and this job." In fact, he'd had it written into the contract that he would have access to the ranch. "Someday I want to build a big spread of my own to live the kind of life I dreamed of as a kid. My folks could come visit. At any rate, tonight I figured the outdoor ride would work better, too, in the event of another traffic jam."

"Better than being stuck in the limo." She tipped back a swig of water.

"Spoken like a person who's grown up wealthy." He couldn't resist commenting, even though that had been his life for a long time, too.

He'd never forgotten his roots. Or how lucky he was today.

She crinkled her nose and set aside her water. "I guess that came out snobby."

"Not snobby. Just…a sign that you grew up privileged."

She tipped her head. "Is that a problem for you?"

"It's just a challenge figuring out ways to romance you." He threaded his fingers through her ponytail.

"And we've established you like a challenge." Her eyes held his.

"Don't start with the negative." He tapped her lips. "Just be in the moment."

"You really are charming under all that gruff business exterior." Her mouth moved against his fingertips. "How did you stay single so long?"

His hand fell away and he looked forward at the blank movie screen, due to glow to life at any minute. "I was married, but we got divorced ten years ago."

She went still beside him, her long legs straight beside his, almost touching. "I'm sorry."

"Me, too." And he was. He hated how much they'd hurt and disappointed each other. Most of all, he hated what had happened to their child. His throat threatened to close. "But we married too young. We gave it a good shot, and it just didn't work out."

"Do you have children?"

His blood turned to ice in his veins. "I have no children."

He could practically hear her thinking through that. His heart slammed harder.

"Do you not like kids?" she asked, her voice tentative.

"I like kids fine." He paused, stared up at the sky then back at her, needing to be honest if this stood a chance of…what? Anything. So he told her as much as he could force past his lips. "I had a daughter. She died."

"Oh, Preston, that's so sad." She rested her hand on top of his on the blanket. "Do you mind if I ask what happened?"

His publicity people had done a damn good job keeping those details hidden from the public, even better than he'd known if the McNairs hadn't discovered those details in the background search they'd undoubtedly conducted before hiring him.

"It was an accident." He cleared his throat. He couldn't talk about this, not the rest. He scrambled for something, anything— "Look, the first movie is starting."

A black-and-white film crackled to life on the screen, the projected version maintaining the authenticity of the original as the Western-style font blazed across the screen with a lasso frame decorating the title. It wouldn't be the first time Preston had lost himself in a place where Gary Cooper and Roy Rogers could still make sense of the world.

She looked as if she might press for more, so he slid his arm along her back and pulled her to his side, wanting just to be with her. Enjoy this.

"Amie. Movie. Okay?"

She relented, leaning against his chest with a sigh. "Right. Sure. I didn't mean to push you to talk about something painful."

"It's all right. Another time, maybe."

For now, he had her in his arms and that helped ease the pain inside him in a way he hadn't felt in a long time. A way he looked forward to exploring more fully when they returned to their hotel.

Six

Nerves pattered in Amie's stomach as the elevator doors slid closed on their way up to their penthouse suite in Midtown Manhattan. The evening in the park had been amazing, romantic, fun. Everything a first real date should be. And surprisingly, he hadn't made a move on her other than sliding his arm around her, being a gentleman but undeniably interested in her. She hadn't felt so mellow and happy in…she couldn't remember when.

Was this the real Preston? Was this what they could have had if she'd dated him rather than impulsively leaping into a coat closet with him? God, that night was so surreal now. But they'd actually been together, no denying their impulsive coupling.

She leaned back against the mirrored wall, just looking at him, soaking in the sight of him. Casual. Approachable. His hazel eyes softened as he held her gaze. Heat flushed through her. Everything felt right. Natural. Could she just indulge for a little while longer and see where it went?

The high-speed elevator brought them to their floor in record time, the doors opening on the west half of the tower, thanks to the private code they'd keyed in for their room. The east-side doors went to a different suite.

She took a deep breath and reached to take Preston's arm as she stepped off the elevator on their private quarters. Only to have Roscoe bolt into the elevator—something that shouldn't have happened because she'd secured the kitty in her bathroom before she'd left.

Alarms sounded in her head as she squeezed Preston's hand. She went rigid, cold. "Someone's been in our suite. I locked up Roscoe…maybe a maid let him out?"

Preston's arm shot out to block her path. "After what happened in LA, I'm not taking any chances. Get back in the elevator. Call Security while I go in. What the hell is it with all the security around these places?"

He charged forward and her stomach knotted with fear for him. The events of last night replayed in her head. She had the baby to consider, but she couldn't just leave him here. She held the elevator door open while reaching for her cell phone.

Across the room, someone sat up on the sofa. A familiar someone in jeans, cowboy boots and a plain black T-shirt.

Her twin.

"Hey there, sister." Alex stood, sweeping a hand through his dark brown hair. "I happened to be in the neighborhood and figured I would say hello."

* * *

Suspicion seared through Preston as he strode toward Amie's twin brother. Here. In Manhattan. In their suite. Did the guy have some kind of brotherly radar that Preston was making progress with Amie? Their night at the park had been everything he'd hoped it could be.

He'd had plans to take things further tonight, but clearly that had been blocked by a towering, suspicious cowboy sibling.

Preston sauntered toward Alex McNair, aware of Amie rushing up behind him. "What are you doing here in New York?"

Alex extended an arm and hooked his sister in for a quick hug before backing up and keeping his arm draped protectively over her shoulders. "I brought Nina and Cody to see a matinee on Broadway, like Gran and Gramps used to do with us. Cody okayed the plan once he heard the show has animals in it. And my fiancée could use some pampering with a shopping trip in New York, some spa time along with that show. Amie, you're welcome to join in."

Amie narrowed her eyes, sticking her brother with an accusatory stare. "And you just happened to choose the day I would be here as well? The hotel staff must have fond memories of you from past trips that they gave you access to my suite."

Her brother shrugged. "I think our family has made a favorable—and lucrative—impression on the management in the past. I spent almost a whole summer here once when I was determined to leave the rodeo life behind." He huffed out a long breath. "Anyhow, there's the Diamonds in the Rough show tomorrow. I figured why not bring Nina and show our support for the family business."

"Where is Nina?"

"Settling into the other penthouse suite next door, getting Cody unpacked and oriented before he goes to sleep." Nina's son had autism and changes in routine could be difficult.

"I'll see if she needs help." She slipped from under his arm, but pinned him with a laser gaze of matching blue eyes. "But we're still going to talk later."

As Alex gave her the code to access the other suite, Preston couldn't help but watch the sway of her hips when she left, wishing like hell this evening could have ended differently.

Alex cleared his throat. "That's my sister you're ogling. Eyes up."

Preston pivoted on his heels and walked to the bar, pulling out two beers. The last thing he needed was this oversize cowboy brother breathing down his neck personally—or professionally. "Did your grandmother send you to check on the event tomorrow?"

And did this have something to do with the McNair matriarch calling her granddaughter yesterday? Preston passed his uninvited guest a longneck.

Alex took the Belgian brew. "My grandmother has nothing to do with this. It's all me. I'm checking in on my sister. You and her together?" He shook his head. "That worries me."

"Amie is an adult. Perhaps you should listen to what she has to say on the subject." He tipped back the yeasty brew.

"I realize that. Doesn't make me any less of a protective brother." He took a long drag from the bottle.

"You're known for being a distant dude. I don't want my sister to get hurt. She puts on a tough act, but she's been pushed around by the family for too long."

"I think you underestimate your sister if you think anyone can push her around." Preston tilted his head to the side.

Alex's eyebrows shot up in surprise. "You have a point there. But that's the Amie you know now and you haven't known her that long." The child's voice echoed from the other suite and Alex looked away quickly. "Let's go next door to check on them. I want to make sure Cody's still okay with all the change." Preston wanted to push for more now, but Alex had already started for the door leading to the second penthouse through the shared elevator. He punched in the code. The doors swept open to reveal the two women sitting on the living room floor with a young, blond-haired boy—Cody. An intricate puzzle lay on the coffee table.

The suite was much the same as its mate, other than the use of silver and blues rather than reds and golds for the lavish accommodations. Preston hadn't grown up in this sort of world, but he'd earned his way into the life of the rich and famous. He hoped he'd kept his feet and priorities planted, much like the young mom over there with her child. There hadn't been much time for him to get to know Alex's recent fiancée and her son, but he'd been impressed by her down-to-earth ways and her devotion to her child.

Amie glanced up, her eyes lighting as she looked at Preston before she shifted her attention back to the puzzle self-consciously. Nina reached up to clasp hands with Alex briefly, connecting without taking her attention off her four-year-old son. Alex kissed the top of her head full of red curls before dropping to sit on the window seat overlooking the buildings lighting up the night skyline.

Preston joined him, curious what this gathering held in store—and what he could learn about Amie.

She helped Cody match pieces in the puzzle, a Monet image far more advanced than a four-year-old could normally put together. But Mariah had told him Cody was a savant at art, and Amie had a gift for helping tap into that connection with the child. She was good with kids and that touched something in him he hadn't thought about in a long while.

Alex set down his bottle on the window ledge. "You asked about my sister," he said softly. "Do you want to know as a boss or for more personal reasons?"

Might as well be honest. He wasn't having any luck hiding his attraction to her. And maybe Alex would respect the straight talk. "This has nothing to do with business. I would like to get to know her better."

"Okay then." Alex nodded slowly, his eyes settling on his sister, fiancée and future stepson. "Did Amie ever tell you about the time Stone and I put Kool-Aid in Amie's showerhead right before the Miss Stampede Queen pageant? I didn't think she would ever forgive either of us for turning her hair pink. Not to mention her skin."

Where was he going with this story? "Seriously?"

"Mom never could figure out which one of us to blame. I did it, but she was convinced Stone egged me on." A smile twitched.

"And the truth?"

His grin faded. "I wanted to help her, and Stone was more of a rebel, the idea man behind the prank. He left a gag book open to a particular page right on my desk."

Preston envisioned Amie stepping out of that shower covered in pink dye—um, better not to think overmuch on that image. "I bet Amie was furious."

"Not really. She wasn't as into the pageant gig as Mom likes to think. It was pretty much the only way she could get attention from our mother."

"That sucks."

"It was worse when she was little. As she got older, she started to rebel." He rolled the beer bottle between his palms. "When we were seventeen, she didn't want to win the Miss Honey Bee Pageant—and given how many pageants she'd won in the past, it wasn't arrogant of her to assume she would run away with that crown. But back to that time. She didn't want to go because the Honey Bee Queen had to attend the county fair and she wouldn't be able to attend homecoming."

"What did you do that time?" He was getting an image of these three growing up together, protecting each other from dysfunctional parents but bonded by the love of their grandparents.

"Nothing too terrible. We went boating the day before the competition, and we stayed out so long we got sunburned. I told Mom the engine stalled. Amie looked like a lobster." His reminiscent grin went tight. "Mom made her compete anyway. Just slathered her in more makeup. Amie got second runner-up."

"Seriously?"

"Scout's honor." He held up his fingers. "I offered to cut her hair but she nixed that, so we opted for the sunburn instead. I was never sure if she opted out of the haircut idea out of vanity or because Mom would have just bought a wig."

Preston studied the beautiful, eclectic woman sitting on the floor patiently piecing together a puzzle with Cody. She was focused on the child's wishes, on the child himself. She was an amazing woman in so many ways.

But he also could see how her upbringing would have left her with some hefty trust issues. Was her brother right to be worried? Because Preston was beginning to wonder if he had enough left inside him to give this woman who deserved—and would demand—one hundred percent.

Amie had felt jittery all evening watching Preston and her brother huddled together talking. What was Alex telling him? What did Preston want to know? She would find out soon enough now that Cody had calmed down enough to go to sleep. The puzzle had helped soothe him in the new locale. Nina was tucking him in now.

Preston had stepped onto the balcony to take an overseas business call. A breeze swept in through the open balcony door, carrying in his low and rumbly voice.

Amie rushed over to her brother as he straightened the puzzle on the coffee table, Monet's *Water Lily Pond*, a puzzle she'd gifted Cody with to connect through their love of art.

She knelt beside her brother. "Alex, be honest. Did Gran send you here to spy on me?"

He rocked back on his boot heels. "No, but that answers a big question. So Gran sent you on this trip for your inheritance test."

"I didn't say that," she hedged, crossing her arms.

"You don't have to."

She sank back onto her bottom, hugging her knees. "You tricked me."

"You fell for it…" He sat beside her and tugged her ponytail. "I just want to make sure you're okay. Preston is a shark. It's clear you two have something going on and I don't want you to get hurt."

Her heart hammered as she hugged her knees tighter. So it was that obvious. Their attraction was visible. But…that also meant Preston looked equally interested, enough to be noticed. And though Alex was playing the protective brother, the confirmation of Preston's interest gave her hope.

"If you think Preston's such a bad guy, why haven't you said something to Gran? You have influence with her."

"He's one helluva businessman and he will make the company successful, which is good for all of us. That doesn't mean I want him having anything to do with my sister."

She appreciated that he cared, but at the same time it bothered her that no one in this family seemed to think she could look after herself. Her pageant days might be long behind her, but people in her family were still so intent on making decisions for her. She didn't even want to consider her brother's reaction if he found out she was pregnant.

Deep breath. That wasn't important now. Not yet. One crisis, one task at a time.

Preston stepped back into the suite, closing the balcony door. He might be a shark, but damn, he took her breath away and set her senses on fire.

And time was running out fast to figure out how to deal with that.

* * *

Preston palmed Amie's back and led her into their suite, all too aware that her brother was so damn close. This whole dating ritual felt alien at forty-six years old. He wasn't a high schooler to sit on the sofa and be grilled by dad.

But Amie was tight with her family and there was no dodging all those concerned relatives. Truth be told, Alex's insights helped, even if he'd meant them as a warning.

Amie stepped into their suite and spun on her heels fast. "I can't wait another second to know. What were you and Alex talking about while I played with Cody?"

"Business." Images of Amie with pink tinged hair and a sunburn filled his mind, making her all the more approachable. Vulnerable.

Beautiful.

"That's all?" She perched her hands on her hips. "Somehow I'm having trouble believing you just talked about Diamonds in the Rough. My brother's known to be protective. It can't be coincidence that he showed up here now."

"Of course it's not a coincidence. He cares about you." Preston guided her deeper into the room, over to the balcony and their view of the Hudson River. He missed the outdoors. Needed the clarity. "But I can handle a worried relative."

"I hope so." She gripped the balcony railing, the NYC skyline lighting up the night, glittering like manufactured touchable stars. This was as romantic a setting as the park. Maybe the evening wasn't lost. Not yet. "I don't need any more conflict in my life right now."

A rogue thought struck him. "Did you tell him what happened between us?"

"No, of course not." Her eyes went wide with unmistakable horror. She shook her head. "I do *not* share that kind of information with him. That would be…creepy. But we're twins. There's an instinct between us. I'm certain he's here to check up on me. So I'll ask again. What did you two talk about?"

"Business—and yes, we talked about you." He skimmed his fingers over her high cheekbones and along her silky ponytail. "He shared stories about your pageant days and pranks you pulled to get out of attending some."

She angled closer, her feet tucked between his. "Why in the world would he do that?"

"I suspect he was lobbying to make sure I know you're more than a pretty face." He cupped the back of her neck. "But I already knew that."

"How so?" Her hand flattened against his chest, no hesitation.

There was a physical ease growing between them. It felt familiar. Comfortable. Natural.

"I work with you. You're damn smart." He tapped her temple. "Underestimating you would be a big mistake on anyone's part."

"Still—" she swayed even closer, bringing her lips inches away from his mouth "—it wasn't my brain that landed us in that coat closet together, since we hadn't even met."

Unable to resist her, all of her—body and brain—he sketched his mouth over hers. "Don't I know it."

Seven

His kiss sent Amie's already simmering passion into a full flame. She was so tired of fighting the attraction and had precious little time left to explore it before she told him about the baby. Tonight had been magical in a million ways, from their date in the park, to seeing him hang out with her brother and future nephew. In his own way, Preston fit. Or rather, she wanted him to fit.

But thinking that far ahead threatened to send her into a panic, so she focused on the present. On the warm stroke of his tongue with the taste of beer and pizza. The bold stroke of his hands along her spine, over her bottom to cup her hips and bring her closer. The press of his arousal sent a rush of power through her. This was real, happening again, not just another dream at night that left her feeling frustrated and aching.

He angled back to meet her eyes. "Are we headed for the bedroom?"

"Is that where you want to be?"

"You don't even have to ask that question."

"Neither do you. My only suggestion—" she looped her arms around his neck and she walked backward, sidestepping her cat "—let's begin in the shower."

His eyes flamed. "I like the way you think."

Their clothes fell away, leaving a trail of clothes as they walked into the Florentine-marble bathroom with an oversize steam rain shower and multiple body jets. He pulled a condom from his leather shaving kit, setting it inside the shower stall as he turned on the sprays, but stayed outside while the water heated.

"You're even more beautiful than I remember." He held her at arm's length, his eyes sweeping her curves and bringing tingles of awareness along her skin as surely as if he'd stroked her. "It's been driving me crazy the past two months thinking about that dark coat closet, wishing we had chosen a place with light and time. Hating like hell that it seemed we wouldn't get another chance."

She savored the breadth of his shoulders, the hard cut of muscles along his chest covered in dark hair. His narrow hips drew her eyes, her attention held by the thick arousal against his stomach.

She trailed her fingers down his chest, lower, his stomach muscles tensing visibly. "That night seems so surreal now."

With one finger, she traced the rigid length of him. His hard-on twitched against her touch and he groaned low in his throat.

His hazel eyes went steely with desire. "It happened."

"Believe me, I know." Her fingers wrapped around

the length of him. "I remember every detail, every moment."

He stepped closer, his hands cradling and caressing both her breasts. "This is going to be even better. I'm going to take my time."

She arched into his touch. "Promises?"

"I'm a man of my word." Dipping his head to kiss her again, he backed her into the shower.

No more reservations. She would have this and worry about the consequences tomorrow.

Preston backed Amie against the tile wall, taking the shower spray against his back. Her breasts filled his hands, the hardened peaks pressing into his palms as he stroked and caressed, then plucked with his thumbs... and mouth.

The spray pelted over their naked bodies, the beads of water mingling with sweat and need. Steam filled the shower stall, creating an even greater sense of privacy, a barrier between them and the outside world. For so long he'd ached for her, dreamed of having her totally. To learn every curve of her that he hadn't had time to explore before. She'd shut him out for so long. He wasn't a hundred percent sure why she'd changed her mind now, but he sure as hell wasn't turning his back on the chance to win her over.

He took a bar of soap in his hands, savoring the task in front of him. He applied all his focus to taking his time. Discovering all her secrets. All the places she liked to be touched best.

Steam surrounded them, a misty warm cloud along her wet skin while he worked up a lavender lather. She shifted from one foot to the other, drawing his eye toward long, slender legs slick with shower spray. Setting down the bar of soap, he reached for her shoulders and massaged the suds all over her.

Preston grinned hungrily, watching as her eyes drifted closed for a long moment, her muscles easing beneath his touch. He brushed kisses across her spiky, wet lashes while he slid his hands lower, kneading her high, full breasts until her knees seemed to give out from underneath her, making her sway. He pressed her to the tile wall with his hips, holding her upright.

Her breath caught as she reached for the soap, too, her fingers fumbling with it somewhere behind his back while he thumbed one dusky pink nipple to taut attention. She sighed in his ear, a throaty rush of breathless pleasure that only deepened when he took her in his mouth.

The soap fell from her hands and landed somewhere around his feet, but he couldn't stir himself to retrieve it. Not when her back arched the way it did right now, her whole body attuned to his slightest movement. Just like that first night when they'd danced. When they'd made love.

The chemistry at work was undeniable.

Still, she'd wanted a shower and he planned to deliver. So he forced himself back to hunt for shampoo.

Water saturated her hair, deepening the dark brown to ebony, and he squeezed the fruity-scented concoction into the locks, working it through, massaging her scalp while she hummed her pleasure. His hands slicked along the soaked strands, down her back to cup her bottom and bring her closer again. Skin to skin.

She sipped a kiss from him. "No more waiting. Now."

"And again in bed."

"Yes," she whispered, passing him the condom from the ledge.

He pressed inside her, moving, claiming.

The clamp of her around him was better than memories. The warmth of her body, the writhing of her hips was perfection. Bathroom lights and moonbeams streamed through the panes over her curves. No darkness. No shadows.

Just steam carrying the scent of soap and sex.

Her gasping breaths ramped, faster, her breasts pressing against him as her desire grew. He could feel it. Sense it. Her hand slapped against the glass wall as she braced herself, sliding down the condensation. Her head falling back, neck vulnerable.

As she unraveled with her orgasm, it was difficult to tell what was hotter—her or the steaming water. Finally, finally, he let himself go and thrust faster, deeper, wringing fresh sighs of pleasure from her as he found his own mind-shattering release.

And he knew he'd made the right decision. They would date, sleep together, work together, keeping it all civil and incredible.

They had all the time in the world.

Time was moving so fast. Knowing she was stuck in a twilight dream and unable to pull herself out, she rolled from side to side in the sheets, the Egyptian cotton sliding against her skin like Preston's touch. Her mind filled with an out-of-control reel, the past and present tangled, the night in the closet meshing with their encounter in the shower. Their clothes on from that night, but wet and plastered to their bodies. The

*peach-colored satin dress clung to her skin and shower
spray slid from the brim of his Stetson.*

*She breathed in his scent, clean but spicy, too. Mas-
culine. Heady. His touch warmed her where he touched
her waist. Her hand.*

*The energy between them crackled like static through
a rainstorm, crackling, dangerous along her skin. The
music from that evening mingled with the percussion of
the showerheads hitting the wall, their bodies, the floor.
She breathed in and he breathed out. The writhing of
their movements—dancing, making love, synced up effortlessly, her body responding to the slightest movement of his, shadowing his steps as she fell deeper into
the spell of his hazel eyes.*

*The dim lighting of the coatroom and shower cast
his face in shadows as she arched up into his kiss, his
arms strong around her but loose enough she could
leave if she wanted. But the last thing she wanted was
to stop even though her mind shouted that she couldn't
see his face, she didn't know who she was with. She
needed to wipe away the water, let in the sunshine and
see him. Know him.*

*Except pleasure pulsed through her at the angling
of his mouth over hers, the touch of his tongue to hers.
The kiss went deeper, faster, spiraling out of control.
She pressed herself to the hard planes of his body. She
lost herself in the kiss again, in the dream. In the feel
and fantasy of this torrid dream that had her pressing
her legs together in a delicious aching need for release.*

*Her breasts tingled and tightened into hard beads
and her hands moved restlessly under the covers
searching for him...but they were in the shower and
the closet. And the hard length of his erection pressed*

against her stomach, a heavy pressure that burned right through the silky dress she'd worn.

She couldn't deny how much she wanted this. Him. Now.

He started to ease back and she stopped him, gripping his lapels. Slipping her hand into his tuxedo jacket, she let her fingers stroke across the muscled heat of his chest, water sloshing over them in her tangled mind. This was a man, the very best kind, powerful in body and mind.

His hands were back on her just as fast, roving, keeping the flame burning and—

Her breath was knocked from her.

She blinked awake, gasping for air as her cat stared back at her, perched on her chest. "Roscoe?"

The rascal must have jumped on her chest, worried over her restless dreams. She reached beside her and Preston still snoozed away, his breath heavy with sleep. She ran soft fingers on his forearm, unable to quiet her mind.

Eyes bleary, she stared at the digital clock on the nightstand: 1:30 a.m. A sigh escaped her lips. She needed to move. To think. To find clarity rather than thrash around in dreams she didn't understand.

Lifting Roscoe off and setting him on the floor, she carefully slipped out of the bed. He didn't stir. Neither did Preston. After the shower, they'd moved to the bed, slept, woken to make love again, taking their time, learning the nuances of each other. Then drifted off again. But still, she was restless.

From the floor, Amie grabbed Preston's T-shirt and put it on. It fell midthigh, like a short dress from her pageant days. But it smelled like Preston's musky cologne. It reassured her. Steadied her.

On tiptoe, she moved to the white chaise lounge across the room. The hand-stamped Venetian velvet made a gorgeous addition to the suite, and the kind of textural art that she loved best. She ran an appreciative hand along the pattern as she plopped down, clutching an oversize silk pillow to her stomach. Roscoe pattered over to her, tail straight up, shaking with excitement and affection. He jumped up, pawed at her until she lowered the pillow. He sat in her lap, purring, squinting his blue eyes at her. Roscoe always knew when she needed someone. When she needed comfort.

And damn. She needed that now more than ever.

Light from the city poured in through the window, allowing Amie to see Preston's figure in bed. He was a wonderful man. Caring. Confident. And more important, he seemed to believe in her. In her designs—at least the ones that she'd openly shared with him— and in her ability to make decisions.

Reaching for her stomach, Amie sighed deeply. There were too many unknowns.

For a moment, she allowed herself to think about what it might have been like if they had dated over the past couple of months. What they would be like. Would he be helping her pick out a nursery theme? Would he be offering names?

"Roscoe kitty, why is this so complicated?" she whispered. Roscoe simply looked up at her, purring still, and stretched his front paws to her belly. "We used a condom. I never sneak off into coat closets. And it's so hard to regret anything."

She scratched his head, wondering about what her

baby would look like. What life with her baby would look like. No, life with *their* baby. With his hazel eyes and her thick dark hair, chubby cheeks. Her heart went tight at the image of Preston smiling, rocking that child in his arms. If only life could be that simple, that easy. Had she blown her chance at it already?

Roscoe jumped from her lap and sprinted back to the bed, curling around Preston's head. Amie stayed for a moment on the chaise lounge before crawling back into bed, wanting to have Preston's warmth against her skin.

He stirred as she found her way back into his arms. He squeezed her tightly, and kissed the nape of her neck.

His breath was warm against her neck. If only things were different, less complicated. Somehow she would have to find a way to fix things between them. Wishing wasn't enough. She needed to act and soon.

Amie watched the clock for another few minutes before drifting to sleep.

After a catnap, Amie curled up against his side, the Egyptian cotton sheets tangled around their legs.

They were so good together it almost scared her, making her want to hesitate pushing for action and savor this just a while longer. It was just one night.

Preston stroked her bare shoulder while moving his toe under the sheet to entertain Roscoe. The cat pawed and pounced at the movement. "I'm disappointed your brother thinks I'm the bad guy."

"Well, you have cut a wide swath through the staff, firing off longtime employees we've grown to know and care about for years," she pointed out, tugging lightly at his chest hair.

He closed a hand around hers as Roscoe waddled slowly up the bed. "You mean, I saved the corporation."

"*Saved* is a strong word." She flattened her palm to his chest, his heartbeat steady and strong. "I would say you bolstered things."

"Semantics."

And likely why her grandmother had put him in charge instead of her.

Still, she frowned. "We lost a lot of talented people. Talented loyal people. I feel they deserved better from the company."

"It wouldn't help those talented and loyal people if the company started losing money. And that's what we were looking at. The employees don't thrive if the organization isn't thriving." He spoke with surprising passion, opening their blinds a bit with the remote control beside the bed, exposing an incredible view of the city lights in the middle of the night. "You know how many companies reorganize and then leave their people sweating it out for months afterward, worrying about their jobs? I happen to think it's kinder to circumvent the drama and the questions, making cuts as quickly and painlessly as possible."

"None of it was painless." Although she understood his point. She'd had friends who had been caught in corporate takeovers, worrying about their jobs for months while they navigated shifting seas at work.

"That's what severance packages are for." He shrugged. "I take personnel issues very, very seriously. I honestly believe the people are the backbone of any good company. That's not lip service. That's a fact. I happen to think it's one of the things your grandmother liked best about my philosophy when we first met."

"I believe you." She could see what had won over her grandmother. Preston might seem bottom line oriented. And he was. But he did care. "You just…look at things differently than me."

She wondered what he saw out that window overlooking the city right now. While she saw the lights and play of the moon over the river, he no doubt focused on other things.

"Different is not bad. Most artists are empathetic by nature. It's what makes them thrive in their work."

"Oh, really?" She grinned for a moment, realizing she'd never separate the man from the arrogance for long. But he was a smart man. And he'd obviously spent some time thinking about this kind of thing.

"Really."

They were quiet for a moment as she tried to process this new side of Preston. A side, she had to admit, appealed to her.

"I'm trying to see your take on things. My whole family has been more on edge recently because of Gran's cancer, so maybe not all the McNairs have given you a fair chance." That worry inside her—the fear that dogged her about the woman she loved most in the world—had been a large part of what had driven her into Preston's arms in the first place. "You're an outsider, so it will take us a while to trust you."

He lifted a strand of her hair. "Do *you* trust me?"

What a loaded question. She tugged the sheet up farther over her breasts, avoiding his eyes. "I trust you can lead Diamonds in the Rough."

"But you still wish it was in family hands."

Except then she wouldn't have met him and she wouldn't have this baby she loved more and more every day. Life was complicated. She opted for an honest answer—about the company. "I understand where my area of expertise falls at the company, but I still resent that I was not even considered for the CEO's position. I wasn't consulted about the choice. It stings."

"I'm sorry to hear that." He sat up, studying her face with those perceptive CEO eyes of his. "Your cousin didn't want the job. Did you?"

"I wanted to be considered." She sat up as well, hugging her knees to her chest.

"What makes you think you weren't?"

She rolled her eyes. "My family has never taken me seriously." Roscoe curled under her hand to be rubbed. "I'm the eccentric one, the airheaded beauty queen."

"You've proven you're at the top of your field at Diamonds in the Rough. Your more rustic designs are catching on like wildfire across the country and in England. You deserve to be proud of that. We all have a role to play."

She thought about the designs that weren't rustic. The ones he hadn't asked her much about. They might be all wrong for Diamonds in the Rough.

"I guess I just feel all the more need to prove there's no nepotism. My grandmother gives my father an office with a title and his name on the door."

"Your father's position is as a figurehead," he said matter-of-factly. "We know that. You contribute work, founding entire design lines. Sounds to me like you don't take yourself seriously."

She snapped back at the observation. One that was perhaps a little too astute for her peace of mind.

"Maybe you're right. And maybe you're not." She slid

off the bed, taking the sheet with her. "But I do know one thing for sure. I'm starving."

Seemed she was hungry all the time lately once the morning sickness passed. Her time was definitely running out to tell him about the baby. She'd rambled on about trust and yet she was lying to him in one of the worst ways possible.

They'd taken a big step here tonight. She just hoped the connection they'd made was enough to carry them through the news she had to tell him.

Preston leaned against the wet bar, facing the bay of windows looking out over one of the best views in Manhattan, but his eyes zeroed in on Amie. She perched on a leather bar stool wrapped in a sheet and eating a sliced pear, cheese and crackers from the cut-crystal dish as though she were a starved athlete. He'd learned to read people over the years, a survival skill in his job world. And he could see something huge weighed on her mind.

Nudging aside her empty plate and sliding it across the smooth granite countertop, she dabbed a napkin along the corners of her mouth with overplayed care. She folded the crisp linen napkin, set it down and pressed the crease nervously. "We need to talk."

Damn. He'd known something was off with her from the second she'd rolled out of bed. "Forget the speech about how we shouldn't have done this and it will never happen again. There's an attraction between us we've tried to deny and that hasn't worked. I say it's time to quit fighting it."

"Things aren't quite that simple." She pressed the napkin crease again and again.

"They can be. You can't deny what's between us any

longer, especially not after tonight." He picked up her hand and linked fingers, even the simple touch crackling the air with attraction.

"I hear you." She squeezed his hand, a sadness creeping across her face and catching in her eyes. "And in a different world things could have played out over the months."

"Different world?" He struggled to follow her words and for an astute CEO, he just wasn't getting it. But he wasn't letting go. "Is this because I head the company? It's not like I'm your boss any more than you're mine, since your family owns the business. That puts us on even footing."

She shook her head, tousled hair sliding over her cheek. "It's more complicated." She jerked her hand free and pushed her hair back with agitated fingers. "I've been looking for the right time—the right way—to tell you."

Tell him what? To go to hell? That she was seeing someone else? "Just say it."

She sat up straighter, her hands falling away from her head and settling to rest over her stomach. "I'm pregnant. And the baby is yours."

Eight

"You're pregnant?"

Preston's flat tone and stunned expression didn't give Amie much hope for an enthusiastic reception. She tucked the sheet more securely around her, wishing she'd chosen her timing better to make the announcement, when she felt less vulnerable from making love with him.

When she had on some clothes and he was wearing more than sweatpants low slung on his sexy narrow hips.

Arming herself with a bracing breath at least, she met his shocked gaze head-on. "Apparently the condom didn't work—welcome to the world of the two percent fail rate. And before you ask, I haven't been with anyone else in over six months, so I am absolutely certain the baby is yours."

He gave a rough nod. Swallowed visibly.

"I wasn't questioning. I trust your honesty." He thrust his hands through his tousled dark hair, the dusting of silver strands on the side a hint more pronounced in his stress. "I'm just…stunned."

She tipped her chin, trying to squelch the ache of disappointment in her heart that he hadn't…what? Just turned a cartwheel? Or hugged her and asked how she was feeling? Make her feel connected to him since they'd created this new life together? She knew better than to hope for those things. But that didn't stop the sting of hurt just the same.

"I don't expect anything from you. I'm able to support myself. I would hope for the baby's sake you would want to be a part of his or her life, but if you decide otherwise, I am not going to force you to pretend to care."

"Whoa, hold on. I didn't say I'm out of the picture." He started pacing restlessly around the luxury suite, the same way he did whenever he went into thinking mode in the boardroom. "I've had less than a minute to process this. I'm forty-six years old. This isn't the news I was expecting. I'm past that stage of my life."

She remembered his child who'd died and her heart softened. No doubt her baby would stir all the more difficult emotions for him. Yes, she understood that. Wished he would have confided more in her when she'd asked him about it. But he hadn't wanted that kind of intimacy between them.

His decision. And damn it, this wasn't easy for her, either. This baby was coming no matter what.

"Fine then." She clasped the sheet between her breasts and slid off the bar stool. "My baby. I'll take care of him or her and you can move on with the next stage of your life."

He clasped her elbow gently and stopped pacing. "Lower your defenses, Amie. This is my baby, too. And I may not be as young as most new parents, but I'm not Methuselah." He massaged her arm, his touch tender but his face still guarded. "I'm all in. Whatever you and the child need, I'm here for you both. I will be an active part of his or her life."

"Thanks for doing your duty," she said dryly, easing her arm away.

He sighed heavily. "Apparently I'm not expressing myself well."

"No, I'm hearing you just fine. And more than that, I can see in your face this news doesn't please you in the least." A knot started in her throat. Damn hormonal emotions.

"Are *you* happy?"

His question caught her off guard. She hadn't spent a lot of time thinking about her own emotions. She'd focused more on Preston's and her grandmother's reactions. "I'm nervous. But yes, there are days I have these images of what he or she will be like, and I'm happy."

"Pardon me for being human. You've had a while to process this surprise." He clasped her hand, holding firm. "Give me time to get over the shock of your being pregnant and I'll get to the happy part."

She eased a step closer, not quite ready to relent. "Well, forgive me if I'm skeptical."

Holding her gaze, he sat on the sofa, tugging her hand carefully until finally she sat on his lap and he held her close. They didn't speak and she let herself soak up the feeling of his arms around her. Maybe, just maybe, they could work things out in a way no one would be hurt or feel disappointed.

He rubbed his hands up and down her back. "Holy crap," he said slowly, realization lighting his eyes. "This is why you've been avoiding me lately."

"Ya think?" She pressed her cheek against his steady heartbeat.

"What about before you found out you were pregnant? Why did you give me the deep freeze then?"

Now, *that* surprised her. How could he be so clueless? "You honestly don't know?"

He shook his head. "Afraid not. Enlighten me."

"You were firing Diamonds in the Rough employees at the speed of light." She slid off his lap to sit beside him, the warm fuzzy moment over as indignation crept up her spine. "The poor staff was literally put on the island watching people voted off every day."

"You don't agree with the business decisions I made." He arched a dark eyebrow.

"Not all of them. No," she admitted.

"But you can't deny the company is thriving now. Those who are still working for us have jobs that are more secure than ever. With luck, we'll be able to hire more back."

Could that be true? Could she trust him? "When will that happen?"

"When the numbers speak."

She stifled disappointment at his typical double-talk answer. "Numbers don't talk. People do."

He spread his hands. "That's why you're the artist and I'm the CEO."

"And we're both now parents of this baby." She shot to her feet, feeling more hopeless than before that they could find a middle ground together. "I need to shower and rest. I just can't talk about this anymore."

Before she did something weak and vulnerable like curl up and cry against his chest. She dashed back to her bedroom and closed herself inside, alone with her cat and an even bigger tangle of emotions.

Maybe a better man would have gone after her.

Preston could not be that man. Not right now. Not when this news had ripped him raw.

Charging into his bedroom, he found his workout clothes and pulled on a clean T-shirt and running shorts. Socks. Shoes. He focused on the routine to keep himself from putting a hole through the nearest wall.

Amie pregnant. His daughter had died giving birth... The two events spun together. Clouded his mind. He needed to move.

He sprinted out of the suite and down fifty-two flights of stairs from the penthouse suite. He headed west on East Fifty-seventh Street and picked up his pace. Midtown was far quieter in the small hours of the morning. While it may be the city that never sleeps, 4:30 a.m. didn't attract the same kind of crowds. Cabs raced to the stoplights in the freedom of no traffic. Bars and clubs in unlikely places spilled music and colored lights out onto the sidewalk, making him dart around the occasional red velvet ropes set up on the street.

And Amie was pregnant.

Lungs burning, he hit Central Park before he realized where he'd been headed. Maybe not the wisest place to run after dark, but he pitied anyone who tried to mess with him. He'd love an excuse to throw a punch. Or ten. Anything to make this ache in his chest go away. The fire behind his eyes.

He'd lost his baby girl to a pregnancy. And now *Amie was pregnant*.

Tripping on a tree root as he darted off the sidewalk into the grass, he almost fell onto a homeless guy sleeping on a green painted bench, his face covered with newspaper.

"You okay, man?" the guy asked, a hand shoving aside last week's sports section as he stared up at Preston.

He nodded. Started running again.

Slower.

He spotted the pond up ahead and followed the path around it. Now and then a cab pulled onto one of the roads through the park, headlights flashing over him. A few street lamps lit his way. Nocturnal birds called out from the trees all around the pond, the conservancy efforts having made this portion of the park feel like being out in the country. Exactly what he needed.

Space. Air. Stillness.

Slowing his steps even more, he paced alongside the water's edge until he'd circled almost the whole way around. He hoped he'd sweat out the worst of the crushing fear for Amie. For his unborn child. He'd loved his daughter so much. Even during the years where he hadn't gotten to see Leslie much, he took joy and pride in knowing she was in the world. A small piece of him, but better than him. The very best of him.

Losing Leslie had cut so deep he'd barely stood it. There was the pain of losing her. Compounded by the fact that she'd died without getting to hold the infant she'd given up everything to have. And made even worse by the pain of knowing how much she hadn't wanted her own father in her life.

When Leslie had died, he'd taken time off from work—something he'd never done. Listless weeks he could hardly remember. But a company crisis had saved him. Forced him to dedicate everything he had to bending the corporate world to his will. There had been a grim satisfaction in that. And it had saved his sanity.

Now, he was going to face all that again. With Amie.

"You sure you're okay, man?" a gruff man's voice shouted to him from several yards away.

For a second, Preston figured voices in his head was just about right for the hell of the past hour. But then he saw a flash of newspaper waving at him from another bench surrounded by bushes and flowers. Lights illuminated the plantings—and the homeless man he'd almost tripped on before. The guy's grizzled beard and shaggy hair were so long they flowed over his T-shirt, but he held up both hands as if to show him he meant no harm.

"I'm good. Thanks. Just out for a jog."

But was it too much to ask to be alone with his thoughts?

"Sorry, dude," the scratchy voice rasped in the quiet of predawn when the sounds of night bugs were still more prominent than the rattle of diesel engines and squealing brakes in the distance. "Had a friend that came here to…er…end it all." The guy scratched his beard. "Got that same feeling when you sprinted past me."

"No problems here—" he started. But seeing the older guy's patches on a tattered jacket—military badges, Preston stopped with the bs answer. "Running off some old ghosts. But I'm…okay."

Scared spitless of having another child. Worried he might fail this baby the same way he'd let down Leslie… but he was going to find a way to get himself together.

Man up.

"Hard to keep 'em off your heels some days. I've had that kind, too." The man nodded thoughtfully, staring out at the pond.

Laughter nearby interrupted as a young couple stumbled past, sounding intoxicated as they held on to one another, doubled over with hilarity while the street lamps glinted off their matching face piercings.

Preston needed to get out of here. Get his butt back to the hotel and be there for Amie. For his child.

And the only way to do that? Wall off those emotions—the ghosts on his heels—and just focus on her. Getting through this. He was a man of honor and he would stand by her. His family.

His eyes burned even as he thought it.

Striding over to the older man, Preston took a deep breath.

"Thank you for your service." He held out his hand, knowing in his gut the man was a veteran fallen on hard times.

Sure enough, the guy grinned. A few teeth were missing. But his eyes held plenty of wisdom.

"You're welcome, son." His weathered grip was strong. "You might try surprising those ghosts sometime, by the way. Stop and turn instead of running. One of these days, you'll give them hell."

"I'll remember that." With a nod, Preston launched into a run, turning his feet back toward the luxury hotel that seemed a million miles away from this place.

He wasn't ready to battle any ghosts today. But for now he would count it a victory if he could talk to Amie about this child without breaking out in a cold sweat.

First, though? He needed to run faster, arrange with the concierge to find help for his veteran angel.

Then Preston would be ready to ask Amie to marry him.

The next day passed in a blur for Amie. She couldn't get a read on Preston. He'd been the perfect gentleman, but it was all so…perfect. Too perfect. He'd closed himself off from her in a way she couldn't explain but couldn't miss.

Technically, he'd done nothing wrong. They'd shared breakfast in the hotel dining room with Alex, Nina and Cody, then attended a Broadway matinee together. In fact, they'd spent the entire day together, leaving not one free moment alone to talk about the baby.

In another half hour, they would be leaving for the Diamonds in the Rough gala being held at the Waldorf Astoria. For now, Preston sprawled on the floor with Cody, playing with action figures from the children's performance they'd seen today. They were watching her future nephew while Alex and Nina got dressed. The sitter would be arriving soon—one of the camp counselors Cody had met and grown fond of. She was from home being flown in so Cody would have a familiar face to care for him.

Meanwhile, Preston looked too damn enticing playing in tuxedo pants and his shirt. No jacket or tie yet, just his suspenders and cummerbund. His broad hands moved the little lions, marching them over a mountain they'd built from throw pillows.

He was clearly at ease with children. But then, he'd told her he'd been a father and that his daughter had died. This new baby had to be bringing up old memories—good and painful ones. She should have thought of that before now.

The elevator door opened and Amie glanced over to see Nina walking through, wearing a floor-length black dress, simple other than the plunging neckline with a long yellow diamond pendant. Her red curly hair was upswept in a riot of spirals.

Amie rose from her chair and greeted Nina, grasping her hands. "You look amazing. I'm sorry if Alex caused you any trouble dragging you here to check up on me."

"A woman's never too old to play dress up. This is a fun break." She grinned, twirling, her silky dress swirling around her feet, a flash of gorgeous Jimmy Choo heels beneath. "And you, oh my, you do have a way of making a statement."

"This old rag?" Amie winked, but she couldn't deny she'd dressed to the nines, too. It was a kind of armor, a way to stabilize herself. The Grecian-style red dress was gathered on one shoulder, leaving the other bare, exposed. The gown was cinched on one hip with a brass medallion, a long slit up one leg. She hooked arms with her future sister-in-law and walked to the window seat where they could talk without Cody overhearing. And where she could gain a little distance from the appeal of Preston.

Amie sat in the window seat, cars below moving at the typical New York snail's pace. "How's Cody adjusting to your decision to stay at the ranch?"

"It's a love hate thing." She smoothed her dress over her knees, her eyes lingering affectionately on her blond son. "He likes that we're going to live there now that Alex and I are engaged. He adores being around horses all the time. He gets along so well with Alex. Your brother is wonderful at getting through to him—and willing to learn more every day. He wants to go with me to interview new doctors and therapists for Cody. But it's all happened so fast, which makes it tough, because new routines upset Cody tremendously."

Amie chewed her lip before asking, "I hope you don't take this the wrong way, but why choose to come to New York now?"

"Alex is worried about you, and Cody was upset over him leaving, so we came along. Your brother says you haven't been yourself lately. I don't know you well enough to compare, but you do seem very…stressed."

Having someone to confide in felt good, but she didn't know how much she could tell her brother's fiancée, a woman none of them had known for very long at all, given the whirlwind romance. She needed to share the news with her grandmother first. And before she did that, she wanted to have things in order with Preston, to have a plan in place. Amie settled for a general—and still truthful—answer. "Gran's cancer progressing has us all worried."

"I can understand that. I mentioned the same to Alex, but he says it's different. He can sense it because of the twin connection."

Amie glanced down at her hands, anxiously twisting the four gold and topaz rings she'd chosen to go with her dress. "Things have been difficult at work."

Nina glanced at Preston, then back at her. "It's clear there's a chemistry, but I can see how that would be complicated. I'm here if you ever need someone to talk to."

She clasped Nina's hands, noticing they both wore one of the newest Diamonds in the Rough pieces, a sun and moon facing each other in silver and gold. "Thank you. I appreciate it and am sure I'll be taking you up on that soon."

"Just not today?"

Amie shook her head, smiling warmly. "Soon."

The elevator slid open again and her twin strode into the suite. Cody shot to his feet, carrying one of the lions to show him, chattering about the imaginary game he'd been playing with Preston.

Amie rose quickly. Too quickly. Her head started swimming and the room spun. Oh God. She reached for the wall, but her line of sight was narrowing to a pinpoint. Damn it, damn it, she was going to pass out.

Dimly, she realized Preston was rushing toward her. "Amie? Are you okay?" He caught her under the arms as her legs gave way. "Is it the baby?"

"Baby?" Alex barked.

"Baby?" Nina whispered.

"Baby, baby, baby," Cody chanted.

Preston swept her up as she fought back the dizziness. He settled her onto the sofa. "Amie?"

"I'm fine," she said, the room already stabilizing. "I just stood up too fast, and I could use some supper."

"Baby," Alex said again in a menacing tone, walking closer. "What the hell is going on here?"

Preston shot him a dagger glare. "Do not upset Amie."

Still, Alex walked closer. "My *sister* is pregnant?"

Nina gripped his arm. "Alex, I don't think this is the time or the place. When Amie's ready to talk, we can have a civil discussion. Maybe we should give them some space?"

Alex kept walking toward Preston as if Nina hadn't

spoken. "I'm asking you now. Is my sister pregnant and is the baby yours?"

Preston stood, his shoulders broad and braced, staring down her angry twin. "Yes, the baby is mine."

Oh God. Her twin was the quiet one in the family, but fiercely protective. So it was no surprise when he drew back his fist.

And punched Preston in the jaw.

Nine

Amie launched forward, shouting at her brother, tugging on his arm as he pulled back for another hit. "Alex, what the hell are you doing?"

Preston stumbled a step but stayed on his feet. His eyes went steely as he stared down Alex but pointed to her. "Amie, step out of the way." He zeroed in on Alex, that same alertness in Preston's body that she'd witnessed right before he took down a criminal on an LA street corner. "McNair, get yourself under control. Think about how this is upsetting your fiancée and Cody."

The young boy with autism was sitting on the floor with wide eyes, hugging his knees while rocking back and forth. Alex cursed softly, then kneeled beside his future stepson, all his focus shifting. "It's okay, Cody. I just lost my temper. Grown-ups do that sometimes. I'm sorry, buddy. Would you like to go back to our room with your mom?"

Cody nodded, standing, moving over to his mom. Nina cast a cautious look over her shoulder before shuttling her son out of the suite.

Alex took a deep breath, but his tense face said he wasn't backing down as he stared at Preston. "You knocked up my sister."

Amie gasped, stepping between them, hands raised. "Excuse me, but I am an adult. I make my own choices, and while I am expecting a baby, I take offense at the phrase 'knocked up.' I would also appreciate it if you didn't shout the pregnancy to the world. This is my business. I don't know why you're going all Cro-Magnon."

"Seriously? It doesn't take a math whiz to realize that since you haven't been around very long, the kid was conceived before you even had a chance to really get to know my—"

Preston growled, "Watch where you're headed with what you're saying. I let you have that first punch free and clear. But push me or say anything to Amie and I'm taking you down."

Alex's jaw jutted. "You can try."

Amie pressed a hand on each man's chest. "Stop. Both of you. You're both stressing me out and that's not good for the baby."

Alex's eyes narrowed, but she felt him ease a fraction. "Sister, you're manipulating me. I don't like that."

She patted her twin and looked into his familiar eyes, finally seeing more love than anger. "But I'm right. Thank you for your concern, but I'm okay. Go see Nina and Cody before you say something you'll regret. Your family needs you."

With a tight nod, Alex hugged her quickly. "Love you, Amie." He leveled a look toward Preston before backing away. "Be good to her or there will be hell to pay."

He stalked away and the elevator doors slid closed, leaving her alone with Preston. She reached to touch his jaw carefully along the red mark turning light purple. "Are you hurt?"

Her gaze ran all over him, taking in the powerful shoulders and chest. But his hands were impossibly gentle as they landed on her arms.

"It's nothing. I've taken worse. I just need to know you're all right."

Was she? Not really. Her heart pounded double time and she just wanted life to settle down. But there was nothing she could do about that. "I'm fine, and we have the party to attend."

His hand brushed her cheek, smoothing away a tendril that had slid out of place.

"We'll talk later," he promised.

A good thing or bad? She honestly didn't know. His expression was impossible to read. Cool despite his warm touch, and that worried her. Life had been so much simpler when they were in a coat closet and shower.

Five hours later, Amie put together an ice pack from the limo minifridge. The gala had been a success from a business standpoint, with the displays echoed by edible-desert versions the guests feasted on with relish. But the event hadn't been nearly as pleasant from a personal perspective. Nina and Alex had opted to stay at the hotel with Cody. And Preston had been distant and remote but utterly in control. He'd done his job impeccably. He'd been a consummate gentleman and efficient CEO as he chose a few key people to speak with, applying just the right amount of charisma on a night that called for a personal touch. He'd even laughed off questions about his bruised face, saying he'd run into a street light while jogging.

But even so, there was still no sign of the tender lover, the man she'd started to think she could have a relationship with. He'd shut down on her ever since the baby news. She needed to get past that polite wall again, for her child's sake—and yes, for her own peace of mind.

Preston sat in the plush leather limo seat, collar unbuttoned, looking handsomely disheveled. Clutching the ice pack, Amie inched next to him, closing the space between them.

She pressed the bag of ice against his jaw and the light purple bruise. "I'm so sorry my brother hit you."

"He loves you. He didn't break anything. It's okay." He seemed to have turned the explosive moment into a simple math equation, reducing it to a balance sheet with a measurable figure. Always a businessman. Calculating.

"It's not okay. It was awful." She shivered thinking of the moment her brother had taken a swing at Preston. She dabbed the ice pack along his jaw while the limo slowed for a red light. "Can we at least talk honestly here instead of this cool and distant approach? If you've decided you're not okay with the baby, after all, just tell me. I can't take living in limbo." Her heart slammed as she waited for his response. In what way had he decided to coolly solve this complicated equation?

"I've already told you I'm going to be a part of the

baby's life." He smiled, then winced, his jaw clearly sore. "I want to be in your life, too."

"I hear the words, but your eyes are not the same." He was still closed off. She could see it in the way he refused to really look at her. "Something's wrong and you're not telling me. I know this has happened fast, but we don't have the luxury of unlimited time. Not with a baby on the way."

He tugged the ice pack from her hand and tossed it aside in irritation. "I'm giving you everything I have."

"*Giving* me?"

"Everything I have. Yes," he said, his voice clipped. "This is all there is."

"What does that mean?" she pressed, not even sure what she was searching for from him, but certainly not this. "You either want to be with me or you don't."

His jaw flexed, his stormy eyes darting back and forth for an instant before he finally exhaled, his head falling back against the leather seat. "I told you I had a daughter and that she died. This new baby has brought up a lot of memories. Tough memories to deal with."

Her heart softened. She'd suspected this, but to hear him say it—it took the fight right out of her. She smoothed a hand down his arm, the fine fabric of his tuxedo warm from his body. "Tell me, Preston, please. Let me know what's going on inside you. Your daughter is my baby's sister. I want to know—I need to know."

The car started forward, the tinted windows muting the headlights and street lamps on Park Avenue, past an older residential section of the city. She saw the lights reflect on Preston's face while he seemed to debate what to tell her.

Finally, his throat moved in a long hard swallow. "Leslie was just eighteen when she died."

So young, so tragic. And at the same time, Amie realized he'd lived a whole other life before walking into hers just two months ago. He'd told her more than once he considered himself too old for her. She didn't agree but could see right now why he felt that way.

Hoping he wouldn't close her out again, she kept rubbing his arm. "You said she had an accident. I can only imagine how that must still hurt." Her voice was soft, gentle. She brimmed with the ache to be someone he could trust. The car slowed to a stop again, and this time, the flood of red brake lights nearby created a crimson glow inside the limo.

He shook his head. "I don't think anyone gets over losing a child. And the fact that Leslie's death was preventable eats me alive every day."

Preventable? He'd said it was an accident, but clearly he'd said so to brush people—her—off. But not tonight. They'd moved past that. They were tied together for life through this baby. "What happened?"

"It's a long story without a simple answer." He turned his head toward her, his eyes full of pain.

"I'm listening." A sympathetic, encouraging smile brushed her lips as she squeezed his hand.

"Her mother and I split when Leslie was just finishing elementary school. They both hated me for leaving." He winced over that part, the pain flashing again. "And Leslie hated her mother for staying. There was no reasoning with her. She became an out-of-control teenager. Some say she would have been that way regardless, but I worked too much and missed so many of my schedulcd visitations. Time I can never get back." He rested his elbow on his knee, dropping his head into his hands.

"I'm sure you did the best you could." She rubbed circles along his broad back, their car stuck in gridlock just a few minutes from their hotel.

She suspected they wouldn't be moving anywhere for a while. And this time, she had no intention of leaving the limo.

"How can you be so certain?" he asked softly.

"You're a perfectionist. You hold yourself to a standard so high most would be crushed."

His laugh was bitter as he sat up again. "That's my business persona. My parenting skills were sorely lacking. I thought by giving her nice things I didn't have as a kid, I was being a good dad. Trust me, I see how screwed up that is now."

"How did she die?" she pressed again.

"She ran away from home at seventeen with her loser boyfriend," he said, the bitterness in his voice unmistakable. "She got pregnant, didn't get proper prenatal care. She died and the baby didn't make it. Something callcd placenta previa. She went into premature labor and by the time she got to the ER…it was too late."

Amie stifled a gasp, the story so much worse than she'd expectcd, so painful. So terribly tragic. "No wonder you're worried about becoming a parent again."

Losing his daughter through a pregnancy added a whole other layer to his emotions where Amie's baby was concerned. It made sense now that he'd looked so rattled when she'd told him. The lines of worry that etched in his jaw all evening made more sense. Seemed more reasonable.

"It's tough not to worry about your health and the

baby. It's all I can think about sometimes, all the things that could go wrong." His eyes sheened over. He stared out in front of them.

An ambulance honked nearby, lights flashing while it went up on the sidewalk to get through the jam.

"I'm taking care of myself and am absolutely getting the best care available." Clasping his hands in both of hers, she pressed his to her stomach.

He froze again, his palm broad and warm through her silky dress. Preston stared at her stomach before meeting her gaze. His face was contorted with a sadness she could not quite comprehend. "That's not what's scaring me most."

"What then?"

"I'm scared as hell of loving another child and screwing up—" his voice came out ragged, tortured "—of having my soul ripped out if something happens to him or her. I can't go through that again. My heart died that day, Amie. I don't think I have anything left to give the two of you and that's so damn unfair."

He squeezed his eyes closed, no tears escaping, and she knew that just meant he kept them bottled up inside with all that pain and misplaced guilt.

"Preston? Preston," she said again until he looked at her. "You seem to care a lot more than you like to let on. I can see it in your eyes."

"You're seeing what you want to see."

"Trust me—" she cupped his face and couldn't help but notice he left his hands on her stomach where their baby grew "—I may be an artist, but I'm the most starkly realistic one in the family."

She was far more practical than people gave her credit for, a side effect of having her every move scrutinized by a stage mother—a mother she did not intend to emulate.

Her thoughts were cut short by the soft chime of a bell that preceded an announcement from the driver.

"Excuse me, Mr. Armstrong. My apologies for choosing this route, sir. There's an overturned bus ahead. Looks like we may be stuck here for a while."

Preston hit the speaker button. "Not a problem. Thank you for the update."

Releasing the light on the communications panel, he stared at her in the dim light of the luxury car, his eyes bright with inscrutable emotions slowly shifting to…hunger.

It was her only warning before he leaned closer and pressed his mouth to hers, kissing her. Not a quick kiss. But the kind that promised more.

So much more.

The old hurt and anger roiled inside him. But this time, instead of running it out, he had Amie's hands on him. Amie's soft voice in his ear and slender body shifting beside him on the limo seat. It was tough to resist her on a good day. And this day? The last twenty-four hours had shredded him.

All the emotions surged and shifted into one inescapable need.

He kissed her hard. Deep. But he made sure to be gentle with his hands and his body. He skimmed a touch along her bare shoulders, feeling her shiver and tremble. She was exquisitely sensitive. He'd been an ass not to see the signs of her pregnancy earlier. But now? It seemed written all over her body.

In the way she quivered against him when he did

something small, like nip her ear the way he did now. Or when he licked his way down her neck and her skin broke out in goose bumps.

The limo windows were the blackout kind. No one could see in. The partition window was secured, he'd double-checked it on the communications panel. Doors locked. Traffic jam keeping them right here for a long time.

So he didn't quit kissing her. He laid her back on the seat and stretched out alongside her, never breaking his kiss down her chest to the swell of her breast. More delicious evidence of her pregnancy. He'd just thought her curves were even more lush than he'd remembered from that first wild night together. But now, he cupped the weight of them in both hands, savoring the way she felt almost as much as he liked hearing her breath catch.

Dipping his head to the valley between her breasts, he nudged aside the pin on her red Grecian gown, essentially undoing all her clothes with just one touch. A red lace bra molded to her curves, but a flick of the front hinge had that falling away, too.

Impatient as hell, needing to lose himself in her—in this—he circled one tight crest with his tongue even as he slid his hand up her thigh. She arched and sighed beneath his touch, totally on board with this plan. He nudged aside the lace panties she wore, feeling her warmth right through the thin fabric.

"Amie." He said her name so she would open her eyes.

Put all that brilliant blue focus on him as he touched her. She was a beautiful woman, but damn…so much more than that. He watched her lips part as he slid a touch inside her. Her eyes fell closed again. Her thighs clamping tight to his hand to hold the touch there.

As if he was going anywhere.

He covered her mouth with his again, working her with his hand until he felt the rhythm of her sighs and throaty little hums of pleasure. Finding the pace she liked best, he took her higher. Teased her. Tempted her.

He wanted to draw it out. To make it last, but she had her own ideas. She captured his wrist in her hand. Held him right where she wanted him most.

"You like that?" He repeated the circling motion, bending to draw on one breast. Then the other. "I like it, too."

"More," she demanded, voice rasping, her blue gaze landing on his.

Complying, he drove her right where she needed to be, her cries of completion sweet music in his ear as she found her release.

Another day, he might have given her a little time to recover herself. Or taken her to that peak a second time while she was so delectably willing in his arms. But just then, that dark, hungry need returned, his emotions churning to the surface. Reminding him how damn much he needed her.

"Preston?" She smoothed her fingers along his shoulder, making him realize he hadn't even removed his jacket.

He ditched it now, sitting up on the seat.

"I'm going to bring you up here, sweetheart," he crooned as he peeled away her panties and then lifted her. Gently. Carefully. He moved her onto his lap so she straddled him.

Her thighs splayed over his, remnants of her red silk

gown still clung to her thighs and waist. She unfastened his belt and tuxedo pants, freeing him from his boxers. He watched her, her dark hair mostly falling around her shoulders, the updo sacrificed to their frenzy.

She stroked him, fingers cool and nimble as she guided him closer to where she wanted him.

Grasping her hips, he lifted her high and then eased her down. Down. Deeper.

Perfect.

Everything else fell away. Her slick heat surrounded him, holding him tight. Her hands fell to his chest where she steadied herself. She brushed a kiss along his cheek, urging him on. Telling him what she needed in a way that only fueled him up. His hands molded to her waist. Smoothed up to her breasts.

He had a lot of other ideas for his hands, too. But she gripped his wrists again. Pinned them to the limo seat on either side of his head as if she had him captive. She arched an eyebrow at him. Teasing.

But then things got crazy. She swayed her hips in a dance that about turned him inside out. Lifting up on her knees, she found a rhythm she liked and took them both higher. Faster. And he let her. Not thinking right now—great idea. He took everything she was giving him.

When her grip slipped on his wrists, though, he sensed she was close. He held her waist, taking over, pushing them the rest of the way. Her release squeezed him hard, spurring his own. With no condom between them, the pleasure seemed to last all the longer, the pregnancy issue moot at this point, and hell if that didn't feel…so good.

Wrung dry, he shuddered a deep sigh and folded her

against him. Holding her. Kissing her bare shoulder as a silk strand of her dark hair teased his nose. He spanned a hand along her back, rubbing slow circles while he tried to find his breath again.

He couldn't bear to think about the past anymore. And thinking about the future raked him raw with fears as well. Walling off the past didn't mean he had to wall himself off from the future. He just wanted to lose himself in the present, with Amie.

"I'm sorry for being distant earlier today. I just needed some time to myself to think."

"I know." She shifted against him, resituating herself so she sat beside him, her head tucked against his chest. Her hand covering his heart. "I've had more time to process this than you, and even for me I feel like I can't wrap my head around it. Everything is changing so fast. Both with my grandmother and the baby."

"Let me help you. Your whole family works together and depends on each other. We're tied now through this child, so let me into that circle." He hoped it was the right time for this —the most important pitch of his life.

But it needed to happen and he couldn't fail. She meant too much to him.

"What do you have in mind?" She lifted her head, eyeing him as the limousine finally inched forward.

Preston took her hands in his and hoped his eyes didn't betray his fears. The time had come to tear down some walls and start letting her in if they would stand a chance at building a future together.

"Let's get married."

Ten

"**M**arried?" Shock chilled Amie to the core, the leather crackling under her as she inched back to look into Preston's eyes. She'd expected him to pursue her because of the baby. But she hadn't expected this. It felt too forced, too sudden. Too rehearsed. "You have got to be kidding."

"I'm completely serious." His voice was steady, eyes trained on her face.

Amie shook her head in disbelief. "We've only known each other a couple of months. That's a huge leap to take just because I'm pregnant."

She knew he was only proposing because of the baby, and maybe even to secure things at the company, too. Old insecurities flamed to life inside her and she couldn't shut them down no matter how much she wanted to believe their connection was special. That given more time, they could have gotten to this place on their own. And maybe they would have. But now there was no way to separate fact from fiction.

Preston reached for her hand. He ran his thumb over her knuckles. His face etched calmness. Stability. Reminding her of his boardroom demeanor, where he focused on the goal and calmly maneuvered his way there. Her gut wrenched.

"Sure, it hasn't been long, but you can't deny we have something good going here. We have an attraction beyond anything I've experienced. We get along now that you're not icing me out at the office. We work well together. I know we can build a future together for ourselves and this baby."

A part of her heart leaped at the idea of being married to Preston. He was a good man. Protective. Confident. Sexy as hell. But she wouldn't settle for being his end goal just because he felt as if he should marry her. Ever since her pageant days, people had taken it upon themselves to judge what was best for her. To tell her what she needed, what she desired. For so long, she hadn't cared about the outcome of the pageants, so she let herself be told what to wear, what act to perform a how to answer interview questions.

Was Preston just like that, deciding this was t logical outcome to their problem? Deciding best for her? She couldn't allow herself to t of least resistance just because it was si man in question was irresistibly appe her baby better.

She wanted to trust what he said from him. Was it so wrong to wa and company aside? "We don't have to decide now. We have a few months to think this through."

"I take it that's a no." He still held her hand, but his grip loosened.

"I just want us to make the right choices—for ourselves and the baby. We still have time with the Atlanta event before we have to face the family at home…"

"Family." He slumped back in the seat, dropping her hand. Running his fingers through his hair, he let out a pent-up sigh. "I hadn't thought about all of them."

"And your parents. Do you have other family?"

He shook his head. "Not since Leslie died."

"Do you still communicate with your ex-wife?" Amie knew so little about his life before the company. Before her. They were tied together through this child. And if he was going to make hasty decisions, she would make sure she balanced that with all the important angles he was overlooking.

He blinked in surprise but answered quickly. "Not ~~or~~ regularly. Last I heard, she and her new husband ~~G~~eorgia. They adopted two children, ~~b~~aned."

~~~~ying and having ~~~~t, heart pounding

~~~~ I want her to move

~~~~imself. Or was that ~~~~o tough to tell when ~~~~or his past. "What was ~~~~s little?"

~~~~aughed out the words. ~~~~ inward. Thoughtful.

Amie knew in that moment how much he had loved his daughter.

"Sounds like her father." Amie grinned at him, placing her hand on his knee, leaning closer. This was a hard subject for him. She wanted to make sure he didn't close up on her. And that he knew she was here to listen.

"Except for the pigtails."

"Now, that's an image." Her smile widened. "What color was her hair?"

"Dark, like mine. She was an active child. She walked early, loved her trike. I bought her a pony, a fat little bay mare from Chincoteague, Virginia. She loved the books about the ponies from that island. It seemed suited that she had a formerly wild pony as her own." He hung his head. "My ex said I used gifts to make up for lack of time."

"That could be true, but it also sounds like you knew her and her wishes. Time together doesn't always translate to a quality relationship anyway. My parents spent plenty of time with me and never had a clue what I wanted to do or what gifts I may have preferred."

"I appreciate you trying to let me off the hook. But I made mistakes. I have to live with that. I'm going to do my best not to make the same mistakes with this child." Genuine promises shone in his eyes.

Amie desperately wanted to believe that's what she was seeing. "My baby's lucky to have you as a father."

"Our baby," he softly corrected her.

"Right, I'm still adjusting, too." She was fidgety. Her fingertips smoothed back her hair, but nothing was out of place—unlike her insides that were a mess.

"I want to be more than the dad. I want to be there. With you and the baby."

"I told you, I need more time to think about the proposal." Her voice edged with more steel than she intended. While she was starting to have a clearer picture of Preston the father, the image of Preston the husband was still elusive. And she would not settle. She needed someone that genuinely wanted her.

Preston considered her words. Amie could see him recalculating. "Well then, how about we move in together and if we decide to get married one day, we can head to the courthouse. Let me at least be there to help you through the pregnancy day by day."

"I have a houseful of servants." She was thinking practically, suspecting he was doing the same.

"Good. Because I suck at doing laundry." He offered her a causal grin. "So is that a yes to moving in together?"

She studied his face, trying to get a read on him. If only she had spent the past two months getting to know him. She might have been able to tell something from the light in his hazel eyes. "Let's enjoy the next couple of days and decide after the Atlanta show so we have a plan in place when we talk to our families."

He studied her at length as if he intended to press, then nodded. "I can live with that." He slid his hand behind her neck, fingers massaging her scalp. "In the meantime, I intend to make the most of every second to fully and completely seduce you."

She looped her arms around his neck. "Maybe I intend to seduce you first."

Preston lint rolled cat fur from his tuxedo, making sure not a stray hair was in sight. Tonight was important. And not just for the gala. It meant more than selling jewelry and making this line succeed.

He needed to sell Amie on the idea of them. She hadn't outright rejected the idea of them together, but she wouldn't commit to the proposal. He could see hesitation and questions in her eyes.

If she would just say yes, he could do away with so many of those fears. He had meant what he said about wanting to be there for their baby. For her. He wanted to do this right.

There had to be a way to convince her that he was serious about her. That he wanted to pamper and take care of her and their unborn child.

She was an amazing woman. Independent. And she was smarter than she gave herself credit for. Her artistic instincts were brilliant and he hated that she couldn't see how much she was worth to the company. To him in particular.

Amie riled him, made him want to try harder. There was something in the way she carried herself, in her sarcasm and eclectic flair that drew him in. No one but Amie would ever consider taking an elderly and sickly cat on a business trip just to ensure proper care was administered. Her heart was so big. He wanted a place in it.

He'd been racking his brain on how to show her he cared. How to prove to her practical nature that he cared. Or maybe.

He stopped the mindless brushing of his tuxedo jacket and put the lint roller down on the floor for Roscoe to play with—the cat was a primo escape artist, sneaking out of Amie's room. Maybe he didn't need to show her he cared so much as show her that he believed in her.

Hadn't she said that no one in her family took her seriously? That she wasn't even asked about heading the company? A plan came together in his mind as he thought of ways he could show her just how much he valued her. She might think his efforts to prove his faith in her were just corporate maneuvering. And— he had to admit—the plan he had in mind was straight out of his boardroom toolbox. But for a woman who felt as if she hadn't been taken seriously in the business world, it might help her to understand that he saw her differently.

That he recognized more than her legendary beauty or her obvious wealth. He respected the hell out of her.

Picking up his cell phone, he tapped the lint roller into motion for Roscoe again while trotting out some instructions to his personal assistant to get the ball rolling on his idea.

A few moments later, his work was interrupted when the door to his suite clicked open and Amie stepped through the threshold. She was radiant.

Yes, beautiful, but so much more.

He would convince her to marry him, one way or another. He had to.

Amie was used to working close to home, which meant she wore casual business attire some days and ranch clothes on others. All these galas so close together gave her flashbacks to her pageant days. Except at least she got to choose her own clothes now. No more traditional stage garb like the kind her mother insisted on as her "manager."

Now she could let her creative impulses run free. And yes, she had to confess, she enjoyed watching the heat flame in Preston's eyes every time she made an entrance.

Since she'd pushed the edgy boundaries before, she went for a simpler look tonight, a fitted gold lace dress that flared around her feet. Her hair was slicked back into a tight bun. Simple, classic cat eyeliner and nude lips. Dangling hammered-flat gold earrings and multiple wide bracelets were engraved with her favorite quotes from her favorite poets. All the words of encouragement and perseverance were strung around her wrists. There to remind her to breathe.

She walked down the grand winding staircase at the Saint Regis Hotel where they were staying and holding the event. No getting trapped in a limo together tonight.

Her body heated at the memory of making love in the backseat. And continuing through the night when they'd returned to their hotel. The trip on the private jet had been too quick and full of business for any deep conversation, but that marriage proposal still hung in the air between them.

Could she really just move in with him and see what happened over the next few months? She wished she knew the answer or saw some kind of sign. She felt adrift with nowhere to turn. Her mother wouldn't be a help at all. Her brother had made his adversarial position clear. And she didn't want to burden her grandmother.

Her fingers clenched around Preston's elbow as they reached the bottom of the staircase, noise from the jewelry show already drifting down the hall along with music from a string quartet.

Preston glanced at her. "Are you feeling all right? Tired? Or dizzy?"

"I'm feeling fine," she said quickly. Of course, he'd meant the baby, not the proposal or her feelings. "I'm taking my prenatal vitamins religiously. I promise."

"Just making sure you aren't overdoing it. It's been a hectic week." He patted her arm. "Let's get to the party and find some food."

Okay, more pregnancy concerns, but it was thoughtful and she was starving. She spotted a waiter heading into the ballroom with a silver platter of persimmon pear caprese toast. Another with what looked like goat cheese and beets. Her mouth watered.

"Definitely food. Sooner rather than later."

He smiled down at her with such light in his eyes she felt hope flutter to life inside her. Maybe, just maybe, they could be happy, sharing great sex and working hard to build a future together. They were both driven people. If they set their minds to this…

He dropped a quick kiss on her lips before escorting her into the ballroom teeming with jewelry displays on models strategically seated and standing on small themed stages throughout the room. As songs changed, they changed jewels from the display cases beside them. More than just a runway event, they'd created an interactive jewelry fashion show to play throughout the evening. She was quite proud of the execution of this idea, the thematic podiums echoing the various Diamonds in the Rough lines.

She snagged an appetizer from a passing waiter. Cheese truffle with chives. She could have eaten a dozen. Her mouth full, she looked around the domed space, searching for the contacts she needed to make.

Taking her time to work the room, she sampled her way along the perimeter.

Preston went still beside her, stopping her short of her goal of a mini lobster soufflé.

"What's wrong?" She followed his gaze and realized his attention was focused on a lovely blonde in a pale blue dress walking toward them on the arm of a distinguished-looking man in a conservative tux. "Preston?"

"Amie…" He paused, his forehead furrowing. "I'm not sure how to tell you this or why she's here, but—"

The woman stopped directly in front of them. "Hello, Preston, it's been too long, but you're looking good." She extended her hand to Amie. "I'm Dara West. I used to be married to Preston."

After an awkward introduction to Amie, Preston cornered his ex-wife by the triple chocolate fondue fountains surrounded by fruit and small delicacies. She always had adored her sweets. That had gotten him out of trouble more times than he could count. He'd known they were through the day she'd thrown a box of her favorite Godiva's exclusive G Collection chocolates at his head after he missed Leslie's fourth-grade dance recital because he'd worked late. No good excuse.

"Dara, what the hell are you doing here?"

"I do keep up with your life thanks to the internet and an occasional Google search. I saw photos of you and Amie in the social pages. I know you, and I could see there's a connection between the two of you. I was curious." She picked up a glass of champagne from a passing waiter.

"And your husband doesn't mind?" Preston raised his eyebrows in disbelief.

"Bradley and I are secure. Solid. Besides, coming here gave us an excuse for a weekend away together. Mom and Dad are thrilled to watch the kids."

"The kids are—" he swallowed hard, thinking back to the photograph she'd sent—a family, a complete family "—beautiful. Thank you for the Christmas card."

"I'm happy…" Dara's voice trailed, became leaden. She shook her head. "Well, there was a time I didn't think that happy was possible. But I love Bradley, unconditionally, and I've worked hard to find happiness again after what you and I went through. I keep hoping you'll find a way to be happy, too."

Leslie's death had shredded Dara as deeply as it had hurt him. He knew that.

"So here you are, checking up on my happy meter." Preston's arms crossed over his chest.

"Checking up to make sure Amie McNair is worthy of you." She gestured with her champagne flute to Amie, who was standing chatting with a potential client. She took Preston's breath away with her understated charm and love for the company, for people.

He threw back his head and laughed. "You are something else, Dara. But thank you. I can take care of myself. Truth be told, Amie's too good for me."

"Spoken like the gentleman you've always been."

"Not always." Preston's eyes darkened, muscles tensing. He had spent years ignoring and burying his past. His ex. His dead child and premature grandchild. These past few days had brought every painful memory lurching back to the surface. "I'm sorry I let you and Leslie down. Sorrier than you'll ever know."

"Casting blame takes away from thoughts of remembering her. I want to remember her and smile." She looked thoughtfully at him. And she seemed to be at peace.

"How did you do it?"

"Do what?" Dara's green eyes looked back inquisitively.

Preston let out a long-held breath. He shrugged his shoulders. "Get up the guts to have another child in your life?"

She nodded her head in understanding. "I have a mother's love to give and nowhere to pour it. There are children who need that love."

"You're a good woman. I was an idiot to let you get away."

"You aren't about to hit on me, are you?"

"Our time passed before Leslie died. I know that." The weight of the past threatened to drag him under. He needed to lighten the mood. Fast. "Besides, your husband would kick my ass."

"He would try. But we both know you could take him." She winked at him, tossing her blond hair over her shoulder with a dramatic flick of the hand.

"Flattery? You surprise me." He laughed. The conversation was easier than he could have ever imagined, than he felt he deserved.

"I've realized our breakup wasn't entirely your fault. I had my part in how things went south between us."

"That's kind of you to say, but I know—"

"Stop. You don't have to protect me from myself. I take responsibility for my own actions. That's a part of how I was able to move forward and enjoy my future." Dara smiled at him.

If she could move on, could he? Could he stop running from those old ghosts?

He sighed, the words falling out before he could weigh the wisdom or why of speaking them. "Amie is pregnant. The baby's mine."

Her eyes flashed with only an instant's surprise, then total joy. "Congratulations. That's wonderful news."

"It is." Pain crept into his words.

"Then why aren't you smiling?"

"Amie won't marry me. I'm having to work my ass off just to get her to agree to let us move in together."

"She doesn't love you in return?"

He scratched the back of his neck. "We, uh, didn't talk about love."

Dara rolled her eyes. "She won't marry a man who doesn't love her, who only proposed to her because she's pregnant. Hmm…" She tapped her chin in mock thought. "I wonder why she said no. That would have been enough to sell me."

Sarcasm dripped. And yet, the theatrical delivery helped him get the message. Sometimes he needed things spelled out for him.

Damn. How could he be so successful in the business world and such a screwup in the relationship department? Of course Amie wanted more from him. How had he overlooked that? "Okay, I hear you. And by the way, you're funnier than I remember."

"And I'm hoping you still remember how to be romantic. There was a time you were quite good at that. You do love her, don't you?"

"This is not the way I saw this conversation going," Preston admitted.

She raised an inquisitive brow at him. "But you're not denying it."

"Because I can't." Realization bubbled in his stomach.

She rolled her eyes, tilting her glass back to Amie. "Well, don't tell me. Tell her."

Eleven

Amie kept her cat in her lap on the flight back to Fort Worth, needing the comfort of stroking Roscoe. The rhythm of Roscoe's purring was the only thing anchoring her. The last week had left her raw. Vulnerable. She had spanned a year's worth of emotions over the course of a few days. How could it have only been a week since her grandmother gave her orders to travel with Preston, to make peace with him for the future of the company?

She felt anything but peaceful after seeing the way Preston greeted his ex-wife. It was obvious he had feelings for her. It didn't matter that Dara had moved on with a new family. Amie hadn't been able to take her eyes off Preston with his former wife at the party in Atlanta, mesmerized by the emotions she saw broadcast through his hazel eyes.

Emotions she'd never seen for her.

She'd hardly slept afterward, her stomach churning all night, knowing that Preston didn't care for her that way. Knowing she didn't have a fraction of his heart. His offer to stay, to marry her, was not out of desire or longing for her.

Roscoe nudged closer, standing to make his feline presence felt. She brushed her fingers behind his ear, doing her best to keep herself from shedding tears on the flight home. Instead, Amie concentrated hard on Roscoe's purring. She could only imagine the turmoil that would erupt over her news, especially with the memory of Alex's reaction weighing on her heart.

She needed to do what she could to control the family response. Which meant talking to Preston. And she wasn't ready to face more questions about marriage or moving in. She needed time and space to think.

Stroking the senior Siamese, fur soft under her fingers, she hoped it was a good time to broach the topic. On her terms. "Now that Alex and Nina know, it's only a matter of time before word gets out."

Preston stretched out his long legs, crossing his boots at the ankles, wearing faded jeans with his suit jacket now that the galas were done. "Do you think they would talk, even if you asked them to keep their silence? I assume you asked them to wait for you to make your own announcement."

"I did ask before they left. Nina won't say a word and no one will guess from her behavior. But Alex? Even if he keeps his silence, I'm not so sure he can hold back his emotions. He's mad—which I think is ridiculous because I'm a consenting adult. I am damn tired of this family treating me like a flighty nitwit who doesn't know her own mind. So it's going to be time to tell them soon."

"They're your family," he said, his hand resting on his Stetson beside him as if he took comfort from it the way she did her cat. "You have my support in however you decide to handle the announcement. I do want to be there with you."

"Okay, I'm all right with that. I think we need to tell them about the baby after the final event in Fort Worth. We can say we're still working out the details between us, but that we're committed to doing the best by our child."

"You can say that and I'll support you. That doesn't mean I agree with you." He leaned forward, elbows on his knees, eyes skimming her turquoise and gold–trimmed maxidress, taking in every inch of her as he always did. "I want to marry you. I would like them to know that."

"No, absolutely not." She shook her head adamantly, remembering the way he'd looked at his ex. The shine in his eyes and warm quality of his face as they slipped into easy conversation. That, more than anything, had assured her she was making the right decision. She would not rush into this and wind up with only a shell of a man doing his duty. "They'll all pressure me to say yes and I can't take all of them coming at me that way."

He frowned.

"What?" Did he know she was withholding her deeper concerns?

"If they say so much as a cross word to you, I'm going to have trouble with that. I don't relish the notion of all of them coming swinging at me, but I'll handle it."

The thought of another fight breaking out made her shiver. A follow-up thought popped to mind. "Is that why you proposed? Because you care what they think?"

"Hell, no, and frankly I'm offended you think that of me." He held her eyes with unwavering intensity. "I proposed because I want us to be a family. I want us to bring up the baby together, no split-time parenting."

Something she wanted, too. But was that enough to build a marriage on?

"And if it doesn't work out between us and things turn acrimonious?"

"It will work out. I care about you, Amie." He said it so earnestly she wanted to believe he meant more than that. "I won't fail again."

He wouldn't fail? Like they were a work project? The thought sent her spiraling. His honor and protectiveness weren't in question. But she wanted more from him than just "caring" about her. She wanted... Her heart lurched as if the plane had lost altitude, realization making her unsteady.

She loved him. She loved Preston Armstrong. And she wanted him to propose because he loved her, too.

Preston was losing control fast. Something had shifted with Amie during their discussion on the flight. She'd shut down and clammed up. He'd seen this volatile woman go through many emotions, but closed off? That was never one of them. Even when she was icy, it was that cold ice that burned. This shutdown came from buried emotions. She'd left the plane as quickly as possible, abandoning her luggage except for her cat. She'd even taken the waiting limo and said she needed to leave immediately, mumbling an excuse about needing to get a vial for the cat.

He didn't know what he'd done to flip things so fast other than asking to marry her, for heaven's sake. He'd even told her he cared about her, as Dara had reminded him to say. And it hadn't made things better. In fact, they were worse off than before, and he wasn't sure what move to make next.

He'd caught a ride from one of the flight-line crew back to the ranch to find her. She wasn't answering her phone. He got out to the ranch, a buzz of activity with vacationers taking riding lessons and the kids' camp off to the side. The resort side of the main lodge was busy, as well, but the private living quarters looked quiet.

He saw the limo backing up beside the barn, attempting to turn around to leave. He jogged over and knocked on the chauffeur's window.

The electric window slid down. "Yes, Mr. Armstrong? I was just coming back to pick you up. Miss McNair said you were conferring with the pilot."

"I found my way back. Thanks. Which way did Miss McNair go?"

"She handed the cat to one of the staffers and headed to the barn. She said she needed to ride Crystal to clear the cobwebs."

Riding? Pregnant? Was that wise? Panic rolled in his gut.

"Thank you for the information," Preston said, already jogging toward the main barn. He readied his personal sorrel quarter horse, Chance, waving aside the stable hand that offered to help. Leather creaking, he swung up into the saddle. He looked down at the stable hand. "Which way did Amie ride off?"

The employee pointed toward the forest to the east, away from the kids' camp. Off to privacy and away from the more beaten trails. Preston urged Chance forward. The horse leaped instinctively, digging hooves into earth with as much desperation as Preston felt. He set off after her, unsure what he would say when he found her but knowing he couldn't leave things this way.

The wind whistled in his ear as his horse galloped. He gave Chance his head, pressing his legs into the horse's sides. He needed to find her. Quickly. While the speed was safe for him, it made him afraid to think of Amie racing over trees and creeks—afraid for their child and for her.

Finally—thank God—finally, he saw her in the distance, her dark brown hair streaming behind her as she took the trail with her white Arabian.

She sat deep in her seat, a saddle of black and silver with a bridle to match. She looked like something out of some Western fairy tale. Her long dress flowed and rippled, hints of bare leg flashing above her turquoise cowboy boots. She was intriguing. Gorgeous. Wild and untamable. Infuriating.

Irresistible.

He galloped alongside, shouting, "Amie, slow down. Let's talk."

"Let's ride," she shouted back, hair whipping across her face.

Crystal's pace opened up and the space between them doubled. Tripled. Her grace, even here, was perfect. The way her arm fell casually to her side. She moved in perfect time to the mare's beat.

God, how he wanted to take her up on that offer and just let loose on their horses, riding the expanse of the land. But he had to be careful, for her sake.

He pushed Chance onward, making sure he was close enough to be heard. "Are you sure this is safe for you and the baby?"

Her face creased and she didn't stop, but she slowed to a trot. She sat perfectly balanced, reins gathered in one hand as she swiveled to face him. "You know, pregnant women ride horses, drive cars and even go swimming. It's quite the revolution."

"I'm not laughing." He eased his quarter horse to a trot in step with hers and reached to take her reins.

Her eyes flashed with fury at his taking the lead. "Duly noted and not surprising."

"Please, get off the horse," he said through clenched teeth.

"I wouldn't risk my child," she snapped.

"*Our* child," he snapped back, slowing Chance to a halt.

"Walking up the stairs is more dangerous than riding this horse." Still, she slid off Crystal's back, her boot thudding the ground beside his.

"Then I guess you'll be taking the elevator."

"Are you one of those smothering kinds?" Her chin jutted, challenge in her eyes as she took her horse's reins back. She stroked the Arabian's arched neck and clucked softly to her. Crystal sprung to attention as Amie guided her around Preston.

"I'm one of those careful kinds. It's how I've become such a successful businessman. Why would I take more care with work than with my personal life? I'm learning about balancing that."

"Good point. If it makes you more comfortable, I won't ride again once I return my horse to the stable." She withdrew from him again.

Shutting down.

"What's wrong?" he probed, dropping his horse's reins, effectively ground tying the well-trained mount.

"Nothing." She tightened her grip on the polished leather of her horse's reins, not slowing down. Continuing away from him, to the forest line.

"Damn it, Amie, you're upset about something."

"We don't know each other well enough for you to read my emotions." She stopped. Turned.

"Are we going back to that again? Fine, I won't press for marriage. We'll go back to dating."

"I'm not some fragile flower." She dropped the reins at her feet, leaving Crystal as she stomped toward him. "I'm not an airheaded person who's too stupid to live. Treat me like an equal, damn it."

He didn't have a clue what she meant. Why she was so angry. Or what the hell had gotten under her skin. But he knew a spark when he saw it, and she was sparking all over him.

"Treat you like an equal?" He fought for calm. Control. Couldn't seem to find any as he dragged in a harsh breath. "Remember—you asked me to."

Her brows furrowed for all of an instant before she seemed to guess his sensual intent. He angled toward her.

But she beat him to it, lunging closer to fling her arms around his neck and damn near kiss his socks off.

His brain raised a protest for about a fraction of a second—shouldn't they be talking?—before his body got fully on board with this plan.

He wanted this. Needed this.

Lifting her off her feet, he backed her up against the trunk of a massive bald cypress tree, hiding her from view, even though they were far from the ranch and not close to any trails. Her hands already worked the buttons of his shirt, her lips dipping to follow where her fingers had been. He reached to skim a hand under her hem, letting the dress bunch around her thighs while he cupped a palm between her legs.

Her head fell back, eyes closed, lips parted. She was so responsive. So hot and ready for him. Despite everything that didn't work for them, this did. The electric connection that torched away anything else.

With one hand he palmed her thigh, lifting her leg to wrap around his waist and giving himself better access. With his other hand, he slipped beneath her panties to stroke her until she went breathless, her fingernails catching on his back as she held herself still for his touch.

She amped him up so much. Unfastening the fly of his denim, he shoved aside her underwear just enough to take her. The thin strip of lace gave way anyhow, leaving her naked as he sank deeper inside her.

His groan mingled with her soft whimper, the pleasure undeniable. He cupped her cheek with one hand and slid a palm behind her back, making sure not to press her into the tree bark. She didn't seem to notice, though, her hands stroking through his hair and down his back. She kissed his chest and breathed along his skin, warming his flesh, driving him out of his mind with her sweet, sexy ways.

A breeze rose, scattering a few old leaves around his feet and plastering his shirt to his back. Amie's hair lifted, blowing around him, too. She tipped her head back as if she enjoyed the feel of it. The wildness of it. He edged a shoulder sideways a little so he didn't block her from the brunt of it, letting her feel the force of it on her face.

Her eyes popped open then, blue gaze meeting his

for one fierce, unguarded moment, and she smiled at him in a way that dazzled the hell out of him. Made him want her more. Forever.

Fueled by frenzy and too much emotion, he thrust into her again. And again.

"Preston!" She called his name in a hoarse rush right before she found her release, her body convulsing around him in the soft clench of feminine muscles.

He followed her a moment later, his own fulfillment slamming through him. His heart pounded hard against his chest, their bodies sealed together while they twitched through aftershocks of a passion bigger than the Texas sky.

When she went still against him, he could almost feel the taut strain creeping into her shoulders and back. Just like that first time they'd been together, the aftermath went tense as she relegated him to a place outside her life. He settled her on her own feet.

His head rested in the crook of her neck, his breath coming in pants as he struggled to get his galloping heartbeat under control. "Amie, you're tearing me apart here."

He remembered that moment of connection when the wind had kicked up. He hadn't imagined that.

Yet now, her hands smoothed along his hair, over his shoulders, but her eyes were distant. "I'm sorry, Preston, I'm so sorry." A sigh shuddered through her. "I just think this is all too much too fast. We should keep our distance until we figure out a plan. It's the only way to stay objective."

A cold lump settled in his gut as he angled back. "Are you dumping me?"

She smoothed her dress into place, not meeting his gaze. "I'm protecting us and our child from heartbreak."

Too damn stunned to know what to say. It wasn't often he'd been struck speechless, but right now was one of those times. He could only stare at her as she moved away from him, talking softly to Crystal as she approached her horse and then stroked the animal's muzzle.

She swung up on her horse again. She didn't race off, giving him time to make the trip with her. She kept the pace at a slow trot, but she didn't look at him or speak again all the way to the stable. Once they returned, she slid off her horse, handed the reins to a stable hand and walked away.

Her silence and stiff spine spoke louder than words. Preston waved off the stable hand, insisting on untacking Chance on his own. He needed time to think. Spending time in the barn was more productive then locking himself up indoors.

Inhaling the smell of sweat and hay, Preston attached his horse to the crossties. He loosened the girth, gave Chance a pat on the shoulder and heaved the saddle off. The sorrel shuddered from withers to tailbone as his saddle was removed.

Preston dutifully brushed and hosed the horse down. Once again, he found himself escaping in a rhythm of routine. Avoiding ghosts.

His window of time to win her over had closed unless he came up with a Hail Mary fast. A way to break through her insecurities and let her know how much she meant to him. How much he cared.

Cared?

With a sinking sensation in his chest, he knew that

was far too tame to describe the way he felt right now. Her rejection gutted him after lovemaking that had been one of the most incredible experiences of his life. After a week of witnessing her talent, her generosity and her warmhearted ways up close.

"Cared" was the cop-out of a man too scared to face his own ghosts. But he was ready to do battle now. Because he knew that he felt a whole lot more than that for Amie.

He loved that woman. Heart, body and soul.

Twelve

Amie had never felt less in the mood for a party.

But this final wrap-up of the Diamonds in the Rough promotional tour was crucial to finishing off her deal with her grandmother. And beyond any "deal," she wanted Gran to be happy. This would likely be her last celebration, a fact that tore at Amie's already raw emotions.

Preston's overprotectiveness, his anger, then his tender lovemaking had been every bit as much of a roller coaster of feelings as her own. What were they doing to each other? How could love be so damn complicated?

She stepped into the largest barn, an open space used for entertaining, the same location her cousin had used for his wedding just a week ago. Rustic elegance. The signature of Diamonds in the Rough.

Bales of hay and leather saddles made eclectic showcases for high-end jewelry with pricey stones and intricate carvings. And not just women's jewelry but men's as well, along with belt buckles and boots. Light from the chandeliers refracted off the jewels, sending sparkles glistening throughout the room and over the guests. The room was bathed in splintered, glittering light. All the indications of a lovely evening. One she couldn't enjoy.

Amie had reached into the back of her closet for a gown, barely registering what she wore. Somehow, she'd ended up in one of her old pageant gowns. A black strapless number, fitted at the top with a floor-length, poofy tulle skirt studded with tiny diamonds and silver flecks. She'd always felt like the bad Disney princess in this gown. And it was too darn tight across the chest now, thanks to her pregnancy breasts. Her cleavage was getting more attention from some men than the jewels.

She just had to get through the evening without crying over the mess she'd made of things with Preston. And then she saw him across the room, looking as sexy and brooding as ever in a black tux with a bolo tie and Stetson, cowboy boots polished. He looked so…

How could she love him so much and still have so many doubts?

Her stomach rumbled and she realized she'd been so upset she'd forgotten to eat. She turned toward the buffet, only to stop short. Her parents were standing there. On a good day, dealing with them was taxing. But tonight? Tonight they threatened to send her nerves out of control. Undo what little stability she had.

She and her brother had always thought her mother's collagen-puffy lips and cheek implants had changed her appearance until she looked like a distant-relative version of herself. Not her mother, yet eerily familiar. Her father always worked to look like an efficient businessman. Ironic as hell, since Garnet McNair carried an in-name-only title with the company, some kind of director of overseas relations. Which just meant he could pretend he worked as he traveled the world. Mariah only requested that he wine and dine possible contacts and charm them. On the company credit card, of course. Her parents were masters at wringing money out of Gran. But they would have to learn to live within their trust-fund means soon enough.

Her eyes burned with tears at the thought and she turned away fast, searching for Gran. She found her grandmother in the back of the room, away from the noise, sitting in her wheelchair, holding court with different loyal business contacts.

Amie angled through the crowd, smiling and nodding, her full-skirted gown brushing tables, chairs and people on her way past. As she neared, Gran ended her conversation with two jewel suppliers and turned her attention to Amie.

Gran patted the chair next to her. "Your business trip seems to have been a success."

"We completed the events." She smoothed the back of her dress and sat in a cloud of black tulle. Her hair was swept back on one side with a large pewter-and-diamond comb, leaving half the silky mass to fall over her shoulder.

"So you believe you and Preston can work together? You can accept him as the CEO of Diamonds in the Rough?"

It would be so easy to just say yes. Instead, she found

herself asking, "Gran, why didn't you ever ask me if I wanted to be considered for the job?"

"Did you want the job?"

"God, no," she answered quickly, surprising even herself. "I believe I could do it, but I'm like Gramps. I'm the artist. I just wanted to be considered. To be asked."

Her grandmother took her hand and squeezed, her grip still firm in spite of her thin frailty. "I know you could have handled the job, but I also knew you wouldn't want it. I assumed you understood that. You are my amazing girl, everything I could have hoped for as the next matriarch to lead the family. *The family.* You know that's much more important than the company. You are the McNair glue that's going to keep our empire cohesive—Diamonds in the Rough, Hidden Gem Ranch and HorsePower Cowkid Camp."

Her grandmother's words surprised—and touched—her. "You really think so?" Amie's own words came out in a half whisper.

"I do." She nodded with confidence. "And if you feel the artist well is drying up and you need a change of pace, I can also see you on the board of directors, even leading the table someday. You're a force to be reckoned with, my girl."

Tears welled in her eyes that had nothing to do with hormones and everything to do with a lifetime bond she felt to this woman who'd been the true mother figure in her life.

She leaned in to hug her grandmother. "I love you, Gran."

Her grandmother wrapped her in a hug, the familiar scent of gardenias enveloping her with memories. "I love you, too, Amie dear."

Amie held on tighter, her voice choking. "I'm going to miss you so very much."

"I know, sweetie." Gran pulled back, brushing the two fat teardrops from Amie's cheeks. "And I'm sorry we didn't have more time together. But I am at peace about all of you and the legacy your grandfather and I built. I miss him. We're going to have a beautiful reunion in heaven, he and I."

Amie smiled, wobbly but heartfelt. "Say hello to him for me."

"I will." She touched Amie's stomach lightly. "If it's a girl, will you name her for me?"

Amie blinked in surprise. "You know?"

"I suspected, yes, and I am assuming Preston is the father." She narrowed her gaze. "I didn't miss the quick exit you two made for a certain coat closet that first night."

Oh, but those eyes had always seen so much, hadn't they?

Amie could only nod slowly, her eyes darting to Preston then back to her grandmother. "Is that why you sent me on the trip?"

"I didn't know then, actually, just knew there was something between you and Preston. I guessed about the baby when you got back."

"How?" She had to know what gave them away.

"He treats you like spun glass."

Amie winced. Now, wasn't that a sore subject? "I don't want him to be with me because of the baby or the business."

"Good Lord, Amie, have you looked in that man's eyes when he's watching you? He's been in love with you since day one."

Amie shook her head, wanting to believe but still too scared to hope. "You're just seeing what you want to see."

Her grandmother took her face in her cool hands. "You're afraid to see what's really there. But take a look. Take a risk. The payoff is beyond anything you can imagine. Watch with your heart rather than your eyes." Her voice softened and she cut off any chance of response as the chandeliers dimmed. A spotlight illuminated the dais where the band finished their song and Preston stepped up to the microphone.

Amie's throat burned as she looked at him. And wished.

"Thank you, everyone, for joining us here this evening." His voice still made her nerve endings twitch to life, just like that first night when they'd met. "For those of you who may not know my face, I'm Preston Armstrong, the CEO of Diamonds in the Rough. I'm also known as the interloper brought into a tight-knit family business."

He paused as laughter rippled through the room. Once the silence settled again, he continued, "I'm a man of numbers, a businessman, but in my soul I appreciate the beauty of art my skill set could never create. However, it is my honor to use my experience in the business world to bring that beauty into the lives of others."

That's what she wanted, too. She found herself nodding, embracing his company philosophy in a way she hadn't allowed herself to before. She'd been so busy avoiding him, she truly hadn't let herself hear the good things he was doing for the business.

"And on that note," he continued, gesturing toward a

screen that immediately illuminated. "The art speaks so much better than I ever could. So I'll turn over the stage now for our presentation of Diamonds in the Rough's most popular brands—as well as unveiling an exclusive first look at a new line in development by our top designer, Amie McNair. It is our hope that this new direction will add a division to the company that will bring new jobs into our community." His gaze found hers in the audience. Warmth radiated from his eyes. "And now, if you'll all turn your eyes to the screen, I give you… the heart and lifeblood of Diamonds in the Rough."

Fingers sliding into her grandmother's hand, Amie's heart leaped into her throat at his words.

The film presentation held so many of her designs, even Amie hadn't realized until then just how large her stylistic imprint had been on the company. Guests oohed and aahed as audibly as they had over the fireworks at Stone and Johanna's wedding, the jewelry brought to life with cinematic flair.

And then the screen scrolled an announcement for the future, images from her sketchbook fading in and out, the snake-themed coils she'd designed, the patterns of their markings inspiring interlocking pieces for multicolored chains in precious metal. They were more urban and sophisticated than the rustic-luxury items that were the company cornerstone, potential crossover items for a younger, more international market, while staying true to her roots.

This was the new program he'd spoken of. The new division that could create jobs and bring some of their former employees back. Realizing how well this man knew her—how well he had listened—made her heart swell. Truly listened to her wishes, her choices, even her style. He let her be—herself. Something she didn't take for granted after the way she'd grown up. He didn't stuff her into a category.

He accepted her. Flaws and all. And she owed him the same acceptance. She needed to take her grandmother's advice and be brave, take the future waiting for her.

Shining right before her eyes.

Preston sat on a bale of hay on the stage, the barn quiet in the aftermath of the final stop on their gala tour. A success in attendance, and the feedback on his presentation had been unanimously positive from the board of directors.

But there was still one person left to hear from, the opinion that mattered most.

Amie's.

As if conjured from his thoughts, she walked into the empty barn, weaving around the tables and chairs that would be cleared away in the morning. She was a vision, wearing her version of a "little black dress." So very Amie. She was one of a kind and he wouldn't have her any other way. He needed to tell her that, in no uncertain terms, to let her know he loved her. No more running. No more cop-outs. No more ghosts. She was worth every risk. Had always been worth the risks.

Her dress swished as she walked. "Thank you."

"For what?"

She stopped in front of him, her gown brushing his knees, blue eyes shining. "For the presentation. For your faith in my work. For loving me."

Her pronouncement stunned him. How did she…? Hell, he wasn't sure what to think. He slid off the stage and stood in front of her. "You know that? I was about to tell you and you've preempted my speech. But you trust that I do love you, right? I have since the first time I saw you. I can't explain it, but I do." He gathered her into his arms and held her close, something he'd feared he might never get to do again.

She tucked closer against his chest. "It would have helped if you'd told me sooner."

"My ex-wife said something a lot like that," he muttered under his breath.

She angled back to look up at him. "You talked to your ex about me?" She waved and shook her head. "Never mind. That doesn't matter. Why didn't you listen to her?"

"I guess I'm thickheaded."

"But not unteachable. The McNairs are strong-willed people, too. We can be difficult, but we are so worth the effort." Her smile was brighter than diamonds.

He cupped her waist and lifted her to sit on one of the saddles that had been used to display studded reins.

"Amie, I want you to marry me. This is about you. Nothing and no one else. You've turned my life upside down from the moment we met. I haven't been able to stop thinking about you, and yes, wanting you. But for so many more reasons than the fact that you're hot as hell. You're smart and strong. You're loyal and loving. I need that—I need you—in my life. Please make me the happiest man alive and say we can spend the rest of our lives together."

She tugged him close until they were face-to-face, close enough to kiss. "I want nothing more than to marry you. I've fallen crazy, impulsively, in love with you. No matter how hard I've tried to fight it, I can't help myself."

He listened to her, hardly daring to believe how fortunate he'd been to find her. To win her.

"I can't help myself, either." He traced the line of her jaw. The soft fullness of her lips. "I've built a reputation on being the most controlled person in the room, the CEO with the cool head, and yet you took one look at me and undid all that without saying a word."

Angling his lips over hers, he brushed a kiss along her mouth. A tender, forever kind of kiss.

He gathered her in his arms, trailing hands across her silky bare shoulders. Through the soft fall of dark hair that blanketed one arm. He breathed her in, her scent imprinted on his brain the way the feel of her had imprinted itself on his body.

Deepening the kiss, he stroked along her lower lip, demanding entrance she was only too willing to give, her whole body sighing into his as the tension left muscles at last. He kissed and kissed her, not caring about anything else but this moment with her. They might have forever, but he wanted to savor every moment with her, not taking any of this for granted.

He pulled her hips to his, knowing his whole world was in his arms. In her. He was a lucky, lucky man.

Ending the kiss with a final nip on her bottom lip. "Mind telling me why you fought something this amazing?"

"You know why," she said, her blue eyes swimming with emotion. "The fear of losing love is scary."

Of course. The answer was so simple and so complex at the same time. He'd fought against those same fears. "I can't promise a perfect, trouble-free future.

But I can promise you'll never have to doubt me or my love for you."

"You're a man of your word."

"That I am. And I look forward to proving that every day."

Epilogue

Nine months later

Amie smiled with pride as her husband thanked the family for attending the outdoor baptism held at their private new spread on the Hidden Gem Ranch property. Their home—having built a house of their own on five acres, away from the resort activity.

Preston stood with her in the landscaped gardens full of multicolored flowers, their own private jewel box of petals. He spoke to their guests as they stood together under a bower of roses holding their twins. "Amie and I can't thank you enough for joining us in celebrating the joy of our two precious—vocal—bundles of joy, Mariah Armstrong and McNair Armstrong."

He paused for the laughter before continuing the speech he'd spent more time preparing for than any boardroom presentation. He was excited—and so proud. She'd never known she could be so exhausted and happy all at once. She took her squawking son from Preston, while her husband held their daughter and kept speaking to their families—hers and his. His parents were regulars now, flying up for visits.

Amie inhaled the sweet scent of baby shampoo, McNair's unbelievably soft cheek pressed to hers. Perfection.

She should have considered she might be pregnant with twins, given she was a twin herself, but she'd still been stunned when the doctor picked up two heartbeats and then the ultrasound showed two babies. Her pregnancy had been blessedly uneventful. She'd even made it to thirty-eight weeks pregnant, giving birth to a seven-pound daughter and six-pound son.

Alex had joked she'd always been an over-the-top kind of person. Preston had just smiled, declaring her and the babies perfect.

As much as she'd missed her grandmother that day, she could feel her spirit smiling down in happiness. She felt that feeling even now, all around them, celebrating the family. With the sun shining on their happy haven, their family and closest friends beside them to help them celebrate, Amie had never felt more blessed. Family truly was everything.

She smiled up at Preston as he talked about the joys of second chances, expressing his gratitude for being a part of their family. She snuggled McNair closer, her heart overflowing with love for her babies. Their babies.

Johanna and Stone had adopted a toddler daughter six months ago and since seeing the babies, their little girl was already asking for a sibling. Alex and Nina had married last month, and Cody was already calling her Aunt Amie. He was a McNair in all the ways that counted. He had taken his job of watching over Roscoe the cat very seriously today, and Amie was pretty sure Roscoe the cat took his job watching over Cody darn seriously, too.

The cat twined around the boy's feet where they played together in the rock garden between the lilies of the valley and the gardenias.

And what a treat to have their house complete in time for the baptism. The three-story stucco home had airy porches and large rooms with plenty of space for the children to play while she and Preston watched in awe. She couldn't imagine the awe would ever go away.

She worked on designs from home three days a week, and Preston had installed an office for himself in their house to spend more time with his family. They were making it work, being with their children and keeping the McNair legacy alive. She wasn't sure she was ready to call herself a matriarch any time too soon, the way Gran had mentioned, but then again, it felt right to host all of her and his family here, under her roof. She had large shoes to fill, but she would enjoy trying.

Her parents might not have given her the upbringing she'd hoped for, but they seemed to be embracing the grandparent role with Alex's stepson and now with little Mariah and McNair. They'd come today and so far had been pleasant—maybe they'd all learned the importance of family and acceptance after losing Gran.

Preston wrapped up his speech and waved for everyone to help themselves to the brunch buffet by the pool. The beautiful chaos commenced. Preston kissed her cheek before stepping away to speak with his parents.

Alex stepped beside her, sliding a brotherly arm around her shoulder. "Gran would love all these kids playing on the lawn."

Amie could swear she smelled her grandmother's gardenia cologne on the breeze. "A familiar sight, that's for sure."

Their cousin Stone joined them, the three as close as siblings, having grown up under Mariah's care. "Our parents all seem to be better at grandparenting than taking care of their own children. I can live with that."

"True," Amie agreed. "Gran would be happy about that, too."

Stone nodded to her husband. "Preston's working out well on a lot of levels." High praise from the former CEO of Diamonds in the Rough. "You look happy. And the company's in capable hands."

Alex shook his head wryly. "Funny how that all worked out. Hell, I even like the guy."

Amie grinned up at her brother and cousin. "Love you guys."

They both tugged her ponytail at the same time.

Alex said, "Love you, diva."

Stone said, "Love you, brat."

And the teasing didn't bother her in the least. She heard the affection. They both rejoined their wives as Preston brought Mariah over, one tiny foot peeking out of a pink lightweight blanket.

"Everything okay?" he asked.

"Absolutely perfect." She leaned back against his shoulder and kissed her daughter's foot before tucking it back under the blanket. She felt the studious weight of his gaze and looked up to find his eyes serious. "What?"

"You've made me happier than I ever thought I could be. I hope you know that."

"I do," she promised. And meant it. "That's a very reciprocal feeling. Do we still have a date later tonight after the babies are asleep and the nanny can watch over them?"

"Yes, ma'am, we do." He skimmed a kiss over her lips. "I have a surprise cooked up for you, something to do with a nighttime picnic in the backyard, complete with a private showing of a Wild West film on an outdoor screen. I might have even arranged for someone's favorite pizza in all the world to be specially flown in for the occasion."

Amie laughed, remembering their perfect date in Central Park. "You wouldn't be so extravagant."

"Possibly just this once." He brushed a kiss along her lips. "I'm still in the honeymoon phase of this marriage, Amie. You're going to have to excuse my indulgent side."

Her heart warmed that he took so much time to think about what she liked.

The rest of the party fell away — even with family and babies and a senior cat at their feet.

"I think I can make special accommodations for you," she whispered, gazing up into the hazel eyes that captivated her. Fascinated her. Loved her. "I wonder how long this honeymoon phase lasts."

"I have it on good authority it can last a lifetime if we're careful." He brushed a kiss on her cheek. Her nose.

"Is that so?" Happiness curled her toes as she looked out over their party. Their family. "I wonder who told you such a thing."

"Those words of wisdom came from Mariah Mc-Nair herself. She was one of the two smartest women I've ever met."

Amie's heart squeezed tight. Happy tears threatened. So she laid another kiss on McNair's head and then kissed Preston, too.

Sometimes, no words were needed.

* * * * *

LET'S TALK
Romance

For exclusive extracts, competitions
and special offers, find us online:

f facebook.com/millsandboon

○ @millsandboonuk

🐦 @millsandboon

Or get in touch on 0844 844 1351*

For all the latest titles coming soon, visit
millsandboon.co.uk/nextmonth

Want even more
ROMANCE?

Join our bookclub today!

'Mills & Boon books, the perfect way to escape for an hour or so.'

Miss W. Dyer

'Excellent service, promptly delivered and very good subscription choices.'

Miss A. Pearson

'You get fantastic special offer and the chance to get books before they hit the shops'

Mrs V Hall

**Visit millsandbook.co.uk/Bookclub
and save on brand new books.**

MILLS & BOON